CARLA CASSIDY

COLTON NURSERY HIDEOUT

DANA NUSSIO

MILLS & BOON

Stalker In The Shadows © 2021 Carla Bracale
Colton Nursery Hideout © 2021 Harlequin Books S.A.

Special thanks and acknowledgement are given to Dana Nussio for her contribution to *The Coltons of Grave Gulch* series.

ISBN:978-0-263-28327-3

0221

MIX
Paper from
responsible sources
FSC™ C007454

This book is produced from independently certified FSC™ paper to ensure responsible forest management.

For more information visit: www.harpercollins.co.uk/green

Printed and bound in Spain
by CPI, Barcelona

STALKER IN
THE SHADOWS

CARLA CASSIDY

Chapter One

"Ainsley, order up," Eddie Burwell, aka Big Ed, called from the pass-through window between the kitchen and the dining area of the Dusty Gulch Café.

Ainsley Meadows hurried to the window to pick up her order. "Hmm, looks good, Big Ed," she said of the day's special of an open-face hot roast beef sandwich with a special slaw on the side.

Big Ed flashed his wide, toothless grin in response. He told everyone he had gotten rid of his teeth to better taste the food he cooked. But the rumor was he'd really lost his teeth in a bar fight years ago when he'd been young and courting the wrong side of the law.

She carried the order to Jim Nelson, one of her regulars. Jim was an attractive older man with snow-white hair and a sweet disposition. She always enjoyed waiting on him.

"Here you go, Mr. Nelson," she said as she placed the plate before him. "Can I get you more coffee?"

"Not right now," he replied. "You always take good care of me when I come in."

"I try," she replied with a smile.

She definitely tried to do the best job she could as a

waitress here at the Dusty Gulch Café. She was hoping to make the small Kansas town her forever home.

When Big Ed, who not only cooked for the café but was also the owner, had hired her as a waitress, he had quickly learned she was alone with her eight-year-old daughter. They were stranded in town with car trouble and had no place to stay. So he'd offered her the apartment in the back of the café, which had been emptied by his daughter when she'd left town a couple of years ago.

Ainsley had been thrilled with the accommodations and considered it her first real bit of luck in a very long time. She'd been in town for two and a half months now, and she prayed that finally she and her daughter, Melinda, would be safe here, that this was finally the place where they could put down roots and not live in fear.

The noon rush had just passed when fellow waitress Lana Kincaid sidled up to Ainsley at the coffee machine. "Don't look now, but your man just walked in."

Ainsley flashed a quick glance over her shoulder to the café's front door, where Deputy Sheriff Hunter Churchill had just entered.

She quickly looked back at the older waitress. "He's not my man," she protested even as her heartbeat quickened at the sight of him.

"He wants to be," Lana replied and then cackled. "Trust me, I've been through four marriages. I know when a man has the hots for a woman, and that man definitely has the hots for you."

"Stop it," Ainsley protested. "I think the coffee fumes you inhale all day long have made you delusional," she added with a laugh of her own. Still, if Ainsley was honest with herself, she'd confess she had a bit of a crush on the handsome deputy.

When she turned around and saw the deputy seated in one of her booths, she couldn't help the warmth that filled her cheeks.

She pulled her order pad from her apron pocket and approached the booth. "Good afternoon, Deputy Churchill," she greeted him.

"Afternoon, Ainsley. How's my favorite waitress doing today?" His deep green eyes seemed to smile at her just before his lips curved into the gesture.

"I don't know, I'll have to ask Lana how she's doing," she replied teasingly.

He laughed. "Oh no. Don't even mention my name to that man-eating woman. I have no desire to be her husband number five."

"I'll do my best try to protect you from her," she replied with a grin.

Deputy Hunter Churchill's rich dark hair was short and neat, and his features were classically sculpted. He was tall and lean and broad shouldered. He wore his khaki uniform with a confidence that instantly portrayed strength and only added to his overwhelming attractiveness.

He'd been playfully flirtatious with her since the first time she'd waited on him, and it had only been recently that she felt comfortable enough to tease and flirt back a little.

"What can I get for you today?" She looked down at her order pad. Even with all the different odors in the room—the frying onions and hot coffee, the baking meats and aromatic sauces—she could still smell his enticing, slightly spicy, slightly woodsy cologne.

"How's the special?" he asked.

She gazed at him once again and smiled. "We've had lots of orders for the special and so far no complaints."

"So, what you're telling me is nobody has died from eating the special today." He grinned again, and the temperature in the room seemed to shoot up a hundred degrees.

She laughed. "That's exactly right."

"Okay, then, I'll take the roast beef with a regular soda," he replied.

"I'll be right back with your soda." She hurried away from the booth, put his order in and then went to the soda machine. As she drew his drink, she released a deep breath.

Hunter was the first man in years who made her remember she was a twenty-nine-year-old single woman who had been alone for a long time.

Is it safe? The familiar words jumped into her mind. They were words that had haunted her for a little over three years. She hoped it was safe to make a home here in Dusty Gulch.

It was important for her daughter that they put down real roots and try to build a normal life without fear. Deep in her heart, she wasn't even sure that was possible.

She shoved these troubling thoughts aside and hurried back to Hunter's booth to deliver the drink. "Here we go," she said as she put the glass in front of him.

"Thanks. How's your day going?" he asked.

"Good, what about you? Are you catching all the bad guys in Dusty Gulch?"

He laughed. "Right now the bad guys have all been fairly quiet…just the way we like it."

"That's good. Uh…let me just go check on your food order."

"Ainsley, before you go, I was just wondering if you ever go out on your days off or in the evenings after work?"

"In the couple of months that I've been in town, nobody has asked me out," she replied, her heart quickening by the spark in his eyes.

"What if somebody did? Would you be interested in going out?"

"It would depend on who was asking," she replied with a teasing smile.

"What if I'm asking? Would you be interested in maybe going out to dinner someplace else on your night off? And of course your daughter is invited."

Is it safe? It's just a dinner out. The two voices whispered in her head. Surely it was safe after all this time. "I'd be interested, but not with Melinda," she replied. Her cheeks warmed with a blush.

She'd never really thought about dating, but she definitely didn't want to invite her daughter into spending time with some random guy Ainsley went out to dinner with.

Hunter smiled. "Great, so when is your next night off?" The man had a gorgeous grin that involved not only his lips, but every other muscle in his face. It was a smile that welcomed you in, one that warmed the person it was directed at.

"Ainsley?"

"Ainsley, order up," Big Ed yelled.

She flushed, realizing she'd been staring at Hunter in silence for too long. "Thursday," she said. "I'm off on Thursdays."

"Do you like Chinese?"

"I love it," she replied.

"Then how about I pick you up Thursday around five and we'll go to the Red Wok and over dinner we can get to know each other."

"Ainsley," Big Ed hollered again.

"That sounds good," she replied. "And now if I don't pick up your order, Big Ed is going to have a heart attack." She hurried away from the booth with the sound of Hunter's deep, pleasant rumble of laughter warming her.

Once he'd been served, she continued to wait on the patrons that continued to trickle in, but in the back of her mind she thought about the date with Hunter that would occur in two days.

She'd never really considered what life might look like if they ever managed to settle in somewhere. Working at the café she'd met a lot of the Dusty Gulch natives, and for the most part she'd enjoyed her interaction with all of them.

However, she'd never thought ahead enough to see herself in a position to make real friends or to date anyone. And now a handsome deputy had asked her out.

Of all the people she could choose to hang out with, anyone in law enforcement would be the last she would pick. If she didn't play things right, he could be very dangerous to her.

Still, she couldn't help that something about Hunter Churchill drew her. Besides the fact that she found him drop-dead gorgeous, there was something in the very depths of his green eyes that pulled her in, that made her want to get to know him better.

It was a whisper of pain and Ainsley knew all about pain…both the physical and the emotional kind. It was that pain that had forced her to make decisions she'd never dreamed she would have to make.

As she thought about her date with Hunter, there was both an excitement and a sadness inside her. She was excited to spend time with him and get to know him better.

And the sadness came from knowing she was going to lie to him about who she was and where she'd come from.

The faint stir of misery came from the fact that everything about her was a complete lie, from the color of her hair to her very name.

HUNTER LEANED BACK at his desk in the Dusty Gulch police station. There were only five large desks in the room, shared by a total of fourteen deputies. Sheriff Wayne Black's private office was behind a closed glass door just in back of the five deputies' desks.

Lanie Byrant was the first person anyone interacted with when they came into the station. She was a charming brunette with sparkling blue eyes and met everyone who came in with a problem with dignity and respect. She was also the gatekeeper between the public and the officers.

Although Hunter found the twenty-three-year-old attractive, he'd never had a romantic interest in her. Instead she was more like a little sister to him.

That was the sum of the Dusty Gulch police force, and over the past two months they had been stretched thin with the murder of an old man while he slept and the sensational story of terror and attempted murder among the powerful and wealthy Albright family.

Thankfully things were back to normal with the usual crimes of speeding, stealing, mischief and public intoxication. It was as if the winds of September had blown away the evil that had possessed some of the town people in the month of August.

Hunter looked up from a report he'd been writing as the door opened and Deputy Nick Marshall walked in. "Hey, buddy," he greeted as he sat at the desk across from Hunter. "What's happening?"

Nick and Hunter were the only two single men on the force. They had grown up together on neighboring farms. Nick was thirty four years old, two years older than Hunter and one of his closest friends.

"I'm just finishing writing up a report about Ben Wilkins being drunk and disorderly last night in front of the grocery store," Hunter said.

"I thought he'd moved to Makenville," Nick replied, referring to a small town about twenty miles away from Dusty Gulch.

"Yeah, well he's back. He's living in the motel and supposedly looking for a job."

Nick shook his head. "With his reputation for drinking, he's going to have trouble finding any work."

Hunter leaned forward. "So, ask me what else is new."

"What else is new?"

"This Thursday I have a date with Ainsley." Hunter couldn't help but smile.

"Ah, you lucky dog," Nick replied. "I was thinking about asking her out, but I had the distinct feeling if I did she'd turn me down."

Hunter's smile fell as he looked at his friend. "Ah man, I'm sorry. I didn't know you were even interested in her."

Nick laughed. "A new gorgeous single woman moves to town? I imagine every single man in Dusty Gulch is interested, but she said yes to you. I hope you aren't planning on taking her to the café."

It was Hunter's turn to laugh. "I doubt she'd be happy with me if I took her to the place where she works all the time. Actually, I'm taking her to the Red Wok."

"Seriously man, I hope it goes well."

"Yeah, me too."

The two men visited for a few minutes longer, and

then Nick left to go back out on the streets and Hunter finished up writing his report.

The rest of the workday passed peacefully, and finally Hunter was on his way home. Home was a three-bedroom ranch house he'd bought eight years ago. At that time he'd had his dream job and a beautiful wife. He'd been filled with happiness, and the future had looked so bright.

Those dreams had all shattered four years ago, leaving Hunter alone and with so many emotions to sort through. He'd been grieving and had become bitter and had isolated himself from everyone and everything.

A year ago he'd suddenly awakened to the fact that he was still young, that it wasn't too late to achieve the dreams he'd once had.

Ainsley was the first woman who had stirred something inside him, something that had been dormant for a very long time. Was she the right woman for him? He had no idea. Right now he just wanted to get to know her.

Physically he found her very attractive with her long black hair and beautiful blue eyes. More than that, her smile warmed him in a way he hadn't felt with any other woman in town. Maybe it was because her smile seemed so open and her eyes shone with honesty.

He didn't know much about her. Her full name was Ainsley Meadows and she had a young daughter, but there had been no gossip about her to tell him anything else.

He wasn't expecting much of the date. It would be nice to find out if there could be something between them, something good and long-term. He was ready for that in his life. Of course, there was also the chance that the date could be a total bust and they would quickly realize they weren't right for each other.

He walked into his living room and was greeted by his black miniature schnauzer, Zeus. The little dog danced at his feet and then ran to the black recliner where Hunter usually sat and petted him.

"Okay, okay, I'm coming." Hunter laughed and sat. Zeus jumped up in his lap, and Hunter stroked down the dog's back. Zeus seemed to smile with utter happiness.

He remained there only a few minutes and then got up and opened the back door that led into the fenced backyard. Zeus darted outside.

About a year ago when his loneliness had become too heavy to bear, he'd found Zeus at the local shelter. At that time Zeus was only three months old and had been abandoned by a transient couple when they'd passed through town.

The dog had certainly brought Hunter a lot of joy, but there was still a core of loneliness inside him that yearned for somebody who could talk to him, somebody who might share his hopes and dreams.

Even though he knew it wasn't a good idea, he walked down the hallway and opened the door to the smallest bedroom. This room had once held a little boy's laughter and a toy box full of dreams.

It now held nothing except a photo on the wall, a crib and a teddy bear in a rocking chair to indicate that a little boy had lived two years of his life in the room.

Danny. His heart squeezed tight as he thought of that little boy…his son, who had died of childhood leukemia four years ago.

Hunter picked up the teddy bear and sank down in the rocking chair as memories of Danny took away all other thoughts. He'd handled his wife's betrayals and gotten past them. But this…this absence of the child he'd loved so much was another animal altogether. There were moments when it clawed at him, when it stabbed at his heart with a real, physical pain.

He'd grieved the loss of Danny all alone. His wife, Emily, had left him, but not before delivering one final devastation as she'd walked out of his life.

He raised the teddy bear to his nose and took a deep breath, imagining that he could still smell Danny's little-boy scent on the furry animal.

He remained that way for several long minutes and then finally stood and placed the teddy bear back in the chair. Before he left the room, he stared at the framed photo on the wall.

Danny had been a happy child, and the photo depicted a year-old Danny with Hunter. They were both laughing. Even though the disease had ravaged him, the little boy had remained a happy child who never complained.

And it was that particular spirit of Danny that Hunter now embraced. Danny would have wanted his daddy to be happy. As he left the room and closed the door behind him, he tucked his grief away, not to be entertained again until the next time he went into that bedroom.

He returned to the back door, where Zeus was waiting to come back inside. "Come on, boy." He opened the door, and Zeus greeted him all over again as if he hadn't seen Hunter a few minutes earlier.

Zeus had been Hunter's first step in reaching out for happiness once again. Now he was looking for more. He wanted to fall in love again, to get married and have children.

He just wanted to find an open and honest woman to

share his dreams of home and family, and he was hoping that's what he would find with the new woman in town. He was desperately hoping Ainsley Meadows could be the new forever love in his life.

Chapter Two

Ainsley's nerves sizzled in her veins as she stood in the bathroom and spritzed on her favorite perfume. In fifteen minutes Hunter should show up for their date.

The Red Wok wasn't a dress-up kind of place, so she had on a pair of black skinny jeans and a long pink blouse that hugged her in all the right places.

Melinda had been picked up a few minutes before by Juanita Burwell, Big Ed's wife. The couple had five children, including an eight-year-old named Bonnie whom Melinda considered her very best friend in the whole world. Juanita had made it clear to Ainsley that Melinda was welcome in their house anytime. It was only one more thing that made Ainsley desperate to make this place her permanent home.

She left the bathroom and went into the small living room to await Hunter's arrival. Although she was excited about the night to come, in the past two days she'd changed her mind a dozen times about going out with him.

One part of her thought it was foolish to start a relationship when she didn't know if or when she might have to pick up and run. And then she reminded herself that it was just a simple meal out and nothing more.

It was exactly five o'clock when a knock fell on the door. A new burst of nerves shot through her as she answered. "Hi," Hunter greeted her.

For a brief moment she was speechless. Any time she'd ever seen him before, he had been in his khaki uniform. Now jeans hugged his long legs and a black polo shirt stretched across his broad shoulders and emphasized his slim waist and hips. He looked so handsome he nearly took her breath away.

His smile faltered slightly. "Ainsley, are you ready to go?"

"Yes…yes, I'm ready," she quickly answered. "Just let me grab my purse." Gosh, he probably thought there was something wrong with her when all she'd been doing was taking a brief moment to enjoy the view.

She grabbed her purse from the sofa and then went back to the door. "Now I'm ready." She closed and locked the door behind her.

His off-duty vehicle was a king-cab pickup truck. The inside was pristine clean and smelled of leather and the faint scent of his cologne.

"Are you hungry?" he asked once they were on their way.

"Definitely," she replied. "What about you?" Now that she was alone with him, she felt unaccountably shy.

He flashed her a quick smile. "I can always eat. So, how did you spend your day off?"

"The first thing I did was slept later than usual. It's always a luxury when I don't have to open the café at six in the morning."

"What else did you do?"

"Mostly fairly boring things, like laundry and cleaning." She released a small laugh. "If you're looking for me to tell you something exciting I did today, you're out of luck."

Once again he shot her one of his smiles. "Boring isn't all bad."

"What about you? How was your day?" she asked.

"Fairly boring," he replied, and they both laughed.

By that time they had arrived at the Red Wok. The restaurant had a cozy feel, and a pretty young waitress led them to a table for two. The air was redolent with the scents of exotic spices and simmering chicken and beef.

They were each given a menu and drink orders were taken and then the waitress left them. "One of my favorites is crab Rangoon," Hunter said. With the dim light in the restaurant and a candle flickering on the table, his eyes glowed with what appeared to be a preternatural light.

"I love them, too," Ainsley replied. "Anything deep-fried and filled with cream cheese is a winner in my book."

"So, besides a couple orders of crab Rangoon, what sounds good to you?"

She closed the menu and set it on the table. "I'm in the mood for sweet-and-sour chicken."

"Hmm, that sounds good, but I'm partial to General Tso's chicken. How about we make these specials so we get the soup and the appetizers with the meal?"

"That's fine with me."

The waitress served their drinks, took their orders and then left them alone once again. She returned a moment later with their soup.

Ainsley began to relax as they ate the soup and talked about favorite foods and cooking skills.

"I have to confess, my favorite kind of cooking mostly

involves a microwave," he said. "But I do some pretty good work on my grill."

She laughed. "So, for the most part you're a zap-it kind of guy."

"For the most part, but I'll bet you're a good cook."

"I'm not a world-renowned chef, but I can hold my own," she replied. "Although I have to admit it's very easy to step out of the apartment and eat meals in the café. Big Ed lets me and my daughter eat for free, but the best part of that arrangement is there are never any dishes to clean up afterward."

"You cook but don't like to clean up dishes afterward, and I wouldn't mind doing dishes but don't really enjoy cooking. It sounds like we're a match made in heaven." He smiled at her, that devastating smile that half took her breath away.

Thankfully, at that moment the waitress appeared to serve their entrées and their orders of the crab Rangoon. "Tell me all about Ainsley Meadows," he said when the waitress had left.

"What do you want to know?" she asked. She picked up a piece of red pepper and popped it into her mouth. Now was the time she had to be on guard.

"Dusty Gulch isn't really a destination for anyone in the world, so what brought you here?"

"A flat tire," she replied with a small laugh. "After my divorce three years ago, I wanted a change of scenery, so my daughter and I were on a road trip to find a new place to live. As we were driving through Dusty Gulch I got a flat tire, and Mike, down at the garage, had to order a new tire, so we had to wait here for a couple of days. In those couple of days I realized this might be a nice place to live, and so here we are."

"Thank God for flat tires," he replied with a smile. "Where were you coming from originally?"

Let the lies begin, she thought with a touch of sadness. "A small town in Nevada." In truth she was from Portland, Maine.

"And your ex-husband was okay with you just taking off with his child?"

"He was an extremely uninvolved father and didn't really care where we went. I don't even know where he is now." Lie number two.

She shoved away any thoughts of her ex-husband, Peter, that tried to enter her mind. If she got caught up with thoughts of him, this night, this time with Hunter would be completely ruined.

"I'm sorry to hear that. I would give anything to be a husband and a father again," he replied.

She looked at him curiously. "Again? So you were married and have children?"

"No children, but I was married for about four years. But we divorced a little over four years ago." He took a bite of his dinner and then asked, "Do you want more children?"

She laughed. "To be honest I haven't given it much thought." She frowned. "If I found the right man and was married, I would maybe consider having more children. It would depend."

"Okay, now that those questions are out of the way, why don't you tell me what kinds of programs you like on television?"

The conversation grew less personal as they enjoyed the meal and talked about television and movies and music. It was a light, easy conversation that once again put her at ease.

She hoped Hunter didn't ask her any more questions that would require more lies. She liked him, and lying to him felt all wrong. But she couldn't tell him the truth—she couldn't tell anyone the truth about her past and the things she had done to survive.

If he knew the truth about her, Hunter would have to arrest her for breaking dozens of laws. But that wasn't the worst that would happen. She fought the shiver that threatened to race up her spine as she thought of the consequences of getting found by the man she had once married with such hopes of being loved for the rest of her life.

"Would you like something for dessert?" he asked.

"Goodness no, I'm absolutely stuffed." She wished she wanted dessert to prolong their time together.

"What do you think about parking on Main Street? We could take a leisurely walk together and maybe we'd work up our appetites for a visit to the ice cream parlor."

"That sounds nice." So, he wasn't in a hurry to end their time together, either. That warmed her in a way she hadn't been warmed in a long time.

They left the Red Wok, and he drove to the middle of Main Street, where they got out of the truck and began to walk. Within minutes he reached for her hand.

He had a big hand that swallowed hers in a pleasant grasp. She couldn't remember the last time a man had held her hand. It felt good, like a promise of something nice to come.

If he wanted to see her again, if he wanted to build something with her, could she allow it? There was a part of her that wanted it, but there was another part that told her it was foolish to continue to see him.

It was a beautiful September night, warm enough not

to need a jacket or sweater. It was just after seven, and the people on the streets were starting to thin out.

Still, the people they passed greeted Hunter and offered friendly smiles to Ainsley. They talked about the various shops they passed, many of them Ainsley hadn't been in yet.

They finally came to the ice cream parlor. "Now could you eat some ice cream?" he asked.

"Maybe a cone."

He smiled. "Good, let's go inside."

Within minutes they were seated at one of the high round tables inside the shop. She had a chocolate ice cream cone in her hand, and he had a banana split.

"I have to confess, ice cream is one of my weaknesses," he said.

She smiled at him. "My daughter and I have been in here several times since we moved here. Ice cream is one of her weaknesses, too."

"Maybe sometime the three of us could come here together."

"Maybe," she replied. The idea that he saw them being together sometime in the future thrilled her more than it should. In fact, she liked Hunter more than she should.

He was funny and charming, and when he looked at her there was not only an interest, but also a bit of flame in the depths of his eyes that excited her, that made her feel pretty and desirable. He felt dangerous to her in a decidedly delicious way.

Once they'd eaten their ice cream, they headed back to her apartment. It was almost nine, and not only did she still have to go and pick up Melinda, she also had an early morning the next day in the café.

"Thank you, Hunter, for such a nice evening," she

said once they stood in front of her apartment door at the back of the café.

"I really enjoyed it, Ainsley." He took a step closer to her, invading her personal space just a bit. "I'd like to see you again."

"I'd like that," she replied, half breathless with his nearness.

He smiled. "I'd also like to kiss you. May I do that?"

She was surprised and pleased that he respected her enough to ask her permission. She did not hesitate in giving him an answer.

"You may," she said and raised her face to him.

His mouth covered hers in a kiss that lasted long enough for her to know his lips were soft and warm. He didn't wrap his arms around her or pull her into him. It was just a sweet, soft kiss that, when it ended, made her want more.

He stepped back from her. "So, when can we do this again? Do you have any days off coming up?"

"I'm off on Sundays, but I reserve that day for time with my daughter. Other than that, I'm always off on Thursdays."

"What do you think about pizza?"

"I love pizza," she replied.

"Then how about next Thursday night I pick you up and we go to Antonio's Pizza? Same time as this evening?"

"That sounds good to me," she replied. Once again his eyes held that glow that warmed her from her head to her toes.

"In the meantime, I'll see you in the café."

She nodded. "Good night, Hunter."

"Good night, Ainsley."

She watched as he got into his truck and then pulled away. She went inside, shut the door and then leaned against it. She raised her fingers to her lips, remembering the thrill of Hunter's kiss.

There was a part of her that had hoped she wouldn't like him and the date would be a total bust. But that's not what happened.

She dug in her purse for her keys so she could run over to the Burwell residence to pick up Melinda. Minutes later as she drove across town, her thoughts lingered on Hunter.

Was it wrong for her to wish for a healthy relationship with a man? Was it wrong for her to be hungry for love in her life? A love she'd once hoped for but hadn't found in her first marriage?

Surely it was time for her to be able to breathe, to stop her constant vigilance and relax. It had been a little over a year since he'd last found her.

Enough time had passed that she was starting to feel safe for the first time since she'd escaped from him. But if she was wrong, if she somehow let down her guard and he found her again, she knew he would kill her and not break a sweat.

"TELL ME WHAT'S going on today, George." Hunter shot a quick look at Sheriff Wayne Black, who stood some distance away with his gun drawn, and then he looked back at the man who held a large butcher knife at his own throat.

George Calvert was a big man who suffered from chronic depression. He did pretty well when he was taking his meds, but Hunter could usually figure out how long he'd been off them by how dirty and how many stains rode his T-shirt.

They all stood in the front yard of George's attractive ranch house that was located only a block away from Hunter's own home.

As Hunter studied George's filthy shirt and greasy hair, he figured the man had been off his meds for a week to ten days. When he went off his meds, he medicated himself with booze, and it was evident now that George was drunk.

"I got nothing to live for," George said, tears streaming down his face.

"Come on, George, put the knife down and let's talk," Hunter replied. Although the sheriff stood ready to protect his deputy, Hunter was grateful he didn't try to interfere. Wayne didn't have a rapport with George like Hunter did.

"I'm not going to put the knife down. Just shoot me." He took an unsteady step forward and pointed the knife at Hunter. "Shoot me or I'm going to stab you."

Sheriff Black took a step forward, obviously concerned for Hunter's safety. "Come on, George. I'm not going to shoot you," Hunter replied, keeping his voice calm and steady. "Hell, George, I like you too much to shoot you."

George turned the knife back to his own neck. "I just need to die."

"Has Marybeth been around to see you?" Normally George's daughter kept a close eye on her father.

"She's gone…took the kids to visit their other grandparents in Kansas City." George looked even more miserable. His knife hand trembled, and although Hunter didn't fear the man would really cut his throat, he did fear he might accidentally hurt himself.

"When is she coming home?" Hunter asked.

George frowned thoughtfully. "I think maybe tomorrow."

"Now, George, you know she wouldn't be happy to find you like this. Why don't you drop the knife and we'll go inside. You can get cleaned up, and I'll make you a pot of coffee so you can sober up."

To Hunter's relief, he dropped the knife. Hunter hurried forward and kicked the knife far enough away that George couldn't pick it up again.

Hunter could have arrested George, but a little time in jail wouldn't help this situation. So instead, for the next forty-five minutes Hunter helped George get into a shower and change into clean clothes. He found the bottles of his medicine and got George to take it and promise that he would take it again in the morning.

Hunter sat and drank a cup of coffee with the man, then got him settled on the sofa so he could sleep it off. Finally, as George began to snore, Hunter left the house.

Depression was a crappy thing, he thought as he headed back to the station. Hunter had definitely suffered situational depression when he'd lost his son, but thankfully as time had passed and with a few counseling sessions, he'd managed to climb out of the darkness that had stolen all the joy from his life.

He had a couple more hours of work, and then he'd get to eat lunch and see Ainsley. After last night's date, he was really looking forward to spending more time with her.

He'd found her refreshingly authentic. She was also

intelligent and funny and the type of woman he could see himself with for the long-term.

Of course all those were first-night impressions—they certainly needed to spend more time together and see how things went. Still, for the first time since his divorce, he was excited about the possibility of a relationship with a woman he found warm and exciting.

Although he'd wanted to wrap her up in his arms last night and give her a real, deep kiss, he'd restrained himself. Her lips had been so soft and incredibly hot. Kissing Ainsley again was definitely something he was looking forward to.

It was just after one when he entered the café. His gaze immediately found Ainsley taking orders from a group of four. He sat at one of the other tables that he knew she worked and waited for her to turn around and see him.

When she did, her lips curved into a smile that seemed like it was just for him alone, and her cheeks flushed with a charming shade of pink. God, she was so gorgeous.

She'd looked incredible the night before. He had been used to seeing her wearing the red-and-black apron that all of the waitresses wore. But last night the pink blouse had hugged her curves and her jeans had fit tight on her long, slender legs.

Within minutes she stood at the side of his table. "I heard you had an exciting few minutes this morning talking down a man with a knife."

He looked at her in surprise. "Where did you hear that?"

"Sheriff Black was in here earlier extolling your patience and great police work."

Hunter felt his cheeks warm as a wave of embarrassment washed over him. "I was just doing my job."

"Maybe so, but according to Sheriff Black you went above and beyond today. Therefore, your lunch is on me," she said.

"Oh no, I can't allow you to do that," he protested.

"Please, Hunter, I insist. It's the least I can do to thank a member of law enforcement who keeps us all safe. Now, what can I get for you this afternoon?"

Although he didn't like the idea of her paying for his lunch, he also didn't want to argue with her. "I'll take one of Big Ed's big burgers with cheese and fries on the side."

"And what about to drink?"

"A cup of coffee," he replied. "I've still got a long night ahead of me, because one of the guys called in sick and I'm picking up his shift."

"That's good of you," she replied. Her blue eyes sparkled with such brightness. He wanted to fall into the crystal clear depths.

"Yeah, well, Zeus isn't very happy about me being gone all night."

Her gaze turned quizzical. "Zeus?"

"My dog," he replied.

She laughed. "I was wondering why the god of thunder and lightning would be mad at you. I'll be back in a minute with your coffee."

Once again he was struck by her intelligence. He could ask a half a dozen women on the streets of Dusty Gulch who Zeus was, and they would probably think he was some kind of new dress designer.

He found himself even more curious about Ainsley's background. As he thought back to their date the night before, he realized for the amount of time they'd spent together, he'd really learned very little about her.

The only thing he really knew was that she was originally from Nevada, divorced from an uncaring, uninvolved husband and father, and she loved crime dramas and old rock and roll music.

They hadn't really started to get into the meat of each other's lives yet, but hopefully that would all come in time. He smiled as she returned to his table with the coffeepot.

"So, you know all about my morning, but I don't know anything about yours," he said as she filled his cup.

"Let me think… I served about twenty people for breakfast, double that for lunch and all I can think about is in half an hour or so I can take my break and get off my feet for just a few minutes." She gave him a charming grin. "What can I say? It's another normal day at Big Ed's."

"Have you always worked as a waitress?"

"I was a stay-at-home mother until my divorce, and then I went to work waitressing because I knew how to hustle for tips and I could pretty much pick my schedule."

"Are you telling me after all this time you've just been hustling me for tips?" he teased.

She raised a hand up to her lips as if she'd just let a big secret escape. "Oh, I wasn't supposed to tell you that part."

He laughed and then held her gaze for a long moment. "Have I told you today that I find you really attractive?"

"Hush, you're making me blush," she replied. Sure enough, that pink hue leaped into her cheeks.

"I find your blushes utterly charming."

"Ainsley?" Big Ed's voice boomed from the pass-through window.

"Maybe that's your order up." She whirled away from the table and headed to the back.

She returned a moment later with his burger and a deeper blush on her cheeks. "I picked up your order, along with a bit of a scolding."

"Scolding?"

Her gaze didn't quite meet his. "Big Ed said we can flirt with each other a little less and I need to work a little more because I have other patrons to attend to."

"So basically what he's saying is we have to flirt faster," Hunter replied with a grin.

She laughed. "And on that note, I'm leaving your table now."

He watched her scurry away to another table and enjoyed the slight sway of her hips. He looked over at Big Ed, who grinned at him and then shook his head.

Sure to her word, she didn't give him a check when he finished eating, so he tipped her not only the cost of the meal, but also his usual twenty-five percent.

When he left the café, he was even more excited for their next date. He had a feeling that Ainsley Meadows just might be the right woman to help heal the pain of his past.

Bingo.

Peter Waverly closed his computer down and leaned back in his chair in his spacious home office in Portland, Maine. Success…it tasted even better than the thousand-dollar bottle of wine he'd opened to celebrate.

It was true that money could buy you almost anything, and he'd thrown a ton of money out on the dark web to find the answers he'd needed.

A big help in achieving what he needed was the fact that his father had passed away eighteen months before. Jeffrey Waverly had been a very successful businessman worth millions, and upon his death Peter had become a very wealthy man.

Peter now took another sip of his wine and then rose from his desk. He walked down the hallway to the master bathroom and stared into the mirror over the sink.

A stranger stared back at him. Gone was the blond hair, replaced with a dark brown color. That had been only the beginning of his transformation.

In the last year and a half he'd had a nose job, cheek and chin work done, and implants to fix two crooked front teeth. If his parents were alive right now, they wouldn't recognize him…and neither would *she*.

She wouldn't see him coming. Tomorrow he would begin arrangements to arrive in Dusty Gulch, Kansas. It was past time he have a reunion with his ex-wife, Colette.

He had to teach her a lesson for leaving him. He had to teach her an even bigger lesson for taking his daughter away from him.

He grinned at the man in the mirror. Thoughts of Colette rushed through his head…the intense love he'd felt for her, the all-consuming passion and utter need of her. She had been his entire world, and when she'd given him his daughter, he'd been over the moon with happiness.

Sure, there had been times he'd needed to discipline Colette because she broke one of his rules, but he always told her exactly why she was being disciplined.

And then she'd left him.

The last night they had been together, he'd admit, he lost it. She had made him so angry he'd almost killed her then. Luckily, he had friends in high places, and he'd managed to escape an attempted murder charge. He'd assumed he and Colette would pick up where they'd left off, but while he'd been locked up for a day, she had run.

He balled up his fist as a white-hot rage gripped him. He slammed his fist into the mirror, shattering it into a million pieces.

That's what he was going to do to Colette. First he intended to break her…and then he was going to kill her.

Chapter Three

"What is this? Date number three?" Juanita's dark eyes twinkled.

"Officially it's date number three, but I kind of feel like we're been on one extended long date," Ainsley replied. "When he comes in for lunch every day, it's like we're having mini-dates."

Once again Juanita was keeping Melinda for the evening so Ainsley could go out with Hunter. The two women were seated at Juanita's kitchen table, and the sound of children's laughter drifted in from the living room.

"You like him." It wasn't a question, it was a statement of fact.

"Oh, Juanita, I do," Ainsley confessed. "Tonight he's grilling steak for me at his house."

"If you've already eaten Chinese and pizza together, other than the café you've hit all the hot eating spots in town," Juanita said with a laugh.

"That's what Hunter told me."

The sparkle in her eyes and her smile dimmed somewhat as Juanita reached across the table and covered one of Ainsley's hands with hers.

"Try not to break his heart, Ainsley. He's had enough

heartache in his life for any one man to carry. Hunter is a good man who deserves much better than what he's been dealt in his past." Juanita pulled her hand back.

"I know he's divorced and that must have been painful for him, but is there more?" Ainsley asked curiously. Hunter hadn't appeared scarred or badly hurt when he'd mentioned his divorce to her.

"There's more, but it's Hunter's story to tell when he's ready. And now, you'd better get out of here or you'll be late for your date with him."

Ainsley nodded and stood. "I feel like I should be paying you for babysitting for me," she said as she walked toward the back door.

"Nonsense, I've told you one more in this household is no big deal. Besides, Melinda is really good with helping with the younger ones. I should probably be paying her for all her help."

Minutes later as Ainsley drove home to get ready for her date, thoughts of her mother and her sister filled her mind, and a deep ache swept over her. Ainsley's father had passed away over ten years ago. Thankfully, he hadn't lived to know the brutality his daughter had gone through.

However, her mother and sister were very much alive, and she missed them terribly. When Ainsley had first gone on the run, she'd made the mistake of believing herself safe and she'd called her mother. It had almost been a deadly error, for the phone call had been traced and he'd nearly found her.

At that time she'd realized she had to function as if her mother and her sister were dead. This had been and continued to be absolutely heartbreaking, but Ainsley was determined to protect not only herself, but more importantly her daughter.

By the time she got back to her apartment, her thoughts were consumed by the man who would pick her up in thirty minutes. There was no question that she was quite smitten with Hunter.

Their last date had gone as well as their first. At the end of that date, he'd once again given her a short, sweet kiss. Her desire to get a real, deep kiss from him was growing by the minute.

As she put on her makeup, she thought about what Juanita had said about Hunter. She'd already believed she'd seen a core of sadness inside Hunter's eyes, and now Juanita's words intrigued her even more.

Try not to break his heart. Juanita's words echoed in her head. That was the last thing Ainsley wanted to do. But she didn't know what the future might hold. She knew Hunter liked her, as she liked him. Should she just stop seeing him to make sure she didn't hurt him? Maybe he would be the one to hurt her.

She was hoping to just let things develop naturally between them. The only way she could see that she might break his heart was if she had to pick up and leave town in the blink of an eye. And she was hoping that wouldn't happen.

She finished getting ready, and by the time she stood in the living room to await Hunter's arrival, all other thoughts of anything else had vanished beneath a rush of sweet anticipation.

Promptly at five o'clock, the knock fell on her door. She grabbed her purse and then opened the door. As always her breath hitched at the sight of him.

"Hi," he said, his eyes sparkling.

"Hi back," she replied.

He grinned. "Ready to go?"

"Ready." She closed the door behind her, and together they walked to his truck.

"Hungry?" he asked once they were on their way.

"I can't wait to see if you can really grill a mean steak as you promised me yesterday at lunch."

"The pressure is definitely on. I'm also baking potatoes and making a salad."

"Sounds like a perfect meal to me." As always the scent of his fresh cologne mingling with a faint hint of minty soap and shaving cream half seduced her.

Within minutes they pulled into the driveway of an attractive beige ranch house with chocolate-brown trim. The lawn was neatly manicured, and a large maple tree stood in the center, sporting the beautiful red leaves of autumn.

"This is lovely," she said as they walked to the front door. "How long have you lived here?"

"About eight years."

"You must have been a baby when you bought it," she replied.

He laughed. "I was young." He unlocked the door and turned to her. "You told me yesterday at lunch that you liked dogs. I have to warn you, when I open this door, we will be met by a small bundle of fur who will threaten to lick you to death."

She playfully straightened her shoulders. "I think I'm ready."

He opened the door, and they stepped inside. Sure enough, a little black dog flew past Hunter and instead began to dance at Ainsley's feet.

"Oh my gosh, aren't you the sweetest thing." Ainsley

leaned over, and Zeus jumped into her arms. Zeus kissed her neck as if he was thrilled to see her.

"Uh-oh, you just made a big mistake."

"What's that?" she asked, giggling as Zeus continued to kiss her.

"You picked him up and made nice with him. Now you'll be his slave."

She laughed and put the dog back on the floor. As Zeus finally greeted Hunter, she looked around at her surroundings. The living room was a nice size. The black recliner chair and overstuffed gray sofa suggested this was a room for comfort.

A large television hung on the wall above a gray stone fireplace, and a nearby bookshelf held not only a variety of books but also a framed photo of all the men and women who worked together for the sheriff, and one picture of Hunter with the sheriff and Jake Albright.

"You know the Albrights?" she asked. She had heard about the wealthy, powerful family who owned most of the town. She also knew there had been a huge scandal when Jake Albright's brother had tried to kill Eva Martin, the woman Jake loved and had since married.

"Not well. You heard about his brother and the whole mess?"

She smiled at him and nodded. "Gossip is not in short supply around Dusty Gulch."

"That was definitely a gossip-worthy crime. Anyway, when the dust finally settled, Jake donated money for body cams and for updating other ancient equipment in the department."

"That was nice of him."

"He seems like a real nice guy."

"Are you going to give me the full tour of the house?"

She was interested in seeing all the rooms, especially his bedroom.

"Sure," he replied. "Just follow me." He led her down the hallway and gestured into the first door on the left, which was a bathroom done in navy blue.

"Nice," she said.

He grinned. "I'm not much of a decorator, so everything is pretty basic."

"There's nothing wrong with basic."

He smiled at her. "That's one more thing I like about you. No judgment." He opened a door on his right. "This bedroom I'm using as a home office." There was a desk with a computer and a small bookcase with stacked paperwork.

He gestured to the closed door on the right. "That's just an empty room."

She thought she detected some sudden emotion in his voice, but before she could really process it, he opened the door to the master bedroom.

A king-size bed was covered with a spread in light and dark grays. Two nightstands flanked the bed, each holding attractive lamps. Several black-and-white pictures of landscapes hung on the wall. There was a doorway that led to an adjoining bath.

He gestured toward the bed. "This is where I dream about you."

"Don't you know it's against the law to try to seduce a woman before you feed her?"

He laughed. "I have to confess, that's a law I'm unfamiliar with, but I hope you let me off with just a warning. Maybe it's time I take you to the kitchen before I break that law again."

She followed him back through the living room and

into a large airy kitchen with gold-speckled black granite countertops and a center island. The dining table was smoked glass, giving the whole room a sleek, contemporary look. "Please, sit down." He gestured her toward the table.

There were glass sliding doors that led onto a deck. He opened the door, and Zeus ran outside.

"This is really nice, Hunter."

He grinned. "You say that like you thought I might live in a cave."

She laughed in protest. "I definitely didn't mean it that way."

He opened the refrigerator and pulled out a bottle of red wine. "How about a glass?"

"I'd love it."

"Or, if you prefer, I have beer."

"A glass of wine is good."

He pulled a bottle of beer from the fridge. "I'm more of a beer kind of guy."

"Is there anything I can do to help with dinner?"

"No. Just sit tight and relax." He poured the wine and set the long-stem glass in front of her. "I've got the potatoes baking and the salad chilling. All I have to do is put the steaks on the grill."

He joined her at the table. "Did I mention how lovely you look tonight?"

"No, you didn't, and thank you." She'd worn jeans with a lightweight lavender sweater that she knew somehow accentuated the blue of her eyes.

"I didn't really get much of a chance to talk to you when you came into the café yesterday. So, how was your day? Anything exciting happen?" she asked.

"The most exciting thing today was trying to tell

Madge Renfro that it wasn't an emergency calling for excessive speeding to get her dog Pookie to her grooming appointment. She was going fifty-eight in a thirty-mile-an-hour speed zone. She then proceeded to tell me that Pookie had poopie on her bottom and needed the groomer to clean her up, because it was stinky and Madge doesn't do stinky." He grinned and shook his head ruefully. "The life of a small-town cop…"

Ainsley laughed. "Did you give her a speeding ticket?"

"No, I wound up giving her a stern warning."

"Ah, so at heart you're just a softie," she replied teasingly.

"Don't mistake my compassion as weakness." His eyes glittered with a look of determination and strength. "If anyone comes after me or the people I care about, they will be met with a force they've never seen before. And now I think it's time I get the steaks on."

He was the kind of man she'd once dreamed of being with…strong and confident. He made her feel safe and protected, but nobody could protect her from her ex-husband. She could only hope she was truly safe in this small town and that the two men would never, ever meet.

SHE WAS EVERYTHING he'd hoped to find. Hunter was definitely crazy about Ainsley. As they ate dinner, he told her about some of the funny things he'd encountered in his work.

He loved the sound of her laughter and the way her eyes sparkled with mirth. He found himself reaching for stories that would make her laugh again and again.

She, in turn, shared with him funny things that happened in the café. He was thrilled that their humor was very similar. It was important in a relationship to be able to laugh together.

Their conversation grew more serious as they spoke about their parents. "Mine moved to a senior living place in Kansas City two years ago," he said. "I try to drive out and see them about once a month or so."

"That's nice. Unfortunately my parents passed away in a car accident five years ago."

"Do you have siblings?" he asked.

She shook her head and stared down at her plate. "No, I'm an only child." She gazed back up at him. "What about you? Do you have brothers or sisters?"

"Nope, like you I'm an only child."

"When I was younger I made up a sister. Her name was Lily, and she was a year older than me. She played with me, and as I got a little older she gave me fashion advice and we would talk and giggle long into the night."

He smiled. "You definitely talk about her like she was real."

Once again she looked down at her plate. "She was definitely real to me for a little while." She looked back up at him, and there was a touch of embarrassment in her eyes. "You probably think I'm crazy."

"Not at all," he assured her. "You sound like you must have been a lonely child."

She shrugged. "That was then and this is now."

They finished the meal, and he insisted she remain seated as he cleaned up the dishes. Then he poured her a fresh glass of wine and he grabbed another beer. He let Zeus back inside, and they went into the living room.

Zeus jumped up on the recliner and looked at Hunter expectantly. However, for tonight Zeus was out of luck. Hunter would much rather sit on the sofa next to Ainsley.

He sat close to her, smelling the heady scent of her and feeling her body heat warming him. For the last three weeks, a tremendous desire for her had been building inside him.

He desperately wanted to pull her into his arms and feel her body against his. He wanted to kiss her lush lips until they were both breathless. But he didn't do any of that.

Their conversation was light and easy. Zeus finally gave up, jumped down from the recliner and curled up in his bed next to the fireplace.

"Tell me about your daughter," he said when the conversation between them momentarily stalled.

Her face lit up with a beautiful smile. "She's the absolute best thing that ever happened to me. She's smart and funny and has the sweetest heart in the whole wide world. Of course I might be just a wee bit prejudiced."

"Mothers are supposed to believe their children are all that and a bag of chips," he replied with a smile. "Because she's your daughter, I believe she's smart and funny and has a sweet heart. I would also believe that she's beautiful like you."

Her cheeks dusted with color. "Why, Deputy Churchill, you sweet-talk me like that and I'll think you're trying to seduce me again."

"Maybe that's exactly what I'm trying to do." His heart suddenly raced as he held her gaze. There was a stillness about her. Her tongue slid out as if to dampen overdry lips, and then those moist lips opened slightly and she raised her face to his.

Even though he saw open invitation in her mouth, in her eyes, he still wanted to make sure. "May I kiss you, Ainsley?"

"Please," she replied.

He leaned forward and placed his lips on hers. Heat swept through him and his heart raced faster, especially as she raised her arms and wound them around his neck.

He pulled her even closer to him and deepened the kiss by swirling his tongue with hers. This kiss was everything and more than he'd imagined it would be.

It was a confirmation that this was a woman he wanted more from, not only physically but also emotionally. He was all in to see where this relationship would go, and he was hoping it would go the distance.

The kiss continued for several long moments, and then he softly kissed across her jawline and down her throat. She clutched at his shoulders as if afraid he'd stop, and that only shot his desire for her even higher.

She was close enough to him now that he could feel the press of her full breasts against his chest. He wanted her...he wanted to pick her up and carry her into his bedroom. He wanted to feel her naked body next to his.

He captured her lips once again with his, and when the kiss ended she unwound her arms from around his neck and leaned back from him.

"You're a dangerous man, Deputy Churchill," she said half breathlessly.

"And you're a dangerous woman," he replied. He reached out and touched a length of her long, black hair. "I have to confess, Ainsley, I have a lot of desire for you."

"And I have a lot for you." Her eyes glistened as she held his gaze. "But I...we need to take things slowly."

"I can do that. Whatever you need from me, Ainsley. You're in charge of our physical relationship. You tell me if and when you're ready."

"Thank you. I appreciate you understanding."

"Is it too soon to ask to meet your daughter?" he asked. "Or am I rushing things?"

A small frown danced across her forehead. It smoothed out and she smiled. "How about next Thursday you come to my place for dinner and then you two can meet."

"That sounds great." He knew her agreement was a deepening of their relationship. He felt as if finally fate was casting down a light of positivity on his life, and he was excited about what the future would bring.

"Unfortunately, it's time for me to get home," she said and stood from the sofa.

Reluctantly Hunter stood as well. "Just let me grab my keys and gun, and I'll get you home."

Minutes later they walked out of the house together. "It's a beautiful night," she said.

He was about to answer her when movement next to his porch snagged his attention. Immediately he saw a man hiding in his bushes. He grabbed his gun and pushed Ainsley behind him. "Who's there? Step out where I can see you with your hands up."

Adrenaline pumped through him as he held his gun steady, ready for anything that might happen next. While he knew many of the townspeople liked and respected him, he also knew there were some who took offense when they or their loved ones were arrested.

"I said, come out of those bushes with your hands up," he commanded again.

The shadowed figure moved out of the bushes, and Hunter swore and lowered his gun. "Jeez, George, you were just about to get yourself shot. What are you doing skulking around out here?"

"I didn't mean no harm," George replied. He held out a package of cookies. "I just wanted to give these to you to thank you for taking care of me when Marybeth was gone. Then you stepped out here with your lady friend and I thought maybe the time wasn't right."

"Next time make yourself known and don't hide in the bushes." Hunter holstered his gun. He then took the package of cookies from him and introduced him to Ainsley.

"You didn't have to bring me cookies, George," he said.

"I just wanted you to know that I'm mighty thankful for your friendship." He offered a shy smile to Ainsley. "He's a mighty good man, Miss Ainsley, and now I'll just leave you two to carry on."

As they got into Hunter's vehicle, George meandered down the sidewalk back to his house. "That was sweet of him," Ainsley said.

"He's a nice guy. He's just got some issues," Hunter replied.

"Must be kind of strange to work law enforcement in a town where everyone knows where you live," she said.

"It has its moments. I occasionally get my vehicle egged, but most of the time people respect my privacy, and I haven't had any real trouble."

"That's good."

They small-talked on the rest of the way to her apartment, and then it was time to tell her good-night. "Thank you, Hunter, for another wonderful night."

"I really look forward to Thursday nights when I get to spend time with you."

She smiled up at him. "Me too." She leaned toward him, and he gathered her into his arms.

"Is it too soon to tell you that I see a bright future ahead of us?" he asked.

Her eyes darkened and seemed to shutter closed

against him. It lasted only a moment, and then she gave him one of her beautiful smiles. "I feel the same way. And now it's time for a good-night kiss."

"With pleasure." This time he kissed her softly and then stepped back from her. "I'll see you tomorrow for lunch."

"I'll be here."

Minutes later as Hunter drove back home, he thought about that moment when her eyes had darkened as if hiding secrets. Had he only imagined it? Had it somehow been a trick of the night shadows?

He hoped so, because the last woman he'd been involved with had had a ton of devastating secrets, and he never wanted to engage with a woman like that again.

Chapter Four

Ainsley sank down on the edge of Melinda's bed. "Did you have fun tonight with Bonnie?" She swept a strand of her daughter's honey-colored hair away from Melinda's beautiful blue eyes.

"We had lots of fun. We played pretend and I was the queen and Bonnie was a princess. We decided to make Henry the king and we colored him a crown, but he tried to eat it."

Ainsley laughed. Henry was eighteen months old, the youngest of Juanita's children. She leaned forward and kissed Melinda on her cheek. "Have sweet dreams, my little angel."

"I will," Melinda replied. Ainsley started to get up. "Mom, last night Daddy talked to me."

Ainsley's breath caught in her chest. "Melinda, honey, you know Daddy can't talk to you. I told you, Daddy went away and he's never coming back."

"But he told me last night that he *was* coming back for me because he loved me more than anything else in the whole wide world." Melinda looked at her earnestly.

"You must have had a dream," Ainsley said.

"It wasn't a dream. I wasn't even asleep when he talked to me," she replied.

"You tell me if he talks to you again, okay?" Ainsley stood. "Now you need to go to sleep. It's getting late and you have school tomorrow."

"Okay, good night." Melinda turned over and closed her eyes, and Ainsley left the small bedroom.

It was only when Ainsley was in her own bed that she allowed herself to think of what Melinda had said. It had been at least a year since Melinda had even mentioned her father.

At that time Ainsley had seriously considered telling the little girl that her father was dead, but ultimately she hadn't done that. Instead she'd told Melinda that her father had been sent far, far away and would never be able to see them again.

There was no question in her mind that either Melinda had dreamed of her father talking to her or it had been the fantasy of a little girl who didn't have her father around.

Still, the mention of her ex-husband stirred all kinds of memories in Ainsley, horrible memories that transferred into nightmares that plagued her for what felt like the entire night.

She awakened late the next morning. She threw herself together, checked on Melinda and then raced into the café to get things going for the day.

By the time Lana came in so that Ainsley could go back and get Melinda up and ready for school, Ainsley was still flustered and off-kilter because of the nightmares that had chased her through the night.

"Girl, sit down and I'll pour you a cup of coffee. You need to calm down before the breakfast rush really starts," Lana said. "You're as shaky as my third husband wearing a pair of my high heels."

Ainsley laughed. "I'm not sure I want to hear that whole story."

Lana pointed to the end stool at the counter. "Sit." The gray-haired woman poured Ainsley a cup of coffee. "What's going on with you this morning?"

"Nothing really. I had nightmares all night and then overslept this morning, and I've just been off since then."

"I hate nightmares. One of my worst nightmares involves my second husband, a plucked pink chicken and a horse wearing a big straw hat."

Ainsley couldn't help but laugh, which she knew was exactly what Lana had wanted. "You're the best, Lana."

Lana grinned and then her smile faded. "So, what were your nightmares about?"

"The boogeyman chasing me through the shadows."

"Ah, boogeyman dreams are the worst. Sit and drink your coffee. I've got the diners in here right now."

Lana got up as Big Ed yelled, "Order up!"

Ainsley sat for only a minute or two and then she slid off the stool. The breakfast rush would begin in earnest in the next fifteen minutes or so.

She released a deep sigh when Richard Adams walked in and sat at one of her tables. Ainsley guessed Richard to be in his midsixties. He was a big, burly man and more than a bit of a curmudgeon. He was also a crummy tipper—if he tipped at all, it was usually a single dollar.

"Good morning, Richard." She greeted him with a smile.

"What's good about it?" He scowled at her.

"The sun is shining and good food is cooking, so I'd say that's a great start to the day. Now, what can I get for you?"

"I'll take the breakfast special, but I want some

cheese in the scrambled eggs and extra onions in the hash browns. I want the bacon extra crispy and the toast light. I'll also have a cup of coffee and a glass of orange juice. Think you can get all that right?"

"I'll do my very best," Ainsley replied. She placed the order and then hurried to get his coffee and juice. "Here we go," she said as she served his drinks.

"I hope the coffee is fresh. Last time you served me, the coffee tasted burned and nasty."

Ainsley suppressed a sigh and kept her smile in place. "This coffee was brewed fifteen minutes ago, so it should be nice and fresh for you."

She had no idea why Richard always chose to sit in her section when he obviously didn't like her. She smiled as she approached the table next to Richard, where Jimmy Miller sat.

Jimmy was a young, friendly man who worked as a ranch hand for Eva and Jake Albright. "Hey, Jimmy. We don't usually see you here in the mornings," she said.

"Jake gave me the morning off, so I decided to come in here and see you." His blue eyes twinkled. "I can't think of a better way to start my morning than to see your pretty face."

Ainsley laughed. "Have you ever considered bottling that charm?"

"It's just too good to be bottled." Jimmy's smile faltered. "But I guess it's not enough to win you away from Hunter Churchill. He's got a badge and a gun…kind of hard to compete with a man like that."

"Let's talk about food, Jimmy. What can I get you this morning?" she asked, hoping to get off the personal turn of the conversation.

An hour later the dining room was almost empty as

the breakfast crowd left and the lunch group had yet to show up.

"I hope you didn't let that turd Richard get under your skin," Lana said as the two stood next to the soda machine.

"I have to admit, it's hard not to take his complaints personally," Ainsley admitted. "He acts like I never do anything right."

"At least you had that young buck Jimmy making goo-goo eyes at you."

Ainsley laughed. "Jimmy seems like a nice guy, but…"

"But it's that fine Deputy Churchill who floats your boat."

"Hey, ladies, why don't you come back here and we can have a tea party together and socialize all you want," Ed said sarcastically.

"Don't get your underwear twisted," Lana yelled back. "You know we're the best darned waitresses in town."

The two women parted ways at the coffee machine and readied the tables for the lunch rush. Immediately anticipation started working inside Ainsley. She knew once the lunch rush was over, Hunter would be in.

A thrill swept through her as she thought of the kisses they had shared the night before. There had been a part of her that had wanted to throw caution to the wind and make love with him. But when they did make love, she didn't want to have to rush because she had to leave to get Melinda by a certain time.

She was excited about taking the next step with him, and that was introducing him to Melinda. She couldn't imagine her daughter not liking Hunter. And she certainly hoped that Hunter would love her daughter.

For the first time in what felt like years, there was real

hope in Ainsley's heart. Sure, eventually she'd have to tell him about the lies she'd told him. But she hadn't lied to him about anything except a couple of factual things.

She'd been truthful with him about everything that formed the very core of her. She'd shared deep feelings with him about a number of things that shared her code of ethics, her sense of morality and the kind of woman she really was. Besides, hopefully by the time she decided to tell him the truth, he'd be so madly in love with her it wouldn't matter.

Is it safe?

For the first time since she'd run from the home she'd shared with her abusive husband, she believed the answer was yes. It was finally safe for her to pursue life to its fullest.

And she desperately wanted to do that with Hunter.

TONIGHT MARKED A month of Hunter and Ainsley officially dating. As he dressed for the date, adrenaline rushed through him as he anticipated spending more quality time with her.

He'd bought a stuffed pink unicorn for Melinda and a bouquet of a variety of flowers for Ainsley. The bouquet was bright and colorful and reminded him of Ainsley's playful, beautiful spirit.

He knew that tonight was the most important date he'd have with Ainsley. It was so vital that Melinda liked him. He knew that if the little girl didn't like him then the odds of the relationship further deepening were probably nil.

Nerves jangled through him as he drove to her place. He was interested to see the apartment she called home. He'd never been inside the living quarters at the back of the café, and his interest was piqued.

There was no question in his mind that he was falling in love with Ainsley. All the barriers he'd had up after his ex-wife's betrayals had been tumbling down since the first date he'd had with Ainsley.

He was ready to trust again. He was ready to love again, and the place he found himself in both mentally and emotionally excited him.

By the time he pulled up behind the café, his nerves had calmed and he just felt the sweet anticipation of seeing her once again.

He got out with the flowers and stuffed unicorn in hand. He was about to knock on the door when it opened and Ainsley greeted him with a smile. "Punctual as always."

"I always try to be on time." He thrust the flowers toward her. "These are for you, and the unicorn is for Melinda."

"Ah, do you always bribe the women in your life with gifts?" She took the flowers from him with a teasing glint in her eyes.

"Not always, but sometimes."

"Come on in." She opened the door wider to allow him inside. "Melinda is in her room. I'll call her out in a few minutes."

"Hmm, something smells really good," he said as he stepped into a small living room.

"Homemade enchiladas with cheesy refried beans and rice on the side. Come on into the kitchen."

The living room held a navy sofa, where he placed the unicorn, a coffee table and an entertainment center that held a small television. The kitchen was small as well, a square wooden table shoved against one wall taking up most of the room. She motioned him into one of the three chairs. The table was already set with navy blue plates and silverware.

"This is called intimate living. I can almost sit at the table and stir something on my stove at the same time," she said with a laugh.

"I find it quite nice," he replied. He watched as she placed the flowers on the counter and then reached into a bottom cabinet and retrieved a vase.

"You're very nice," she replied with a sweet smile. "This place is just a resting place. I'm hoping eventually to rent a house or at least get into a bigger apartment. While I really appreciate Big Ed for letting us stay here, I don't want Melinda to grow up in this tiny apartment."

While she was talking she arranged the flowers and then set them on the table. "There, a nice bright note to the room," she said and then moved to the oven, opened the door and then closed it again. "This should all be ready in the next fifteen minutes or so."

"Is there anything I can do?" he asked.

"Just sit. How about a beer?" She opened the fridge and brought out the brand of beer that he drank.

"I wouldn't turn my nose up at that," he replied.

For the next few minutes, they caught up on their days as she stirred the contents in two saucepans on the stovetop. Despite the odors of Mexican spices that filled the air, he could still smell the floral fragrance of her perfume. It was a scent he found incredibly sexy.

She was clad in a pair of black jeans and a fitted royal blue blouse that did amazing things to her eyes. Yes, he was definitely on the verge of falling helplessly and hopelessly in love with her.

She took another peek into the oven and then pronounced

the meal ready to serve. "Why don't you come with me to get Melinda? That way you can give her the unicorn."

"That sounds good to me." He was eager to meet her daughter, who would surely become an important part of his life and heart in the future.

As he followed her back through the living room, he picked up the unicorn from the sofa. There were three doorways, one that led to the bathroom, one that apparently was Ainsley's bedroom and the third room where her daughter slept and played.

He would have liked to get a glimpse of the bedroom where Ainsley slept. He wanted to know the color of her bedspread so he could imagine himself beneath it with her.

"Melinda, our guest is here, and he has a surprise for you," Ainsley said.

"A surprise for me?" Melinda stepped into her doorway. She was a petite girl with blond hair and her mother's beautiful blue eyes.

"Hi, Melinda. My name is Hunter." He held out the unicorn. "This is for you. It doesn't have a name yet. I thought you might want to give it a name."

Melinda took the unicorn from him, but her eyes held more than a bit of distrust. She looked at her mother and then back at him. "Thank you."

"Why don't you put the unicorn on the sofa and you can think about a name while we eat dinner," Ainsley said.

They left the small hallway and headed back to the kitchen. Melinda sat in the chair opposite him, and Ainsley opened the oven and pulled out a large baking dish and set it in the center of the table.

"There's both meat and cheese enchiladas," she said

as she spooned beans into a serving bowl and then did the same with the rice.

"Do you like Mexican food, Melinda?" The girl hadn't made eye contact with him since they'd sat down.

"I like pizza better," she said, not taking her gaze off the plate in front of her.

"Pizza is also a favorite of mine," he replied. "What kind do you like? I like pepperoni."

"Just cheese. I like cheese pizza," she replied.

The rest of the meal made it to the table, and then Ainsley sat. "Dig in," she said.

"How about I serve you two," he said and picked up Melinda's plate. "What would you like? Meat or cheese?"

"Cheese," she replied.

Hunter ladled out a cheese enchilada on the plate. "Would you like some beans and rice?"

"Some beans."

Hunter fixed the plate and then slid it in front of her. "What about you, Ainsley?"

"I can serve myself. You go ahead and fill your plate," she replied.

He took one meat, one cheese and a helping of the side dishes. Once Ainsley had served herself, they all began to eat. "This is delicious," he said after a few bites. "Does your mother always cook this good?" he asked Melinda.

She shrugged. "Mostly we eat in the café."

"And mostly that's true," Ainsley said. "Most nights I'm so tired from working all day, and the café makes it easy for us to have dinner there."

He hated that she had to work so hard, that when she worked she had very long hours. If they married, he'd make sure she would waitress only if she wanted to.

As they ate he tried to engage with Melinda, but she

was having nothing to do with him. Each time the girl answered him in monosyllables and with no eye contact, the frown on Ainsley's forehead increased.

They finished the meal and Melinda jumped up from the table. "Can I go back to my room now?" she asked.

"Before you go, did you come up with a name for the unicorn?" Hunter asked.

"I'm going to name her Ella." For the first time Melinda made eye contact with him. "Just because you bought her for me doesn't mean I have to like you."

"Melinda," Ainsley said in obvious surprise.

"Well, it's true. Daddy said I shouldn't like him because Daddy is coming to get me and Mr. Hunter just wants to get into your pants."

Hunter wasn't sure who gasped louder, him or Ainsley. "Melinda Marie, march yourself into your bedroom right now."

"I'm just saying what Daddy told me to say," Melinda protested as her eyes began to glaze with tears.

"Go." Ainsley pointed to the bedroom.

Melinda released a little sob and then raced to her room and slammed the door behind her. Ainsley turned to look at him, her cheeks pink. "I'm so sorry... I don't know what's going on with her."

"If you need to speak to her, I can cool my heels right here."

She looked at him with relief. "I'll be right back."

He watched as she hurried to her daughter's bedroom. Wow, there was no question he'd been shocked by what the little girl had said. It made him wonder where she had heard the adult, rather nasty words.

He hadn't expected it to be love at first sight with Melinda, but he certainly hadn't expected this. Ainsley was gone about fifteen minutes, and then she came back into the kitchen.

She sank down in her chair and shook her head. "I'm worried about her. She insists that my ex-husband talks to her at night, but of course that's impossible. For the last couple of years, after the divorce, she didn't really mention my ex-husband, even though she'd thought of herself as a daddy's girl at one time. I don't know if she's just imagining or dreaming about him or if she's having some sort of strange psychological issues that include auditory hallucinations."

"I'm not sure if this helps, but there is a psychologist in town who works with adults and children. Her name is June Atkins. She used to practice in Kansas City and moved out here to retire, but she is still taking patients here in town."

Hunter knew June because for a couple of months after his child had died and his wife had left him, he'd had sessions with the psychologist to help him climb out of his depression.

"Can you give me her information?" she asked.

"I'll text it to you, and now I'll help you clear the dishes."

"Oh no, you don't. You're my guest, and that means you get to just sit while I do the cleanup. Besides, it won't take me long at all." She got up and began to clear the table.

"The meal was really delicious," he said.

"Thanks. Mexican food is one of my very favorites. Too bad we don't have a Mexican restaurant in town."

He laughed. "As small as this town is, I'd say we're lucky to have the café, the Chinese restaurant and a pizza place, plus a couple of drive-through hamburger joints."

"I suppose you're right. The town isn't big enough to have cuisine from all around the world." She grew quiet as she continued to work to put the dinner leftovers away.

He knew she was probably still worried about her daughter, and as much as he would like to spend the rest of the evening with her, he believed at this point she'd rather be alone.

"Why don't we go back into the living room?" she suggested once the kitchen was completely cleaned up.

"Why don't I get out of here?" He stood and walked over to her. He gently stroked down the side of her face with two fingers. "I really don't think you're in the mood to entertain tonight."

She sighed, but she didn't object. Instead she captured his hand with hers and squeezed tight. "Thank you, Hunter."

They walked to the front door. "I'll text you Dr. Atkins's information as soon as I get home."

She nodded, and he bent down and kissed her on the cheek. She leaned against him for a long moment and then straightened. "Let me know if I can help in any way," he said.

"You're helping right now." She smiled up at him, but the smile wasn't as bright as usual. "I'll see you tomorrow for lunch."

"I wouldn't miss it," he replied. He stepped out of the apartment and into the night air.

Worry rode with him back to his house, the worry that his relationship with Ainsley was now threatened by a pint-size little girl who apparently had no intention of allowing him into her life.

Chapter Five

Ainsley pulled up in front of a two-story house just off Main Street. Her heart beat with anxiety as she parked and then turned off the car engine.

"I don't know why you just don't believe me," Melinda said from the back seat. "I don't want to talk to anyone who is going to try to make me believe I'm just dreaming when Daddy talks to me at night."

"I'm sure that's not what Dr. Atkins is going to try to do," Ainsley replied, although she really had no idea how Dr. Atkins was going to try to help Melinda. All she knew was something needed to be done.

It was late Wednesday afternoon, and Ainsley had taken off work to bring Melinda here. Since the disrupted date with Hunter the Thursday before, Melinda had continued to talk about her daddy coming to get her soon and how he spoke to her at night. She was also becoming more and more disrespectful to Ainsley, per Daddy's instructions.

"It's time for us to go in and meet Dr. Atkins," she now said and opened her car door.

"I still think this is dumb," Melinda grumbled as she got out of the car.

Maybe it was dumb, but Ainsley was desperate to get

somebody else's opinion about what was going on with Melinda. June Atkins had been very nice on the phone when Ainsley had called her and explained what had been happening with her daughter. When Ainsley had made the appointment, she was instructed to walk around to the back of the house, where apparently the garage had been converted into an office.

Ainsley knocked on the door, and June Atkins answered. She appeared to be in her late sixties or early seventies. Her hair was a beautiful silver and she had kind blue eyes.

She ushered them into a little waiting room painted in pale blue and with a blue flowered love seat. A coffee table held several magazines for both men and women.

"Please, have a seat." She pointed to the love seat, and she sat in a wing-back chair that matched the love seat. She offered them a warm smile. "It's so nice to meet you both. Melinda, I'm especially excited to get to know you better."

Melinda didn't respond.

The smile on Dr. Atkins's face didn't waver. "Mom, why don't you relax out here while I take Melinda into my office for a private chat?"

She stood, and Ainsley prodded her daughter with her elbow to get her up. "I promise I don't bite," Dr. Atkins said.

A small smile crossed Melinda's lips. "I didn't think you would bite me."

The two disappeared behind a door, and Ainsley blew out a deep, weary sigh. It was exhausting to worry about a loved one. Melinda was her very heart and soul, and she didn't know what was happening to turn her sweet, loving child into a stranger.

Had the trigger for Melinda's odd behavior been the knowledge that her mother was now dating? Something that hadn't happened since the two of them had run from Portland? Run from Peter?

If she had to give up Hunter to fix Melinda's mental health, then she would do that. But even thinking about that option made her heart twist with an ache she hadn't thought possible.

In four short weeks, Hunter had already worked his way deep into her heart. She hadn't realized how deep until this moment, when she had to contemplate telling him goodbye.

She'd had such hope that finally she was going to get to live the fairy tale of love with a good man. But there was no way she could sacrifice her daughter for her own happiness.

The minutes ticked by with agonizing slowness. What were they talking about in there? Would Melinda inadvertently say something that would bring a scrutiny to Ainsley's life that she couldn't afford?

Peter had always been good at keeping his abuse of Ainsley under wraps and separate from their daughter. Many nights Ainsley had suffered in silence and lied to her little girl about black eyes and split lips so Melinda wouldn't know the truth about her father.

In any case, Peter hadn't been a hands-on kind of father, and often several days and nights would go by without him even asking about his daughter. Even though he'd been the one who had told Melinda she was a daddy's girl, the truth was the two hadn't been close.

For the past three years Melinda had seemed to accept that their vagabond lifestyle was normal and they were just seeking the perfect place to call their forever home.

She hadn't talked much about Peter, and Ainsley just assumed with the passing of time that Melinda had very few memories of her father and didn't miss him at all.

Until this…these nighttime disturbances that had Melinda believing her father was coming for her. Once again Ainsley released a deep sigh as she stared at the closed office door.

She didn't know how long these sessions lasted, but she did know how much they cost. Unfortunately, health care wasn't in the budget at the moment. That was a whole different worry. She was hoping to at least be able to make enough in the near future to get Melinda some kind of health-care coverage, but that hadn't happened yet. Still, she would work as many shifts as possible, sell whatever little she possessed to see that Melinda got the help she needed.

Finally the door reopened, and the two walked back out. Both were smiling. "Melinda, can you wait out here for a few minutes so I can talk to your mother?" Dr. Atkins asked.

Ainsley dug her phone out of her purse and handed it to Melinda. "You can play your games while I'm gone." Melinda grabbed the phone and sat on the love seat while Ainsley followed Dr. Atkins into her office.

The inner office held a nice oversize chair with a coffee table next to it and a small desk with a computer on top and a black swivel desk chair.

"Please sit." Dr. Atkins gestured her to the overstuffed chair. Ainsley sat and leaned forward.

"First of all, you have a charming and very bright daughter," Dr. Atkins said.

"Thank you," Ainsley replied.

"She's also very stubborn in her belief that she talks

to her father at night, but I gave her some things to think about and hopefully we can start working to make her see that this is a fantasy."

"So, that's what you believe it is?"

"I believe it's the longing of a little girl who doesn't have her father in her life."

"But why now? Do you think this has something to do with the fact that I'm dating? Should I stop seeing the man?"

"I would not recommend you stop dating. We don't want to give that kind of power to an eight-year-old girl. It's possible it was triggered at school or whatever. What I recommend for now is that you continue to listen to her, but don't engage in a battle with her. I'm hoping I can appeal to her intelligence."

The psychologist smiled. "I don't think this is a long-term issue. I'd like to see her next week at this same time, if that's okay with you."

"That's fine. I feel so much better now that I've spoken to you," Ainsley replied. "We'll definitely be here next week."

She stood as the doctor did the same. "I'm confident we can get this cleared up in just a couple of sessions." She opened the office door, and they stepped out.

Melinda got up from the love seat and handed Ainsley back her phone. "Melinda, it was nice visiting with you," Dr. Atkins said.

"Thank you," the young girl replied.

Minutes later mother and daughter were back in the car and heading home. "Did you like Dr. Atkins?" Ainsley asked.

"She was nice. She didn't believe me about Daddy, but she was still nice," Melinda replied.

"How do you know she didn't believe you?"

"'Cause of the questions she asked me." Melinda frowned. "I don't want to talk about it anymore. Can we stop for ice cream on the way home?"

"I think I can make that happen," Ainsley replied.

The rest of the evening passed peacefully. Even though it was early, once Melinda was in bed Ainsley took a long hot shower, changed into her nightgown and then got into bed.

She held her cell phone in her hand, and after several moments of thinking about it, she punched in Hunter's phone number.

He answered on the first ring. "I was just thinking about you," he said.

His deep voice smoothed all the rough edges inside her. "And what were you thinking?"

"Since I didn't get into the café for lunch today, I was just thinking how much I missed seeing you and wondering if we're going to get together tomorrow night?"

"I'd love to get together tomorrow night," she replied.

"I was afraid you might not want to see me again."

"I was afraid about that, too. But we had our first appointment with Dr. Atkins today, and she assured me that it was okay for us to continue to date despite Melinda's current attitude toward you."

"That's good to hear." There was obvious relief in his voice. "I'm hoping Melinda will warm up to me as time goes on."

"We stopped on the way home to get ice cream, and I told her that no matter what her father said to her at night, she knows the difference between right and wrong and good behavior and bad. I told her I expected her to act appropriately."

"Did she listen to you?"

"I believe she did. Time will tell. So, what are the plans for tomorrow evening?" She cuddled down in the blanket, happy that she was ending the night with a phone call with the man who was quickly winning her heart.

"Whatever we do together, I'll be happy," he said.

"Why don't we go to your house and hang out watching television and eating popcorn," she suggested.

"That sounds good to me," he replied. "But I think I'll order pizza for us to eat before I break out the popcorn."

"How about you let me get the pizza, Hunter?"

"That's not necessary, Ainsley."

"I know it's not necessary, but it isn't always necessary for you to pay every time we get together."

"I'm an old-fashioned kind of guy. I like taking care of the woman I'm dating. I'll let you know if and when it becomes a problem, deal?"

She hesitated a moment. "Deal," she finally replied.

They spoke a few more minutes and then hung up. Ainsley plugged her phone into the charger and then settled in to sleep. She was falling fast for Hunter Churchill. He was everything she'd ever wanted in her life.

She loved his patience and his kind heart. She adored his smile and the sound of his deep, rumbling laughter. She absolutely loved the sound of her name falling from his lips. She just wished it was her real name.

The closer she got to him, the more she worried about the lies she'd told him. Could she go the rest of her life living the lie? As she drifted to sleep, she had no answer.

PETER HAD BEEN busy since he'd learned the location of his ex-wife. He'd bought himself a farm fifteen minutes from Dusty Gulch. It was a simple three-bedroom house, nothing like what he was accustomed to, but it was completely isolated and perfect for what he had in mind.

He now stood in front of the bank of computer monitors that showed him images of Colette's little apartment. Both Melinda and Colette were asleep, so there would be no more activity happening tonight.

He'd been enjoying having conversations with Melinda after he knew Colette was in her own bedroom at night. It had been particularly fun to watch her misbehave at his command.

Having the cameras and microphones installed there had been fairly easy. All he'd needed was to find somebody who could give him access to the café attic.

He'd found that person in Ted Johnson, the janitor/maintenance man who worked at night at the café. Ted was sixty-three years old and worked hard to earn just a little bit more than minimum wage.

When Peter offered the man ten thousand dollars for two nights of access to the attic and not telling a soul about it, Ted had jumped at the opportunity.

The two nights had allowed Peter to set up the electronics he needed to watch and listen into the tiny two-bedroom apartment where his angel and his bitch of an ex-wife were staying.

He now stretched with his arms overhead and then left the bedroom. He locked the door behind him and then looked into the master bedroom, where Sheila Turrel was sprawled across the bed.

Sheila was the perfect woman he needed for now. He'd gone trolling for somebody just like her at a dive bar in Dusty Gulch called the Wrecking Ball.

The thirty-six-year-old woman was thin as a rail and

not pretty, but she was also a heavy drinker and a heroin user, which made her very attractive to him.

As long as he kept her hooked up, she would be the best alibi he could have if for some reason he came under suspicion.

She stayed nodded out most of the time and had no idea when he was home and when he wasn't, but she would swear he'd been with her if anyone from law enforcement asked. Although he found her a weak, disgusting waste of a human being, he needed her right now to assure his own safety.

He continued walking down the hallway and into the kitchen. He flipped on the light against the darkness of night and then opened the back door and stepped out on the back porch.

The smell struck him first. It was an odor of musk and filth, of urine and feces. Grunts and rustling filled the otherwise silent night.

He didn't have to see the pigs to know they were there. When he'd bought the farm, he'd paid extra for the herd of pigs the farmer owned.

According to what he'd read, there were far too many pigs in the small pen where they were kept and Peter was making sure they all stayed nice and hungry.

The most important thing he'd learned about pigs was that sixteen of them could completely eat a human body in eight minutes. There were currently twenty-five pigs in the pen.

This pen of hungry pigs was perfect for tying up any loose ends. Right now there were two—Ted and Sheila.

Ultimately the pigs were his ex-wife's fate.

Colette had wanted to disappear from his life. Now

he was going to make sure she disappeared from life altogether. He drew in the nasty scent of the pigs.

Yes, it all smelled bad…but it also smelled of sweet revenge.

"THE PIZZA SMELLS DELICIOUS," Ainsley said as she walked into Hunter's kitchen.

"Half pepperoni and half mushroom and green pepper," he replied as he got out two plates and napkins.

Ainsley sat at the table. She was touched that he had remembered the kind of pizza she liked. It meant he paid attention, and that made her feel very special.

"Beer or soda?" he asked.

"Soda is fine for me."

Within minutes they were both seated at the table and enjoying the pizza. "It was another fairly quiet day for me, which is just the way I like my days," he said between bites.

"My day started with me having to deny service to Ben Wilkins. He came in highly intoxicated. He was loud and belligerent, so I told him he needed to leave," she said.

"Did he comply?" Hunter asked. His green eyes darkened as he held her gaze.

"He screamed and cursed at me, and then Big Ed escorted him out of the building," she replied.

"Big Ed should have called me. You should never have to endure that kind of abuse."

"Down, tiger," she replied with a laugh, although she was secretly thrilled by the protective light that shone from his beautiful eyes.

"I don't like anyone talking disrespectfully to you," he replied.

She laughed once again. "It's a hazard of working in food service."

"Then you should get hazard pay."

She grinned at him. He looked amazingly handsome tonight in a pair of jeans and a forest green shirt that did wonderful things to his eyes.

She'd never dreamed it could be so easy, that a relationship could feel so warm and comfortable. She'd never believed she was worthy of a man like Hunter. He made her feel so many ways she hadn't felt before...witty and funny, smart and beautiful. Whenever she was with him, she felt protected and safe.

She wished she had met him years ago. She wished she had met him instead of Peter. But then she wouldn't have Melinda, and she would never, ever wish her beautiful daughter away.

Once the pizza was eaten, they moved to the sofa, where he pulled her close to his side. She relaxed into him, loving the feel of his nearness and the scent of him that stirred her on so many levels.

He turned on a movie they both had wanted to see, but she was more focused on him than the action taking place on his television. As they cuddled together, she stroked her hand back and forth across his broad chest.

It didn't take long for her to sense a growing tension in him. His heartbeat accelerated beneath her touch and his breathing became quickened.

"Being this close to you does terrible things to me, Ainsley," he whispered into her ear.

She raised her head to look at him. "Like what terrible things?"

"You make me think about kissing you until we're both positively breathless. You make me try to imagine what it would be like if I swept you up in my arms, carried you into my bed and made sweet love with you."

Her breath half caught in the back of her throat. "Why, Deputy Churchill, are you trying to seduce me again?"

"I definitely am. How am I doing?" His eyes glittered with the burn of desire.

"You are doing wonderfully well. I'm just wondering why you aren't following your words with actions?"

His lips immediately captured hers in a kiss that seared her right to the bottom of her feet. She was ready to take the next step with Hunter. She was ready to be completely vulnerable and make love with him.

When he finally lifted his lips from hers, she smiled. "Ah, that was good for a beginning, but what happened to the part where you sweep me into your arms and carry me to your bed?"

His eyes widened and then blazed with a passion that only confirmed to her that this was right. It was obvious he wanted her and oh, how she wanted him.

He stood and then picked her up into his arms and walked down the hallway. When he reached his bedroom door, Zeus tried to follow them in.

"Sorry, buddy. This is a party of two." He closed the door to shut the dog out, and then he walked across the room and gently deposited her onto the bed.

He stepped back and gazed at her for a long moment. "I must say, you look amazing in my bed."

"It will be a better picture when you join me here."

He grinned and leaped onto the bed. Her laughter was stolen by another one of his toe-curling kisses. Their tongues swirled together in a heated dance of sensuality.

His hands moved up the back of her blouse, his palms

hot against her bare skin. She wanted his hands touching her bare skin everywhere...and she wanted to touch his.

As the kiss ended, she pushed away and sat up and then began unfastening the buttons on her blouse. He sat up as well and watched her. When she was finished with the last button, he reached out and pushed the garment off her shoulders, leaving her clad from the waist up in only her lacy bra. The blouse fell to the bed behind them.

He then grabbed the bottom of his shirt and pulled it off over his head. His bare chest was gorgeous. It was smooth, and his muscles were sculpted and perfect.

They came back together for more kissing and touching, and within minutes her bra went the way of her blouse. Finally, he kicked off his shoes, took off his socks and then shucked his jeans. He looked completely hot clad only in a pair of black boxers.

He moved next to her and unfastened the button on her jeans and then unzipped them. She raised her hips to help him pull them off her, and then there was nothing between them except his boxers and her lacy, pale pink panties.

"You are so beautiful," he whispered. "And I want you so badly."

"Show me," she replied half breathlessly.

He pulled her back into his arms for a deep kiss. After several minutes he slid his lips to kiss behind her ear and then on down her throat.

He melted her with the flames of desire in his eyes, with the heat of his lips and hands on her. When his mouth captured one of her taut nipples, she couldn't help but moan with the sweet sensations.

Her hands gripped his shoulders as he licked and nipped at first one nipple and then the other. This was what she'd wanted...this complete and total closeness with him.

As his hand slid down her stomach to the waistband of her panties, her breath caught in her throat. He slowly moved his fingers from left to right, teasing her and heightening her need for him.

She reached down and found him fully aroused within his boxers. She plucked at the material, wanting the boxers off him so she could stroke his bare hardness.

Before that could happen, his fingers slid beneath her panties and found her moist center. She cried out as electric shocks of pleasure ripped through her. His fingers moved with just the right pressure, with just the right tempo. Her need climbed higher and higher, and then a climax shattered her.

She cried out his name and reached for his arousal once again. "I need more, Hunter," she gasped. "I want you inside me."

He rolled away from her and took off his boxers. He then reached into his nightstand and grabbed a condom. He quickly rolled it on and then positioned himself between her thighs.

He slowly eased into her and held her gaze. His eyes were like a primal forest, dark and wild. He buried himself in her and then remained unmoving for a long moment.

As he continued to look down at her, she felt connected to him not only physically but also emotionally as well. It was as if their souls were uniting as well as their bodies.

Slowly he began to stroke into her, and the tension inside her began to build once again. Their breaths became pants as he increased the quickness of his strokes. She was lost in him…in them.

She'd never felt these incredible feelings before, certainly not in all the years of her marriage. This was more intense, more meaningful, and while he masterfully took control, there was also a wealth of gentleness coming from him.

With a gasp, she felt another climax begin to build inside her. She urged him faster and met each of his thrusts with her own. She felt him surging inside her and the tension stiffening his entire body right before he climaxed sent her back over the edge again.

After several seconds he rolled off her and onto his back next to her. It took a few minutes for them to both catch their breaths.

He propped himself up on an elbow and smiled down at her. "That was better than in my best dreams," he said.

"For me, too."

He reached out and stroked his fingers across an old scar on her abdomen. "What's this from?"

"Oh, uh, a splenectomy due to a car accident," she said. The lie tripped from her lips and she hated herself for it. She still had her spleen, no thanks to Peter, who had tried to kill her by stabbing her to death. Thankfully all the other wounds and broken bones she'd received from him were no longer visible.

Once again he stroked his fingers over the old scar. "I'm sorry that happened to you."

"It was a long time ago," she replied. She sighed and looked at the clock on his nightstand. "It's almost time for you to get me back home."

"I thought it was women who always wanted to bask

in the afterglow," he said teasingly. He leaned over and kissed her tenderly.

When the kiss ended, he swept a strand of her long hair away from her face and frowned. "I wish you could stay right here for the whole night. I would love to cuddle you all night long and then wake up in the morning with you in my arms."

She sighed with wistfulness. "I would love that, too, but unfortunately reality intrudes and we need to get up."

"Go ahead and use my master bathroom, I'll use the one in the hallway." He rolled off his side of the bed, grabbed his boxers, jeans and shirt from the floor and then left the bedroom.

Ainsley grabbed her clothing from the bed and the floor and then went into the adjoining bathroom. As her heart finally found a normal rhythm, she dressed and then stared at her reflection in the mirror.

She looked like and felt like a woman who had just been thoroughly loved. Making love to Hunter had been magical. This evening, this experience, had just confirmed what she'd seen coming…she was falling head over heels in love with Hunter Churchill.

She wanted this relationship to thrive and grow. She wanted this healthy and happy relationship. She desperately wanted a future with Hunter. Right now she felt as if it was within her fingertips—she just hoped nothing happened to mess it all up.

Chapter Six

"Deputy Churchill, somebody is out here to see you," Lanie said when she stuck her head into the bullpen.

He gazed at her quizzically, but before he could ask her who, she disappeared again. "Ainsley?" Nick said from his desk.

Hunter shrugged. "She's never shown up here before." But they hadn't spent the kind of night they had shared last night before.

He'd spent far too much of the morning thinking about how much he'd loved the taste of her, the feel of her bare silky skin against his and the evocative scent of her.

He sprang to his feet and hurried to the door. "Go get her, tiger." Nick's laughter chased behind him.

Hunter stepped out into the reception area, disappointed not to see Ainsley but surprised to see Marybeth Wilson. "Marybeth, your dad doing okay?" he asked, instantly concerned about George.

She was a petite blonde and had an aluminum foil–wrapped platter in her hand. "He's doing fine. I should have done this before now, but I wanted to thank you for taking care of him while I was gone. He told me how kind you were to him." She held out the platter. "These are homemade chocolate chip cookies fresh out of the oven."

"Marybeth, you didn't have to do this," he said as he took the platter from her. He made an instant decision not to tell her about his father's visit to his home with his cookies. George apparently hadn't told her, and Hunter wasn't going to rat him out.

She smiled. "Trust me, I needed to do this. You've been so kind to my father on so many occasions. It was about time I did something to show my appreciation."

Hunter smiled. "These cookies smell delicious, but still, I was only doing my job."

"We both know that you have gone above and beyond just doing your job for him many times. Anyway, enjoy the cookies." She gave him another smile and then turned and left.

"You'd better give me one of those cookies before you take them back to the other guys," Lanie said. She jumped out of her chair, ripped the aluminum foil off the cookie plate and then sighed with pleasure. "Look at them…all warm and gooey with chocolate chips." She grabbed two off the platter and then returned to her desk.

"This was really nice," Hunter said.

"Way better than that time Betty Simon brought you her special cauliflower casserole," Lanie replied.

"Yeah, her thoughtfulness was appreciated even if her cooking skills weren't," Hunter said with a laugh. He returned to his desk, where Nick immediately grabbed two of the cookies. "If these are from Ainsley, then you better marry that girl," he said after a bite.

"Actually, they're from Marybeth Wilson for me taking care of George whenever he goes off the rails. But I am considering marrying Ainsley."

Nick paused with the cookie halfway to his mouth. "Seriously, dude?"

"Seriously," Hunter replied. He didn't know exactly when he'd realized he was completely in love with Ainsley, but he had reached a point in their relationship that love for her filled his heart. Making love with her last night had just confirmed it.

"So, are you going to propose to her soon?"

Hunter frowned. "Not yet. We've got a major issue we need to get past before I'll ask her."

"What's the issue?"

"Her daughter hates me."

Nick's dark brows danced upward in surprise. "Seriously? She hates the most well-liked deputy in the entire county? What did you do to her?"

Hunter laughed. "Nothing. I bought her a stuffed pink unicorn, thinking that would break the ice between us."

"So apparently she isn't into unicorns," Nick said.

"Oh, she was into the unicorn, she just wasn't into me. I'm hoping it's just going to take a little time."

Nick took a bite of the cookie. "Good luck with that, man."

Minutes later Hunter was back patrolling the streets, but his mind was still filled with Ainsley and Melinda. He hoped Dr. Atkins would be able to sort things out with Melinda and the little girl would give him a chance to be a part of her life. Without that, he knew there was no hope for a future with Ainsley.

Still, last night had confirmed to him that she felt close to him. He didn't believe she was the kind of woman who would go to bed with him if she wasn't falling in love with him, and that excited him for the future.

When it was time for his lunch break, he was more than happy to head to the café. He stepped inside, grateful that as usual the lunch rush had passed and the café was relatively quiet.

He spied Ainsley by the soda machine, and he slid into a seat at one of her tables. When she turned around, her beautiful smile lit up her features. She delivered a soda to one of the other diners and then walked over to his table.

"I've been waiting all day to see you," she said.

"That's funny, I've been waiting all day to see you, too," he replied.

"I couldn't wait to thank you, although you shouldn't have." Her eyes twinkled brightly.

"You're welcome, but what is it I shouldn't have done?"

"You know…the roses," she replied with one of her charming blushes rising up to color her cheeks.

"Uh…what roses?"

"Stop playing," she replied and gave him a playful smack on his shoulder. "They were delivered in here this morning."

He gazed at her solemnly. "Ainsley, I'm not playing with you. I didn't send you roses. What exactly was delivered to you this morning?"

"A dozen red roses in a beautiful vase with no card. I just assumed after last night…" Her voice trailed off.

"I wish I had sent you roses, Ainsley, but I didn't." He reared back in his chair and then grinned at her. "So, it looks like you have a secret admirer and I have some competition."

A deep frown cut across her forehead. "It isn't funny. I don't like secrets."

"I'm sure if you give it a little time whoever sent them to you will let you know."

"I hope you're right," she replied. Her frown smoothed out somewhat. "Now, what can I get you for lunch?"

He placed his order with her, missing the flirtatious small talk they usually indulged in. He watched her taking care of the other diners in her section, and a sense of disquiet suddenly filled him. Despite the way Ainsley had reacted to the roses, maybe he shouldn't be so sure of himself when it came to her.

Who in the hell was her secret admirer, and how much did he have to worry about him?

AINSLEY SAT AT her kitchen table and stared at the vase of red roses that had been delivered to her in the café that morning.

When she'd realized the gorgeous roses beautifully arranged in a white vase were for her, she'd been thrilled. She'd also been certain they had been from Hunter even though there hadn't been a card.

Lana had teased her unmercifully, and the other waitresses, both married and single, had looked at her with a bit of envy. She'd quickly carried them back to her kitchen table and then had hurried back to the floor to continue working.

She'd spent the rest of the morning anticipating seeing Hunter and then when she had and he'd told her he hadn't sent the roses, a sick feeling had swept through her.

She definitely didn't like surprises. She'd had enough of them during her marriage to Peter. She'd never known whether he was going to stroke her hair or pull it, smile at her or smack her. The secrets that only he could hear and see in his own head kept him unpredictable and dangerous.

She shook her head to dispel any further thoughts of Peter. She couldn't allow herself to be pulled back into memories of his brutality and utter madness.

If not Hunter, then who had sent her the roses? The longer she stared at them, the higher her anxiety climbed. They were such a deep red…like the color of blood.

Now why would she think that? The flowers might represent a special thank-you to her or a budding romantic interest from somebody. She just wished the sender had sent an identifying card as well.

She glanced at the clock. It was just after eight. There was only one flower shop in town, and they might still be open. Maybe she could get some answers from somebody there.

She found the number and then called. "April's Flowers," a pleasant female voice answered. "This is Megan speaking, how can I help you?"

"Hi, Megan. My name is Ainsley Meadows, and I work at the Dusty Gulch Café. This morning a dozen red roses were delivered to me there, and I was wondering if you could tell me who sent them."

"I'd love to help you out, but there was no order for a dozen roses that came out of my shop today," Megan said.

Ainsley paused in surprise. "Are you sure?"

The woman on the other end of the line laughed. "Honey, I've been here all day, and a sale for roses is a good day for me. Trust me, no roses went out today or any time in the last few weeks."

"Thank you anyway," Ainsley said. She hung up and then stared at the roses again. She hadn't paid much attention to the young man who had delivered them. He'd worn a hat, so she didn't even know if he'd been blond or brunette.

She jerked up from the table and carried the roses to the trash can. If they weren't from Hunter, then she didn't want them. The flowers finished filling the trash bag, and she tied it at the top and then carried it to her door.

The dumpster for the café was just at the back of the property. She regularly carried her trash bags out to it, but for some reason she was particularly on edge tonight.

You can always take the trash out tomorrow when there's more daylight, a little voice whispered in her head. *You've taken the trash out at this time of night a hundred times before,* another voice chided.

Irritated with herself, she unlocked the door, grabbed the trash bag and stepped outside. The cool night air wrapped itself around her as she scurried across the parking lot toward the dumpster.

The night seemed deeper…darker than usual as the moon was covered by clouds. The streetlamp on the corner provided only the faintest illumination into this area.

She reached the dumpster and threw in her bag. A rustling behind the dumpster froze her in her tracks. Was somebody there? Was somebody hiding behind the trash receptacle? Watching her? Waiting for her?

Her heart began to pound as she took a step backward, keeping her gaze shooting from the dumpster to the area just around it. Somebody had sent her roses…was it possible that somebody was stalking her?

She jumped and released a sudden laugh in relief as a mouse scurried out from behind the dumpster and raced across the parking lot. Jeez, what was wrong with her?

She went back inside the apartment and sank down on the sofa. She was being ridiculous. Just because she'd gotten roses from an unknown person didn't mean that something was wrong…that something was somehow threatening.

Hunter was right—somebody would probably come

forward by the end of the next day to claim the roses and say why they had sent them to her.

Her negative reaction was from her past. Peter had always gotten her roses...sometimes as an apology for beating her, and sometimes in anticipation of beating her. But Peter wasn't around. And hopefully he had no idea where she was. Most men would assume any woman loved that particular flower.

She had just gotten into bed when her phone rang. She saw the caller identification and immediately answered, unable to halt the smile that curved her lips.

"I've decided I love the sound of your voice right before I go to sleep," Hunter said.

"Same," she replied simply.

"I've been kicking myself all day long," he said.

"Why is that?"

"After last night I should have been the one to send you roses."

"Hunter, making love to you was all the gift I needed. I don't need you to send me roses or gifts. You're all I want."

"God, I'm crazy about you," he replied.

She laughed. "You're just happy because I'm a cheap date."

"Well, there is that," he returned with a laugh of his own. "I just wanted to tell you to have sweet dreams."

"Thank you, Hunter. Sweet dreams to you, too."

Her smile continued to ride her lips long after the phone call ended. Making love with Hunter had been like fulfilling a fantasy. He'd been so gentle, so wonderfully tender and everything she had hoped he would be.

She awakened the next morning feeling well rested and more centered. She was especially pleased that over breakfast Melinda didn't mention hearing her father talk to her the night before. Maybe the appointment with Dr. Atkins was already making a difference.

Since it was Saturday, Melinda settled in at a small two-top table next to the kitchen with Ainsley's phone for playing games, a pack of crayons and several coloring books, and colored pencils with drawing paper. Melinda was always good about keeping herself occupied on Saturdays when Ainsley worked and Melinda was out of school.

As Ainsley started her workday, she couldn't help but speculate about the sender of the roses. When she told Lana that Hunter hadn't sent them to her and the local florist hadn't delivered them, Lana played sleuth with her.

"Maybe Jim Nelson sent them to you," Lana said when the Ainsley met her at the coffee machine. "You know that man thinks the world of you."

Ainsley thought of the elderly man who she served breakfast to each morning. "He's a sweet man, but I don't see him sending me roses for getting his order right each day. Besides, he also doesn't strike me as a man who has that kind of money to throw away. I'm sure a dozen roses aren't cheap."

"That's true. Hell, most of the men in this town wouldn't spend the money to send a woman a dozen daisies. Bunch of cheapskates, if you ask me," Lana grumbled and then brightened. "What about Jimmy Miller? You know that boy makes a good salary working for Eva and Jake Albright, and he definitely acts like he might have a crush on you."

"Lana, order up," Big Ed hollered, effectively halting their conversation.

Was it possible Jimmy had sent the flowers to her?

He was definitely a flirt when he came in. He also always sat in her section. The more she thought about it, the more convinced she was that Jimmy had bought her the roses. He'd told her that Hunter was a hard man to challenge…was he attempting to do just that by sending her the flowers? When he came in for lunch today, he'd probably confess that he'd sent them.

She smiled when George Calvert walked in with another man she didn't recognize. The two remained standing and talking to each other just inside the door. She assumed the two were together, but then George took a seat in her section and the other man sat in Lana's.

"Hi, George," she said. "For a minute I thought you would be sitting at a table for two with a friend."

"Nah, I just met that gentleman outside the door. He's new in town and his name is Hank Bridges," George replied. "He's single and bought the old pig farm just outside the city limits."

"Well, it's nice to see you again," she said. "You look good."

"I'm feeling pretty good. I decided I needed one of Big Ed's breakfast specials this morning."

"Would you like the one with the pancakes or the biscuits and gravy?"

"I have a hankering for pancakes, so I'll take the special that includes them."

"And to drink?"

"A cup of coffee will be just fine."

"I'll put your order in and get your coffee right away."

Ainsley placed George's order and then once again met Lana at the coffee machine. "Don't look now, but the new man in town has been checking you out," Lana said. "I swear, Ainsley, you could have your pick of a dozen single men in town."

Ainsley laughed. "I've got the single man I want."

"And a good one he is," Lana replied.

Suddenly Ainsley was reminded of what Juanita had said about Hunter's past, something Hunter hadn't shared with her yet. Everything had been going so well with Hunter, she'd forgotten what Juanita had said.

What could it be that Hunter hadn't told her yet? They'd shared so many conversations, shared so many things about each other. What might he be hiding? And was it something that might play a negative role in their relationship?

Ha, she was worried about him having secrets when she probably had more secrets than anyone else in town. Definitely double standards. She expected him to come clean about everything while she was lying to him about almost everything.

As she served George his coffee, she glanced over to the new man in town. The single ladies should be happy with a new, attractive man in town.

His dark brown hair was nicely cut, and he had high cheekbones and a perfectly straight nose. When he smiled at Lana, his teeth were straight and white…altogether he was quite a hunk.

But, despite his good looks, he stirred absolutely nothing in her. Her heart was already completely taken by a very hot deputy sheriff named Hunter.

The breakfast rush passed, and then it seemed like just a minute went by and the lunch rush was on. Ainsley scooted from table to table along with Lana and two other waitresses who worked on the weekends.

"How's the best-looking waitress in the county doing

today?" Jimmy Miller greeted her with his usual smile when she arrived to take his order.

"I'm doing just fine. What about you?" If he'd been the one who had sent her the roses, surely he'd say something about them now.

"I'm doing pretty good, although it sounds like we're supposed to get some nasty wet days next week."

"I hate to see the weather turning cold," she replied.

"Me too. Winters in Dusty Gulch can sometimes be pretty brutal," he replied.

"What can I get for you, Jimmy?"

He ordered, and if he was the one who had sent her the roses, apparently he wasn't ready to confess to her yet. If not Jimmy, then who? The question continued to haunt her.

With a pause in the patrons, Ainsley went over to Melinda's table. "Hey love bug, are you ready to order some lunch?"

"Yes, but first look at the picture I drew for you." Melinda scooted over a picture of a pink house with lots of purple flowers amid a bright green lawn.

"That's awesome, honey."

"Do you think we could find a pink house for our forever house?" Melinda asked.

"It might be easier to plant pretty pink flowers in front of our forever house. Would that be okay, too?" Melinda nodded. "Now, tell me what you'd like for lunch."

"Grilled cheese with chips," Melinda said.

"How about grilled cheese with an apple?"

"Okay," Melinda replied. "But I'd rather have chips."

"Maybe tomorrow you can have chips," Ainsley said. "While you wait for your lunch, I want you to think if maybe you could give Hunter another chance if we all go out for pizza. We can talk more about it later this evening."

Once Melinda was finished with her lunch, she returned to the apartment to watch television. She knew the rules as far as keeping the door locked and not answering it if anyone knocked.

While they'd been in town with Ainsley working the hours she did, she and Melinda had fallen into a good routine for Saturdays.

Melinda spent the mornings in the café and then got to watch television in the afternoons until Ainsley got off work before the Saturday evening rush. Throughout the afternoon it was easy for Ainsley to step into the back to check on her daughter.

Hunter came in for his lunch break, and as usual, he flirted with her as she took his order and then served his meal. "I'm hoping maybe Thursday we could try to do pizza with Melinda," she said.

He looked at her in pleased surprise. "That would be nice. I'm willing to do and try whatever to make her like me. Maybe I should get her a pink teddy bear."

"No more gifts for her," she said sternly. "I don't want you trying to buy her affection."

She didn't hang around for more conversation with him. The café continued to stay too busy for chitchat. "Fifteen more minutes and then the two of us can get out of here," Lana said as the two stood side by side and watched the diners. "You have any plans for the rest of the weekend?"

"Tomorrow I'll probably take Melinda for a drive around town just to get out of the apartment for a little while. We'll shop a bit and then wind up at the ice cream parlor for a treat," Ainsley said. "What about you?"

"I figure it's time for me to do a changeover in my closet. You know, pack away the summer clothes and pull out the winter," Lana replied. "In other words, I'm going to have a damned boring day."

"Sometimes boring is good, especially after the busy day we've had here today."

"Hey, Ainsley." Rhonda Carlton, one of the waitresses who had come in to work the dinner rush, hurried toward her.

"Hi, Rhonda. What's up?" Ainsley's smile faded as Rhonda didn't offer her one in return.

"Uh... I was cleaning off the table back by the restrooms and I found this." Rhonda's blue eyes were troubled as she held out a folded piece of paper.

For a moment Ainsley didn't want to take it from her. The look in Rhonda's eyes scared her. Finally she took the note and opened it. A frightened gasp escaped her as she read the bold block letters.

AINSLEY MEADOWS. YOU ARE A WHORE AND WE DON'T LIKE WHORES IN THIS TOWN.

Chapter Seven

Hunter held the offending note in his gloved hand. Around him the sounds of people laughing and glasses clinking sounded like a normal Saturday night in the café.

But this note wasn't normal, and he hated to see the fear that kept Ainsley's eyes darkened. "How about we go into your apartment where things will be quieter," he suggested.

"Okay," Ainsley agreed.

He looked at Rhonda. "If you could come back with us, I'll just keep you off the floor for a minute or two."

Rhonda shot a look at Big Ed and then looked back at Hunter. "Can't I just talk to you right here? My section is full of people."

"Okay, just tell me exactly where you found the note," Hunter said.

She pointed to a two-top table in the back. "It was just sitting there. I thought it was just somebody's trash, but then I opened it." She frowned. "I don't even know who has sat at that table today. I had just come in for work when I found it."

"Thank you," Hunter said. "I may need to talk to you later, okay?"

Rhonda nodded. "Can I get back to work now?"

"Yes, that's fine." Hunter turned back to Ainsley. "Let's get out of here."

She led the way through the door that entered into her apartment. "Melinda, could you please go play in your bedroom for a little while? I need to talk to Deputy Churchill."

Once Melinda was gone, Hunter gestured Ainsley toward her small dining table. He placed the note into an evidence bag he'd carried into the café when he'd arrived and then set the bag down.

"What's happening, Hunter? Why would somebody leave that note for me?"

"Did you have any problems with anyone today while you were working?" he asked. He hated the tension that wafted from her and the simmer of fear in her eyes.

"No…nobody. It was a good day. First the roses and now this… What is going on? Why is somebody doing this to me?"

"I don't know, but I'm going to figure it out." He pulled off his gloves and then reached across the table to cover her hands. They were icy cold. He rubbed them in an attempt to warm them, even though he knew their coldness had nothing to do with an outside chill.

"I just can't imagine who would think such a terrible thing about me. What have I done that would give anyone the impression that I'm a whore?"

"Nothing…absolutely nothing," Hunter replied. "Ainsley, I don't want you to overreact to this. It's not a threatening note, it's just a nasty one, and I'm going to do my very best to try to figure out who left it."

She pulled her hands from his and instead wrapped her arms around herself. "Whore…that's what my husband used to call me when he was angry with me."

"Well, then he was a nasty man, too. But as far as I know, your ex-husband is nowhere around. Was Ben Wilkins in to eat today?"

"He was in for lunch. He seemed sober and he sat in Lana's section."

"Then I'll be having a chat with him today. Do you remember who sat at that specific table during the day?"

She frowned. "I don't think anyone did. We try not to seat anyone there unless we absolutely have to. It's so close to the restrooms."

"So it would be easy for anyone who went to the restroom to just drop the note on the table," he said.

She nodded. "And that's going to make it impossible to find out who left it," she replied. "It's probably not even a crime."

"That doesn't mean I'm not going to investigate it," Hunter countered. "But you're right. No crime has been committed, and at least the note isn't threatening."

"It's definitely character assassination," she replied darkly.

He laughed. "Honey, anyone who knows you knows what kind of good woman you are, and you are not what that note said. That note was just somebody venting in a childish manner. It definitely sounds like something Ben Wilkins might do."

Hunter rose from the table and then pulled her up into his arms. She remained stiff against him for a long minute and then released a deep sigh and rested her head against his chest.

He stroked her hair, and when she looked up at him he kissed her gently. After the kiss, he held her gaze. "I don't want you to worry about this. I don't want you to give it any more thought. Deal?"

She hesitated a moment and then nodded. "Deal."

He released her, and together they walked to the door that would take him outside. "Now, before I leave, can I see one of your sunshine smiles?" he asked.

She smiled, but the gesture didn't quite lighten her eyes. "You'll let me know what you find out?"

"Of course. And even if I don't have any answers, I'll call you before bedtime."

"I'd like that." This time her smile was more relaxed.

Once he left he immediately drove back to the station to speak to Sheriff Black. He had a good working relationship with Wayne, mostly because Wayne was a hands-off kind of boss. He trusted the people who worked for him, but Hunter knew Wayne could also be a bit lazy.

Once back he knocked on Wayne's private office door. "Enter," Wayne yelled. "Hunter, isn't it time for you to be heading home?"

"Yeah, but something has come up and I just wanted to discuss it with you."

"Well, sit down and discuss."

Hunter sat in the straight-back chair facing Wayne's desk and explained about the note directed at Ainsley that was found in the café. He relayed his feeling that Ben Wilkins could have left it.

"What I'd like to do is hunt Ben down tonight and question him about it and also question anyone else who might possibly be responsible for it. Naturally it has Ainsley a bit upset."

Wayne frowned. "A nasty note isn't a crime."

"I'm aware of that, and I certainly won't take away any time from my normal duties. Tonight I'll be on my own time, but I just wanted for you to be aware of what I'm doing about this."

Wayne shook his head and then leaned back in his chair and scratched the top of his head. "Why would Ben have it in for Ainsley?"

"He went into the café drunk and disorderly one morning, and she basically had to kick him out."

"I wish when Ben left town a couple of months ago he would have stayed gone."

"That makes two of us," Hunter replied.

"Your plan to do a little sleuthing on the side is fine with me. So, go…get out of here so you can get to it."

"Thanks, Wayne."

Minutes later Hunter was in his patrol car hunting down Ben Wilkins. His first stop was the Dusty Gulch Motel, a sad six-unit that rented out nightly or monthly to whoever would make the choice to live here.

He parked in front of the office and stepped out of his vehicle. The air smelled faintly of marijuana and spoiled garbage, of hopelessness and neglect.

The motel was owned by Jeb Harness. When Hunter entered the office, the old man sat behind the counter reading a tabloid magazine. "Deputy," he said in greeting. He didn't bother to get up. "Who you looking for tonight?"

"Ben Wilkins. What room is he in?"

"What's that drunk done this time?" Jeb asked.

"Just the kinds of things that drunks do," Hunter replied.

Jeb shook his head. "He's in unit three."

"Thanks, Jeb."

Hunter left the office and walked the short distance to Ben's room. No lights shone from the window to indicate that anyone was inside.

Hunter knocked on the door and waited. No answer.

He knocked again, this time harder. Still, there was no response. He was just about to knock a third time when the door to unit four opened and Jane Landers, an older woman who also liked her booze, leaned out.

"He ain't there. He took his bottle and went off somewhere. His stingy butt didn't even want to share with me," she said, her voice slurred enough to let him know she'd been drinking heavily as well.

"Thanks, Jane." At least when she got drunk, she didn't leave her room. She didn't cause issues like Ben often did.

Hunter got back in his car and headed for Main Street. He knew the places where Ben often parked himself to drink his bottle. He didn't find him on the bench in front of the post office or in the doorway of the grocery store.

He did find him seated in the alcove in front of the drugstore. Hunter parked his vehicle, got out and approached him. "Hey, Ben," he said in greeting.

"Ah, Deputy Churchy, are you here to arrest me?" Ben asked, his voice heavily slurred.

"I don't know, Ben. Do you need to be arrested?" Hunter asked.

Ben frowned. "I don't think so. I'm just sitting here not bothering anyone," he replied. "I'm being quiet, so I'm not disturbing the peace."

"That's good, Ben. So tell me, what do you think of Ainsley Meadows?"

Ben's frown deepened. "Who?"

"Ainsley at the café," Hunter said.

"At the café…oh, her." Ben's rheumy eyes narrowed. "She's a mean witch. She doesn't like me and I don't like her. She threw me out of the café just because I was a little bit drunk and a little bit rowdy."

"Did you maybe leave her a nasty note when you were in the café earlier today?" Hunter asked.

"A nasty note?" Ben frowned. "What kind of a nasty note?"

"You tell me," Hunter replied.

Ben's frown creased his forehead again. "I didn't leave no nasty note in the café for her or anyone else."

"You sure about that, Ben?"

"I'm positive," he replied, and then laughed. "Heck, I wouldn't even know where to get a decent piece of paper or a pencil."

Hunter stared at him for several long minutes. He believed him. Despite Ben's inebriated state, there was an innocence shining from his eyes that Hunter believed.

Ben stayed drunk enough most of the time that to believe he'd had the foresight to get a piece of paper and a pen and actually write a note about something that had happened in the past seemed impossible.

As Hunter finally headed home, his thoughts were troubled. When he'd seen the note and heard that Ben had been in the café that morning, he'd been sure that the man had written it in retaliation for Ainsley having him thrown out of the café.

Now, with Ben off the table, the note somehow seemed a bit more ominous. Who might hold such a strong negative feeling toward Ainsley?

It was just a hateful note, he told himself, but there was a small thought that niggled in the back of his head. Was the note the end of it, or was it the beginning of something much bigger, something that might be more dangerous?

LONG AFTER HUNTER had left, a chill continued to fill Ainsley as she thought of the note. Although she succeeded in keeping things normal for the rest of the evening for Melinda's sake, once her daughter was in bed, Ainsley wandered the small space they called home.

She checked to make sure that both doors were locked and then checked the locks on all the windows. She told herself she shouldn't take a stupid, anonymous note so seriously, and yet she couldn't help how much it had unsettled her.

Finally exhausted, she flopped down on the sofa. Her thoughts continued to fly through her head as if a tornado had lodged there.

Who had written the hateful note? Other than Ben Wilkins, whom had she offended so badly? As much as she wanted to believe it had been written for spite by Ben, she found it hard to believe that he'd actually carry a grudge through his alcoholic haze to write it.

If not him, then who?

Or was it possible this had little to do with her and more to do with Hunter? Did the secret Juanita had hinted about have to do with another woman? A woman now displaying an ugly jealousy toward Ainsley?

She mentally picked through everything that had ever happened between her and Hunter, and a new question popped into her head. What was behind the closed door in his house?

Both times she'd been there, all the doors in his house had been wide-open except one. He'd indicated it was just an empty room, but was it? And if it was, then why not keep the door open?

Knowing her thoughts were going way left field, she got up and headed to bed. She'd just changed into her nightgown when her phone rang.

She sat on the edge of the bed and answered. "Hi, Hunter. I hope you have some information for me."

"I wish I had some information for you, but I don't. I caught up with Ben Wilkins and questioned him. He was drunk, but he said he didn't write the note, and unfortunately I believed him."

"So, we're back to square one." Disappointment swept through her.

"I'm going to keep questioning people, but I'm inclined to chalk this up to a juvenile, disgruntled diner and nothing more."

"I've been thinking, and I was wondering if maybe that note wasn't so much about me, but maybe about a woman you dated who sees me as a threat…a woman you haven't told me about."

There was a long moment of silence. "Ainsley, I haven't dated anyone since my divorce. There are no women I'm keeping secret from you."

"I just know Juanita mentioned to me there were things in your past, things that I don't know about and she wouldn't tell me."

Again there was a long pause. "There are some things I still need to share with you, but they aren't things I want to tell you over a phone call. Is it possible for Juanita to watch Melinda tomorrow evening so you could come over here and we can talk?"

"I can probably arrange that. What time is good for you?" A touch of anxiety replaced the disappointment that had filled her when he'd told her Ben wasn't the note writer.

"I'm working tomorrow, so why don't we say around six thirty," he said.

"That should work. Instead of you coming here to pick

me up, I'll just drive over to your place." She'd prefer to have her own car to escape in if things somehow went south between them.

"Okay, I'll see you then."

Ainsley hung up and frowned. Whatever he was going to tell her, it must be serious, and that filled her with even more anxiety.

Things had been going so well with Hunter. She should have known there would be a glitch. Right now she just didn't know if the glitch was a deal breaker or not.

Yes, she should have known something would happen to screw up the happiness she'd been living. It was as if the fates refused to allow her to live happily.

The next day she and Melinda headed out for a day of fun, and Ainsley refused to allow thoughts of nasty notes, the mysterious roses and Hunter's secrets to ruin the day.

They took a drive around town, exploring areas they hadn't yet seen. It was a beautiful day, but rain was supposed to move in later in the evening.

At lunchtime they went into one of the two drive-through hamburger places in town. Once again that morning Melinda hadn't mentioned her father "talking" to her.

Ainsley certainly didn't intend to bring it up, but she and Melinda hadn't had a chance to talk about Hunter. "I asked you yesterday about you giving Hunter another chance," Ainsley said. "Have you thought about it?"

Melinda dragged one of her fries through a puddle of ketchup and then popped it into her mouth. At the same time she nodded and chewed.

"So, you have thought about it?" Ainsley pressed.

"Yeah. I guess I could give him a chance. Even though

Daddy doesn't like him, I know he makes you happy, and I did like the unicorn he bought for me."

"So, if we all went out for pizza this Thursday night, you could be nice to him?"

"I could be nice," Melinda agreed. "But if Daddy comes for me, I want to go with him for a while. I'd come back to be with you again after I'm with Daddy for a little while. That's only fair."

Ainsley bit her tongue, not wanting to ruin the day by arguing with her daughter. What Melinda didn't know was if Peter ever got hold of her, he would never let her go.

Peter didn't want a daughter. He wanted a possession he could control. He wanted Melinda solely to hurt Ainsley, and she would die before she allowed Peter anywhere near Melinda. The scar on her stomach suddenly burned, reminding her that she'd nearly died at Peter's hands before.

After eating lunch they went into a clothing store that sold children's fashions as well as women's. Even though it was Sunday, the stores along Main Street were all open for business. They bought Melinda two new sweaters and a cute pair of jeans, and Ainsley bought herself a lightweight turquoise sweater to wear later that evening with Hunter.

She'd already talked to Juanita about babysitting for a couple of hours, and Melinda was looking forward to spending some time with her friends.

They ate an early dinner at the Red Wok and then topped off the day with a stop at the ice cream parlor. It was after five when they got home, and Ainsley immediately began to get ready to go to Hunter's house.

She'd managed to stay out of her own head for most of

the day, but now her anxiety returned. What did Hunter have to share with her and how might whatever he told her affect their relationship? First the roses, then the ugly note and now this. What was going on in her world?

An hour later as she was on her way to his house, the level of love she had for Hunter slammed into her and nearly brought tears to her eyes.

He was the man she'd been waiting for…a man who treated her with respect, a man who made her feel protected and loved. She'd fantasized about a man like him, had spent many nights dreaming that a man like Hunter would appear in her life.

She'd believed she was marrying a good man who loved her when she'd married Peter. She'd had no idea what kind of a monster he was. Her dream of happily-ever-after had quickly become a horrendous nightmare.

She believed Hunter was the real deal. Looking back, there had been a lot of red flags where Peter was concerned, but she'd seen no such red flags with Hunter. Now that he was in her life and her heart was so involved, she feared something was going to happen to spoil it all.

And she had a terrible feeling that tonight might be the night it all fell apart.

Chapter Eight

Hunter paced the length of his living room as he waited for Ainsley to arrive. He probably should have told her more about his past before now, but he hadn't really spoken about the loss of his baby boy to anyone.

He wasn't ashamed of his grief—he'd just held it tightly inside him. But now it was time for him to share. Part of that sharing meant not only allowing himself to be more vulnerable than he'd ever been, but also showing himself as being stupid and incredibly naive.

It was time. It was past time. He wanted to be one hundred percent open and honest with her. Tonight he was putting it all on the line for her. He was going to share his sorrow with her and hope she didn't see him as a weak man.

At exactly six thirty, his doorbell rang. He opened the door, and as always his breath caught at the sight of her. She was absolutely stunning in a pair of jeans and a turquoise sweater that enhanced the bright blue of her eyes.

"Come on in." He stepped aside so she could step into the entry. "Why don't you have a seat on the sofa."

"Thanks," she replied.

"Want something to drink? I have wine and soda."

"No, thanks, I'm good." She settled in on the sofa, and he sank down next to her.

"Is it raining yet?"

She shook her head, her beautiful long hair rippling with the movement. "The skies are definitely clouding up, but so far no rain. Hunter, I don't want to talk about the weather. I've been worried all day that you have secrets that are going to tear us apart. I really care about you."

"Ainsley, I don't have any deep, dark secrets. I know what Juanita was probably referring to, and it's time I share it with you so you know all the pieces of me and my past." He rose and held out his hand to her. "Come with me."

He took her down the hallway to the bedroom that held his tears. He drew a deep breath and then opened the door and turned on the light.

She pulled her hand from his and looked around the room and then up at him in obvious confusion. "What is this, Hunter? Do…do you have a child?"

"I used to." He waited for the soul-wrenching sorrow to overtake him, but the ragged, rough edges of grief had finally softened.

"Did your wife get custody of him?" she asked.

"No, God got custody."

She stared at him for several long moments and then took a step toward him. "Oh Hunter, what happened?"

"Let's go back to the living room to talk." He didn't want to talk about Danny here in the room where the little boy had spent part of his short life.

They returned to the sofa, and this time she sat close to his side, her warmth and familiar scent a balm to him as he dived into the pain of his past.

"We didn't plan for Emily to get pregnant so quickly

after we got married, but despite our precautions, it happened. I was thrilled. All I'd ever wanted was to be a deputy and to have a family." He paused a moment, trying to swallow against the emotion that rose up inside him.

As if she sensed his sudden struggle, she reached out and took one of his hands in hers. Her gaze was soft and gave him the strength to continue.

"I was thrilled when Danny was born. He was the most perfect little boy. He was such a happy baby. He rarely fussed, and I would have given my life for him." Hunter's chest tightened.

"When he had just turned a year old, we discovered he had leukemia. For the next year, he was in and out of the hospital for chemo, and we'd hoped that he'd beat it. But just after his second birthday, we lost him."

"Oh Hunter. I'm so very sorry. I can't even imagine the pain of losing a child." She squeezed his hand and then leaned closer and wrapped her arms around his neck.

He pulled her close and buried his face in her sweet-smelling hair. He found comfort in her embrace. He'd grieved so long and so hard all alone. It was oddly soothing to share this horrible event in his life with her.

Tears burned at his eyes, but he swallowed against them. He had already shed more than enough tears over losing Danny.

He finally released her. "I've heard that the loss of a child often causes a divorce," she said. "Is that what happened to you and your wife?"

"No, although certainly we did grieve separately, but I had every intention to try to make the marriage work after Danny was gone. Unfortunately, she didn't. The same day we buried our son, she told me she'd been having an affair since the day we got married and she wasn't even sure Danny was mine."

Ainsley gasped. "What kind of a woman was she? To do that to you? To do that to any man at a time like that." Anger fired in her eyes.

"It didn't matter. That little boy was mine the moment a nurse handed him to me after his birth. She couldn't take that away from me, no matter what she said or what she had done."

"Love is what makes a child yours, not genetics," she replied fervently.

"Another point of pain was I guess everyone in town except me knew that Emily was cheating on me. In retrospect, the signs were all there. She was often unavailable to me. She never let me see her phone. There were dozens of flags… I just didn't want to see any of them."

"Hunter, I'm so very sorry for you." Sympathy replaced the momentary anger in her gaze. "You deserved so much better than that, and I'm so sorry you had to go through so much."

"I have no other secrets, Ainsley. I was just afraid if I told you about all this, you would somehow see me differently."

"Differently how?" She looked at him curiously.

"I don't know… I thought you'd somehow see me as weak and stupid," he confessed.

"Oh Hunter. Rather than making you look weak and stupid, all this makes you look incredibly strong and compassionate and loving. It takes a strong man to shed tears, to be vulnerable with his emotions."

Once again he pulled her into his arms and held her close. The sound of rain began to patter at the windows as if it were his tears for Danny.

Still, there was a new peace inside him where his past was concerned. There would always be sadness in his heart when he thought of his little boy, but he was truly ready to move on from that and seek new happiness in his life.

He leaned back from her. "Maybe one day you could come over and help me pack away the last of the items in Danny's room."

"Are you sure you're ready to do that?" Her gaze was incredibly soft.

He nodded. "Actually, it's past time. I don't need the things to remember him. Besides, maybe someday in the future it would make a great bedroom for a little girl."

"That would be nice in time," she replied. "But of course I'll come over and help you whenever you're ready."

"Thanks, Ainsley, and I promise there are no more secrets in my life."

"I'm glad you shared with me." She smiled at him. "While I waited to talk to you this evening, I'd almost convinced myself that you had an insane wife locked up in that room—although your wife had to have been insane to cheat on you."

He laughed. "Ainsley, you are good for my heart and soul."

She held his gaze for a long moment. "Hunter, I... I..." She looked down and then back up at him. "I... I probably need to get back home since I have Melinda at Juanita's on an unexpected night." She stood from the sofa.

"I really appreciate you coming over tonight." He got up as well to walk her to the door. "And I really hate to send you out in the rain."

"It's not raining that hard, and I don't melt when wet,"

she replied with another one of her smiles. She stood on her tiptoes and gave him a kiss on the cheek. "Thank you for sharing with me tonight, Hunter."

"Thank you for your caring and support." He opened the front door and peered out into the dark, rainy night. "Why don't you call me so I know you got home safely?"

"I can do that," she replied.

"At least let me get you an umbrella."

"That's not necessary. I'll be fine. I'll call you when I get home." With those words she stepped outside and hurried to her car.

He watched until she backed out of his driveway, and then her car lights disappeared, swallowed by the darkness of the rainy night.

He finally closed the door and with his cell phone in hand, he went back into Danny's room. The sorrow that had lived here was now tempered by the scent of Ainsley that lingered, by the support of her caring arms around him.

Yes, it was time to pack away the items in this room and put his past truly behind him. He no longer needed these things to remind him of what he'd gone through. Ainsley was partially responsible for him moving on and looking forward instead of backward.

He left the bedroom and returned to the living room. He sank down on the sofa and checked the time. The rain was now coming down in torrents, although there was no thunder or lightning. He hoped Ainsley remembered to call him when she got home.

There had been a moment when he'd thought she was going to tell him something, but then she apparently changed her mind. What might she have to share with him? He pushed that moment out of his head. If she did have something to tell him, then hopefully, eventually she would.

He still hoped to get to the bottom of the roses that had been sent to her and the nasty note left at the café. Both left a bad taste in his mouth and unsettled him, and he knew she was worried about the same things.

He wouldn't feel better until he solved the mystery of who had sent the flowers and left the note. It was so odd, to get beautiful roses and then the horrible note. Were they from a single person or two separate people? Once again he wondered if and when something more might happen, and if there would be a dangerous escalation?

SHE'D ALMOST TOLD HIM. There had been a moment when she'd been comforting him that Ainsley had wanted to come clean and tell him the truth about herself. But the moment had passed without her confessing anything.

Did she really have to tell him anything? The people from the battered-women underground had assured her that her new identity would stand up under any scrutiny. Could she go forward with Hunter and never tell him the truth?

She didn't believe she could. But she had to pick the perfect time to tell him about Peter and how she had violated a child custody order and gone on the run.

She felt like she just needed a little more time. She wanted to see if her daughter would come around where Hunter was concerned—once she did, then it would be time for Ainsley to come clean with Hunter.

The rain pelted her car window as she drove down Main Street, making visibility difficult. But it was easy to see the car lights that fell in too close behind her.

She frowned. It was too dark for her to be able to tell

what kind or color of car followed her. Were they actually following her? Or was it just a coincidence that somebody was driving so close to her?

Her heart beat an uneven rhythm as she tightened her fingers around the steering wheel. Was it possible the person who had left the nasty note was behind her right now? Were they going to run her off the road? Try to get her out of her car?

She shuddered with relief as the car turned off on a side street and disappeared from her sight. She released a deep sigh. God, she had gotten herself so worked up, and it had probably just been somebody in a hurry to get home in the rain.

The next couple of days passed without incident. Hunter told her he was still hunting down the sender of the roses and the note, but she knew he had nothing to go on and so was expecting no real results.

She now sat in Dr. Atkins's office, waiting for Melinda to get finished with her latest therapy session. On the way over Melinda had told her mother that Peter had stopped talking to her every night, but he still talked to her every other night or so. Ainsley hoped that this was a sign that slowly Melinda was giving up the fantasy of her father talking to her at night.

Tomorrow she, Hunter and Melinda were set to go out for pizza, and Ainsley definitely didn't want any repeat of the last time the two people she cared about had tried to spend time together.

Dr. Atkins had spoken to Ainsley first to see how things had gone over the past week. Ainsley had told her that for the most part Melinda had stopped talking about Peter, but Ainsley wasn't sure if that meant Melinda was putting away the fantasy or if she'd simply stopped sharing with Ainsley.

Forty minutes later Dr. Atkins and Melinda walked out. Once again they were both smiling, and Ainsley felt herself relax. "If you don't mind, I'll call you later in the week to touch base with you," Dr. Atkins said to Ainsley. "Unfortunately I've had an emergency come up, and I need to leave right now and head to the hospital."

"Then I'll talk to you later and we're out of here," Ainsley replied.

"How are you feeling?" Ainsley asked once she and Melinda were in the car.

"Good, but I'd feel better if we went to get ice cream."

Ainsley laughed. "Is this going to be a thing every time we see Dr. Atkins?"

Melinda giggled. "Yeah," she replied.

"Then I guess we're going to get ice cream." Ainsley would have liked to hear from Dr. Atkins after she'd spoken to Melinda, but she'd just have to wait to hear from the doctor. Although her first instinct was to ask Melinda all kinds of questions, she refrained from doing so.

While the two ate their ice cream, Melinda talked about school and the friends she had made since they'd been in Dusty Gulch.

"Don't forget that tomorrow night we're going out to the pizza place with Hunter," Ainsley said.

"I know, and I told you I'll behave," Melinda replied.

"Honestly, Melinda, Mr. Hunter is a really nice man."

"I can be nice to Mr. Hunter and still go with Daddy when he comes for me," Melinda replied.

"That's true," Ainsley said even though she wanted to protest and tell Melinda her father wasn't coming for her. "And I would appreciate you being nice to Mr. Hunter."

"Can we go for ice cream tomorrow night after the pizza?" Melinda said hopefully.

Ainsley laughed. "Girl, you're pushing your luck with all this ice cream." Melinda grinned at her and licked at the cone she held in her hand.

Both mother and daughter were in good moods as they returned to their apartment. As they stepped out of the car, darkness had begun to fall.

Despite the shadows by the door, the square package on the stoop was hard to miss. Wrapped in bright pink paper and sporting pink and yellow ribbons, it looked like a birthday present waiting to be opened.

"Mom, is it your birthday?" Melinda immediately asked.

"No, honey. It isn't my birthday." Ainsley stared at the box, her heart thudding loudly in her ears. She knew Hunter was on patrol tonight, but there was no way he'd drop a package outside her door and not tell her about it. So, who had left it? And what was inside?

"It looks so pretty. Aren't you going to pick it up?" Melinda's voice reached through Ainsley's racing thoughts.

Ainsley bent over and picked it up and then unlocked the door and together they stepped into the little apartment. Ainsley carried the "present" into the kitchen and set it on the table.

She stared at it, unsure if she should be afraid or not. With the roses and the note, she had no idea what to expect. She suddenly became aware of Melinda staring at her curiously. "Mommy, aren't you going to open it?"

"Maybe later. Right now you need to go get ready for bed. You have school tomorrow."

Melinda looked at her curiously. "So, you aren't going to open it now?"

"No, honey. I might even wait and open it tomorrow night when Hunter gets here," Ainsley replied. "Now, run in and get a quick shower."

An hour later Melinda was in bed, and Ainsley sat at her table and eyed the package. She hadn't wanted to open it in front of Melinda in case it was something inappropriate for a young girl to see.

Just because the packaging was fun and pretty didn't mean there was something fun and pretty inside. Or did it? Dammit, who had left it for her?

There was no way she was going to wait until the next night to find out what was inside. She picked the present up and shook it. It had a little weight to it, but made no noise when she moved it back and forth.

Just open it, she told herself. Whatever was inside couldn't hurt her. She was being completely childish in being afraid of what she didn't know.

The present had obviously been wrapped with care. The ends were perfectly folded and taped. She opened one side. Beneath the wrapping paper was an ordinary brown cardboard box. Carefully she took off all the paper and folded it neatly.

She then eyed the cardboard box. She thought of the beautiful roses she'd received and then the nasty note. There was absolutely no way to anticipate what might be inside the package.

Just open the damned thing, she repeated to herself. She grabbed a pair of scissors, cut the tape across the top of the box and then opened the flaps.

A scream rose up inside her, and she slapped her hand over her mouth to keep it inside. She shoved away from the table, nausea threatening as fear and horror shot through her.

Hunter. She needed him. She leaned forward to grab her purse straps and then pulled it into her lap. She fumbled for her phone and then hit the button that would call him.

Chapter Nine

Hunter raced across town to get to Ainsley's place. Her tearful call had been nearly incoherent. All he really got out of it was that something had happened and she needed him.

Because there were few people out on the streets, he could push the speed limit to get to her. Unfortunately, he'd been on the other side of town when he'd gotten her call.

He wasn't supposed to be on duty at all, but he had taken on an extra shift because of another officer being off for a family death. With so few deputies in the town, it wasn't uncommon for all of them to pick up extra shifts to make sure the town was protected at all times.

He finally pulled up by her door. He'd barely gotten out of his car when she flew out of the apartment and into his arms. She cried into the front of his shirt, her body shaking as he pulled her close.

He let her cry for several moments and then he unwrapped her arms from around him. "Ainsley...honey, what's going on? What's happened?"

"I...we went to Melinda's a-appointment and then g-got ice cream and wh-when we got home there was a p-present on the doorstep." The words jerked out of her amid her tears.

"A present?"

She nodded and drew in several deep, long breaths in an obvious attempt to calm down. "It was wrapped up pretty like a present."

"Why don't we go inside so I can see it," he suggested.

"Melinda is asleep. I wanted to scream, Hunter." She grabbed his arm. "I still feel like screaming."

"You try not to scream and I'll try to keep it down so neither of us wake up your daughter," he said gently. He wrapped an arm around her shoulders and led her toward the door.

"It's on the kitchen table," she said. "I… I'm not sure what it is. All I saw was blood and fur." A sob choked out of her.

He went directly to the table where a square cardboard box set next to some ribbon and pink wrapping paper. She stopped behind him.

He opened the flaps and almost jumped backward. He forced himself to lean in to get a good look at what was inside. He grabbed gloves out of his back pocket and pulled them on, then moved the contents inside the box to better identify what it was.

"It's a dead rat," he said softly. It was a dead, bloody rat with the throat cut. He closed the box and retaped the lid. "Do you have some sort of a sack I can carry all this out in?"

She went to the cabinet beneath the sink and pulled out a café takeout sack. "Hunter, please help me make sense of this," she said, her voice shaking as she handed him the sack.

"There is no sense to make of it," he replied tersely.

Dammit, who was doing this to her? And why? A dead rat to him implied a threat even though no note was included. He quickly placed the box and the wrapping paper into the sack and then carried it out into the living room and set it just outside her door on the stoop.

He turned back to find her looking at him. She looked so small, so achingly vulnerable clad only in a pink nightshirt. Her eyes were filled with fear, and as she reached up to tuck a strand of hair behind her ear, her fingers trembled.

He took her hand in his and pulled her down to the sofa. He sank down next to her. Even though he was on duty, there was no way he could just walk away and leave her so frightened.

What he wanted to do was take her to bed and warm her body with his. He wanted to hold her through the night if that was as long as it took to make her fear ease.

"Ainsley, I swear I'm going to do everything in my power to get to the bottom of all this." He took her hand in his, hating how cold and small it felt in his.

"I just can't imagine why this is happening to me. I've been nice to everyone I've met. I haven't caused any trouble for anyone." She held his gaze, and her eyes were filled not only with fear, but also confusion.

"I'm just as confused by all this as you are," he admitted. "But the good thing is nobody has tried to physically harm you."

"Not yet," she said darkly.

"I'm going to find this creep, Ainsley. It's possible I'll be able to pull some fingerprints off the wrapping paper or the box itself."

"I hope you can." She released a deep sigh. "I just want

this all to end. I don't know who is doing this to me or why, but I want it to stop."

"I'm going to figure this out, Ainsley." He felt like he was saying the same words to her over and over again. "But in the meantime, if you get anything else like this, don't touch it and call me immediately."

"Trust me, I'll call you," she replied.

Reluctantly he released her hand. "I wish I could stay here with you, but I've got to get back to work. I'll make an official report on this, and I'm going to start interrogating people to see if somebody might know what this is all about."

She stood as he did, and she walked with him to the door. He pulled her into his arms and held her for several minutes. The trembling in her body finally ceased and reluctantly he released her.

"Ainsley, try not to worry. I won't let anything happen to you or your daughter. This is somebody who must just like the idea of freaking you out. Don't let them win."

"I'm trying not to be freaked out, but I am," she admitted.

"I know. Now, try to get a good night's sleep, and I'll talk to you tomorrow." He leaned forward and gave her a kiss on her forehead.

Minutes later he was back in his patrol car, seething with anger and hoping like hell the culprit had left a few fingerprints behind on the package.

Right now about the only thing he could arrest the perp for was trespassing. If he couldn't get the person in jail, then he'd make sure the person knew that to bother Ainsley again meant he was risking his health and well-being.

As he thought about Ainsley's fear, it ticked him off

enough to want to beat the hell out of somebody. He now clenched his hands on the steering wheel.

Dammit, he didn't know whom to question. He'd never heard anyone speak negatively about her, so who was behind this reign of terror? He certainly didn't believe Ben Wilkins was capable of carrying out this kind of harassment.

A dead rat with its throat cut. Who was holding that kind of madness inside them? Who would think about catching a rat, slitting its throat and then packaging it up in pretty paper? It was such a disgusting and heinous thing to do.

He thought he knew the people of this small town. He knew the people who suffered from various mental issues and the ones who liked to cause trouble. But none of the people he knew had a mind so wicked as to do this to a vulnerable single woman.

He drove directly to the sheriff's station, eager to give the wrapping paper and box to fellow deputy Larry Knight, who was an expert at lifting fingerprints, among other lab-related things.

Unfortunately, Larry wasn't at work right now. Hunter called him and told him where to locate the items the next day when Larry came on duty.

Once that was finished, Hunter hit the road again. The first place he drove was to Lana Kincaid's house. The woman had worked as a waitress at the café for as long as Hunter could remember.

Lana knew practically everyone in town, and because gossip was rampant in the café she was the keeper of many secrets. She also probably knew more about the people in Dusty Gulch than he did.

She lived in a small ranch house on three acres just

outside the main district. As he pulled in, lights shone out of her windows, letting him know she was still awake.

He parked and got out of his car. The front door opened just before he reached it, and Lana greeted him with a look of surprise. "Well, it's not often one of Dusty Gulch's finest comes visiting. Come on in." She opened the door to allow him entry.

He'd never been inside Lana's place before. He stepped into the living room and was vaguely surprised to see a pink zebra-striped sofa and a purple zebra-striped chair. The end tables and coffee table were glass, and the lamps on the end tables held enough sparkly crystals to blind a man.

Lana laughed. "It's all pretty unique, right?" She laughed and gestured him toward the sofa. "I bought all this stuff online after my last divorce. I know I don't have much decorating sense, but I just bought what I loved. I don't give a damn what other people think. If my next husband doesn't like my furniture, then he can stay in my garage. Now, can I get you something to drink?"

"No, thanks, I'm good. I just want to ask you a few questions." He sank down on the edge of the sofa.

She sat in the purple zebra chair, the light from the garish lamp glittering on the side of her face. "Questions about what?"

"About Ainsley."

"Has something else happened since she got that terrible note?" Lana leaned forward, obvious concern on her wrinkled face.

"Somebody delivered a rat with its throat cut to her doorstep this evening. It was wrapped up like a present."

"Oh my goodness. Who on earth would do such a thing?" she asked.

"I was hoping you could help me answer that," he replied.

"I can't imagine. Everyone at the café loves her. Not only is she gorgeous, but she's also a hard worker and very pleasant to be around."

"So, you haven't heard anyone speak ill about her?"

"Nobody." Lana laughed. "Hell, all the men want to date her and all the women want to be her." She sobered. "Honestly, Hunter, other than the skirmish she had with that drunk Ben Wilkins, she hasn't had any trouble with anyone."

"Do you know anyone who might be capable of doing these kinds of things to a vulnerable woman? Be honest, Lana. You've been around this town for a long time."

"I have, but I swear I don't know who is capable of this kind of crap. Slitting a rat's throat? That takes a particular kind of sick mind." Lana shook her head. "Is she in danger?"

"Let's hope not," Hunter replied even as a burn of anxiety lit his stomach on fire. He got up, and Lana walked with him to her door.

"I wish I could have been helpful, but honestly I've never heard anyone say a bad word about Ainsley. I care about that girl. I think she's a real sweetheart."

"Yeah, I kind of like her myself," Hunter replied with a small smile.

"I'll keep my ears to the ground for you," Lana said.

"I appreciate it, Lana."

As he drove away from Lana's place, her words echoed in his head. All the men wanted to date Ainsley, and all the women wanted to be her.

He'd just assumed the perp he was looking for was a man. But Lana's words made him wonder if it was possible it was a woman behind everything that was happening to Ainsley?

Maybe somebody who was jealous that she was gorgeous and friendly and had stirred up all the single men in town? God, it was bad to think there was a man who could do these horrible things, but somehow it was even worse to believe it was a woman.

EARLY THURSDAY MORNING Ainsley and her daughter went into the café for breakfast. While they ate she became aware of Big Ed sounding angry as he called out orders.

"What's up with the boss?" she asked Lana when she stopped to top off Ainsley's coffee.

"Ted didn't show up last night to do the cleaning," Lana said.

"That's a first. He's always been so reliable," Ainsley replied.

"Ed called his house this morning, and his wife said he'd left to meet a friend after dinner last night and she'd just assumed he'd gone ahead and come in to work after that. When she woke up this morning and he wasn't home, I guess she called the sheriff."

Ainsley shook her head. "I wonder what happened to him."

"Hopefully, Sheriff Black will be able to figure it out," Lana replied.

Ainsley found herself thinking about the missing janitor once Melinda had left for school and Ainsley was back in her apartment.

Even though she hadn't had much contact with him, she'd always found Ted to be an affable man. She hoped nothing bad had happened to him. However, even her concern about Ted couldn't halt the simmer of fear that had been her companion for what felt like forever.

Last night after Hunter had left, taking the horrendous "present" with him, she'd remained awake long into the night. There was no window in Melinda's room, but there was one in the kitchen and one in Ainsley's bedroom.

She'd spent half the night going back and forth between the two windows, peering out to see if anyone was lurking outside in the shadows of night. She saw nobody, but even when she got into bed, sleep continued to elude her.

She found herself going over everyone she had spoken to, all the people she had served since the moment she had landed in town and started working as a waitress.

There had to be somebody she had offended, somebody who now felt the right to torment and frighten her. Despite her need to identify somebody, she couldn't.

She hadn't spoken to Hunter yet today, although she knew they were still on to get pizza that evening. He'd been so sure in asserting to her that he was going to get to the bottom of this madness. But even though she believed he was a great deputy, he was only human, and if there were no clues to follow then how could anybody find the person responsible?

She tried to empty all that from her mind as she cleaned the apartment. Once she'd finished with her chores, it was just after noon. She made herself a tuna sandwich for lunch and then sank down on the sofa and tried to read a book.

No matter how hard she tried to concentrate on the words on the page, her thoughts kept going back to the dead rat that had been delivered to her doorstep.

What did it mean? Was it a warning to her? A warning about what? Aside from the horror of getting something like that was the confusion of wondering what, exactly, it meant in the long run?

Hunter called at two to make sure the plans for the evening were still a go. He also told her that they'd been able to pull fingerprints that they believed to be hers but had been unable to find any others.

Whoever the creep was, apparently he was smart enough not to leave a clue to his identity behind. Who in the heck was it? Her head hurt from trying to figure it all out.

By the time Melinda got home from school, Ainsley had her happy face on. The last thing she wanted was for Melinda to know things were happening that frightened her mother.

"Are you ready to go out with Hunter for pizza?" she asked her daughter. Melinda looked so sweet in a blue sweater that matched the pretty blue of her eyes and a pair of jeans. Her hair was in pigtails with blue ribbons streaming down the lengths.

"Sure." Melinda sank down on the sofa and smiled at her mother. "And I promise I'll behave."

"That's nice. I'm hoping you'll get to know Hunter better, because he's somebody important in my life and I'd like to think that he might become somebody important in your life."

"Like a stepdaddy," Melinda said. "Lisa at school has a stepdaddy and she likes him okay, but she still loves her real daddy."

"And you can still love your real dad," Ainsley said.

The conversation then turned to everything that had

happened at school that day. They were still seated on the sofa when Hunter arrived for their evening out.

"Are you two ready for some pizza?" he asked. "Melinda…cheese pizza, right?"

"Right," she replied. "And I promised I'd be nicer to you tonight."

"I appreciate that." He smiled at Melinda.

Ainsley was grateful that he was keeping things light, although when he looked at her she saw his concern for her in the depths of his eyes.

Minutes later they were in his truck and headed to the pizza place. "I had to chase Ben Wilkins away from the café dumpster," he said softly.

She looked at him in surprise. "What was he doing back there?" Had she been wrong about Ben? Was it possible the drunk was behind all the things that had been going on?

"He was drunk and dumpster diving for food. He told me the café threw out better food than they sold. Apparently whenever he gets hungry he goes to the dumpster."

"Do you think that was all he was doing there?" she asked.

"Yeah, I do. I honestly don't think Ben is the person we're looking for." He looked in the rearview mirror and smiled. "How are you doing back there, Melinda?"

"I'm good," she replied.

Ainsley just hoped Melinda stayed good for the duration of the date night. "I heard about Ted going missing. Did you all manage to find him today?" she asked Hunter.

He grimaced and shook his head. "No. We aren't even sure who he was meeting before going into work last night. His wife had no clue, and so far Ted is still missing. I feel like lately law enforcement is striking out all over the place."

"Hopefully, Ted will show up safe and sound," she said.

"And we'll figure out what's going on with you. That would be a big win-win."

He pulled up in front of the pizza parlor, and they all got out. They went inside and settled in one of the empty booths. Melinda sat next to her mother, and they both faced Hunter.

Facing him, Ainsley once again noticed what a handsome man he was. He could probably have his pick of any of the single women in Dusty Gulch, but he'd chosen her.

It just made the pressure to tell him the truth about herself all the harder to bear. She'd decided she would wait until they figured out who was behind the things that had been happening to her. Once they had that answer, then she would come clean to him about her past. She only prayed he would understand and forgive her for lying to him.

They ordered their pizza, and while they waited the conversation was light and easy. She was pleased by how easily Hunter included Melinda, asking her questions in an obvious effort to get to know her better.

The pizza arrived, and Melinda remained on her best behavior. Hunter even managed to make her giggle several times. They finished their meal and then got back into Hunter's vehicle.

"I'm feeling like a little ice cream for dessert," he said as he started the engine. "Does anyone else in this car like ice cream as much as me?"

"I do," Melinda replied eagerly.

"Not me. I'm way too full of pizza to eat ice cream," Ainsley said.

Hunter laughed. "There's always room for ice cream, right, Melinda?"

"Right. Mr. Hunter, we could still go to the ice cream parlor and Mom doesn't have to get anything but you and I could get something."

"That sounds like a good plan to me," he replied. For the next five minutes, he and Melinda argued good-naturedly about what was the best kind of ice cream.

As Ainsley listened to the two of them—the two most important people in her world—laugh and tease each other, a sense of rightness swept through her.

This was what she wanted for her future. The man she'd escaped had been a monster…a nightmare, but Hunter was her dream man and she could only hope that when everything was said and done, they would share a bright and future together.

"WHAT'S IN THAT bedroom where you spend so much of your time?" Sheila asked Peter.

The two of them were in the living room. He was in a chair and she was half sprawled on the sofa, on her way to drinking herself into oblivion. She held a tall glass of gin in her hand, and her voice was already slurred.

Pig, Peter thought to himself. She was a waste of air and space and he was sick of her. But he still needed her here. "It's my work," Peter replied and forced a smile to his face. "It's what keeps you enjoying all the goodies that you like."

She laughed and raised the glass to her lips. "I do like my goodies."

"Maybe it's time you call it a night," he suggested. The

last thing he wanted to do was sit and talk to the woman. He'd much rather be alone with his thoughts of Colette.

"Just let me finish this glass," Sheila said and took another deep swallow.

Peter waited patiently. Once she'd drained the glass, she was toasted. He helped her to the bedroom, where she collapsed on the bed and within minutes was snoring.

Peter returned to the living room and his chair. It had been a good week. Twice he'd sat in the café eating while Colette had been serving tables on the other side of the room. She'd even looked at him several times, but no recognition had widened her eyes.

Then watching her reaction when she'd opened the present he'd left for her had been priceless. Her fear, her utter horror, had fed his very soul.

But he was tiring of the games. He'd already taken care of one loose end. It had been pathetically easy for him to lure Ted Johnson out here with the promise of more money. Ted had arrived and Peter had invited him into the kitchen. Thankfully, Sheila had been in one of her dope-enhanced nod outs and had no clue that they'd had a visitor.

He and Ted had shared a few drinks, and then when good old Ted was feeling nice and mellow, Peter had stabbed him. He'd slid the big, sharp knife in just under Ted's armpit and then had ripped it downward.

"Wha…" The single syllable had fallen from Ted's lips, and his eyes had widened. Before the man could say anything more, Peter carried him out to the porch and threw him into the pigpen.

It was true. Pigs could dispose of a human body in a very short time. He'd stood on his porch and listened to the pigs' frenzy. They squealed and fought each other to get a piece of the meat, and the sound of bones crunching filled the air.

When it was all over, there was nothing much left of Ted. Peter had then driven Ted's truck to an old shed on the property and parked it inside. And that was the end of Ted.

He was ready for his ultimate revenge. He was ready to make Colette learn the price for leaving him and shattering his world.

By listening in on her, he'd heard her make plans to go out with some girlfriends tomorrow night. Melinda was spending the night with a friend, and Deputy Do-Right was working. It would be a perfect night for a reunion.

And the pigs were still hungry.

Chapter Ten

Although Ainsley would much rather be spending her Friday evening with Hunter, he had to work, and so when Lana had approached her about several of the waitresses going out for drinks and to chill out, Ainsley had agreed to go with them.

Melinda had already made plans to spend the night with Bonnie, and in truth a little downtime with friends sounded good. It fact, it sounded wonderful. She hoped for just a little while she'd be able to get out of her own head and leave all the drama that had become her life at home.

Thursday night pizza had been a huge success. She believed real strides had been made between Hunter and Melinda. At the end of the night there had been no new "present" waiting for her, making the evening a real success in her book.

She now stood in her bathroom, putting on her makeup for the evening out. She had noticed there were two bars in the small town. The one on the edge of town, the Wrecking Ball, was supposed to be a nasty dive.

The other one, just off Main Street, was called Barney's Place and was supposed to be a nice place to get a drink, relax or do a little moving on the dance floor.

Ainsley certainly didn't intend to do any dancing unless it was with Hunter, and since he wasn't going to be there, she'd be cooling her heels in a booth and visiting with Lana and the two other waitresses who were going.

She didn't intend to make it a late night. She had to open the café as usual the next morning, and she knew Lana wouldn't want a late night, either. They were all supposed to meet at eight, and she figured she'd probably be home by around ten.

At seven forty-five she walked out of her apartment and headed to her car. Already the shadows of night were beginning to fall. As she got inside her vehicle, she looked at the dumpster, but thankfully she didn't see anyone lurking around.

It was sad to think that Ben Wilkins lived on food out of the dumpster. Apparently he had nobody in his life who cared for him. He needed help, but there was nothing Ainsley could do about it.

Barney's Place was a fairly large bar with plenty of parking in front. Already the parking lot was filled with pickup trucks and cars, indicating that the bar was a popular place on a Friday night.

She scanned the area for Lana's car. The two had agreed to meet in the parking lot and enter the bar together. She finally spied her friend's car and pulled into the parking space next to it.

Lana got out of her car, looking like a woman on a mission to find her next husband—her purple pants hugged her legs, and her purple-and-white blouse displayed her full breasts.

"Wow," Ainsley said when she got out of her car. "You look hot."

Lana laughed. "I might be old, but I'm not dead."

"Have you seen Betsey and Abby yet?" Ainsley asked. The two women worked the same shifts as Ainsley and Lana.

"They came together about ten minutes ago. I told them to go on in and get us a booth or a table," Lana replied. "Let's head inside and find them."

Ainsley had never been in the bar before, and as they walked into the dim interior her nose was assailed by the odors of bar food, beer and various colognes and perfumes battling for dominance.

There was a long counter where people either sat on the stools or leaned in to order drinks. Booths were against both walls, and tables and chairs surrounded a decent-size dance floor. A live band was on a small stage just off the dance floor, playing a rousing country music song.

They found their friends in one of the booths, both with drinks already in front of them. "Hey, ladies," Betsey said in greeting.

Ainsley slid in next to Betsey, and Lana sat across from her and next to Abby. Almost as soon as they were seated, a waitress appeared to take Lana and Ainsley's orders.

Lana ordered a beer and Ainsley ordered a margarita, and within minutes the drinks were before them as the four chattered about work-related events from over the past week.

"I still can't believe Ted is missing," Betsey said. She twirled a strand of her long blond hair as her blue eyes widened. "I mean, it's like a real mystery."

"Yeah, he just seemed to vanish into thin air," Abby said. Abby was a favorite among the café diners. She was a short, cute redhead who always wore a smile. "Has Hunter told you anything about it?"

"No, we don't generally talk about his work," Ainsley replied.

"You've got your own mysteries going on," Lana said to Ainsley.

"I don't even want to think about all that tonight," Ainsley replied. "Tonight I'm on a mental vacation and all I want to do is relax and not think too much."

"Then we won't bring any of that up tonight," Lana assured her. "Tonight is for fun. We'll all worry about real-life stuff tomorrow."

Ainsley raised her glass. "I'll drink to that."

"Hell, I'll drink to anything," Lana said, making the others laugh.

For the next couple of hours, the women laughed and joked with each other. Lana saw several male friends in the crowd and occasionally got up to grab one and hit the dance floor.

Betsey also got up to dance while Abby and Ainsley remained seated. Abby had a serious boyfriend and, like Ainsley, had no intention of dancing with another man.

None of the women ordered a second drink. They were all responsible women who knew the dangers of driving while under the influence, and all four of them were working early the next morning.

However, that didn't stop them from having fun. Abby did impressions of some of their customers, and the other three practically rolled on the floor with laughter. After all the tension of the past couple of weeks, Ainsley was grateful for the lighthearted fun.

"Hey, Ainsley." Jimmy Miller appeared by the side of their booth. "I've never seen you in here before."

"That's because I've never been in here before," Ainsley replied.

He gestured toward the dance floor. "Why don't you come out with me and let me show you my smooth moves?"

"Sorry, Jimmy. I'm not here to dance. I'm just enjoying some time with my friends," she replied.

"I could be your friend," he returned.

"Buzz off, Jimmy. She's your friend, but her heart belongs to Hunter," Lana said. "And she only dances with her man. But I'll dance with you."

Jimmy backed up, a wide grin on his face. "Oh no, Lana, you know you scare the hell out of me." As he hurried away from the booth, they all laughed.

"I think that's my signal to call it a night," Ainsley said. It was already a few minutes after ten.

"Yeah, me too," Lana said. "As much as I hate to admit it, I can't stay up until all hours of the night and then work the early-morning shift the next day."

"At least we get a day off on Sunday," Ainsley said.

"I think Betsey and I are going to hang out here for just a little bit longer," Abby said.

"Then we'll see you two in the morning," Ainsley said.

They said their goodbyes, and then Ainsley and Lana left the bar together. They stepped out into the darkness and headed toward their cars.

"This was fun, and I needed to have a little fun and relaxation," Ainsley said.

"It was fun," Lana agreed. "It's nice that all of us get along so well."

"Abby and Betsey are so nice it would be hard not to get along with them," Ainsley replied.

"Isn't that the truth?" They reached the two cars.

"Well, girlfriend, I guess I'll see you bright and early in the morning."

"Good night, Lana." Ainsley got into her car, grateful to turn on the heater as the night air was bordering on cold. She waited a couple of minutes for the car to warm up and then headed back to the apartment.

She was grateful that at least for the night she'd managed to put her worries away and really relax in a way she hadn't since she'd received the anonymous roses.

She stifled a yawn as she parked the car. Before she got out, she grabbed her cell phone. She'd promised she'd call Hunter when she got home.

"Hey," he said in greeting. "Did you have a good time?"

"I did. It was fun, but also very laid-back and relaxing," she replied. "And now I'm ready for a good night of sleep."

"I'm glad you had a good time. Are we still planning on the cookout at my place on Sunday?"

"We're up for it if you are." She looked toward the dumpster, grateful that once again she saw nothing and nobody to concern her.

"I can't wait to introduce Zeus to Melinda," he said.

She laughed. "I have a feeling it's going to be a match made in heaven."

"We'll see. In any case I'll come into the café tomorrow, so I'll see you then."

"Okay, good night, Hunter." Her smile still lingered on her lips as she finally left her car and went to the apartment door. She'd just put her key in the lock when, in her peripheral vision, she caught movement rushing toward her. She didn't even have a chance before she was slammed with her back against the door. Her breath whooshed out of her, momentarily rendering her helpless.

It was a man. He was clad all in black and wore a black ski mask. That's the only thing her brain could comprehend before his fist slammed her in the stomach.

Sharp pain weakened her knees, and nausea rose up inside her. Before she could recover, he tried to pick her up. Someplace in the back of her mind it registered that if he managed to pick her up and spirit her away, she'd never be seen again.

Sheer terror shuddered through her. She kicked and flailed her arms in an effort to keep him back. He punched out and connected with her jaw. Her head snapped back as a new pain roared through her and stars momentarily filled her head.

Tears blurred her vision as he continued to pummel her. She tried to kick him again. He grabbed her leg and pulled. She tumbled to the ground. She finally gained enough air to scream.

"Help," she cried. She screamed again. He kicked her in the ribs, and intense pain once again stole her breath away.

Who was it? Dear God, did he intend to beat her to death?

"What do you want?" she yelled with what breath she had left. "Help! Somebody please help me."

"Hey, leave her alone," a voice called out from the distance. "Hey, you…stop what you're doing. We need help over here."

"Help me," Ainsley screamed. The attacker kicked her in the ribs over and over again, making it impossible for her to scream or fight back. She curled up in a fetal ball in an effort to protect herself.

"Stop hurting her," the man cried out of the darkness. "I'm calling the police."

She managed to scream again, the other man continued to yell about getting the police and suddenly the attack stopped. She remained on the ground, sobbing and in so much pain she could hardly think.

"He's gone and I didn't really call the police because I don't have a phone." The words were slurred, and as he came closer to her she could smell the booze. "What can I do to help you?"

Ben Wilkins. Hysterical laughter rose up inside her. The town drunk…the man she had thrown out of the café…was her savior. The laughter quickly changed into deep sobs, and the sobs shot such excruciating pain through her ribs that darkness encroached and she knew no more.

"Boys, I know there's marijuana in this car, because I can smell it." Hunter had just pulled over a car with four boys in it. They had blown through a red light on Main Street.

"I swear there's nothing in the car," the driver, Lenny Nicholas, said. "Maybe it's my cologne you smell."

Hunter laughed. "Right, and maybe you think I was born yesterday." He recognized all four of them—they weren't bad kids. "I know weed when I smell it. Now, do you want to hand it over to me? Or do you want me to call all your parents out here and then I'll conduct an official search of the car?"

They all protested until finally one of the boys in the back seat handed out a roach. "That's all we have left, Deputy Churchill. I swear. We just had one cigarette and we all took a puff off it and then we put it out," he said.

"Honestly, Deputy Churchill. That's the truth. The

guys just wanted to try it," Lenny said. "I didn't have any. And that's all we have."

"You know I could arrest all of you. Weed is still illegal in this state, but I'm going to let you off with a warning tonight. Possessing weed is against the law, and smoking it doesn't make you cool. From now on I'm going to have my eyes on all of you."

"We didn't even like it," Lenny said. "That's why we didn't smoke the whole thing. It tastes nasty."

"I'm just warning you all. Next time I catch you with weed, it's going to be a whole different story. Now get out of here and don't run any more red lights."

As Hunter got back into his patrol car, Lenny eased away from the curb. Hunter placed the roach in a bag to be taken into the station and destroyed. He'd just pulled away when his phone rang.

He frowned as he saw Ainsley's number come up on the caller identification. What was she doing calling again? She should have been in bed and sound asleep by now.

He answered. "Ainsley?"

A male voice replied, his words a jumble Hunter couldn't understand. "Who is this?" he asked, a ring of alarm sounding in his head. Why would any male be on her phone?

"It's Ben. You know… Ben."

"Ben?" Hunter sat up straighter in his seat. What in the hell was going on? "Ben, where is Ainsley?"

The man began to sob, obviously drunk. "I can't wake her up."

"What do you mean, you can't wake her up?"

"She was…you know…attacked. A big man all in black hit her and kicked her. I wanted to call the police, but I don't have a phone. I got into her purse to use her phone, but I didn't take nothing. I swear all I took out of her purse was her phone."

"Ben...where is she?" A sick horror filled Hunter. "Where are you, Ben?" he asked again urgently.

"I was dumpster diving. I know you told me not to, but I came back and I found a couple pieces of good meat, some fries and a whole loaf of bread."

"Dammit, Ben, are you at the café?"

"I thought I told you that," he replied.

Hunter hung up and turned his car around. He flipped on his siren and lights and drove as fast as possible. Blood rushed through his veins as an urgency he'd never felt before filled him.

Ben couldn't wake her...

She'd been attacked...

Ben couldn't wake her...couldn't wake her.

The words buzzed through his head over and over again. How badly was she hurt? Was she unconscious or was she... Oh God, his brain couldn't take him there.

He got on his radio and requested an ambulance to meet him behind the café. He also radioed for more officers to meet him there.

She had to be all right. She just had to be. He continued to speed through the night to get to her, hoping and praying that she would be okay.

He pulled into the back of the café and turned his spotlight on. He immediately spied Ben half sprawled next to a prone, unmoving Ainsley in front of the apartment door.

He jumped out of his car and rushed to them. Ben looked up at him, drunken tears falling down his face. "She won't wake up. I should have done something sooner," he lamented. "I tried to help, but I'm nothing but a stupid drunk and the man scared the hell out of me."

Hunter crouched down, his heart thudding hard against his chest. He picked up one of her cold, lifeless hands and felt for a pulse.

His heart jumped into his throat as he waited to feel any stir of life. Was her heart no longer beating? There... he felt it. It was slow and faint, but it was there.

"I'm sorry," Ben half slobbered. "I should have done something more. I shouldn't have been so scared."

"Ben, move away. You did a great job and I appreciate you waiting here with her, but now I hear the ambulance coming," Hunter said. The ambulance couldn't get here fast enough for him. She needed immediate help.

Ben scooted back, and Hunter stared down at Ainsley. He didn't see any blood anywhere, but he did see a blossoming bruise underneath her chin. The sight made his blood boil. Who had done this to her and what other injuries had she sustained?

Thankfully at that time the ambulance pulled up, and two of the paramedics jumped out of the back and grabbed a gurney. "I'm not sure what injuries she's sustained, but she's been unconscious since I came on scene," Hunter told Matt Daniels, one of the paramedics.

Nick also showed up, along with Zac Ross, another deputy working the late shift. As the paramedics loaded Ainsley onto the gurney and took off for the hospital, Hunter turned to quickly explain the situation to the two deputies.

"Take Ben's statement, see if you can find any evidence around the area and I'll be in touch. Right now I'm heading to the hospital," he said.

"Don't worry, we'll take care of things here," Nick assured him.

Hunter got back in his car and headed for the hospital, his thoughts consumed with Ainsley's condition. Was she going to be all right? What had she suffered before falling unconscious? The thought of somebody beating her…the thought of her in pain tortured him.

Dammit. He clenched his hand around the steering wheel as anger burned in his gut. It was an anger not only directed at the perpetrator, but also at himself.

He should have seen something like this coming. When she'd received the dead rat, he should have recognized the situation had escalated.

And his main question continued to be who was behind all this—who had attacked her with deadly intent tonight? Hopefully Ben saw or heard something that would help them identify the perpetrator. And hopefully Nick and Zac would find some concrete evidence that would lead to an arrest.

The Dusty Gulch Hospital was located in a large brick building that also housed several doctors' offices. Hunter parked and raced into the ambulance bay, but they had already unloaded her and taken her inside.

He walked around and entered into the emergency waiting room. Sandy Silver, a nurse he knew from around town, sat at a desk.

"Sandy, Ainsley Meadows just arrived in an ambulance. Could you tell the doctor on call that I'm out here and need an update on her as soon as possible?"

"It's Dr. Lockwood tonight, and I'll let him know," she replied. She got up from the desk and disappeared through a door that was marked No Entry.

Hunter started to sit in one of the green plastic chairs,

but he had far too much adrenaline rushing through him to just sit. Instead while he waited, he paced the length of the small waiting room.

Sandy returned. "He said he'd be out to speak with you as soon as possible."

"Thanks, Sandy." He resumed his pacing, but as the minutes ticked by, he finally sat and stared at the tile floor beneath his feet.

As he waited, he called Ed to let him know what had happened and told the man that Ainsley wouldn't be in to work for a while. He also asked if it would be okay for Melinda to spend the next day at his house. Ed assured him that it was fine, and Hunter promised to call him the next day.

He hoped Ainsley didn't get angry for him overstepping his boundaries, but he was relatively certain she would not be working and it was important to let Ed know as soon as possible so he could make the necessary adjustments.

When he'd hung up, his thoughts were as scattered as the stars in the sky. There were so many questions and no answers. Fear battled with anger as he waited to find out Ainsley's condition.

The outside door opened, and he looked up to see Sheriff Black walk in. "Wayne." Hunter stood.

"I got here as soon as I heard. How is she?"

The two men sat down side by side. "I haven't heard anything yet," Hunter replied. "She was unconscious when they brought her in, and it looked like she'd taken a punch to her jaw, but I don't know anything else yet."

"Well, I just wanted to come by and let you know I called in a couple more deputies to search the area around the café," Wayne said.

"Thanks, I appreciate it." Hunter raked a hand through his hair. "I don't have a clue who is behind this, but I'm sure it's the same person that left the nasty note in the café and a dead rat on her doorstep. Unfortunately, whoever it is, he's smart and hasn't left any clues behind."

"Hopefully that will change tonight and the men will find something that will help identify the perp," Wayne replied. "In fact I'm on my way over there now." Wayne rose. "Let me know how Ainsley is doing. I'm putting Nick in charge of this investigation."

Hunter looked at him in surprise. "What? Why not me?"

"Hunter, you know there can't be any appearance of bias. You have a personal relationship with the victim, and that means you're off this case."

Hunter wanted to protest, but he knew Wayne was right, and the last thing Hunter wanted to do was give the perp a reason to have a defense due to bias on his part. "At least I know Nick will do a good job," he finally said.

He looked at the door where the doctor should come through. What was taking so long? His nerves jangled. How badly was she hurt?

"I'm off," Wayne said. "I expect to hear from you later, and I'm sure Nick will be in touch."

About fifteen minutes after Wayne left, Dr. Andrew Lockwood walked into the waiting room. Hunter shot up out of his chair and approached the doctor. "How is she?"

"She's alert and we have her resting comfortably," Dr. Lockwood said. "She has a broken rib and bruising all along her rib cage. She also took a pretty good blow to her chin. None of the injuries are life-threatening, but we're going to keep her for the rest of the night and, barring no complications, she should be able to go home tomorrow."

"But she was unconscious. What caused that?" Hunter asked even as an intense shudder of relief swept through him. The relief was short-lived as he thought of what she must have gone through.

"Shock and pain, but again, she's resting comfortably now," he replied. "We've given her something for her pain."

"Can I see her?"

Dr. Lockwood frowned. "Only for a short visit. What she needs right now is rest. She's in room 106."

Hunter raced down the quiet hallway and turned into her room. He paused in the threshold, aching at the very sight of her.

Her eyes were closed and she looked as pale as the white sheets that surrounded her except for the bright purple of the bruise on her chin.

As he stared at the bruise, and thought again of the broken and bruised ribs, a deep rage filled him. Who had done this to her? She was so kind…so giving and yet somebody had put their hands on her.

Her eyes suddenly fluttered open. She held his gaze for a long moment, and then she began to weep. "Honey… don't cry." He hurried to her side. He drew up a chair, sank down and took her hand in his. "Please don't cry. It's only going to make you hurt."

"I'm trying not to," she said and drew in several shallow breaths in an obvious effort to contain her emotions.

"I'm so sorry. Ainsley, I'm so damned sorry I didn't see something like this coming. I'm so damned sorry that I wasn't there to protect you."

"Neither one of us saw something like this coming."

"You want to tell me what happened?"

As she gave him a blow-by-blow account of events

from the time they had hung up with each other to when she had come to consciousness in the ambulance, once again a deep sense of rage filled him.

"Did you recognize anything about him? Anything at all?"

"No, he was dressed all in black and wore a ski mask. The only thing I can tell you is it's definitely a he, and he's strong." Tears filled her eyes once again. "I was terrified that he was going to pick me up and carry me away and I would never see Melinda or you again."

"Thank God that didn't happen. Did he say anything to you?"

"No, not a thing."

"What about smell? Did you notice anything about the way he smelled?"

She looked at him in surprise. "I hadn't thought about it." She frowned and then winced, as if the facial gesture had hurt her. "Now that I do think about it, he smelled… funky."

"You mean like dirty?"

"No, it wasn't the smell of perspiration or dirty clothes—it was a strange, nasty scent that I've never smelled before, and I can't even describe it. I'm sorry."

"Don't apologize," he said.

"Ben saved me. If he hadn't been there and yelled out, I would have either been beaten to death or kidnapped."

"Thank God for dumpster-diving drunks," he replied.

"Thank God," she echoed.

She closed her eyes for a long moment, and when she finally looked at him again, he saw not only exhaustion in her eyes, but also realized whatever they had given her for pain was making her sleepy.

"You get some rest now," he said and released his

hold on her hand. He half rose up and then leaned over and kissed her softly on her forehead. "I'll be back tomorrow, okay?"

"Okay." She closed her eyes once again and appeared to be asleep before he even left her bedside.

He remained in her doorway for several long moments, his thoughts tortured by what had happened to Ainsley. He had to figure out a way to keep her safe. His gut clenched. He had to keep her safe, because he didn't believe this was the end of it. Somebody wanted her dead, and Hunter had a terrible feeling that the man wouldn't stop until he'd achieved his goal.

Chapter Eleven

Ainsley opened her eyes to the early-morning sun drifting into her hospital room. She instinctively knew that to move meant pain, and so she stayed still.

She vaguely remembered Hunter stopping by the night before. She'd felt his concern and caring, and it had almost warmed up all the iciness in her soul…almost, but not quite. And that iciness encased her heart once again this morning.

She was scared. No, she was absolutely terrified. Not only by what had happened the night before, but also about what might happen in the future.

If the man last night had wanted to kidnap her, he'd failed. If he'd wanted to kill her, he'd also failed at that, too. Would he try again? Was he out there now already planning his next attack on her?

And as always, her biggest question was who was it? Who had attacked her last night? She now positively knew Ben Wilkins had nothing to do with it. In fact, if he hadn't been dumpster diving again last night, she would probably be dead by now.

There was obviously something good and decent still left in Ben. He could have stayed hidden behind the dumpster while she was being attacked. But instead, even drunk, he'd done what he could to help her. He'd saved her life.

She tried to draw a deep breath, but pain ripped through her ribs where the man had kicked her. Her jaw ached, and overall she felt as if she'd gone ten rounds with a heavyweight boxing champion.

Finding the remote for her bed, she pressed the button to raise her head. She moaned as her body readjusted to the new position.

At that moment Callie Roberts walked in. "Oh good. You're awake," she said. "I'm just going to take your vitals." She prepared the blood pressure cuff. She plumped it up and then slowly released it.

After a minute or so, she pulled off the cuff and smiled at Ainsley. "A little high, but that's probably due to pain."

"Oh, I'm definitely in some pain," Ainsley replied, even as she tried to smile at the young nurse.

"The doctor ordered something to help with that. I'll be right back in with it."

As Ainsley waited, she thought of her daughter. Thank goodness she was at Juanita's. Once it got a little later in the day, she'd check in there.

An hour later Ainsley felt a little better. The medicine had taken the edge off her pain, and she drifted in and out of sleep.

She came awake again and was surprised to see Hunter sitting in the chair next to her bed.

"Hi," he said.

"Hi," she replied and forced a smile. "Fancy meeting you here."

"I'd rather be meeting you anywhere but here," he replied. His green eyes held such warmth, such caring it took away what breath she had. He reached for her hand and gave it a gentle squeeze. "How are you doing this morning?"

"I hurt, but I'm better than I was last night," she replied. "But I'm not going to lie… I'm scared, Hunter. I just know the man last night first tried to kidnap me, and when he couldn't get me up, he wanted to kill me."

"Nick has been assigned to the case. I haven't spoken to him this morning, but I'm hoping he got something to help us identify this guy."

"And if he doesn't?"

"Then we'll keep digging until we find him." His voice was filled with grim determination, but as much as she wanted to believe his words, in this case she felt like the bad guy was definitely winning.

"Thank God Melinda wasn't with me last night," she said. "But what happens next time?"

"There won't be a next time," he said firmly. "I don't want you and Melinda going back to your apartment. Until we find this guy, I want the two of you to move into my place."

She looked at him in stunned surprise, and then more than a little bit of relief flooded through her. "Are you sure you want to do that?"

"Positive," he replied firmly. "According to the doctor, you're probably going to be released today. My plan is to get Melinda and we'll go to your place and you can pack up what you need."

"What about my work?"

"Ainsley, the last thing you need to worry about right now is your job. First of all, you need time to rest and heal. I already talked to Ed to let him know what's going on, and he knows you won't be working for a while." He squeezed her hand once again. "I don't want you to worry about anything."

She laughed and then winced. "Oh Hunter, right now I'm worried about everything."

"Well, stop it. My shoulders are broad, and you can leave the worry to me."

She studied his features without speaking for a long moment. He was so handsome and so earnest in this moment. "I wish it were that easy," she finally said.

"Me too," he replied.

At that moment Dr. Lockwood entered the room. "On a scale of one to ten, ten being the worst pain you've ever experienced, where are you right now?"

"Before the pain medicine, I would have said about an eight, but now I'd say I'm about a six," she replied.

He nodded. "The good news is I'm going to release you today, and I'm going to write a script for ten days of pain meds. The bad news is that these injuries are going to take some time to stop hurting."

"I figured that," she replied. She'd had broken ribs before and knew they took a long time to heal.

"I'll send the nurse in to remove your IV and will write up the paperwork to get you out of here."

An hour later Hunter helped her walk out of the hospital and to his truck. "I guess they didn't feed you any breakfast. You want to grab something in the café before we pick up Melinda?"

"That's not necessary. I'm really not hungry," she replied.

"Okay, then we'll go get your daughter and head to your place so the two of you can pack."

"Don't you have to work today?" she asked.

"I took the day off. At least when I have to go in to

work tomorrow, I know you and Melinda will be safer at my place. My doors and locks are better than the ones in your apartment. I don't like the idea that not only could anyone come through your front door, but they could also come through the door that separates your apartment from the café."

"How are we going to do this? You only have one bedroom available," she said.

"You and Melinda will have the bedroom, and I'll bunk on the sofa."

"Oh Hunter, I don't want you to make that kind of a sacrifice for us," she protested.

"Nonsense, it's not a sacrifice at all. I can't tell you how many times I've fallen asleep on my sofa. It's really quite comfortable."

She smiled at him. "You'd tell me that even if your sofa was made of rocks."

He returned her smile. "Probably, but thankfully my sofa isn't made of rocks."

They fell silent for a few minutes as he drove to Ed and Juanita's house. A million thoughts burned through her head as she stared out the passenger window.

Surely she would be safer at Hunter's place than at her own. Hopefully the man who was after her wouldn't know where she'd gone. If Hunter kept his usual schedule and she and Melinda didn't peek outside, maybe nobody would even know they were there.

She almost laughed at her own stupidity. Of course everyone in town would know where she'd gone because everyone in town knew she and Hunter were a couple. Still, there was no question she'd feel safer staying there.

She'd have to keep Melinda out of school for a while,

but that seemed a small price to pay for their safety. Or she could pack up their things and run.

God, the very thought of starting over someplace else broke her heart. Despite what was happening to her, she still loved it here in Dusty Gulch. She still believed in the goodness of most people here. This was exactly the place where she wanted to raise her daughter.

She certainly didn't want to give up Hunter and the life she saw here with him because of the actions of a single person. She would give this plan a chance and hope within the next couple of days her attacker would be arrested.

Fifteen minutes later they were seated at Juanita's kitchen table. "You know Ed won't be happy about losing one of his favorite waitresses for a while, but we both want you to take all the time you need to get the healing you need," she said.

"Thanks, Juanita. I couldn't do a good job for Ed right now no matter how much I wanted to," Ainsley replied.

"With that in mind, why don't you let Melinda stay here with us for a week or two? I can get her to school in the mornings, and you know she's always good for me."

"Oh no, that's asking too much," Ainsley protested.

"Nonsense. We'd love to have her. Let me take care of her while you take care of yourself," Juanita replied.

"Are you sure you wouldn't mind?" Ainsley felt the hot press of tears of gratitude. This was why she loved this town…because of people like Juanita and Ed. For all of Ed's blustering, he had a heart of gold.

"If I minded, I wouldn't have brought it up," Juanita replied. "My friend, please, let me do this for you."

Ainsley looked at Hunter and then back at Juanita. "Okay, but I'll need to take her home now so she can pick out some clothes to pack and then we'll bring her back here."

"I'll go get her." Juanita got up from the table and disappeared from the room.

"Are you okay with this?" Hunter asked her softly.

"Actually, I'm a little bit relieved. Melinda will stay in school and Juanita will keep her on a regular routine. I won't worry about her if she's here."

Melinda and Juanita's daughter Bonnie came running into the room. "Is it true, Mom? I get to stay here for a whole week or maybe more?"

"Would you like that?" Ainsley asked.

Melinda and Bonnie hugged each other and bounced up and down with excitement. "Yes, I would like it," Melinda exclaimed.

"Then you need to come with us right now so you can pack a bag and then we'll bring you back here," Ainsley said.

"Awesome," Melinda replied and then frowned. "What happened to your chin?"

"I…uh… I took a nasty fall last night. I hit my chin and hurt my ribs," Ainsley said. The last thing she wanted was for her daughter to be afraid.

Melinda's features softened, and she released her hold on Bonnie and sidled up next to Ainsley. "Do you want me to come home and take care of you?"

Ainsley wrapped an arm around her daughter. "No, honey. I'll be fine. I'm going to stay at Hunter's house while you stay here."

"Are you sure?" Melinda asked. "Will he take good care of you?"

"I promise I will," Hunter said.

Ainsley smiled. "Okay then, let's get going so we can get your clothes for a week."

Within minutes the three of them were headed back to the apartment. When they arrived, Ainsley stared at the door, replaying what had happened the last time she'd stood at that door.

Icy chills raced up and down her spine, and her ribs hurt even more as she remembered the kicks she'd received. "Okay?" Hunter asked softly, as if he knew how hard it was for her to come back here.

She straightened her back and reached for the inner strength that had gotten her through hell in the past. "I'm fine," she replied. "Let's just get this done."

They entered the apartment, and Hunter headed for the sofa. "Melinda, get out your pink suitcase and pack it with school and play clothes. I'll be in to check it in just a few minutes," Ainsley said.

Hunter sat on the sofa while Ainsley went into her bedroom and Melinda went into hers. From the closet Ainsley pulled out a suitcase and opened it on the floor. There was no way with her screaming ribs she could lift it onto the bed.

She paused for a moment, trying to decide what she should take with her for being gone for a week or two. With her ribs hurting like they did, all she wanted was loose-fitting pants and T-shirts.

She quickly packed up what she thought she would need and grabbed her bag of toiletries off the back of the stool in the bathroom. Before going back to her room, she decided to check in on Melinda.

She was about to enter her daughter's bedroom when she heard it…the unmistakable deep voice of her ex-husband coming from someplace inside the room.

Shock and then a wild terror froze her in place. The toiletry bag fell from her hand, and a scream lodged in the back of her throat.

"I'm coming soon for you, baby girl," the disembodied voice said.

Peter...he was here.

Oh God, he'd found them again.

He was not only someplace in Dusty Gulch, he was in their apartment. She backed away from Melinda's bedroom, a scream begging to be released.

After all this time, when she was sure she was safe, she wasn't. He'd found her, and it was only a matter of time before he'd kill her.

HUNTER KNEW THE minute Ainsley came into the living room that something had happened. Her face was white, and her entire body was visibly trembling.

"Honey, what's wrong?" he asked. He jumped up off the sofa.

She motioned for him to step outside the door. When they stood on the stoop, she stared at him for a long moment. "I need to go. I really care about you, but I need to pack up everything in my car and get out of town as fast as I can," she whispered.

He frowned. "Ainsley, what are you talking about?"

"Melinda hasn't been lying. Her father has been talking to her. I heard him just now. Peter is here and I've got to leave town."

The words flew out of her in a rush. Hunter could feel her desperate urgency, an urgency he didn't understand. "You heard him? What do you mean? Where?"

"Just now in Melinda's room." Her voice rose with hysteria. "I've got to go."

What the hell was going on? "I thought your ex-husband didn't care about you or Melinda."

"I lied, and now I've got to leave. I… I've got to take Melinda and run." She whirled around to go back inside, but he caught her by the arm to stop her.

"Ainsley, listen to me. I don't know what's going on right now, but we have a plan. Just get your things to go to my place, and Melinda will be safe with Ed and Juanita."

"You don't understand, but I need to run. It's…it's what we do. I… I need to find a place where he can't find us. He's going to take Melinda and he's going to… to kill me." Her eyes were huge pools of abject terror as she clutched at the front of his shirt.

"Ainsley, try to calm down. You don't have to run. We now know who the bad guy is. We'll get him. We're going to find him and get him behind bars. I just need for you to give me some time and some more information. Can you do that, baby?" He took her by the shoulders. "Can you trust me?"

She held his gaze for several long minutes, and he could feel some of the sick energy inside her ease away. "Okay, I'll try things your way for now."

"Let's go back inside." He pushed his car keys into her hand. "Get you and Melinda packed up and leave the suitcases in your rooms. Then go lock yourselves in my truck. Is there attic access in your apartment?"

Once again she clutched at the front of his shirt. "Don't go up there. He'll…he'll kill you, Hunter. He's a very sick, dangerous man."

Hunter touched the handle of his gun in his holster. "You don't understand. When somebody threatens somebody I love, I become a dangerous man. Now, where's the attic access?"

"In the bathroom," she finally said.

"Thank you." He leaned over and gave her a quick kiss on the forehead. "Get packed and get in the truck, okay? You have a flashlight?"

"Under the kitchen sink." Her fingers tightened on the front of his shirt. "Please, Hunter. Don't let him kill you."

"I won't," he replied firmly.

They went back inside, and within minutes Melinda and Ainsley were packed and locked inside the truck. The moment they left the apartment, Hunter grabbed the flashlight beneath her kitchen sink and then hurried into the bathroom.

He stepped up on the toilet lid and then onto the edge of the sink, where he had to crouch. He reached up to move the piece of ceiling that gave access to the attic. Once it was dislodged, he pulled his gun. He wasn't about to stand all the way up not knowing if he'd catch a bullet in the head.

"Dusty Gulch Sheriff's Department. Come down with your hands up." He waited and listened. Nothing. He repeated the command and again waited to hear something…anything that would let him know where the man was in what he assumed was a very large attic.

Still he heard nothing. Not a rustle, not any movement that would indicate anyone in the immediate space.

His heart pounded fast and furiously. Adrenaline poured through his veins. He finally straightened up, leading the way with his gun and the flashlight.

He pointed the light to the left and then slowly panned to the right. He didn't see anyone. He stuck the light and his gun in his waistband and then pulled himself up and into the attic. He quickly grabbed the light and his gun once again.

Once again he scanned the area with his light. There didn't appear to be another person up here. Had the perp already escaped through another access?

He was about to take a couple of careful steps forward when he saw them…a tangle of wires that he knew didn't belong up there.

Realization struck him. Ainsley and her daughter had been spied on, and there had to be speakers involved so that the man could talk to his daughter. How long had these things been up here? Who in the hell was Ainsley's ex-husband?

He got down from the attic and went into Melinda's room. He spied the camera in the ceiling, along with a tiny little speaker, and he knew there were others located around the apartment.

He immediately called Nick. "Hey, man, I was going to catch up with you and Ainsley later today. How's she doing?"

"She's sore, but doing okay. I'm moving her into my house right now. You need to get to the café and check out the attic above her rooms. There are cameras and I don't know what else up here to spy on her."

"What?" Nick's voice was filled with stunned surprise.

"Yeah, and we now know who the bad guy is. It's Ainsley's ex-husband. I'm hoping she has a picture of him on her phone or someplace so we can find him and get him in jail." Hunter spoke fast, aware of the two waiting in the car. "I'm leaving her apartment right now. We'll be at my place in just a little while."

"Okay, I'll head to the café right now and touch base with you later."

The two men hung up, and Hunter hurried into Melinda's room and grabbed her small, pink-flowered suitcase and then went into Ainsley's bedroom and picked up her black suitcase. He carried them outside and loaded them into the truck, then got behind the steering wheel with a reassuring smile at Ainsley.

She didn't smile back. She stared out the passenger window and her trembling fingers twisted into knots in her lap. Once they were alone, he had a lot of questions for her.

She'd already confessed she'd lied to him about her ex-husband. What else might she have lied about? He definitely needed some answers from her.

He also needed any information she had about her ex-husband. If he was the person who had attacked her the night before, then he was in town and hopefully Nick and the other law enforcement officials could find him and get him in jail so that Ainsley and Melinda would be safe.

They took Melinda back to Juanita's, and during the ride to his house Ainsley remained silent and withdrawn. He was completely and totally in love with her. The utter depth of his love for her hit him out of left field.

He'd known he enjoyed spending time with her. He knew that he liked everything about her. He'd realized he'd been working toward a future with her. He'd told Nick he was thinking about proposing to her. He was definitely in love with her, but he wondered what kind of secrets she was keeping.

He'd been open and honest with her about everything in his life, and he'd believed she was open and honest with him. Now doubts twisted his gut. Why hadn't she told him her ex-husband was a dangerous man before now?

They arrived at his place, and he carried her suitcase

through his front door. "Come on into the bedroom." He led her into the room and placed her suitcase next to the bed. "You can unpack later. Right now we need to talk."

She gave a curt nod and then followed him into the living room. She sat on the sofa, her arms wrapped around her middle. She looked so beautiful and yet so small and vulnerable.

He wanted to sit next to her and draw her into his arms. He wanted to tell her how much he loved her and that he wanted a forever future with her, but he didn't. He had more important things to do.

He got a small notebook and a pen from his kitchen desk drawer and then joined her on the sofa. "What's your ex-husband's name?"

"Peter Waverly." She didn't meet his gaze.

"Do you have a picture of him?" If they had a photo of him, then they could immediately show it around town. Somewhere somebody had to have seen the guy.

"In my phone," she replied. "It's in my purse in the bedroom. I'll go get it." She got up and left the living room.

This was the break they had needed. Why hadn't she told him more about this man before now? If she knew her ex was dangerous, then why hadn't she shared with him more about the man when inexplicable things had started to happen to her?

She came back in and resumed her position on the sofa next to him. She turned on her phone and flipped through a dozen photos and then stopped.

When she gave him the phone, her hand trembled. "He's going to kill me. He tried to kill me before."

Hunter looked at the photo. There was nothing distinctive about the man. His blond hair was cut short and his blue eyes stared straight into the camera. His front teeth overlapped each other, giving him a slightly crooked smile. Hunter didn't remember seeing the man anywhere around, but that didn't mean he wasn't here.

He grabbed his cell phone and once again called Nick. "I've got a picture of our perp. It's on Ainsley's cell phone. I'm going to send it to you right now," he said when Nick answered.

"I've got it," Nick said after a moment. "I'll get copies printed off and we'll get it circulating. Tell Ainsley we're going to get him behind bars."

"I'll tell her." Hunter hung up the phone and handed hers back to her. For several long moments, they sat in silence. So many questions whirled around in his head, he didn't even know where to begin.

"How long have you known it was your ex-husband behind everything?" he finally asked.

"When I heard his voice in Melinda's room. Before that I just assumed it was somebody here in town who was tormenting me." Her voice was a dull monotone. "I should have known he would find us. He's found us no matter where we've been. He won't stop until he kills me."

She raised her gaze and looked at him, and in the depths of her eyes he saw more secrets—dark secrets he feared might destroy everything they had built between them.

"Why does he want you dead?" he asked.

"Because I left him. I belonged to Peter and he's a narcissistic psychopath. He tried to kill me before I left him, and he's been hunting me ever since."

"So, he was abusive in the marriage?" Anger rose up inside him. He'd never been able to understand how a man could put his hands on a woman…especially a woman he professed to love.

"The physical abuse didn't really start until the last two years of our marriage. Before that there was definitely mental and emotional abuse."

She shook her head and once again looked down at her hands in her lap. "It's a typical story of domestic abuse. First he began to isolate me from my friends and family. I was rarely allowed to go anywhere on my own. I didn't have a car or a bank account."

She sighed, sounding impatient. "And then one day he thought I flirted with a stock boy in the grocery store. That night was the first time he beat the hell out of me. I should have left then, but he was so contrite afterward, and I was desperate to stay together for Melinda's sake."

"And then he kept beating you," he said. When he thought of what she'd apparently gone through, he wanted to find her ex and beat him to a bloody pulp.

"He did. When he beat me the last time, I was sure he was going to kill me. There was no car accident to make the scar on my stomach. He stabbed me there and would have stabbed me to death if the neighbors hadn't heard me screaming and called the police."

She released a sigh that sounded bone-weary. "He was arrested that night and I packed up what I could, used his bank card, which he'd left behind, to withdraw as much money as I could, and I took Melinda and we left."

"Why didn't you tell me all this before now?" He felt lied to—granted, it was a lie by omission, but he didn't understand why she hadn't shared this with him before now.

"Oh, Hunter, I didn't want anyone to know where I'd come from. I have been so afraid for so long, and I've told you so many lies I don't even know where to begin to tell you the truth."

He stared at her. A woman's lies had destroyed his life before. He now had a dreadful sense of déjà vu. Was it about to happen all over again?

Chapter Twelve

Ainsley had been terrified since she'd heard Peter's voice in Melinda's room. She'd hoped Peter had given up on looking for her and moved on. She'd desperately hoped she and her daughter were finally free of him.

She should have known better. He was totally obsessed. He was a sick man who wanted her dead. She should have known when strange things had begun to happen to her that he was behind it all.

She felt Hunter's stare on her, and even though this wasn't the way she'd wanted to come clean to him, she owed him the whole, unvarnished truth.

He was going to hate her for her lies, and then if he did his job, he would have to place her under arrest. Dear God, how had it all come down to this?

"Peter came from money. His father was not only rich, but also influential. After I got medical treatment for the stab wounds I'd received, I took Melinda to a motel to wait to see what happened next."

"So, what happened next?"

There was curiosity in his voice, but she also felt a touch of coolness from him. The dream she'd had of building a future with him was now shattered. As she looked at him and saw that his beautiful green eyes were guarded, she knew the truth. Peter had won. She felt as if she was already dead.

"Peter was out of jail the next morning with no charges levied against him. He'd tried to kill me and he walked away free as a bird."

"Was this in Nevada?" Hunter asked.

"No, I lied about being from Nevada. I'm actually from Portland, Maine. My mother lives there along with my older sister. My name isn't really Ainsley Meadows, it's Colette Waverly."

He winced, as if she'd physically slapped him. "So, he got no charges and you ran," he said flatly.

She nodded. "While I was running for my life, he divorced me and won full custody of Melinda. Apparently, he told the judge that I was dangerous and deranged. A warrant was issued for my arrest and I was charged with parental alienation, among other things. But there was no way I was going to allow my daughter to live with that madman, so for the past three years I've been on the run. I have fake ID and I've broken all kinds of laws to stay one step ahead of the monster. So, I understand if you have to arrest me."

The words burst out of her on a rush, and when there was nothing else left to say, she put her hands up to her face and began to weep.

She was utterly exhausted. Her body hurt from the beating she'd received the night before. Her heart ached with the distance she now felt from Hunter, with the damage she had done to their relationship.

All she could think about now was if he didn't arrest her, then she needed to get out of here and return to her life on the run. She would never, ever allow herself to get close to anyone again, but she couldn't take back the love she felt for Hunter.

She wished he would take her in his arms and tell her everything was going to be okay. She wanted to be in his embrace, where she'd always felt so loved and protected. She stopped crying and dropped her hands back into her lap.

"Are you going to arrest me?" she finally asked. She met his gaze once again.

"I'm betting that if I don't arrest you then you're going to take off again. Aren't you tired of running?" His eyes were dark, unfathomable.

"Yes," she replied as tears blurred her vision. "Oh God, I'm exhausted. I'm sick of the lying and the looking over my shoulder. I don't want this kind of life for Melinda. I know it's not good for her, but I didn't feel like I had any other options. I was really hoping this would be our forever home."

"Then stop running. Stay here and let us do our jobs. We'll deal with your other legal issues once we get Peter behind bars." A knock on the door interrupted whatever else he was going to say.

He got up to answer the door and returned a moment later with Nick. "Hey, Ainsley, how are you doing?" Nick asked her.

"Okay," she replied even though she was anything but okay. At the moment her physical pain was second to the pain that stabbed in her heart.

She wasn't sure what Hunter was going to do, but she was pretty sure any love he'd had for her was gone. Thoughts of that squeezed her heart so hard it made her ribs scream in pain.

"I just wanted to let the two of you know where we're

at in the investigation." Nick sat in the chair facing the sofa, and Hunter eased back down beside Colette. "I've got men up in the attic at the café dealing with all the surveillance equipment." He looked at Hunter. "This guy spent a ton of money on this, and we have no idea where the location is on the other end. We also don't know how he managed to get everything up there."

"Maybe the person who has that answer is Ted Johnson, who's nowhere to be found."

"If he had anything to do with Peter, then he's probably dead," Colette said. If the man was dead, then she was partially responsible for his death. If she'd never come to Dusty Gulch, then Peter wouldn't have killed Ted. "Peter would consider Ted a loose end. I can't emphasize enough to you both what a dangerous, evil human being he is."

She fell silent as Hunter filled Nick in on her real name, the reasons for her lying to everyone in town and about her abusive life with her ex-husband.

Nick listened carefully to everything. "Thankfully we now have his picture being circulated by all the deputies in town. If he's here in town, then somebody will have seen him," Nick said. "It's just a matter of time before we have him arrested."

"I hope so," she replied. And then what? Peter would go to jail, and if it was like the last time, he'd manage to get out of it. He'd be out and she'd be arrested and he'd have full access to Melinda. He would discipline Melinda the same way he had her…with his fists and with his hurtful, damaging words. This thought once again brought tears to her eyes.

"Is there anything else you can tell us about Peter that might help us in locating him and making an arrest?" Nick asked her.

"Nothing. I could never predict what Peter might do," she replied tiredly. Had it only been hours ago that she'd left the hospital? It already felt like it had been months.

"Of course we all know it's possible he's changed his hair color or grown some facial hair," Nick said and then stood. "I'm heading back to the café to check in on the men there. Ainsley…er… Colette, I'll be in touch. Hunter…walk me out?"

She watched as the man she loved disappeared out the front door with Nick. She had found the town she'd wanted to be her forever home and the man she'd hoped would be her forever man. And now it had all been destroyed.

She never should have tried to be happy. When Hunter had first asked her out, she should have turned him down. She never should have allowed herself to care about or to be cared for by another human being.

Right now, even if she got the opportunity, she didn't have the strength to even think about running again. She felt utterly hopeless. If Peter didn't kill her this time, then he would just wait for the next opportunity he got.

She had little hope that they would find him. He was incredibly smart, and it was quite possible he'd already left town. He had to have known she'd heard his voice in the apartment. He had to have seen Hunter going up into the attic and known they would now be looking for him.

She wasn't afraid of dying. What she was afraid of was leaving Melinda in Peter's care. She would willingly give her own life if it would stop that from happening.

She looked up when Hunter returned. He stood in the doorway between the kitchen and the living room. "Why don't you get unpacked now and I'll see about making us something to eat?"

There was nothing warm or supportive in his eyes at the moment, and an exquisite pain of bereavement shot through her. Without saying a word, she got up and went into his bedroom to unpack some of her things.

Before she even got started, she sank down on the bed and was struck by a deep exhaustion. It was an exhaustion created by both mental and physical pain...one of utter despair.

Her body hurt, and at least she could help that. She dug in her purse, grabbed one of her pain pills and dry swallowed it. Maybe she'd just rest for a few minutes before unloading her suitcase. She stretched out on the bed and was instantly enveloped by Hunter's scent.

She closed her eyes, breathing in the essence of him. It was a smell that had always signified love and protection. She began to cry quietly—from the pain, from the fear and finally for everything she had lost.

She drew in several deep breaths to staunch her tears. When she stopped weeping, her eyelids felt too heavy to lift. Her last conscious thought was that it was just a matter of time before all her nightmares where Peter was concerned came true and all her dreams of Hunter would shatter.

HUNTER THOUGHT MAYBE a bowl of soup with some crackers might taste good to her. He had both chicken noodle and tomato. Since he had no clue which one she might like, he pulled them both out of his pantry along with a box of saltines.

He then sat at the table to await her return. Her...not Ainsley, but Colette. He was still trying to wrap his head around everything he'd learned about her.

His thoughts were disjointed and his emotions were

all over the place. Anger battled with disappointment and created an enormous sense of loss inside him.

If she'd lied to him about her name and where she was from, what else had she lied about? Had her kisses been a lie? When she told him that she cared about him, had that been a fabrication?

Had she gone out with him in the first place thinking that dating a deputy was smart given her circumstances? Was it a case of keeping her friends close and her enemies closer? Had she gone out with him simply because she thought he would keep her safe?

He couldn't figure out what was real and what wasn't where she—Colette, not Ainsley—was concerned.

She should have returned to the kitchen by now. She'd had plenty of time to unpack. A small bell of alarm rang in his head. He got up and walked through the living room and then paused and listened.

There was no sound coming from his bedroom. Had she opened a window and taken off? Had she decided that running was better than trusting him? He hurried down the hallway and stopped short in the doorway, relief flooding through him. She hadn't run—she'd fallen asleep.

She was on her back, her dark hair fanned out against his pillow. She looked beautiful in sleep. All the worry and stress lines were gone from her face.

It had all seemed so real with her. He'd really believed he'd tasted her desire for him in her kisses. When they'd made love, he'd truly believed she was falling in love with him.

Had it all been an act? Had she just been using him all along? He couldn't help but wonder what other secrets she might have, although the ones he'd already learned were devastating enough.

The doubts about her and her actions since coming to town created a pool of deep disappointment and loss inside him. He was so deeply in love with her, and now he didn't know what to do with that love.

There was no reason to wake her. No matter how confused he was about everything, the beating she'd taken the night before had been real. The deep-purple bruise on her chin was very real, and it ticked him off that apparently her ex-husband had gotten to her, had beaten her and would have probably killed her if Ben hadn't intervened.

At least she should be safe here. He hated like hell that he had to work the next day, but three deputies were out with the flu, leaving the department too shorthanded for him to take the day off. Still, his locks were good and sturdy. He'd tell all of his fellow officers to do frequent drive-bys, but he also wanted them to be working on finding Peter Waverly. That was the only way she would be completely safe.

He turned away from the bedroom and returned to the living room. He sat in his recliner, and Zeus immediately jumped into his lap.

He stroked Zeus's fur. "I know you like her, buddy, but I don't see how this ends." He was so confused and his emotions were still all over the place where she was concerned. If they wound up catching Peter and getting him behind bars, then Colette would be free to pursue her life anywhere with anyone she wanted.

What he feared was that when this was all over, it would once again just be him and Zeus alone again.

PETER SAT ACROSS from Sheila in the busy café. It was dinnertime, and the place was packed. Word had gotten out that Ainsley Meadows had been beaten up the night before by her ex-husband, and all the conversations around him seemed to be about that.

"That's terrible about that poor woman getting beat up," Sheila said as they waited for their orders to be delivered.

"Isn't it though," he said with a straight face.

"Thank God you aren't that kind of man," Sheila said. "All the other men I've been with have beat the hell out of me, but you're nice to me."

Peter forced a smile to his lips. "You're easy to be nice to, Sheila."

"Are you going to score me a little dessert later tonight?" she asked coyly. She looked at him with eyes that begged and burned with need.

He knew "a little dessert" meant drugs. "I'll have to see what's available." Once again he thought of what a pig she was…driven by her addictions and with no desire to change. She disgusted him. She was weak, and he had no understanding or compassion for weak people.

"I'm falling for you, Hank. I've got to say I'm really falling for you." She smiled at him.

Even her smile was a huge turn-off, displaying bad and missing teeth. How could she really believe that a man like him would be remotely interested in a woman like her?

Their food arrived, and they'd only been eating for a few minutes when two of the deputies from the sheriff's department walked in.

They each had a photo in their hands and they were going from each booth to each table and questioning each and every diner. As one of them, Deputy Nick Marshall, approached his table, Peter felt no tension whatsoever.

He was so much smarter than the law enforcement in this one-pony town. He was smarter than most people. "Evening, folks." Deputy Marshall stepped up next to their table.

"Evening," Peter replied. "What's going on?"

"We're checking with people to see if anyone has seen this man." Deputy Marshall showed Peter a picture of himself. Peter frowned. "No, I haven't seen him."

Sheila looked at the picture and slowly shook her head. "I haven't ever seen him before. Is that the man who beat up the waitress who worked here?"

Deputy Marshall nodded and then looked at Peter once again. "I don't believe we've met."

Peter half rose in his seat and held out his hand. The deputy took his hand and the two men shook. "I'm Hank Bridges. I bought the old pig farm just outside the city limits."

Marshall nodded his head. "I know the place. How long have you been there?"

"Maybe three months or so," he replied. "The place needs a lot of cleanup, and I'm working on it."

"Well, it's nice to meet you and welcome to town," the deputy said and then moved on to the next table.

Peter went back to eating his meal. Oh yes, he was smart enough to know how to get his revenge against the woman who had left him.

He knew where his daughter was, and he knew where Colette was located. He was going to get her. He was going to make her pay. It was just a matter of time. A sweet rush of pleasure shot through him.

"Are you going to eat those French fries?" Sheila asked and gestured to the potatoes left on his plate.

"No, help yourself," he replied and pushed his plate closer to her. *Eat up*, he thought. It would just make the pigs happier. Sheila first…and then Colette.

Oink. Oink.

Chapter Thirteen

Colette awoke to semidarkness in the room. For a moment she was confused as to where she was and what was going on. Then it all slammed back into her.

Peter was someplace in town. She was in Hunter's bed, and Hunter knew all her secrets. She rolled over and sat up and tried to ignore the sharp pain in her wounded ribs. Right now the wound in her heart hurt just as badly.

She got up, and her stomach growled with hunger. She had no idea what time it was, but she hadn't eaten anything all day. While she'd just like to sleep all night to escape her depressing emotions, she was wide-awake now and needed something to eat.

What she really needed was Hunter's arms around her. She needed him to hold her tight against his warm, strong body. She wanted him to whisper in her ear that he loved her and everything was going to be all right. But she knew that wasn't going to happen. He probably hated her now.

She left the bedroom and went into the living room, where the lights were on in anticipation of nightfall. Hunter wasn't in the living room.

She found him in the kitchen, seated at the table with a cup of coffee before him. As she entered the room, Zeus danced at her feet. She bent down and gave him a quick scratch behind his ears.

"I was wondering how long you might sleep," Hunter said. He got up from the table and walked over to open the back door and let Zeus outside. He then returned to the table.

She stood by the table but didn't sit. "I took a pain pill and only intended to lie down for a few minutes, but I guess I was more tired than I thought."

"You must be starving," he said. She felt his distance in his tone, in the blankness of his eyes. She supposed she should have expected it.

"I am hungry," she replied.

"I thought maybe soup and crackers might sound good to you," he said and got up from the table.

"Actually, that sounds perfect."

"Why don't you sit and I'll get it for you." He pointed to the chair across from where he had been seated.

"You don't have to wait on me," she protested.

"I don't mind. All I need to know is if you want chicken noodle or tomato soup. I'm afraid those are the only kinds I have."

"Tomato sounds good. Thank you." She sat at the table and watched him as he got the can of soup, fixed it in a soup bowl and then put it in the microwave to warm.

As the microwave hummed, Hunter opened a package of crackers and placed a handful of them on a saucer. As he worked, he made no eye contact with her, and a heavy silence hung between them.

A ding announced the soup was ready, and he delivered it to the table in front of her and then added the plate of crackers. "Would you like something to drink?" he asked.

"No, thanks, I'm good. Are you going to sit with me while I eat?"

He sank down in the chair opposite her and looked at a place just over her head. "Did anything happen while I was sleeping?" she asked. She'd hoped somehow a miracle would have happened while she was out and Peter had been caught.

"Nothing, although everyone is looking for Peter," he replied.

He finally looked at her, and in the depths of his eyes she saw not only distrust, but pain...pain that she knew she'd put there.

"Hunter, it was all real for me," she said softly. "I might have lied about my name and where I came from, but I didn't lie about how I feel for you. I'm in love with you, Hunter."

Her words hung in the air for what felt like an eternity. She had hoped she'd see a happy smile curve his lips, a warmth fill his eyes, but neither happened.

He studied her as if she were a scientific specimen he'd never seen before, and then he sighed. "Were you ever going to tell me the truth?" he finally asked.

"Of course I was. I almost told you the night we made love, but then I decided I'd wait until we figured out who was doing the terrible things to me. I was going to tell you, Hunter. I swear I was going to tell you." She realized he had no reason to believe her now.

He sighed once again. "Eat your soup before it gets cold. I'm going to make a phone call to check in with Nick." He got up, let Zeus back into the house, and then he and the dog left the room.

She stared down into her soup, her eyes filling with tears. She should have known this would happen, but someplace in her heart she'd hoped for it to be different. She'd hoped that love conquered all, but she now knew that sometimes love just wasn't enough.

When this was all over, when he remembered her, she would just be another woman who had lied to him. She hated that. She'd managed to do exactly what Juanita had asked her not to do—she'd broken his heart.

Although she no longer felt hungry, she ate the soup and crackers because she knew she needed to put something in her stomach. Tears continued to burn her eyes, but she managed not to cry.

She'd hoped that she and Hunter would share a future together. Now she didn't know what would happen next with her life.

Even if they caught Peter and managed to make charges stick, she didn't think she could stay in Dusty Gulch if she and Hunter weren't together. It would just be too painful to see him every day, to love him every day and know that he no longer felt the same way about her.

When she finished eating, she carried the bowl and saucer to the sink, rinsed them off and then loaded them into the dishwasher.

She left the kitchen and found Hunter seated in his recliner with Zeus next to him. She sat on the sofa and looked at him. "Did you check in with Nick?"

"I did, but so far there is nothing new to report."

"I suppose you hate me right now," she said.

"Ainsley… Colette… I could never hate you." A whisper of warmth filled his eyes. It was there for only a moment and then was gone. A frown cut across his forehead. "Right now the only thing I'm focused on is getting your ex-husband behind bars."

"And once that happens?"

"I don't know." He looked down at Zeus and stroked his fur, then returned his gaze to her. "To be perfectly honest, I'm kind of numb right now where you're concerned. I haven't really had time to process everything you've told me today."

"Do you think time will help you to forgive me?" Her heart raced in her chest as she waited for his answer. Was there any hope at all that they would be together when this was all over?

"I don't know how to answer that right now. All I want at the moment is for you to be safe." He held her gaze for a long moment and then looked back down at Zeus. "I need time, Ains... Colette. I just need time."

"I understand," she replied. And she did. She knew all the lies she'd told him had come out of left field. She hated that it had all unfolded the way it had.

She drew in a deep breath and winced as her ribs protested. "Would it be easier if I moved back to my apartment or someplace else?" she asked.

"No," he replied sharply. "You need to be here." His gaze softened. "This is the best place for you right now. Even though I have to work in the morning, I've already instructed drive-bys by my fellow officers at regular intervals to make sure nothing happens here. Besides, your ex would be foolish to try something now. He's got to know by now that he's on the hot seat. I wouldn't be surprised if he's already hours away from here."

"I hope he isn't hours away. I hope this time he's overplayed his hand and believed in his own invulnerability and has stuck around. If he goes into the wind, then I'll never find peace. He tried to kill me last night, and he'll never stop trying until he's succeeded."

"I thought he'd killed you last night." Pain leaped into

his eyes. "Some of the longest hours of my life were waiting to hear from the doctor after you'd been taken to the hospital."

She was so damned selfish, she realized. She'd been caught up in her own drama and hadn't realized what Hunter had been through in the last twenty-four hours.

She now saw the lines of exhaustion on his face. How late had he been up the night before…waiting to hear from the doctor…and then worrying about her recovery?

"Did you manage to get any rest while I was sleeping?" she asked.

"No, I'm not much of a daytime napper. I'll sleep tonight," he replied.

"Are you sure you don't want to sleep in the bedroom and let me have the sofa?" she asked.

"I'll be fine on the sofa," he replied firmly. "So, you mentioned that your mother is alive and you have a sister. Was that the imaginary sister you spoke about?"

"Everything I said about her was true except the part about her being imaginary." She sighed, and tears once again began to burn in her eyes as she thought of her mother and her sister.

"We've always been very close. When I first went on the run from Peter, I was communicating with them regularly, but then Peter appeared in the small town we were staying in and I realized he had to have been tapping their phones. We managed to leave town before he found where we were staying, and after that I realized I had to never contact my mom and sister again."

She swallowed hard against her tears. "I needed to do whatever I could to keep Melinda away from Peter. If he gets his hands on her, he'll eventually destroy her."

"I'm sorry you've had to make the choices that you

have," he said. His eyes filled with compassion. "That's no way for a woman, for a child to live."

"I thought I was finally safe here," she said with a touch of bitterness. "Melinda loves it here, and we were hoping to make it our forever home."

"If we catch Peter, you could still make this your forever home," he said. Once again he looked down at the dog, making it impossible for her to read any emotion that might emanate from his beautiful eyes.

She released another sigh. "We'll see."

She couldn't see into the future, and Hunter wasn't giving any clue as to whether there was any hope for them to come out of this as a couple. Right now it felt unlikely that they would come out of it together. That thought made her want to leave, to run from all the memories of him and love that were in this small town.

But she had Melinda to think about. Melinda loved it here. She'd made good friends and loved school, and it was difficult to contemplate tearing her away from all those good things just because Colette couldn't suck it up and figure out how to live here without Hunter in her life.

She could only hope that with time, Hunter would forgive her and love her once again.

HUNTER BREATHED A deep sigh of relief once Colette finally left the living room to unpack and go to bed. Their conversations had been difficult, and he knew she wanted something from him that he just couldn't give her right now.

Everything he'd learned about her was just too new. She'd lied to him about so many things—how was he to trust that what she was saying to him now was true?

This wasn't over with yet, and it was in her best interest to keep him emotionally close to her. If they got Peter behind bars, then would she confess that she'd lied about loving Hunter? Would she then admit that she'd only been using him?

God, he was so confused. But one thing he wasn't confused about—he wanted Peter Waverly behind bars and facing attempted murder charges for what he'd done to her last night.

He grabbed a blanket and a spare bed pillow from his hallway closet. He tossed them on the sofa and then turned out all the lights except for the light above the stove. If she got up in the middle of the night for a drink of water, at least she'd be able to see what she was doing.

With his gun on the coffee table, he finally got out of his clothes except for his boxers and then stretched out on the sofa with Zeus at his feet.

He was utterly exhausted and yet sleep remained elusive. He found himself thinking about his marriage to Emily. She'd been his high school sweetheart and as far as he was concerned one of the prettiest girls in town.

He'd thought he knew her inside and out. The one thing he hadn't known was just how duplicitous she was. Lies had fallen so easily from her lips, lies that he'd believed because he wanted to so badly.

When she'd left their marriage, he'd walled up his heart, built sturdy fences inside him so that nobody could ever hurt him like that again.

And then he'd met Ainsley Meadows, a woman he'd believed was open and honest, a woman he believed would be his future. And she'd shattered his trust all over again.

He understood the reasons she'd chosen to live undercover, and he recognized why she'd lied to him. But emotionally he was having trouble wrapping his head around things.

Right now he was afraid to tap back into the love he'd had for her. He was afraid to feel at all. All he wanted to focus on for the moment was finding Peter. He wanted to make sure that from this point on Colette and Melinda would be safe from the man who was obviously a brutal monster.

He finally fell asleep and into nightmares of Peter chasing Colette down a dark street. Peter wielded a long knife that glittered in a streetlamp. Hunter held his gun in his hand. He fired it at Peter, only to discover his gun held no bullets.

Knowing he needed to get to Peter before the man could kill Colette, Hunter tried to run, but his feet and legs refused to move. He jerked awake covered in a cold sweat and panting as if he'd just run a marathon.

He swung his feet over the edge of the sofa, aware that the first stir of morning was peeking over the horizon. Zeus sat up and yawned and then jumped down from the sofa.

Hunter got up and let him out the back door and then started a pot of coffee. He was up about an hour earlier than he usually got up on workdays, but there was no way he wanted to doze off again and fall back into the nightmares that had chased him all night long.

Once he got the coffee working, he then went into the office where he'd hung several of his uniforms before Colette had taken over his room. He grabbed one of them and then headed for the shower.

After washing off he remained standing beneath a hot spray of water as if it had the power to unjumble his thoughts. Unfortunately it didn't help.

Once he was finished showering and then dressing, he returned to the kitchen. He let Zeus back inside, poured himself a cup of coffee and sank down at the kitchen table.

He hated having to go in to work today, but one more deputy on the streets made the odds of them finding Peter that much better. However, he believed the man had probably left town. He'd be stupid to stay knowing that everyone in the area was looking for him.

If he had left town and wasn't captured in the next day or two, then Colette would remain at risk. He frowned and sipped his coffee, the idea unsettling to him. How could she live with the threat of him killing her continuing to hang over her head?

How had she lived for the past three years? The mental, the emotional pressure on her had to have been so intense. Had she gone to bed every night with terror on her mind? Had that terror ever released its grip on her?

Compassion for her situation, for what she'd been through and what she might still have to endure, fluttered through him. God, he wished it could end for her here, but there was no guarantee it would.

And then what?

That's the part he couldn't think about right now.

He'd just poured his second cup of coffee when Colette came into the kitchen. She was already dressed in a pair of pink jogging pants and a matching sweatshirt. Her long dark hair was damp, letting him know she'd already showered in the master bath.

The bruise on her lower jaw appeared even more livid this morning. The sight of it made him want to slam his fist into Peter Waverly's face.

"Hmm, that coffee smells wonderful," she said.

"Have a seat and I'll pour you a cup."

"Nonsense, just tell me where the cups are and I can get it."

"Right cabinet above the sink," he replied.

As she walked by him, he caught a whiff of her scent… a clean smell coupled with the hint of her perfume. His stomach tightened with tension in response. Even knowing all the lies she'd told him, his body still yearned for hers. It was his mind that was having problems sorting his emotions out.

She got her coffee and then joined him at the table. "Did you sleep well?" she asked.

"I slept okay." He wasn't about to share with her the nightmares he'd suffered. "What about you?"

"I slept all right."

"You're up early."

"I'm used to being up early to open the café. What time do you go in to work this morning?" She took a sip of the coffee. Above the cup her beguiling eyes begged him to let her back into his thoughts…his heart.

He steeled himself against them. He wasn't ready to untangle his emotions where she was concerned. "I need to leave here around seven thirty or so."

"There's enough time for me to make you some breakfast," she said. "I mean, if I'm not overstepping kitchen privileges."

He couldn't help but smile. "For as long as you're here, you have full kitchen privileges. And while I appreciate the offer, I'm not much of a breakfast eater. Feel free to help yourself to whatever you want."

"I'm not much of a breakfast eater, either. Coffee is good enough for me." She raised the cup for another drink.

"Do you know how to shoot a gun?"

Her eyes widened in surprise, and she lowered the cup to the table. "Point and pull the trigger. That's all I know about guns. Why?"

"I've got a nine millimeter that's for my personal use. I'm going to leave it here for you. Could you actually shoot your ex-husband?"

Her eyes narrowed. "Absolutely. I know his only goal is to kill me, so I could absolutely shoot him to save myself."

He believed her. Her eyes burned with determination. "I'll be right back." He got up from the table and went into the room he used as an office.

He grabbed his keys and unlocked the right top drawer. Inside was the spare gun he kept for security purposes. He took the gun out of the drawer, checked it to make sure the safety was on, and then he carried it back into the kitchen.

As he set it on the table with the barrel facing the wall, she looked at it soberly and then looked up at him. "I can't believe it's come to this," she said softly.

"To be perfectly honest, my gut instinct is he's left town. I think they would have caught him by now if he was still in Dusty Gulch. However, just in case I'm wrong, I want you to be able to protect yourself while you're here alone. Before I leave to go to work, I'll take the safety off so all you have to do is point and pull the trigger."

She nodded. "Aim for center mass, right?"

"Right," he replied, surprised she knew the term.

She grinned at him. "I picked that up while watching police shows on television."

Her grin caught him off guard, and a well of love for her rose up inside him. He stared down into his coffee cup. Damn her for ruining things. Damn her for not telling him the truth as soon as they started seriously dating each other. Damn her for twisting and tangling his emotions to the point where he didn't know what to feel.

"Center mass is right," he now replied. For a moment they sipped their coffee in silence. Then she looked at him, and all her features softened. A soft pleading filled her eyes.

"Hunter..." she began.

He held up his hand. "Don't."

"Don't what?"

It would be so easy to fall into the blue depths of her winsome eyes, but he couldn't allow himself. "Colette, I don't want any heart-to-heart discussions right now. I can't think about us right now."

He saw the pain that dimmed the brightness in her eyes, and he hated himself for putting it there. But at the moment, he didn't know if they had a path forward or not. The last thing he wanted to do was give her any false hope about what might happen between them in the future.

"I just want to tell you thank-you for letting me stay here and for keeping me safe," she finally replied.

"Protect and serve, that's our motto."

"We both know you're going way above your duty," she replied. "You're a great deputy, and you're a wonderful, good man."

He didn't feel like a good man right now. He still felt numb. Once again they fell into an uncomfortable silence. She looked at the clock over the stove and got up from the table. "I'm just going to go back and call Juanita's to check in on Melinda before school."

He drew a deep breath as she left the kitchen. There

was no question that things were going to be awkward between them. Sharing space with so many things unresolved between them was going to create more than a little bit of tension.

When it was time for him to leave for work, he was torn with the desire to get out on the streets and find Peter and remain here with her to make sure she stayed safe.

"Make sure you only touch the trigger if you intend to shoot somebody," he said as he took the safety of the gun off. "Where do you want to keep it?"

"How about on the coffee table. I plan on spending most of the day in the living room."

He placed the gun on the coffee table. "You know how to use the television. Help yourself to anything you want to eat, and I'll bring home dinner for us from the café."

"I would be glad to cook something for us," she offered.

"I'd rather just bring something home. Is there anything in particular you'd like?" As silly as it sounded, he didn't want her to cook dinner for them. It felt too intimate…too much like they were a cozy couple.

"Anything is fine. Just surprise me." She walked with him to the front door. He started to go out the door, but she stopped him by placing her hand on his arm. "Hunter, stay safe today."

"Always," he replied with a reassuring smile. "If you get scared or something doesn't seem right, call me. One of the other deputies or I will come running."

"I'm sure I'll be fine," she replied.

He wanted to touch her. He wanted to pull her into his arms and hold her tight. He needed to run a finger down the side of her soft cheek or touch a strand of her silky hair. He didn't do any of those things.

"Lock the door behind me, and I'll see you later today." He practically ran out of the house with the need to escape her. It was crazy, but he'd rather face down a psycho killer than face his emotions where Colette was concerned.

Chapter Fourteen

The minute Hunter left, he seemed to take all the oxygen, all the life out of the air with him. She locked the front door and then went into the living room and sat on the edge of the sofa.

She stared at the gun on the coffee table. Could she shoot to kill her ex-husband, the father of her child? As she thought of all the times he'd beaten her, of the intense mental and physical pain he'd put her through, the answer was easy. Yes, she could definitely shoot to kill him.

More important than the crimes Peter had already perpetrated against her were the crimes she feared he would perpetrate against their daughter. For that alone Colette could kill him.

If Peter really had left town, then a new nearly insurmountable issue would arise. How could she continue to stay here if he knew where she was? Even if Hunter forgave her and professed his love for her, how could she stay if Peter got away?

She turned on the television in an attempt to escape her depressing thoughts. Hopefully, in the next couple of days, she would know whether Peter was truly gone from the area. Then she would have to make a decision about what to do next.

She had told Hunter she'd slept well, but that wasn't exactly the truth. She'd had trouble getting comfortable. Her ribs hurt and the bruise on her chin throbbed with pain, keeping her awake off and on throughout the night. And if the physical pain hadn't been enough, she'd been unable to turn off her thoughts.

She found a channel with a game show on. She kept the volume fairly low so she could hear any other noises throughout the house. Zeus jumped up on the sofa next to her and curled up at her side.

She stroked his soft fur and tried to keep her mind empty, but it was impossible. She'd dreamed of living here with Hunter and Zeus and Melinda. She'd dreamed of them all being a happy family.

She definitely owed her daughter a big apology for not believing her about her father speaking to her at night. Who could have guessed it was true, that Peter had installed all the equipment in the café attic?

Shoving away these thoughts, she tried to focus on the game show. At noon she let Zeus out of the back door and then opened the refrigerator to find something for lunch.

She'd hoped to hear from Hunter by now and learn that Peter had been found and arrested, but apparently there was nothing new to report. She found a can of tuna in the pantry and made herself a sandwich with chips for lunch.

When she was finished eating, she walked to the front windows and peered outside. She knew from talking with Hunter that most of his neighbors worked and weren't home during the days.

She saw nothing amiss in the area. As she stood there, a patrol car slowly drove by and then disappeared down the street. With a sigh she turned away and walked to the back door to let Zeus back inside.

The dog danced in, followed by a man she'd seen often in the café. "Hank, what are you doing here? What do you want?" Why would Hank Bridges be here? Why had he just come through Hunter's back door?

"Hello, Colette."

The familiar voice shot disbelief through her. She stared at him. Her brain froze. No wonder they hadn't been able to find him. He looked nothing like the photo she'd given to them. He was the new man in town…he'd walked the sidewalks free and easy, he'd eaten several times in the café with Sheila Turrel. Peter!

She stumbled backward from the door. The sight of him here and now shot sheer terror through her.

The gun. She had to get to the gun. She turned to run, but he caught her leg and she fell to the floor. She rolled over on her back and kicked at him. Zeus barked as if to protest what was going on.

He backed up a bit from her and laughed. "Ah, Colette, I've so looked forward to this reunion."

"Go away, Peter," she said breathlessly. "Just leave me alone."

He laughed again, the sound shooting arctic chills up her spine. "Now you know that isn't going to happen. You have to pay for leaving me, for taking my daughter away from me."

"You don't care about Melinda. You never loved her or me."

"Love has nothing to do with this. You belonged to me." He leaned over her and grinned.

She had to get to the gun. She'd been stupid to open the door without the weapon in her hand. She needed to get up. She kicked at him again, needing to gain some distance to get to her feet and run for the gun.

He kicked her, connecting with the rib he'd broken. Pain screamed through her, blurring her vision as she lost her breath.

Before she could fully recover, he grabbed her by her hair and yanked her up to her feet. She screamed but knew there was nobody who would hear her. She was vaguely aware of Zeus running from the room.

"You want that gun?" he whispered in her ear. His grip on her hair tightened. "You want to get that gun and shoot me?" He punched her in her side. Once again pain ripped through her, weakening her knees. "That wouldn't be nice, Colette."

His hot, stale breath made her want to throw up. "If anyone is going to shoot somebody, it's going to be me shooting you. But that would be too easy."

He pulled out a syringe. New horror swept through her. She fought to get away, but he stabbed the needle into her arm.

She flailed her arms and kicked at him, desperate to get free. He laughed at her efforts, his laughter sounding like the devil's happiness.

Within minutes her arms began to feel too heavy to fight and her legs could barely hold her up. What had he given to her? Oh God, what had been in the syringe?

Her eyelids grew heavy. He loosened his grip on her hair, and she nearly fell against him. *Help*, her mind screamed. He laughed as he picked her up in his arms.

He'd won. That was the last thought that drifted through her mind before she knew no more.

HER HEAD POUNDED. Her mouth was dry. Colette came to in confusion. She opened her eyes and frowned. She was in a kitchen she'd never seen before. The floor was an old, faded linoleum, and an old table stood in front of a window with a cracked pane of glass. The air held an unpleasant odor.

Where was she? She tried to raise a hand to her head and realized she was tied to the chair. That's when everything crashed back into her head. Peter...who didn't look like Peter...the stab of the needle in her arm... Oh God, she was in trouble. Peter was actually Hank Bridges, and nobody knew that.

As if to punctuate that thought, Peter walked into the kitchen. He grabbed a chair, flipped it around backward and sat directly in front of her. "Hello, Colette."

It was so disconcerting to hear the familiar voice coming out of the unfamiliar face. But the eyes were the same, dark blue eyes that burned with evil intent.

"Aren't you going to tell me how happy you are to see me again?"

She kept her mouth shut. She had no desire to engage with him in any way. If he was waiting for her to beg and plead for her life, it wasn't going to happen.

How long had she been unconscious? Did Hunter know yet that she was missing from the house? Were they all out looking for her now?

They'd never find her. They could look everywhere, but they'd never suspect she was here. They were all looking for Peter, not this new, improved version of her ex-husband.

She wanted to weep with defeat, but she didn't want to give him the satisfaction of seeing her tears. He'd always gotten off on seeing her cry.

"Gee, I guess you aren't talking to me. Maybe I can make you scream." He started to stand up from the chair.

"Of course you can make me scream. You've got me

tied to a chair and helpless. Congratulations, big man. You're a real hero."

The slap snapped her head to the side. She bit her bottom lip to keep from crying out. "Show me some respect. I've gone to a lot of trouble to get you here," he said. "I've spent hundreds of thousands of dollars to make this happen."

"Why, Peter? After all this time, why come after me at all?" she asked. Her hands were tied behind her back, and she twisted and turned them in an effort to gain some give in the rope.

"You belong to me. Don't you remember that was our song? We danced to it at our wedding."

"We divorced," she replied. "And I never belonged to you. I belong to myself."

She hadn't intended to talk to him, but she now realized she needed to keep him talking. She needed time, time for somebody to find her. She desperately hoped somebody—anybody—would find her.

"A piece of paper doesn't change the fact that you belong to me," he said.

She sighed in frustration. "Why did you marry me in the first place?" she asked.

"I married you because I wanted you. I knew after our first date that you were the woman I wanted to bear my children, the woman I wanted to spend my life with. Why did you marry me?" He looked at her in amusement.

"I fell in love with you, Peter. I thought you were a good man, a gentle man who would take care of me and any children we had. But you became a cruel and abusive man." She stiffened, waiting for another blow from him.

"That's because you failed to live up to my expectations of you as a wife." His eyes were dark and flat, like the eyes of a serpent. "You had to be taught, Colette. It wasn't my fault that you were a slow learner. I hope our daughter doesn't need to be taught."

She wanted to tear his eyes out, stab him in his sick, black heart. As she thought of Melinda in his care, she wanted to scream at the injustice of evil winning. Peter would steal all the sweetness, all the happiness out of Melinda.

Colette would gladly spend a thousand years in hell to save Melinda from him. But the devil was already working with Peter. "Please just let me go, Peter. I'll make sure you get plenty of visitation with Melinda."

"Why should I settle for visitation when I can have her full-time?"

"Please, Peter. If you ever loved me, then just let me go." She had thought she wasn't going to beg, but she was now begging for her life...for Melinda's life. "I won't tell anyone what you look like or that you're living as Hank Bridges. Your identity is safe with me."

His eyes burned into hers. "You were my everything, Colette. I needed you as much as I needed air to breathe."

"You tried to kill me," she replied half hysterically. She continued to work at loosening the rope holding her hands, but so far she'd had no success. Her fingers were numb, but her wrists felt raw and painful. "Peter, you stabbed me in my stomach. You almost killed me."

"I'll admit my need to discipline you got a little out of hand, but that didn't give you the right to leave me. You were mine, and you'll be mine until you die."

He stood abruptly and shoved the chair he'd been sitting in aside. "The only way I'll truly be free of you is for you to be gone...dead. That's the price you pay for leaving me, Colette."

He stalked over to the nearby door and yanked it open.

Immediately a noxious smell wafted in the air. Squeals and grunts could be heard.

Peter turned to look at her. "Hear that? Those are my pets. Did you know that sixteen pigs can completely eat a human being in eight minutes? There are twenty-five starving pigs in my pen. I tested the information with Ted, who got me access to the café attic." She stared at him in horror.

"It actually took seven and a half minutes for Ted to get crunched up and swallowed. Then this morning they got fed again. Poor old Sheila was another loose end that needed to be taken care of. I figure by late this evening the pigs will be hungry again." He grinned at her. "Of course I'll feed my pets… I'm going to feed them you."

As he turned and left the kitchen, she worked desperately on trying to free her hands. She was horrified not only by what he'd already done but also what he planned to do to her.

THEY HAD SCOURED the town for Peter Waverly and nobody professed to have seen him. "How can one man stay so far under the radar?" Hunter asked Nick when they were both in the office for a few minutes.

"You got me." Nick shook his head. "We checked the motel and the few places in town that are rented out. We've asked people if they've noticed anyone in or around their barns and outbuildings, and we've come up empty-handed. We're going to start checking on some of the abandoned buildings in the area, but if you want my opinion, I think he's probably left town."

"That's the last thing Ains… Colette wanted." Hunter frowned.

"This all must have been a shock to you. How are you doing with it all?" Nick asked.

Hunter drew in a deep breath. "To be honest, I don't know how I'm doing with it all. Right now I want to stay focused on minimizing any danger toward her."

"And after that?" Nick asked.

"After that I don't know," Hunter replied honestly. "I kind of feel the same way I did when I realized all the lies Emily had told me."

"But there's a difference. Emily lied to deceive you so she could continue her affair. Colette lied to save her and her daughter's lives."

Nick's words haunted Hunter during the rest of the morning as he worked street patrol. Yes, there was a difference. He tried to put himself in Colette's position. What lengths would he go to in order to protect Danny if the little boy had lived?

He would have lied, stolen and done whatever necessary to save his son from danger. Why would he hold it against Colette for doing the same thing?

It was just after noon when his phone rang and he saw George's caller ID. Why on earth would George be calling him right now?

"Hey, George, what's going on?"

"Hunter, I got something to tell you…something really, really important."

"What's that?" Hunter asked. George had spoken superfast, and Hunter wondered if perhaps George was off his meds again. He didn't sound drunk—rather he sounded amped up.

"I thought today was your day off and I spent most of the morning thinning out some plants and I repotted some because I thought you might like them." The words spewed out of George so fast Hunter could barely digest them. The man was obviously agitated about something.

"So, I took them down to your house and was just about to knock on the door when I heard two people talking inside and then I heard the side gate in your backyard open. I… I peeked around the corner of the house and saw him—he was…he was carrying Ainsley over his shoulder."

A sick burst of adrenaline shot through Hunter. "Who was it, George? Who was carrying her outside?" he asked urgently.

"I can't remember. I know him from somewhere…but right now I can't remember from where. Dammit, I knew she was in trouble and I hid behind the bushes like a damned coward. I'm sorry, Hunter. I'm so sorry. You needed me to save her and I… I failed you." He began to weep.

"George, where are you now?" Hunter asked as he turned his car around to head for home.

"I'm at your house on the front porch."

"I'll be right there." Hunter hung up and raced for home. How in the hell had a man they were all looking for managed to get to Colette? How had this happened? Oh God, where had Peter taken her?

As he drove, he called Nick to let him know what had happened, and the lawman agreed to meet Hunter at his house. Hunter stepped on the gas, his heart thundering so hard he could hear the frantic beats in his head. Dammit, he'd thought she'd be safe in his house. He shouldn't have worked today no matter how much he was needed to do patrol. He should have stayed with her, kept her near to him.

The good news was there was an eyewitness to the kidnapping. The bad news was the witness could be off his medications and might never be able to identify whom he had seen.

Chapter Fifteen

Hunter drove faster than he'd ever driven through town in his life. He was painfully aware that seconds mattered…minutes mattered. The faster George could tell them something, anything about the kidnapper, the faster they might be able to find Colette.

Peter had already beaten her up. Hunter knew the man wouldn't blink twice before killing her. He could have killed her right there in the house, and yet he'd carried her out and away. Why not just kill her?

Where could he have taken her? Where was his lair? The man had apparently moved freely through town in order to leave the items on Colette's porch and to leave the note in the café. Why had everyone who was questioned in town indicated they had never seen Peter anywhere before? Why hadn't he seen Peter in town? The man was obviously a freaking ghost.

Hunter screeched around the corner of the street that led to his house. When he got close enough, he saw George sitting on the front porch. He whirled into his driveway, cut the engine and leaped out of the car.

George stood, tears trekking down his cheeks. "I'm sorry, Hunter. I'm so sorry I didn't do anything to help. I should have tackled him. I should have done something, but I hid like a baby."

"It's okay, George. Right now what I need for you to do is calm down," Hunter said even though he was anything but calm. Every nerve in his body was screaming that he needed to find Colette as soon as possible.

"Come on inside. I need to get some information from you." Hunter tried to stay calm, knowing that would also calm George down, but Hunter wanted to scream with urgency at the only man who had seen Peter Waverly.

As they walked through the living room, Hunter saw the gun still on the coffee table. Obviously she'd never gotten a chance to use it to protect herself. Zeus danced at his feet, and he let the dog out the back door as Nick entered the house.

George began to weep again as Hunter guided him to a seat at the table. "George, we need you to calm down so you can think clearly," Hunter said and tried to keep the panic out of his voice. "You need to tell us exactly what you saw."

"I saw him carrying her over his shoulder," George said.

"Did he have a vehicle waiting for him?" Nick asked.

George nodded. "A black pickup truck. He put her in the passenger seat and then he sped away." Hunter's stomach tightened. Sped away where? Where was the bastard hiding out?

"Was it this man who took her?" Nick showed George the picture of Peter.

"No, it wasn't him," George replied with a frown.

Hunter looked at Nick in confusion. If it wasn't Peter Waverly, then who had taken her away? Were they dealing with two different people? Two separate perpetrators?

George raised a fist and hit himself in the forehead. "I know the man who took her… I just…right now I can't remember who he is. I know I met him. Damn, damn, damn!" He hit himself in the head once again.

Hunter caught his hand. "George, stop hitting yourself. That's not going to get us anywhere. Just give yourself a minute to breathe, a minute to think."

Seconds…minutes…where was she? Hunter's need to find her burned in his belly as his heart continued to beat the rapid rhythm of despair. He needed George to remember, otherwise they had nothing.

"What did the man look like?" he asked.

"Dark hair…nice-looking man." George's frown deepened, and then he snapped his fingers and sat up straighter in his chair. "I know now. I met him at the café. Hank… Hank Bridges. He bought that old pig farm south of town."

Before George was completely finished speaking, Nick and Hunter jumped up from the table and ran outside to their patrol cars.

The pig farm. She'd told them the person who had beaten her had a strange, unpleasant odor about them. A man living on a pig farm would have had that smell clinging to him.

Hank Bridges. What in the hell did he have to do with Peter Waverly? Was he a hired killer working for Peter? Had Peter been living with Hank? Was that how he had stayed under their radar?

It was much easier for Hunter to focus on these kinds of questions than the questions that ate at his guts. Questions like, were they already too late? Had Peter been waiting at the pig farm to bring him Colette and had he already killed his ex-wife? Was Colette already dead?

Oh God, he could scarcely stand the thought that she might no longer be in this world. He couldn't imagine never again seeing her beautiful smile or hearing her sweet laughter. He couldn't imagine her not being there for her daughter.

His heart hurt. All he wanted was for her to be in his arms. He wanted to bury his face in her sweet-smelling hair, feel her heart beating steady against his own. More than anything he wanted her to be alive.

He got on the radio with Nick. "We need to go in quiet," he said. "We don't know whether there's one or two men in there, but either one of them is capable of killing her."

"I've already called in a couple more men and told them to meet us at the old Winchell place next to the pig farm," Nick said.

Thankfully he didn't mention the fact that they might already be too late, that they'd reach the farm and find her dead body and the men would already be gone, never to be seen again.

He gripped the steering wheel tightly. Wasn't it enough that he'd had to say goodbye to Danny? Hadn't life taken enough from him already? He'd lost both his wife and his baby boy. Dammit, he didn't want to lose Colette as well.

Nick followed him down the highway that would take them to the Winchell place, a small farm where the Winchell family had lived and struggled for years. Three years ago they had given up, moved away and abandoned the place to the bank. Nobody had lived in the place since.

He turned in to the long driveway and drove up far enough that the vehicles wouldn't be seen from the road. Nick pulled in behind him, and within minutes two more patrol cars joined them. Deputies Greg McCain and Barry Simpson got out of the cars.

"What's the plan?" Hunter asked Nick, recognizing that ultimately Nick was the lead on the case.

"We need to get close enough to do a little recon," Nick said. "We need to figure out who, exactly, is in the house and where they are in the place. Greg, why don't you and I sneak closer and see what we can see? Hunter, you and Barry wait here. We'll check back here and we can make our ultimate plan to move in."

Before Hunter could protest, the two men were gone, cutting through an overgrown cornfield in the direction of the pig farm. "There isn't time for this," Hunter said to Barry, who was an older, more seasoned deputy.

"Hunter, I know there's a lot at stake here, but we have to have a plan. You know we can't go in blindly. That could cost Colette her life."

"Logically I know that," Hunter replied with frustration. There was a clock ticking in his head, and he had the bad feeling that it was ticking down to Colette's death.

COLETTE KNEW THESE were the final minutes of her life. Her wrists burned and hurt from her trying to get loose from the ropes that bound them. Unfortunately no matter how she tugged and twisted, she'd been unable to make any headway in getting free.

She'd stopped praying for help for herself and instead prayed for some kind of intervention that would keep her daughter away from the evil man who had sired her.

She prayed that Hunter wouldn't carry the burden of her death, something he was in no way responsible for. Finally, she prayed for a quick and painless death even though she knew that wasn't going to happen. There was no way Peter was going to let her die quickly and painlessly.

For the last hour or so, he had berated her, screamed at her and slapped her cheeks over and over again. He told her what a terrible wife she had been, what a horrible waste of breath she was. Then he'd told her how much he had loved her and that she had once been his entire world. He'd finally stalked out of the kitchen, and she was now alone.

She found it hard to believe now that she had ever loved anything about this man…this obsessed sociopath who would go to any ends to get what he wanted.

She found everything about this situation to be surreal. The fact that he'd obviously gone through extensive plastic surgery to change his appearance, the fact that he'd apparently bought this pig farm for the sole purpose of being close to her, to be able to torment her and then to kill her.

Who in their right mind would go to these lengths? It was obvious he wasn't in his right mind, had never been in a sane frame of mind.

She realized now she would have never been able to get away from him. He had enough money to find her wherever she might have run. She could have run for years and he still would have chased her.

Peter was her fate. As much as she'd wanted it to be otherwise, his face would be the last one she'd see before she died. There was no way she wanted that to be so.

She closed her eyes and imagined Melinda's sweet face. She saw the cute little wrinkle in her nose when Melinda smiled, the happy sounds of her giggles when she got tickled. Melinda had been the best daughter a mother could ever want.

She then imagined Hunter's face in her mind's eye. How she loved the way his smile lit up her heart and the beauty of his deep green, dark-lashed eyes made her want to melt into them. His face displayed so much of the character of the man he was. His warm eyes and laugh lines showed him for the good man he was.

Whether he ever found love for her again, she hoped with the information he had about Peter, he would somehow keep Peter from gaining custody of her daughter. She would also hope that after her death he would find forgiveness for the lies she'd told him in an effort to survive.

She wanted to weep for all the dreams she'd wanted to build with Hunter, dreams of happiness and family that had all been shattered. Still, she would take her last breath loving him. She would love him through eternity.

She opened her eyes and tensed as Peter came into the room once again. "It's time, Colette. It's time you pay the ultimate price for running from me. My pigs are very hungry, and I'm eager to end this and get on with my life with my darling daughter."

She fought back a shiver. "You'll burn in hell for everything you have done," she said fervently.

He laughed. "Maybe, but in the meantime I'm having such a wonderful time." He moved behind her and began to untie her hands. "Oof, I see you've been a bad girl and tried to get loose. You've got your hands all bloody, but that's okay. My pet pigs absolutely love blood."

Once he had her untied, he grabbed her by the arm and yanked her upright. She immediately fell to the floor on her butt. There was no way she was going to make this easy for him.

"Get up," he commanded, anger rife in his voice.

She no longer feared his anger. What was he going to do to her? She was going to die within minutes anyway. "Make me," she replied.

He yanked harder on her arm, but she made herself deadweight. "Don't be childish, Colette. Now stand up before I lose my patience."

"What are you going to do if I don't? Kill me?" She laughed. She had nothing to lose now. "You're pathetic, Peter. You're a loser who has wasted the last three years of your life chasing after a woman who didn't give you a second thought. You might have wanted me, but I never, ever wanted you."

Peter's face reddened, letting her know she was making him very, very angry. "Shut up," he yelled.

"Why should I shut up? You've been talking to me the whole time you've had me here. Now it's my turn to talk. You were a terrible husband, Peter. You're a little man who is abusive to women. You really think you're a big man because you can slap around a woman? Because you can get a knife and stab me? You abused me throughout our whole marriage. I ran from you because I hated you and I never, ever wanted to see you again. Even if you hadn't tried to stab me to death, I would have left you anyway. You don't deserve the love of any good woman, and you definitely don't deserve my beautiful daughter."

"Are you through?" A muscle ticked in his jaw.

"Not quite." She drew in a deep breath and laughed. "You also sucked in bed."

She barely got the words out of her mouth when he slammed his fist into the side of her face. An intense pain caused bright lights to flash in her brain, and then there was nothing.

"THERE'S ONLY TWO of them in the house," Nick said breathlessly. He and Greg had just come back to where Hunter and Barry had waited. "It's just Colette and Hank Bridges. We saw no sign of Peter Waverly."

"Was she alive?" Tension pressed tight in Hunter's chest.

Nick nodded affirmatively, and a rush of relief swept through Hunter. "She's tied to a chair in the kitchen," Nick said.

"If there's just one person with her, then this should be an easy takedown," Barry said.

"Are you sure there was nobody else in the house?" Hunter asked.

"Positive. We got eyes on all the rooms in the house. There's nobody else there." Nick looked at Barry. "And there's nothing easy about this. Hank is obviously a dangerous man. If he hears or sees us coming, there's nothing to stop him from killing Colette."

Hunter didn't know what the deal was with Hank Bridges. He and Peter Waverly had to somehow be in cahoots. Hank could only be looked at as an assassin who had been paid to kill Colette. All Hunter really knew was one false move and Colette would die.

"We need to go in carefully and use the element of surprise to take down Hank," Nick said. "Barry, do you have the door ram in your trunk?"

"I do."

"Okay, I'll take it and go in the front door. Greg, you take the south side of the house, and Barry, you take the north side. Hunter, you go around to the back. That's where the kitchen is located. We not only want to get Colette out of there, but I also want to get Hank under arrest," Nick said. "Earbuds in and I'll give the signal to move in when I think everyone is in place."

The four of them took off, moving as silently as they could through the field. Hunter's heart raced with the need to get her out of the farmhouse and to safety. He hoped and prayed that this rescue effort didn't go wrong. One mistake and he knew Colette would die.

Every muscle, every single nerve in his body tensed as a rush of adrenaline flooded through his veins. His need to get to her before anything happened was single-focused and overwhelming.

He changed his direction to come around to the back of the old farmhouse. There was no way to predict what Hank would do when he realized the police were on top of him.

And where was Peter Waverly? Where was the man behind all this? There was no doubt in Hunter's mind that Colette's ex-husband had orchestrated everything that had happened to her. So, where was he? He would think a man with such focus on killing a woman would want to be present when she died.

Still, he couldn't think about that right now. All he wanted to do was bust down the doors, release Colette and hold her warm, breathing body against his.

As he got closer, the smell of the pigs grew stronger. Hunter had been around pigs before, and normally they didn't smell so unpleasant. But this was the odor of neglected animals, of filth and waste.

When this was all over, Hunter would make sure the pigs were removed by the humane society so they could be placed with farmers who would properly care for them.

The farmhouse came into his view. A shed sat between

the edge of the backyard and the house, a perfect place for Hunter to take cover until he got the signal to move in.

Keeping low and moving fast, Hunter raced for the small building. He slammed his back against it and held his breath, waiting to see if anyone in the house had possibly seen him.

When the air remained quiet, he breathed a sigh of relief. So far…so good. The only sound was the grunting and rustling coming from the pigpen.

He froze as he heard the sound of the back door opening. He peeked around the corner of the shed and saw Hank with a prone Colette across his shoulder.

What the hell? Was she already dead? Horror screamed through Hunter as he suddenly realized the man's intent. The pigs squealed as Hank raised Colette high enough to throw her over the porch railing and into the pen.

"Move in. Move in," Hunter screamed through his radio as he raced toward the pen.

Hank looked up in stunned surprise. "Put her down, Hank. Put her down on the porch," Hunter yelled as he drew his weapon.

Hank froze. Colette looked like a limp rag doll in his big arms. "Put her down on the porch!" Hunter yelled again and ran across the lawn toward the two.

"She belongs with the pigs," Hank yelled back. Once again he raised her up to his shoulders. "Say goodbye to Colette," he said and laughed.

A crack sounded in the air, and Hank's laughter stopped abruptly. As if in slow motion, he sank down to his knees and spilled Colette out of his arms and onto the porch.

Nick stepped out of the house and onto the porch, his gun in his hand and a bullet hole through the screen door.

Hunter stumbled forward, his sole concern the woman lying lifeless on the deck. Was she already dead? Had they been too late after all?

His heart nearly stopped as he finally crouched down beside her and felt for a pulse. *Let there be one...please let there be one*, his mind begged.

Her face looked red and bruised, and if Hank Bridges wasn't next to him dead, then Hunter would have killed him with his bare hands.

"She's got a pulse," he cried out to Nick. "We need an ambulance out here."

"Already been called in," Nick replied.

Hunter moved around so he was cradling her head in his lap. "What did he do to her?" he breathed more to himself than to anyone else. Had she been drugged? "The bastard was going to throw her in with the pigs."

"That's why I shot him," Nick replied. "I was afraid he was about to toss her right in, and those pigs look like they are starving to death. Sheriff Black is on his way, and needless to say we've got a crime scene here."

"And where in the hell is Peter Waverly?" Hunter said as he stroked a strand of hair away from Colette's forehead.

"Maybe we'll find something inside that will lead us to him," Greg said.

"We'll ransack the damned place until we find the connection," Nick replied.

"There's got to be something that will lead us to Peter," Barry added.

Hunter barely listened to the conversation. His sole concentration was on Colette. He stroked his fingers over her forehead, down her fevered face. Dear God, why wasn't she awake? What all had she endured in the hands of this madman? It appeared she had been beaten around her face—what injuries couldn't he see?

Thank God he heard the ambulance approaching, the siren screaming with urgency. He needed them to take her, to fix her. He needed to see her smile again. He needed, wanted to see the beautiful blue of her eyes again.

He didn't care whether she had loved him or used him. None of that mattered right now. He just wanted her to be okay. He wanted her to survive this horrendous ordeal and live to thrive.

Within fifteen minutes the ambulance screamed away from the scene with Hunter in hot pursuit. She had regained consciousness as they'd loaded her into the ambulance, although Hunter hadn't been able to speak to her.

It felt like déjà vu as he parked in the hospital lot and ran for the emergency waiting room. Once again Sandy Silver sat at the desk.

"I know why you're here, and I've already told Dr. Lockwood you would be here," she said sympathetically. "He'll be out to speak to you when he can."

Hunter gave a nod and then sat in one of the chairs. Once again he was alone in the waiting room. How badly had she been hurt by Hank? What had she endured in the couple of hours she'd been in captivity? What kind of horrible pain had she suffered?

Thank God Nick had shot Hank and not Hunter. It would make the investigation into Hank's death clean. Hunter just wished they had captured or killed Peter. As long as that man was out there, Colette would always be at risk.

She would probably go on the run again. An aching

hollowness blew through him as he thought of never seeing her again.

Emily lied to deceive. Colette lied to save her and her daughter's lives. Nick's words repeated in Hunter's head. Everything she'd lied about had been for self-preservation from a man who wanted her dead. And Hunter now understood what kind of sick monster she'd been running from.

How could he be angry with her for her lies? All he wanted…all he needed to know was if she'd lied about caring for him. She'd told him she loved him. Had that been a lie?

He wasn't confused about his feelings where she was concerned. He was just confused about hers for him. Not that it mattered. If she chose to run again, then she would just be a happy, yet hurting memory, like that of his son.

The main thing right now was how she was doing. He had no idea what kind of torture she might have suffered. Did she have internal injuries? He'd seen her wrists, bloody and raw, and he wanted to weep as he thought about her being tied up and struggling to get free.

As bad as the physical pain might have been, he couldn't imagine the mental pain she must have suffered. She had to have believed that she was going to die, that her ex-husband would then have custody of Melinda. Those thoughts must have tortured her.

He jumped up from his chair as Dr. Lockwood came out. "We meet again," Dr. Lockwood said.

"Unfortunately. How is she?"

"According to her, she was slapped a number of times and one of her cheeks is definitely bruised. She also told me that she took a hard blow to the head that rendered her unconscious. We did some X-rays and I don't see any permanent damage. We've cleaned up and wrapped her wrists, and we've drawn blood because she told us initially she was drugged. Still, she's alert and doing remarkably well given the circumstances. She's a very strong woman."

Hunter expelled a deep sigh of relief. "Can I see her?"

"Room 109."

Hunter raced down the hallway, his heart beating a quickened pace. He turned into the room and breathed another sigh of relief as he saw her sitting up in the bed. She smiled. "I'm not sure how you all found me, but thank God you did," she said.

Hunter sat in the chair next to her bed. "You can thank George. He was bringing me some plants and saw you being taken from the house. He let us know it was Hank Bridges that had kidnapped you. I'm just sorry that we didn't get Peter."

She looked at him in surprise. "I thought you all knew."

"Knew what?" He hated that one of her cheeks was a fiery red. He wanted to place his hand on it and draw away the redness and pain.

"Hank was Peter."

He looked at her in stunned surprise. "What?"

"Peter had a bunch of plastic surgery done to completely change his looks. That's why nobody saw Peter in town."

At that moment Nick walked into the room. He nodded at Hunter and then smiled at Colette. "How are you feeling?" he asked as he sat in the other chair next to the bed.

"Pretty banged up," she replied. "But I'm happy to be alive."

"Are you up to answering some questions?" Nick asked.

"Absolutely," she replied.

Nick was just as shocked as Hunter had been to learn that Hank was Peter. As Hunter listened to her tell about how Hank had gotten into the house, drugged her and then she'd awakened tied to a kitchen chair, he wanted to kill Hank all over again.

She told them about Peter slapping and hitting her. Hunter wanted to cry for the pain she had suffered and still suffered.

"He planned on feeding me to the pigs," she said. Her eyes darkened. "He fed Ted and Sheila to the pigs." She shuddered, obviously thinking of what could have happened to her.

"It's over now, Colette. Peter is dead, and he'll never bother you again," Nick said.

"Thank God he'll never kill another person," she replied. "He can spend his eternity in hell."

"That's for sure," Nick replied. He got to his feet. "I'm sure we'll have more questions for you as the investigation unfolds. You'll be around?"

"I'll be around," she replied.

"It's finally over," Hunter said to her once Nick had left the room.

"It is. I'm sad that Melinda will never have her father in her life, but she's better off not having Peter in her life," she replied.

"So what are you going to tell her about all this?"

"I'll tell her that Hank Bridges was a bad man who tried to hurt me. I really believe she's too young to burden with the truth about Peter. I'll tell her about her father someday when I feel like the time is right. In the meantime all she needs to know is her father stopped talking to her at night."

"That sounds like a good plan." He gazed at her for a long moment. "You're really free now, Colette. You're free to live your life on your terms. You can go anywhere you want, live whatever life you want."

"Nothing has changed for me. I still want to make Dusty Gulch my forever home." She gazed at him somberly. "I know you probably can't forgive me, Hunter." Her eyes filled with a sheen of tears. "I lied to you about so many things. But I swear I didn't lie to you about my feelings for you."

He searched her face…her beautiful but beat-up face. "You don't need me anymore, Colette. There's no more threat to you."

Her eyes widened and then narrowed. "Is that what you think? That I was only with you for some sort of protection? Oh Hunter, I was with you because I wanted to be. I was with you because I fell hopelessly in love with you. I want my future to be with you. I want to marry you and have your babies. I want you to be the father figure in Melinda's life. I desperately want to spend the rest of my life with you. None of that had anything to do with my fear of Peter." Tears began to race down her cheeks.

"Don't cry, Colette." He reached out and took one of her hands in his. The words she had just spoken caused happiness to flutter in his heart and shot a huge ray of sunshine into his soul.

"There's nothing for me to forgive. You lied to save your life. Colette, don't cry. I fell hopelessly in love with Ainsley, and I'm hopelessly, desperately in love with Colette. I want the same things you do. Will you marry me? Colette, will you be my wife?"

"Deputy Churchill, there you go seducing me again," she said.

"And I intend to seduce you every day for the rest of your life if you'll let me." His love for her nearly took his breath away.

"Nothing would make me happier." She began to cry once again. "But…but I have one more secret," she said through her tears.

Hunter steeled himself, wondering if everything was about to be exploded apart. "What's the secret?" he asked hesitantly.

"I'm really a blonde," she confessed.

Relief whooshed through him. "You know what's amazing? I love blondes. I especially love a blonde named Colette who is the strongest, most amazing woman I've ever met."

Her tears turned to laughter. "I love you, Hunter."

"I'd like to kiss you, but I'm afraid I might hurt you," he said.

She smiled. "My lips are the only thing on my face that doesn't hurt."

"Well, in that case…" He stood and bent over her and gently took her lips in a kiss that fed his very soul. "I can't wait for you to become Mrs. Hunter Churchill," he said when the kiss ended.

"The very worst day of my life has now turned into the very best day of my life," she said. "Kiss me again, Hunter."

"Gladly." The kiss he gave her held all the passion, all the love he had for her, and he knew theirs would be a love, a marriage that would last a lifetime.

* * * * *

COLTON NURSERY HIDEOUT

DANA NUSSIO

To Randy, who feeds me through the crazy days of the deadline period and, let's admit it, the rest of the time, too. It's been a wild ride. Thank you for our first thirty years of marriage—three daughters, four cats, two states, four cities and a mild disagreement or two or three. There's no one with whom I would rather spend the next thirty years.

A special thanks goes to my fellow POTL Critique Group members, Patricia Lazarus, Loralee Lillibridge, Nancy Gideon, Victoria Schab, Laurie Kuna and Constance Smith, who've shared every high-high and low-low of this writerly journey with me.
I adore you all.

Chapter One

As she tucked the plastic test kit just inside the bowl and aimed as best she could at the absorbent tip, her new pencil skirt wadded at her waist, Tatiana Davison grimaced over the irony of the moment. Taking a pregnancy test in the executive restroom was one way to spend her first morning as co–chief executive officer of Colton Plastics. Just not one she would have chosen. Ever.

"Dad would get a good laugh over this," she whispered as she snapped the cap on the kit.

Tatiana shivered more than she had on the drive to the office, not yet reacclimated to Michigan's early-March deep freeze, and then cracked open the solid wood stall door to see if anyone had overheard her talking. Of course, no one had. This plush facility, with pristine granite countertops and waterfall-type faucet fixtures she would marvel over each time she washed her hands, was for her private use. She'd even locked the door to the outer parlor area.

Anyway, her father wouldn't be trying to cheer her up over news she received today or any other day. He wasn't aware that she'd accepted this prestigious position at the fast-growing Grave Gulch company that business magazines had called "one to watch." Nor that she'd moved back to the city of thirty-five thousand that she'd fled last year, overwhelmed after her dad's arrest for murder. He would have known many things about her life if he'd bothered to call her. Other than that *one* time right after the charges were dropped and he was released.

When Len Davison had first been arrested, Tatiana would have sworn there was no way her father could have murdered some guy last fall in Grave Gulch Park. Or any other time or place, for that matter. If only she was so certain of that now. In fact, she was almost convinced he was guilty.

She couldn't think about that this morning. There was no time to feel bad again, either, that her own DNA had connected him to the crime in the first place. She should never have done that genealogy testing…but she had her own problems to deal with at the moment. The ones resulting from her own poor decisions and her too appealing co-CEO. If only thirty-four-year-old Travis Colton hadn't been her favorite kind of male specimen, with toned arms beneath his perfectly pressed dress shirt and a no-nonsense square jaw on his fawn-colored face. And why couldn't his short, dark blond hair have been prickly like steel wool under her fingertips instead of irresistibly soft?

She shoved away memories that had no place in that moment or location, finished up the necessities and readjusted her clothes. Then she carried the test to the sink. She placed it on a paper towel, faceup as the instructions had required, and covered the whole thing with a second towel.

Why she bothered hiding the result, she wasn't sure.

With her stomach rolling just from the scent of the room's lilac air freshener, she had a good guess what the answer would be. And it wasn't a great one.

She washed her hands, scrubbing for longer than was necessary to clean them, and then studied the instructions to determine how soon the test could be read. Three minutes? Shouldn't it take longer than that for an answer that could change her life?

The delicate gold watch she'd purchased in honor of her upward move from celebrated plastics engineer to a corporate leadership role told her time was up. She uncovered the kit and lifted it to get a better look. Two dark pink lines had appeared in the result window. Air froze in her lungs, and her face in the mirror blurred, then sharpened, then blurred. *Pregnant?* That couldn't be true, and yet the proof was right there in front of her, in pink and white.

She lowered the test onto the towel and fumbled with the fancy faucet again, cool water spilling over her hands. Then she pressed her palms to her burning cheeks and forehead. When the heat finally started to cool, she gripped the edge of the counter and glanced up at the glass again. A red-faced woman stared back at her, damp hair clinging to her cheeks and mascara smeared beneath her eyes. The same engineer who'd thought it was a good idea to share a bottle of wine in her hotel suite living room with her corporate equal to celebrate her new executive position. The one who'd foolishly talked long into the night and had ended up happily tangled with him in the sheets of that king-size bed.

What had she been thinking? Well, it was obvious that she hadn't been considering consequences, or this morning she would have been able to march into Colton Plastics like a windstorm instead of cowering in her office as if preparing for a tornado drill. No, she couldn't think about Travis now. It didn't matter that he was unlike any man she'd ever met. That his incisive light blue eyes were also incredibly kind. What good would it do for her to recall that the pressure of his strong arms around her had made her feel safer than she had at any time since her father's arrest? Or that his tender touch might have teased awake parts of her beyond skin and flesh?

He evidently hadn't felt the same. In fact, he couldn't get out of her hotel room fast enough, while she'd been imagining that they'd connected on some deeper level. The test showed they'd connected, all right.

A baby. That explained a lot. Like why she'd been unable to stay awake later than nine the past few weeks and that she'd slept during the whole flight across the Atlantic when she was usually wide-awake on planes. And that it was more than jet lag and a nervous stomach over starting her new position that made saltine crackers her constant companion as she'd unpacked.

"Me? A mother?" Tatiana couldn't wrap her head around it. There was no way she could ever be that unselfish, like her wonderful late mom. She was too preoccupied with her career and would be even more so now. Even at age thirty-two, she still had only plastic houseplants in her apartment for a reason. The real varieties always died quick deaths in her care.

Though she'd always supported other women's reproductive rights, she'd never considered what *her* choice would be in the event of an unplanned pregnancy. But as she listed all the reasons she couldn't and shouldn't be a parent, of its own accord, her hand slid from the edge of the sink to the front of her skirt, just below her waistband. Damp fingerprints marked the cloth over her still-flat belly. No matter what unfortunate decisions had led to this reality, a child was now nestled inside her, growing. *Her* child. The two of them were in this together.

As she brushed her hand down her skirt, the damp prints fading, the test drew her attention again. Those two lines didn't lie. Nor did the hands on her watch. She had ten minutes until her first important meeting in a job she needed now more than ever.

Tatiana shoved the closed test kit and instructions back in the box, wrapped the whole thing in the plastic shopping bag and tucked it inside her designer purse. She pulled out her tiny cosmetics case, and in minutes had reapplied her makeup, combed her hair and brushed away the wrinkles on her skirt. She clipped her hair at her nape again and adjusted the few shorter sections left free around her face. She would appear presentable if no one looked too closely.

Compartmentalizing. She was good at it. Otherwise she never would have survived those weeks after her father's arrest last fall. Sure, she'd fled to Paris after his last cryptic call, but she'd managed to make it a long vacation as well. Even when the chance to interview for the perfect company had interrupted her tour and her unwise affair with Travis Colton had made her miserable upon her return to the romantic city.

If she planned to get through this morning's financial overview with Travis, she would have to harness her concentration skills again and hold an even tighter rein on her emotions. No matter what was going on in her personal life, or her body, she would show him that he hadn't made a mistake in recruiting her for his company.

She could do this, she told herself as she gathered her favorite pen and her leather folio and pulled open her heavy wood office door, nibbling a cracker, just in case. The empty administrative assistant's desk outside her office served as a reminder that one of her first tasks would be to interview candidates for that position.

As she traced the series of hallways that separated her plush office from Travis's, Tatiana ticked off items on the morning's agenda. They would go over cost estimates and discuss the division of responsibilities and their visions for the future of Colton Plastics.

And when those conversations and any other first-day details were out of the way, if she could gather the courage, she would tell Travis that she was carrying his child.

"Welcome to Colton Plastics, Miss Davison." Travis stood behind his desk as she entered his office with his admin, Jan Kennedy. Even as he spoke the words, they sounded ridiculous to him. He and Tatiana knew each other on so much more than a last-name basis, though whatever *that* had been needed to stay in the past where it belonged.

So, why was he staring at that tiny expanse of bare skin that showed between the top of her tall black boots and the hem of her skirt? And why was he following the wavy lines of the deep brown hair that had come loose around her face and recalling how that mass of silk felt spilling through his fingers?

That it had been six long weeks since he'd burned off some steam with any woman was no excuse. Nor that she was the last one with whom he'd shared a bed. Even if as co-CEOs, he and Tatiana were equals in the workplace, answering to the same board of directors, he'd never been one of those guys, who hit on female co-workers, and he wasn't about to start now. He didn't plan to *continue*, anyway.

Besides, they had important matters to address that morning, even more critical than establishing professional boundaries. Only after they'd figured out how to deal with current headlines and the ones to come in the next few weeks could he bring up the amazing sex that should never have happened and vow to never repeat it.

He averted his gaze just in time for her to catch him looking. Her huge hazel eyes narrowing, she lifted her chin.

"Good morning. I prefer Tatiana."

Her movements were robotic as she crossed the room and extended her hand for a brief, professional handshake. Her skin appeared paler than the glowing olive tone he remembered as well. He couldn't blame her, he supposed. The situation was awkward already, and it was about to get worse.

"You said it's casual around here," she continued as she sat in one of the guest chairs across from his desk.

"Right. I did say that. Tatiana, then." He shot a glance at his admin, who stood in her usual pose, notebook and pen in hand, head lowered, as if she didn't see and know everything that happened in his office. Even that he'd just been ogling his new co-CEO. So much for his determination never to let anyone know about their unfortunate attraction.

Travis cleared his throat. "Did you enjoy your six-week vacation?"

Her eyes narrowed, but her lips lifted in a tight smile.

"I did, thanks. I really appreciated the board agreeing to my terms for a start date, though, if I had to repeat it, I wouldn't wait to fly in on the Saturday night before it. The jet lag is rough."

"It's going to be a long first day then." He cleared his throat. "I know that Hartman & Wells was sorry to lose you, but we're thrilled that you'll be sharing your recognized technical acumen with Colton Plastics."

"Thank you. I'm glad to be here."

"You'll have big shoes to fill," he continued. "As you know, we lost our chief engineer, Constantine Niarchos, to lung cancer last year, but I want you to be aware that he would be pleased to see the technical side of our company placed in such capable hands."

"Again, I'm so sorry for your loss. I hope to build on the great work that Mr. Niarchos started."

She smiled then, her plump lips lifting in that mesmerizing way he recalled, but her smile stopped just below her eyes. He wasn't sure what that meant.

"Thanks, Jan. No calls for now, please." He sat again as his assistant stepped out and closed the door. "Okay. Let's get started."

He adjusted his desk pad, though he'd already straightened his desk before she'd arrived, moving his regular clutter into one stack. This would be more difficult than he'd imagined. But in Travis's vision of how this meeting would go, Tatiana hadn't been sitting across from him in that skirt and that filmy blouse. She'd worn one of those camisole things beneath her top to cover the breast cancer pink ribbon tattoo on her rib cage in memory of her mother, who'd died a little more than a year before, but the piece of cloth did nothing to help him forget that or any of her perfect, hidden beauty.

He decided to ease into the subject they needed to discuss. "Since our positions in the company are equal, I wanted to suggest that we should rotate between our offices for our weekly overview meetings."

"Sounds good to me," she said and then opened her folder and balanced it on her crossed legs.

He rubbed the back of his neck as he struggled for the right words. "But before we move on to other subjects, there's a personal matter we need to discuss."

Tatiana shot a glance at the closed door, the foot of her crossed leg bouncing and causing her notebook to wobble. "Can that wait? We have more important things to discuss this morning."

"Unfortunately, it can't. Look, I tried to bring it up when we spoke while you were still overseas, but you didn't want to talk about it."

"It was a bad time then, and it's an even worse time now." She tapped the book in her lap several times with her pen but didn't look up from it. "We need to stick to issues involving only Colton Plastics so that we'll have time at the end of the meeting to discuss another topic."

"This *is* about CP." At least part of it was. Travis shifted in his executive chair where he usually felt cool and in control. Neither of those words had applied to him from the moment he'd met Tatiana Davison. "Have you seen the *Grave Gulch Gazette*?"

Her head lifted at that.

"Not yet. As I mentioned, I only arrived Saturday night. Then I spent yesterday in bed, recovering from, well, jet lag." She stopped herself, her brows pinched together, and then shook her head. "Why? What did I miss?"

"It has to do with your father."

Tatiana blew out a breath. "I thought we'd dealt with this during our meetings in January. I said I'd had no contact with my father since his release, and I don't know where he is now. I was open about my personal life, which should have been off-limits during an interview, by the way. But I understood that the negative publicity could affect the company.

"When will the local paper stop reporting on the murder of that guy? What was his name?" She scanned the stack on his desk as though checking for a copy of the newspaper.

"Vincent Gully," he supplied. He didn't call her on his suspicion that she already knew the answer. No one would forget the name of a victim her father was accused of shooting at point-blank range.

"Oh. Right." She looked up from his desk. "Anyway, the charges against my dad were dropped clear back in December, after their supposed evidence went missing."

"From what I heard, it had help in disappearing." He swallowed, realizing he'd said too much. Just because his PI brother, Clarke, had shared too many details about the investigation of alleged evidence tampering by Randall Bowe, the police department's forensic scientist, didn't mean Travis should share that privileged information further.

"Haven't you heard about the new allegations?" he asked, hoping she would key in on that information instead of that other juicy detail.

The dread in her eyes and her slack jaw suggested she hadn't heard.

"You know of more?" she said finally.

"There's been another murder in Grave Gulch Park. It looked just like the first one. Police believe they're chasing a serial killer, and DNA evidence at the crime scene connected it to one suspect." He glanced down at his hands and had to force himself to look up again. "That suspect is Len Davison."

"My dad? A *serial killer*?"

Her skin was so pallid now that he was tempted to hit his office speakerphone button to ask Jan to bring a paper bag for Tatiana to breathe in. Why was he suddenly feeling protective of her?

"Nothing is proven yet," he found himself saying, though he'd just told her about the compelling evidence.

She wasn't listening, anyway, as she planted her elbows on her thighs and leaned forward, lowering her head in her cupped hands. "No. That's impossible. He *wouldn't*."

Her last word struck him as odd. Shouldn't she have said *couldn't*? But she was in shock. She wasn't choosing her words carefully.

"You okay?" Travis couldn't help himself. He rounded his desk and slid into the chair next to hers. Despite his determination never to touch her again beyond a professional handshake, he leaned forward and reached for her hands.

She jerked them back, crossing her arms as she straightened in the seat. Then she met his gaze. "I'm fine."

He almost believed her. Tatiana Davison might have been petite enough that she barely reached his shoulder, even in heels, but she was no damsel in distress. He needed to remember that. She was a highly qualified plastics engineer, one whose work had impressed him so much that he'd personally recruited her to take the vacant position at Colton Plastics.

"I'm sorry to be the one to give you the news. I was sure you would have heard already. Didn't anyone with the Grave Gulch Police Department get in touch with you?"

She lowered her arms to her lap. "I had a few messages from them on my cell while I was still overseas, but I didn't return the calls."

"Why not?"

"I figured they were just following up on the first case. I'd spoken to them before, so I didn't call back. Since the charges were dropped, I expected them to eventually go away and leave me alone."

"Makes sense, I guess." She also might have been dealing with the implications of her father's arrest by hiding from it. Was that why she'd gone to Paris in the first place? "But, unfortunately, the police aren't going away."

"I get that."

Tatiana stared out his second-floor office window, with a similar view of the snow-covered courtyard that she would have seen from her own office. She squinted as she turned back to him.

"All that new information was in the local newspaper?"

"Only part of it."

"Then how do you know so much?" She nodded as if answering her own question. "Right. You said that the Colton family is like a law enforcement convention. Siblings. Cousins. Everyone except you."

"I also said I was the maverick," he blurted and then

shook his head. He'd shared too many details with her that night, stories of how he'd never fit with his family—with anyone, really. Intimacies that went far beyond just sharing a bed for one night. "Never said police work wasn't an honorable trade. Just not for me.

"Anyway, when I announced at a police department pizza party I'd crashed that our board had hired you as my new co-CEO, my sister, Melissa, and brother, Clarke, nearly pounced on me from across the room. Remember, she's the Grave Gulch chief of police, and he's a PI who works with the department."

"That must have been quite a scene." She settled back in the chair, but her foot rocked again. "Well, what did they say?"

"No specifics beyond what I've told you. In fact, in her position, Melissa can't really discuss active investigations, but Clarke isn't as bound by those rules. He let me know that she believes her department is dealing with a serial killer. Also, Davison—" he paused, clearing his throat, before continuing "—I mean, *your father* has disappeared again. They want to talk to you as soon as possible. They think you can help them find him."

"Haven't I done enough for them?" She reached for the clip holding back her hair, causing more of the strands to fall loose. "You know, by spitting in that tube and registering with that genealogy website."

"I'm sure that helped."

She puffed up her cheeks and exhaled slowly. "I was hoping to learn more about my ancestors. Not send my own dad to prison."

"None of this is your fault." Again, the words came automatically, and, again, he regretted them.

"Doesn't make me feel any better."

He agreed with her on that one. He would have told her that Davison's actions alone would be what put him behind bars, but she didn't seem ready to hear that.

Tatiana tapped her bent forefinger to her lips, appearing deep in thought. She was taking the news better than he would have expected, but then, his board had hired her because she was a proven problem solver. It shouldn't have surprised him that she was freaking out less than the average person. After all, this wasn't the first time her father had been accused of murder.

"So, you're bringing this up now because you're looking for a plan to help Colton Plastics minimize the publicity nightmare. You know, the one that will result from having a co-CEO who's the daughter of a potential serial killer."

"It sounds awful when you put it that way."

She tilted her head to the side. "Or is the board asking me to resign for the company's sake before I even start to make an impact?"

"No. That's not what I'm asking."

"Well, you *should* be. Colton Plastics is still a relatively new company. As CEO—well, *co*-CEO now— you are responsible to our shareholders. A scandal this big could put the whole company at risk."

She was right. This mess made the fact that they'd slept together seem as insignificant as one of the bullet points on the list he could see on her notebook. Yet he shook his head again.

"No. That's not what I'm asking," he repeated.

Tatiana's shoulders relaxed with her sigh. "That's good. Because I need this job. Now more than ever."

Again, her words made sense. Potential employers who did an internet search on her would inquire about the public role she might play in her father's defense. Of course, they would. He had. The label *serial killer* would only make that worse. Human resources managers would have to balance her job skills against the negative publicity she would bring to their companies. Many—*most*—would swipe left before she ever made it to an interview.

"Did you give your brother and sister my start date here?"

Travis blinked. He'd been heading off on a what-if tangent while Tatiana had stayed focused on the current mess.

"I did." Just another on a list of things he regretted doing over the past few months.

"Then we'd better hurry with this meeting. We don't know when they'll try to question me."

Travis had a good idea since his cousin, GGPD detective Troy Colton, had called to confirm that Tatiana had arrived as scheduled that morning. He should have mentioned it, but she was on a roll, jotting more notes on her pad. He'd already given her enough bad news. And he was a coward.

"We need to prepare a statement," she said. "Tragic personal matter. Please respect the privacy of all CP employees. Unaware of Davison's whereabouts. Innocent until proven guilty in a court of law. All that nonsense."

"Are you?"

"Do you mean am I *innocent*?"

She shifted in her seat, and he did the same. They hadn't even made it to the subject of their one-night stand yet. Could this morning get any worse?

"No. I'm asking if you really are unaware of where he is or what he's been doing."

"I told you in my job interview that I haven't spoken with him," she snapped and then shot a look out the window before facing him again. "Do you need me to swear it on the Colton Plastics employee handbook?"

"That won't be necessary." He could have pointed out that not speaking to someone and not *knowing* where he might be hiding were different, but she was already agitated. Anyway, they still weren't finished with their unusual first-day topics.

She beat him to it.

"Okay, then. Let's get onto other matters. As we agreed, I will be interviewing admin candidates this week. Did we receive the prescreened list of applicants?"

"Jan will supply you with that and your passwords following this meeting, but there is still that other personal matter—"

"Can you please stop apologizing for that night?" She gripped the arms of her chair so tightly that her knuckles turned white. "There were two of us in that hotel suite. There was consent as well, if that's what you're worried about, even if the cabernet clouded our judgment. So, *stop.*"

Only when Tatiana's eyes widened did he realize that his jaw had dropped open. He closed his mouth.

"Sorry. It's just that, uh, with everything you just told me and, well, other things…"

"I get it." Okay, he'd overestimated how well she'd taken the news about her father, so he couldn't fault her for overreacting. "For the record, I wasn't planning to apologize. I wanted to set up some ground rules for, uh, our new working relationship."

"Oh. I see." She lowered her gaze to her hands. "I'm

sure we're on the same page about that. A mistake. Won't be repeated. Strictly professional from here on out. Only—"

"So glad to hear you say that." He rushed to end the awkwardness but then couldn't stop babbling. "You should know, that's not something I do— You probably won't believe that. But I've never done anything—" He shook his head, giving up.

"I would tell you to forget about it entirely." She paused, clearing her throat. "But that won't be possible now because, uh, the other matter I needed to discuss with you—"

His office phone buzzed then, interrupting whatever she'd been about to say. He reached for the intercom button. "Yes, Jan. Is it something important? Because I asked for no calls."

"It's important," Jan said. "I have representatives from the local police and the FBI, requesting to speak with Miss Davison."

Travis shot a look at Tatiana, who was rocking in her seat.

"Uh," Jan began again. "One of them says you're expecting him."

Chapter Two

"You knew they were coming this morning?"

Tatiana could only stare at Travis's wide eyes and shiver as she slid forward on her chair. Her already queasy stomach did a full-out roll. The hits just kept coming today. First, the positive pregnancy test, and now her father had been accused of murder *again*? There had been no time to digest either of those bits of news, and now the authorities were there, too?

"My cousin Troy told me this morning," he said simply.

"You could have warned me."

Serial killer. The words replayed again in her thoughts as they had since Travis had spoken them. Like headlines from a dozen news channels and newspapers at once. She wasn't ready to talk to the police again. How was she supposed to answer questions without giving away suspicions she'd harbored since her father's call after his release from jail? What kind of daughter was so quick to believe that claims about her *own father* were true? But how could she not believe them now? Her father had vanished from her life, and the man police and newspapers described didn't sound like the man she remembered at all. As if it wasn't enough that she was still mourning her mother's death, now he was gone, too.

"I hadn't gotten that far." He stood and shifted to face his office door.

Tatiana frowned at him, though she'd already imagined the police descending on her at the office that day. Her head swam as she lifted from the chair, so she steadied herself by resting her hand on the desk as she scooted past the guest chairs to stand next to him.

"Maybe you should sit."

Travis was watching her too closely, just as he had been since he'd delivered the news about the second murder. He'd guessed that she was not okay, though she'd tried to continue the meeting in a business-as-usual fashion. Nothing was *usual* about the events at Colton Plastics that day.

"No. I've got this," she said after a pause that had probably stretched too long.

The police had her at a disadvantage. They'd been aware of the accusations against her dad for weeks. Not *minutes*, like her. No way she would meet them sitting down, even if she had to use the desk to stay upright.

With a click, the door swung open. Jan admitted two men wearing suit jackets, one with a tie, one without. Tatiana recognized the more casual of the two by his short black hair, light brown skin and a scruff on his chin, but she'd never met the clean-shaven guy with a light complexion and dark hair.

"Miss Davison?"

The first law enforcement agent stepped forward, but Travis surprised her by edging between them. Usually, she would have been furious that a man had even tried to defend her. She lived and worked in the engineering world, where she usually went toe to toe with a half dozen mansplainers before lunch, but right now she was grateful that someone at least had her back.

"Please allow me to introduce Tatiana Davison, our new co-CEO at Colton Plastics." He gestured to the man standing closest to them. "Tatiana, I'd like you to meet FBI special agent Bryce Colton. My cousin."

She nodded rather than to have to shake his hand.

"And this is Detective Troy Colton, of the Grave Gulch PD. Also my cousin."

Troy extended his hand, but when she nodded again instead, he lowered it.

"We've met," she said.

Travis looked back and forth between them. "Oh. Right. From the *other* interview."

"We were in the same class at Grave Gulch High, too," she told him.

Just the thought of that awkward first interview made her squirm. The first time her father was accused of murder. When she'd still been positive that her kind, loyal dad could never have committed such a crime.

Troy dipped his head. "Good to see you again, Miss Davison."

"I wouldn't call it good," she tossed back before she could stop herself. She swallowed and then grasped onto something else Travis had said. "You're *all* related?"

"Cousins. From different branches of the family, though. Troy's dad, Geoff Colton, and Bryce's mom, Verity, are brother and sister to my father, Frank." Travis glanced at the two men by turns, but he wasn't smiling. "I tried to warn you about the family business."

"You weren't kidding," she said.

Travis leaned closer to Troy and spoke out of the side

of his mouth. "I thought I asked you to wait for her to at least get settled in."

"Sorry, man, " Troy said. "We've got a job to do. And Chief Colton wants results now."

As if he couldn't wait any longer to get started, Bryce stepped around Travis.

"Miss Davison, you might not be aware, but local police have been attempting to reach you for weeks concerning the whereabouts of your father. He is wanted for questioning in the case involving the murders of Vincent Gully and Jonathan Manelli," Bryce said. "We would like to ask you a few questions."

"Vincent Gully? But my father was cleared—"

Troy made a sound in his throat. "Well, not *cleared*, exactly. Released because of missing evidence."

Bryce picked up the story for him. "Randall Bowe, former forensic scientist for the GGPD, is wanted in connection with alleged evidence tampering in several cases, including your father's. Bowe is currently at large."

"There has to be a mistake."

The expressions on the three men's faces told her otherwise. "I'm sorry, Officers, but I didn't know anything about a second murder until earlier today, and this is the first I've heard about evidence tampering."

Tatiana had learned some other things that morning as well, though the test in the restroom seemed so long ago now. She hugged herself tighter until her chest ached from the pressure.

Troy crossed his powerful arms. "You would have if you'd returned any of the messages I left on your cell while you were overseas. The *same* number where we were able to reach you for an interview regarding the earlier charges. Clarke Colton left several messages as well."

"I didn't receive any messages." It wasn't technically lying to police if she never *listened to* them, right?

"And is this the same phone number you are using now that you have returned to Michigan?" Troy pressed.

"She *said* she didn't receive them."

Tatiana turned her head away from the officers, blinking. Had Travis lied for her, even if it was only a small point in their enormous investigation?

He gestured toward his office door. "Now if you two will excuse us, we were just settling into a budget meeting. Tatiana will have a lot of work to do to shorten the learning curve at CP. Maybe you could schedule this interview at the police department later—"

"That's not going to work out," Bryce said, pulling his notebook and pen out of his suit jacket pocket. "We have to speak to Miss Davison right now. We've already had to wait too long."

"This is an active murder investigation," Troy reminded him. "Impeding a witness falls under obstruction of justice, you know. It's a crime. So, unless you want to be taken into custody yourself—"

"Fine." Tatiana slashed both hands through the air. "I'll answer your questions now. But you're wasting your time talking to me when you could be following other leads. I have no idea where my father is, so I won't be able to help you."

The two law enforcement officers exchanged a dubious look. Bryce spoke for them both.

"Thank you, Miss Davison. Do you have an office where we can speak alone?"

"We have a conference room where you can spread

out a little more," Travis answered instead. "And, if Tatiana doesn't mind, I would like to sit in on the interview."

Bryce shook his head. "I don't think that's a good idea."

"I agree." Troy was staring at Travis, his brow lifted.

His cousins weren't the only ones surprised by that suggestion. Travis had shifted backward so that he stood shoulder to shoulder with her, except his was higher. Was he trying to present a united corporate front or something? It was probably a practical decision. Whatever she said in the interview might affect Colton Plastics, after all. So why did she get the sense that he'd made the offer for *her*?

"Guess that's up to her, isn't it?" Travis said.

All three men turned back to her.

"I'd like my co-CEO to stay," she said. Their relationship was more complicated than that, more than he even knew, but that descriptor was enough for now. No matter what his reason for offering, she appreciated not having to face two officers alone. "That is, if you want to talk to me during my workday. If you'd prefer a private interview, I'd be happy to stop by the police station after work."

Again, their visitors communicated silently. Troy shrugged first, and Bryce did the same.

Troy gave Travis the kind of stare that would have cowed a lesser man, but Travis didn't even blink.

"Do you think you can keep your mouth shut during the whole interview?" Troy asked.

Travis pressed his index finger to his lips. "I'll be as quiet as a church mouse."

"Those aren't necessarily all that quiet," Bryce chimed.

"Quieter," Travis clarified.

"Good," Troy said. "If you cause us trouble, we won't have any problem arresting you. Family or no family."

"We might have to do Rock, Paper, Scissors to decide who gets to cuff you."

Bryce's words were light, but his smile was a tight one. All was not sunshiny in Colton family land, and the fact that Travis was defending her had brought on some of those clouds.

"I'll keep that in mind." Travis gestured to Tatiana. "Now if you'd like to show these gentlemen to the conference room, I'll ask Jan to bring some coffee and be right behind you."

At that, he slid behind his desk and bent to tap a few keys on his laptop. First, he'd stood up to his own family members on her behalf, signaling he wouldn't let them push her around. Now, he was stepping back, offering her the power position with their guests, when he would have been a far better guide through the building than she was. She couldn't have appreciated both gestures more. As strange as it was to admit it, Colton Plastics was the one place lately where she felt safe.

"Right this way," she said.

As Travis's relatives, Bryce and Troy might have been more familiar with CP than she was, but she guided them with authority down the hall around the corner to the conference room. Good thing she'd spent several hours in that room when she'd visited the company, or she might have had them walking around the building, hunting for it.

"Take a seat, gentlemen."

She indicated two chairs near the window, and then, instead of taking the spot at the head of the table, she rested her folio on the position facing them and lowered into that seat. As memories from her last police interview washed over her, she straightened in the suddenly too-hard chair, her silk blouse sticking to her sweaty back. Something seemed to have a vise grip on her lungs, refusing to allow her to take more than shallow breaths. During that first meeting with police, she'd worried that something she said might hurt her father's case, and he would be wrongfully convicted. Now, she was torn between protecting a man who'd become a stranger to her and sharing her own suspicions.

Bryce pushed the button on his pen.

"This won't take long. We just need you to tell us—"

The door clicked then, and Travis hurried through it, carrying his own notebook.

"What did I miss?"

"Not much in the forty-five seconds we've been in this room," Troy grumbled.

"Oh, good."

Travis's gaze moved from the head of the table and to Tatiana's position at the side, and he sat next to her, as she'd hoped he would.

"Now, Special Agent Colton, what were you saying you needed from me?"

At her side, Travis gave a tiny nod. The hold on her lungs decreased by tiny increments. Despite still having to face police questioning, she wouldn't have to do it by herself this time. Someone else was on her team. She wasn't alone. This was the first time she hadn't felt abandoned since her father's arrest. Well, other than when she'd been in Travis's arms.

Just as her traitorous mind needed to forget his tender touch and his kind words from that night, she also needed to drop this naive belief that he was on her side. That his concern for her went beyond his interest in the company he'd built. Of course, he would feel obligated to support her now and help mitigate damage to the business that the news about her father would bring. He'd already been aware of the first case involving her dad, and he'd taken the risk of recommending her to his board, anyway.

She couldn't fool herself into believing that he would continue to stand behind her position with Colton Plastics once he knew about the baby. Was that why she'd been relieved that the officers had arrived to interrupt her announcement? So that she could delay the disbelief on his face when she told him? He might be angry, too, that their protection hadn't worked. But the most difficult thing for her to watch would be his troubled realization that the blood of an accused serial killer would flow through his own child's veins.

No, Travis wouldn't want her anywhere around the company after he learned the news. Sure, he would do the right thing by her and the child. He would probably pay her off for the next eighteen years. And then he would show her to the door.

After twenty minutes of questioning, Tatiana slumped back into the chair and crossed her arms. So much for the interview being a short one.

"Now, Miss Davison, you've said you haven't spoken with your father." Bryce paused, tapping his pen on the paper as he checked his notes. "Since his release. But we need to know more. Tell us about the places that hold special relevance for Mr. Davison. Places he might have gone if he didn't want to be found."

"Come on, Bryce." Travis clasped the arms of his

chair. "How many times are you going to ask her the same question in different ways?"

"Until she answers it," Troy grumbled. "And, anyway, didn't we agree you would be a silent witness? The emphasis on *silent*."

"Right. Don't mind me. I'll just be over here twiddling my thumbs."

Unlike Travis's cousins, Tatiana appreciated his interruption. It gave her a break from having the detective and the FBI agent treating her as if she were the suspect, not her father.

She rested her hands, palms up, on the table. "I've already told you that I don't know where he is."

This time Troy spoke up instead. "We're not asking where he is, though we'd be happy to take that information as well if you're offering. What we want to know is where he *would be*."

That was the question that she didn't want to answer. Not with so many happy memories flooding her thoughts. The escapes to Florida for spring break, during the waning winter months when Michigan was still frozen solid. The stops her dad made on every trip at roadside flea markets, just because her mom loved them. She didn't want to think about the ice-fishing cabin they'd rented near Ludington or the few summers they'd spent at the lake cottage rental up north. Shadows eclipsed every sunny memory now.

"I don't *know*." Her voice cracked on the last word.

"In the file, it says he worked at least for a while at a West Michigan furniture manufacturer until your mother's death early last year." Troy paused and glanced at his notes. "That would be a *Marcia* Davison. Did he travel for work or any of his hobbies?"

"Yeah, like golf?" Bryce added. "Everybody in Michigan golfs, right?"

"Or is he a Civil War reenactor?" Troy chimed.

She shook her head in answers to all their questions. Didn't they get it? She didn't want to tell them anything.

After a long pause, Troy leaned back in his chair and crossed his arms. "We will find your father. Covering for him won't change that."

Tatiana shoved her chair back and stood, immediately resting her hands on the table as her head swam and stomach acid backed up in her throat. Was it the baby or the situation? Or both? She stared at the table instead of meeting their gazes.

"Sorry. I can't do this."

She rushed to the door.

"Miss Davison, wait."

Her hand on the latch, she turned back to find Bryce standing behind the table but making no effort to follow her.

"Look, I get it. This is your dad."

He smiled as though he really could relate to a situation that an average person couldn't begin to understand.

"You *love* your father. Most children love their parents." He pressed his lips into a line, shook his head and then spoke again. "But the sad truth is that same man who brought your mother flowers every Friday after work and took care of her until she died of cancer also murdered two men in cold blood. If the pattern holds, in another two months, he'll kill again."

Troy came to his feet as well. "You wouldn't want to feel responsible if someone else were to be killed because you didn't help us stop him, would you?"

As a sharp sound escaped her throat, Tatiana yanked open the door and ran out. She didn't know where she was going. She barely knew the Colton Plastics facility, and all the closed doors looked the same. But there was one thing she did know: she couldn't stay there.

Chapter Three

"That went well." Travis glared at his cousins across the conference room table.

Troy frowned back at him. "I thought we said—"

"You might not have noticed, but the subject of your interview has left the room. So, I'm guessing your interrogation is over."

"Any idea where she could have taken off to?" Bryce asked.

"She's probably still trying to find her way out of the building." He couldn't blame her if she ran all the way to the parking lot without ever stopping at human resources to complete her benefits paperwork. "She only had the basic tour during her visit in January. I'll have Jan try to find her and ask if she'll come back. I'm guessing no."

He pulled out his phone and tapped out a quick email.

Bryce swiveled his head to look at his partner in the investigation. "What was that all about, anyway? 'Wouldn't want to feel responsible'? Did you really think that would help get answers? I had it under control."

"Did you?" Troy crossed his arms. "Your good-cop tactic wasn't working any better than my bad-cop one."

"You both did a lousy job, if you ask me."

His cousins looked back to Travis and said in unison, "No one asked you."

"Why the hell were you pressing her so hard, anyway? She said she doesn't know anything."

Troy chuckled. "Good thing suspects—and witnesses—never lie to police."

Bryce shook his head. "There was a reason we didn't want you to hang out during the interview."

"So that you two could push her around? I don't think so."

Troy tilted his head to the side, studying Travis the way the officers had Tatiana earlier.

"Why are you so protective of her, anyway?"

"I would be for any colleague being badgered by police." Then why had his whole body tightened over that question? And why had he been tempted to throw himself on the conference table between law enforcement and his *colleague*?

Both men stared down at their notes rather than look at him. They didn't buy his story, either.

"I'd hardly call that 'badgering,'" Bryce said. "You might want to witness a real interview with a suspect." His head lifted. "On second thought, don't."

"Tatiana is our brand-new *co-CEO*. I couldn't have her being harassed at work on her first day." Travis rubbed his sweaty hands on his suit slacks. Why couldn't he stop babbling? He might as well announce that he'd slept with her.

Troy cleared his throat. "About that. Have you considered what impact Miss Davison's presence might have on Colton Plastics?"

"Not that it's any of your business, but of course I have."

In fact, he'd thought about it constantly since learning about her father's alleged involvement in the *second* murder. He could just hear his own dad's I-told-you-so over that one. Nothing like having Frank Colton as his own personal doomsday predictor to provide helpful information like the statistic that forty-five percent of all new businesses failed in the first five years. Or that growing too fast could be the death knell for those few companies that had survived. What helpful tidbit would his dad offer now about the impact of negative publicity in tanking a growing company, even one like CP that was already ten years old? So much for him proving to his dad that he could blaze his own trail outside of law enforcement like so many relatives or even the shipping business like Frank.

Travis shoved those thoughts to the back of his mind, where they belonged. "Why are you asking about her impact now?"

Bryce pointed to the conference room's four windows, all shielded from the morning sun with slatted blinds. "You might want to look outside."

Foreboding settling in his gut, Travis rushed over to the window. News vans from every regional TV station he could name were parked in the Colton Plastics lot one floor beneath them, mobile communications satellites mounted on top, antennae poking into the sky. A dozen reporters and camera operators milled around and through the painted parking spots. They appeared to be setting up cameras for remote feeds.

"What the—" He whirled and faced his cousins. "You brought them all here?"

Troy scoffed. "No, we didn't *bring* them. They just showed up."

Bryce stepped to one of the other windows, out of Travis's reach. "They're obviously following the investigation. Two murders in Grave Gulch? A potential serial killer? There hasn't been news like that around here in thirty years."

"But Melissa, I mean, Chief Colton, said police hadn't released—"

Troy waved his pen to interrupt him. "Two murders. One city. They're sniffing out a bigger story. That's kind of their job. And if they're able to get anyone to speak on the record about this suspect, they'll have their lead stories at five, ten, and eleven."

Travis braced his hand on the wall and stared out the window again. One outlet was already taping, its reporter standing in front of the custom stone-and-brick sign Colton Plastics had added to the campus last year. "What about this morning? How did they know you were coming here *today*?"

"That I don't know," Troy told him. "Someone's not being careful enough with the investigation details or sharing something they shouldn't be with the media."

"Gives me a lot of faith in local law enforcement, family or not," Travis said sarcastically.

He took one last look at the crowd building on the ground below and stalked back to the chair he'd vacated. He should have sat, but he paced instead.

"It's a good guess that she's still somewhere in the building." Travis jutted his index finger toward the windows. "She won't walk out through that. Why didn't either of you mention what was happening in the parking lot earlier?"

Still leaning on the wall next to the glass, Bryce shrugged. "We doubted that information would help us to get the interview we needed. Did we mention we're tracking a probable serial killer?"

"You're willing to do *anything* to get the information you want, too."

Troy shook his head. "Not anything. Anyway, we're just doing our—"

"Jobs?" Travis finished his sentence for him. "Was it your *job* to come bother Tatiana on her first day at Colton Plastics? Only her second back in the country? She isn't even accused of a crime, and yet you're treating her like she's a murderer. It's not her fault that her dad is—could be—you know…"

"Come on, Travis," Bryce said, straightening his tie. "We didn't mean to upset her, but, like Detective Colton tried to say, we're just doing our jobs."

"Well, you're going to have to do them somewhere else."

"What do you mean?" Troy asked.

With a sweep of his hand, Travis indicated the conference room, where no work had taken place all morning. "I mean that you've disrupted our business enough."

Bryce held out one hand, palm up. "It wouldn't have taken so long if she'd just answered our questions instead of trying to avoid them."

"Tatiana just didn't *know* anything. So why don't you search somewhere else for clues and leave her the hell alone?"

He needed to stop, but he couldn't do it, even if his cousins had to be wondering whether he was being so protective over Tatiana for Colton Plastics or for himself.

"You know we can't do that," Bryce said.

He did. That was the most frustrating part. "You can't force her to give you information she doesn't have."

Troy touched his index finger to his lips. "How can you be so sure that she doesn't know anything? You've said you barely know her."

"I am." He straightened his shoulders and glared at them, responding to the first question while skipping the second.

As the detective and the special agent exchanged a skeptical look, Travis refused to listen to his gut, which concurred. He might have been intimately familiar with every curve, dip and taste of Tatiana Davison's body, but outside of bed they were almost strangers. It didn't matter if that night of wine and conversation had tricked them into believing differently.

A chime on his phone announcing a new email saved him from having to answer the question. He nabbed the device off the table before the other men had a chance to sneak a peek at the screen. It was from Jan.

T is in her office and indisposed...

His chest tight, Travis scanned the rest of the message before looking up again. *Indisposed?* What did that mean? He'd worked with Jan a long time and had always appreciated that she never held back details. Was she being vague because she worried that his email might be read by someone else? Travis tilted the phone so that only he could see the screen.

"Is that from Ms. Davison? Will she be returning?" Troy asked.

"Afraid not," he said in answer to both questions.

"She had to go into a meeting and won't be available for the rest of the day."

Bryce's jaw flexed, the first sign that his remarkable cool had been pushed to its limit. "We'll need to talk to her again."

"I'm sure she will be happy to set up another appointment with you tomorrow. She said she will be available after office hours."

Travis was making the story up as he went, but he didn't care. He needed to see for himself that she was all right. If the only way to do that was to toss an FBI agent and a police detective to the curb, where they would be surrounded by hungry reporters, then so be it.

He crossed to the door and pulled it open, indicating for his cousins to exit ahead of him. Both men tucked their notebooks in their pockets and followed his instructions. Instead of waiting for Jan to guide them from the building as was usual practice, Travis led them to the elevator himself, rode with them and guided them to the security station next to the main entry.

Both men slid into their coats and crossed through the exit gate, next to the metal detectors, where they would have had to show their badges because of the weapons they carried.

Bryce stopped and turned to face him. "We'll see Miss Davison tomorrow."

"*Just* Miss Davison," Troy added. "Or she can bring legal counsel, if she prefers."

Travis's chest squeezed at the thought of even more police officers crowding around her and tossing questions that she couldn't answer. Or *wouldn't*. Still, there was no way he could volunteer to accompany her again without raising more questions about her innocence or their connection.

Bryce and Troy left through the revolving door, neither looking back at him. Several reporters rushed toward them and shoved microphones in their faces, but both men declined to comment.

After taking a last look to ensure Bryce and Troy hadn't stopped to speak to the media, Travis hurried to the elevator. Both cars were currently on the third floor, so he took the stairs instead. The interview with his cousins would probably make family events even more awkward, as if he didn't feel maladroit enough around many of them. Mavericks weren't supposed to fit in, he guessed, and not everyone could have the kind of job his father considered honorable. He couldn't worry about that now, or even think about all those media trucks in the parking lot. His only concern was about the woman who'd gone from confidently marching into Colton Plastics on the day of her interview to hiding in her own office now. He had to make sure she was okay.

AT THE LOUD knock outside her office door, Tatiana lifted her head from her hands and patted her damp hair again. She hadn't bothered to fix her makeup a second time. This morning had been a chorus of humiliations, and she still had more rounds to sing.

"Come in."

She hoped it would be Jan stopping by to check on her again, but Travis pushed open the door instead and poked his head inside.

"They're gone."

She let out her breath in tiny spurts. "Thanks."

"They won't stay gone."

"I know."

"Are you all right?"

The worry creasing his forehead as he scanned her face, her hair, and her hands shamed her even more. Whether she had a good reason or not, she'd run out of that meeting. Another shining moment on a glistening first day on the job. Now in addition to worrying about the PR nightmare she'd brought to Colton Plastics, he probably questioned her professionalism, too.

"I'm fine." She was nauseated again from the mint toothpaste she'd used to brush away the evidence of vomiting, but she didn't mention that. "I thought Jan would have passed that along already."

"She did. I wanted to check for myself."

He continued to watch her until she couldn't sit still in her chair. She'd looked for a moment earlier to tell him her news. He probably thought his day couldn't get much worse. It was about to.

"Sorry for running out of the interview."

"Can't blame you for that. It was getting intense in there."

She folded her arms, hating that he would think she couldn't handle a heated discussion, but that only sent sharp pains through her tender breasts. More reminders of the bombshell she had yet to drop.

"I was feeling, well, *ill*."

Concern etched his features. "So, that's why Jan said you were 'indisposed.'"

"I'd hoped she'd missed that." Great. Someone had overheard her while she was facedown in the porcelain throne. Her facilities weren't as private as she'd thought.

"You do look a little pale," he said, watching her again. "Even more so than earlier."

He'd noticed it during their meeting while she'd still believed she was keeping it together?

"Do you need to go home early?"

"On my first day?" She shook her head, though it sounded like an amazing idea. "Some example I'd be setting to the staff."

"We wouldn't want them to catch anything, either. You did just arrive from overseas."

He didn't have to explain that one. Anyone who'd lived through the recent pandemic that affected so many would never take world travel lightly again.

"No, I'm fine. Really. It's just, well…"

As she let her words fall away, Travis nodded.

"It probably wouldn't be a good time to leave the building, anyway."

She'd glanced down at her folded hands, but at his comment, her chin jerked up. "Why is that?"

His gaze shot to her office windows, through which he probably could see into his own office on the opposite side of the courtyard.

"Right. Neither of us have a view of the parking lot." He tilted his head to the side. "Didn't Jan tell you?"

"We didn't exactly have time for a heart-to-heart."

"About the media. They're staked out down there."

She became light-headed as she leaped to her feet too quickly. Travis didn't appear to miss that she held onto her desk to steady herself before rushing past him and out the door. "Can you see them from the conference room?"

She didn't wait for him to answer, continuing down the hall instead. Once inside, she jogged straight to the window. They were there. The vans. The camera operators and reporters milling around and jockeying for the best positions. It was just like last time. Worse.

"Are they all here for *me*? How did they even find me?"

"I don't—"

Tatiana jerked her head to look back at him. "Did you make an announcement in the local paper's business section?"

He shook his head. "Not yet."

"Well, don't," she spat.

"Guess that's not going to make a difference now."

"Who tipped them off that I would even *be* here?" Her cheeks heated, and sweat made her silk blouse cling to her skin.

"No one seems to know the answer to that."

"It's not supposed to be like this." Her head was spinning, and she couldn't make it stop. "I thought the circus would go away when Dad was released. I was going to get a fresh start here. But it's happening again."

"Don't worry. We'll figure—"

"No, it's worse," she said, trampling his words. "Those reporters won't leave me alone. The story's going to be everywhere. People love to read about serial killers. We don't even have time to develop a good media strategy. They're already *here*."

Tatiana hadn't heard his approach, but suddenly his hands were on her shoulders, applying gentle pressure. She knew better than to trust anyone, especially now, but she was tempted to sink back against him.

"It'll be fine," he said. "We'll figure out something."

Only it wouldn't, and they couldn't. She shifted her shoulders until he lifted away his hands and took a step back with a mumbled "sorry."

She shook her head to wave off his apology and stared out at the media frenzy on the parking lot below.

"My dad's status as a fugitive and possibly a serial killer isn't the only problem affecting us."

"There's *more*?"

He stepped to the window next to where she stood and looked out, as if searching for the answers she'd yet to give.

"I won't let them get near you again."

His crossed arms and tight jaw told her he meant it.

Then he drew his eyebrows together, and twin vertical lines appeared on his forehead. "Wait. Are you talking about *us* as in Colton Plastics or as in—"

"*Us,*" she finished for him.

His shook his head. "There's no reason for them to find out about that night. It's no one's business, anyway. And we agreed there wouldn't be—"

"The baby's going to be tough to hide," she blurted.

His hands dropped to his sides. "Baby?"

Automatically, she rested her hand across her tummy and covered it with the other one, shielding the embryo nestled inside her. Then she lifted her chin and met his gaze. "I'm pregnant. And the child is yours."

Chapter Four

"A baby?" Why couldn't he stop repeating that question? He'd heard what she'd said, but the words seemed to be suspended in the air around them. Tatiana was having *his* child? With steps that he hoped looked steadier than they felt, he moved to the conference table and sank into a chair.

"Yeah. It came as a surprise to me, too," she said.

"So, this was the 'other matter' you were trying to tell me about when the SWAT team showed up." At her nod, Travis continued, "How long have you known?"

She slumped into the seat next to his and peeked at her watch. "About two hours and eleven minutes now."

"You just took a test this morning?"

"Right before the meeting in your office. Happy first day at Colton Plastics to me."

Now the subtle differences he'd noticed in her earlier made sense. She'd just been hit with some heavy news. It explained her upset stomach as well. Morning sickness.

"Wait. If you took just one test, then you can't be sure that it's accurate, right? You're an engineer. You know about inconclusive results. Maybe a false positive?"

"The box said ninety-nine percent accuracy from the

day of the missed—" She looked up from her gripped hands. "Anyway, the two pink lines were pretty clear. It's still in my purse. I didn't want to leave it for the custodial staff to find. Do you want me to get it for you?"

"That won't be necessary." He cleared his throat. Could that moment have been more awkward? "It's been over six weeks since we, uh—since you interviewed here. And you're just finding out *now*? I don't know a lot about those things, but isn't that a little late to start being concerned? I hate to have to ask, but are you sure that I'm…?"

She lifted her chin and met his gaze, annoyance simmering in her eyes.

"You're the father, all right. I haven't, uh, *celebrated* with anyone else in—" she paused, shrugging "—more than a year. As for finding out about the pregnancy late, I have irregular periods, and with the stress of moving back to the US, I wasn't paying close attention to my cycles. In case you're getting ready to ask, yes, I have been taking the Pill, just like I said, and, if you recall, you didn't have a condom. Guess this would fall in that nine percent contraceptive failure rate."

He hated to admit he'd had that question about her birth control pills, too. "Thanks. Sorry, I had to ask. We don't know each other that well and—"

"You need to know what I want from you, the hotshot young co-CEO at a growing company. I hold that same title now, by the way. The answer is *nothing*. We don't need anyone."

We? This conversation was going south faster than even the interview with police had, but he couldn't help asking one more thing. "So, you are planning to continue the pregnancy?"

She pushed back her shoulders and glared at him, signaling he'd gone too far.

"Absolutely." She stopped, blinking, and then shook her head. "I haven't had much time to think about it, but, yes, I am having this *baby*. I will be keeping *my* child as well."

"Sorry." That was all he seemed to be able to say today. She had every right to be angry she had to answer these questions. One grilling for the day was enough. "I just didn't want to assume anything. I know it's your choice."

"And I thought you had a right to know that you will have a child living in Grave Gulch. If you need proof that the baby's yours, I'll be happy to have a prenatal DNA test."

"That won't be necessary," he said again.

Her lashes fluttered, as if his words had surprised her as much as they had him. His dad would tell him he was crazy for not demanding that test as a legal precaution in case she later changed her mind and demanded financial support. That would be something else upon which he and Frank disagreed, since he intended to provide it, either way.

His gut told him that everything Tatiana had said was true, anyway. Her reflexive movement—covering her abdomen with her crossed arms again—bothered him even more. She seemed to be protecting her child from everyone. Especially from *him*.

She popped up from the seat and started pacing in front of the windows, which luckily had a protective film that wouldn't allow reporters to shoot photos of her from outside.

"I wouldn't want those test results, either," she said.

"First, it doesn't look great that you slept with someone who'd just been named an executive of the company you founded. Then, you find out her father might be a serial killer. And, to put a cherry on top of that sundae, she announces she's pregnant with your baby."

Tatiana turned back to him, but the earlier defiance in both her features and posture, along with the ruddiness of her skin, appeared to have drained from her.

"It might be too much for you to know for certain that a child with a possible serial killer's blood flowing through his veins is yours."

"We should get married."

Her neck jerked back as if he'd struck her with more than a suggestion.

"What?" She blinked several times and shook her head. "Are you out of your mind?"

That he'd spoken it aloud had surprised him, too, but the idea had been shaping in his mind since she'd informed him about the pregnancy. It was the practical solution. The right thing to do.

He usually kept all his decisions these days to himself until they were fully formed. He overthought details to the point of tedium, too: hard lessons learned during his relationship with his gold-digging ex-fiancée. So, his one-night stand with Tatiana Davison had been his exception rather than his new rule of weighing all information before acting. What did it say about him that the one night he'd felt most himself in seven years had ended in an accidental pregnancy?

"Don't be so quick to answer—"

She swiped both hands through the air. "That's a terrible idea. I thought you wanted to keep Colton Plastics *out* of the news?"

A little late for that. Had she missed all those media types milling around in the parking lot? There was no way the company wouldn't be mentioned or pictured as a backdrop to headline stories, even if they never gave a public statement or confirmed any speculation about her father.

"It's a practical decision. I'm not talking about abiding love or some other nonsense. This is for…" He lowered his gaze to her stomach.

She stalked forward again, spun around, and repeated her steps. "And this is the twenty-first century, not the *nineteenth*. Just because a gal is knocked up, that doesn't mean she has to toss on a veil for her shotgun wedding."

"I know that, but—"

"No one knows yet that it's a *Colton* baby. There won't be an article on 'Baby Makes Three for Colton and Serial Killer's Daughter' if we stay quiet. No one will ask if the law-and-order Colton family has crossed to the dark side."

She appeared to consider for a few seconds and then nodded. "I'll say I had in vitro. Plenty of women choose that when they want a child and don't want to deal with the guy who's contributing half of the DNA."

"You have both the baby and the sperm donor."

"And I remember you saying you were a confirmed bachelor." She stopped again and planted her hands on her hips. "No marriage or family for you. No way."

She also must have recalled when and where he'd shared those personal details as her cheeks were suddenly stained pink.

"The situation is different now."

Tatiana didn't answer. Apparently, she couldn't argue

with that, given the positive test in her purse and the news crews standing between her and her rental car.

"We don't have to make everything worse than it is by adding a marriage of convenience to the mix."

Travis had only said no love. He wisely hadn't mentioned *convenience*, though it would be helpful to the union that they'd already proven they were sexually compatible. A couple of times, in fact.

"If we get married, then I'll be able to watch over you both."

"I told you, we don't need anyone."

"You said it yourself. Your baby is a Colton. At least *half* a Colton. I'd really like to protect him or her. If you'll let me."

She opened her mouth as if to argue and then closed it again, so he pushed his advantage before she produced another point.

"Look, you saw out there." He pointed to the window. "As long as your dad is in hiding, they'll never leave you alone. Maybe not even after he is located. Then you'll have to live through a trial. You'll be caring for a child on your own, and there's always going to be someone waiting outside your apartment window with a camera. You'll have to hire a bodyguard like my brother Stanton, just to keep your family safe."

"Could you make this sound any worse?" She pinched the bridge of her nose between her thumb and forefinger. "I get what you're saying. But almost everything about my life is out of my control, and my choice about marriage is sacred. It's supposed to be for life. No matter what else we discover about Dad, he and Mom had a marriage like that. The real thing. At least, it looked like that to me."

"Some people are just lucky."

Her gaze flicked to his. Travis needed to stop saying ridiculous things around her, but he couldn't help himself when she'd looked so sad. Her mother hadn't been *lucky* to lose her battle with cancer. More than that, if the woman had been blessed at all, it would be because she was blissfully unaware that her husband was a murderer.

"You might call abiding love 'nonsense,' but I don't think it is. I know what it looks like. At least I thought I knew." Though her eyes became shiny, she lifted her chin. "I'll never marry without that forever kind of love. On both sides."

Travis was more curious than he should have been about her parents' story, but he couldn't ask her when they had more critical matters to settle. He held up his hands in surrender. "Fine. I get it. Forget my proposal, but I still don't like the idea of you being alone. You have the police and the media out there. Not to mention, what happens if your dad shows up and expects you to hide him?"

Her shoulders lifted. "I hadn't considered that."

"Well, you should." Like before, he pushed forward while he had the chance. "I think you should stay at my place."

She shook her head. "You're full of bad ideas today."

"I know it's not the best solution, but it's not the worst one, either. You said you were keeping a room in an extended-stay hotel until you found an apartment. My condo is huge. It's a connected walkout ranch, with three bedrooms upstairs and a whole other suite on the lower level. You'd have your own floor."

"It's kind of you to offer. Really. But I still don't think—"

"We wouldn't have to tell anyone about the baby. At least not for a while."

"That part we can agree on, but as for staying there…" She shook her head.

"Let me do this for you, Ana."

Only when her eyes widened did he realize he'd called her by the name he'd used with her just once before. During a moment when neither had been dressed for the office or anywhere else. And one when they were in the process of creating a new life.

The answer was on her lips, the same one they both should have given when they'd considered whether to open another bottle of wine that night six weeks before.

"Then let me do this for our child," he rushed to add. "You're both going to need protection."

He wasn't playing fair, but she'd left him no choice. She faced the window once more and stared down at the frenzy taking place below. She had to be ruling out the lesser of evils, and he hoped he would make the cut.

"I guess that would work for a while. I would expect you to hold up your end of the agreement to keep our relationship strictly professional." Then she turned and met his gaze. "And don't call me that again. *Ever.*"

She strode from the conference room without looking back.

The instinct to chase out after her pulsed through him, just as it had when she'd left the police interview. What would he do? Try to toss her over his shoulder like a modern-day Cro-Magnon, so he could take her back to his cave? He held onto the arms of his seat until the impulse passed and then leaned his elbows on his knees and lowered his head into his splayed hands.

What was wrong with him?

Tatiana hadn't asked for his help, so this overwhelming surge of protectiveness he felt for her and their baby made no sense. He couldn't even use the pregnancy as an excuse. Before she'd told him the news, he'd wanted to shield her from the media, her father and even his own family members.

This was worse. He longed to envelop her and the baby in safety. Just the thought of it made him grin. As if she would ever allow any of that. She was a strong, independent woman. But, for the moment, anyway, he'd won. She would be safe with him at his condo, which offered a good security system, and the neighborhood watch committee was always on volunteer duty.

However, her staying at his place presented a whole new set of problems. They'd just determined that their affair had been a one-off, and now they would be *roommates*? How was he supposed to even sleep, knowing she was in bed a floor away with that mass of silky hair draped all over the pillow and her amazing legs beneath the blankets? Moving her in with him would do just the opposite of cooling his desire for her, just as it would flame rather than extinguish speculation that they were involved or, later, that the child could be his. And what was he supposed to tell his relatives when they found out he was housing a fugitive's daughter?

As he'd told her, it wasn't a perfect solution, but at least she'd be close by, where he could watch out for her. It would also give him more time to convince her that he was right that they should marry. But why was he pushing so hard for this? Instead of running away like some guys did when they learned that the fun and games had made them fathers, he was chasing after a woman he barely knew with a ring she didn't want. He wished he could believe it was only because he loved a challenge. The search for the best deal or a superior product was the nature of his life's work. So why did he suspect that he might have proposed this "marriage of convenience" for his own sake as much as the child's or even Tatiana's?

"THIS ISN'T EXACTLY how I planned to move into my new place," Tatiana called into the void of Travis's condo after work that evening.

He'd vanished down one of the shiny hardwood hallways after he'd let her inside, leaving her standing in the entry under a crystal chandelier that cast geometric patterns of light onto the weave of a Persian rug. She pulled the collar of her long down coat closer around her neck and waited, snow from her warm winter boots melting on the mat. It gave her too much time to think and second-guess.

Why had Travis been so determined that she should stay with him? Worse than that, why had she *agreed*? She'd been off her game since taking the test and learning about the charges her dad faced, but that was still no excuse. She barely knew Travis. At least he'd dropped that marriage nonsense. At first, she'd thought it might have been a joke, or maybe a knee-jerk reaction to the news about the baby, but had it been more than that? Had he been trying to help his family lure her and her father into a police trap?

"You probably thought you'd have more luggage."

She startled as Travis followed his words into the room. At least she hadn't been talking to herself out loud.

"What are you saying?"

He pointed to her purse, computer bag and dress boots, the only items she'd had the chance to bring with her.

"I never expected to have to sneak out the service entrance and escape in the back of a corporate cargo van, either." She stepped out of her boots and set them next to the door, then removed her parka. "Has Miles Kettering ever driven passengers before, or has it only been Colton Plastics products that he delivers in that van?"

"I doubt it."

"You could have mentioned that before I got in. I get carsick in the back seat. That's when I'm not pregnant."

"Sorry about that. And forgive my manners." He took her coat and hung it in the closet near the front door. "I guess you could have stopped and held an impromptu press conference instead."

She responded to his grin with a frown. "That's okay. I've had enough drama for one day, thank you."

Just the thought of having to stand in front of all those cameras, the microphones jammed in her face, made her woozy again, but she didn't tell him that. She wouldn't be able to hide from the media forever, though. Another meeting with the police would be necessary, too, so she was grateful for the reprieve.

She stretched her neck from side to side. Even if by afternoon she'd finally been able to focus on first-day tasks at work, she'd never once relaxed, always sensing that an ambush was coming. Now she had tight shoulders and a headache from the strain, along with new restrictions about what over-the-counter medications she could use.

"Want the grand tour?" he asked.

"I guess so."

"Now don't get too excited about it." He stepped backward into the great room, extending his hands, palms up, like an official tour guide. "We're walking. We're walking."

She followed in her bare feet, regretting her decision to skip tights that morning.

"Wow, you weren't lying when you said your condo was huge," she said as she took in the vaulted ceilings and walls of windows.

What he hadn't mentioned was how nice it was. Decorating-magazine nice if the magazine had been published a few decades back. The luxurious sectional would swallow a youth baseball team, but from the look of it, no sticky little hands had ever smudged its buff color. Same for the massive television on the wall and the elaborate wood tables and lamps. No children would ever be allowed to touch the pricey bric-a-brac methodically arranged around the room. Including theirs.

"I don't lie," he said.

She twisted and pretended to study a bowl filled with blown-glass balls. They both knew Travis had fibbed to the police *for her* just that morning. She'd repeated a lie as well about not speaking with her dad, but he couldn't know that.

"You can still change your mind about having me stay here," she said, brushing her fingertips over the bumpy surface of the glass.

"I won't."

"Because it will create a lot of speculation about, well, us, when there isn't an *us*."

"I said I won't. There's no rush for you to find your own place. Until things settle down around here…"

"Fine." Tatiana was more relieved than she would have expected.

He led her through the kitchen, with its granite countertops and dark wood cabinets too tall for an average human to reach, and then down the hall. He stopped at each bedroom and the bath. The master suite was more of the same but with meticulously arranged clothes and shoes in the walk-in closet. All were perfectly decorated, yet sterile. As if no one lived in the house.

"Is this where you disappeared to when you deserted me earlier?"

"Needed to change out of my work clothes," he said with a shrug. "I wish you could, too."

For the first time, Tatiana noticed that he'd traded the white pinpoint-collared shirt and dark tailored trousers for a pair of crisp khaki pants and another dress shirt, this one in light blue.

"This is you dressed *down*?" She pointed to his sleeves that he'd rolled to the elbows.

"Yeah." He lowered his gaze from shirt to pants to brown wing tips. "Why?"

Even as rough as the day had been, she couldn't help but to smile. Sure, she'd seen Travis Colton impeccably dressed for the office—and then in nothing at all—but she had no idea what he looked like in his regular life. That he was always so buttoned up surprised her. He'd been right earlier. They *really* didn't know each other well.

"Never mind," she said. "Just don't be shocked when you see my sweatpants later. Speaking of clothing, I still need to stop by the extended stay to get mine."

"I'll drive you there after dinner. Then we can pick up your car and drop it off at the rental agency while it's still dark. That is, if you're not too tired."

"That'll be fine," she said automatically. She didn't want to admit that she could have fallen asleep standing right in front of him.

He gestured for her to pass by him into the mammoth master bath, which contained a jetted tub, expansive counter with double sinks, glass-walled shower and private toilet.

"Now you've set my expectations too high." She backed out of the space that, despite its size, felt too small and intimate for them to share. "The lower level probably has concrete floors and a washtub sink to soak my laundry."

"Hardly."

Travis finished off showing her the upper level and then headed downstairs, opening a door and flipping the light switch when he reached the landing.

Another TV viewing area greeted them, less formal than the one upstairs. Down the hall, Travis showed off another sumptuous bedroom suite and bath, plus a fully equipped home office.

"Where's the laundry tub?" Tatiana asked when the tour ended.

"I could install one if you like."

She smiled. "I'll see if I can get by without it."

As they returned upstairs, he spoke over his shoulder. "Will it do for your temporary lodging?"

"I guess it'll pass." In the great room, she glanced around again, more curious than she cared to admit. "Did you decorate it yourself, or did you hire a professional?"

Why didn't she come out and ask if his girlfriend had selected the furniture and décor? Or more than that, if he had a significant other whom he might ask to make those choices for him? His private life wasn't her business, though, even if she was carrying his child. He waited until they were upstairs to answer. "Professional. My sister, Melissa, recommended that I hire one when she stopped by six months after I moved in. She noticed my abundance of unopened boxes. And lack of furniture. I'd been putting most of my energy into growing Colton Plastics, so I wasn't home much."

"Looks like your work at CP paid off if you can afford a place like this."

He slowly scanned the room as if trying to see it through her eyes.

"It's a little fancy for me," he said with a shrug. "Maybe I should have been more involved with the process, but at least it's finished. I usually spend most of my time downstairs, anyway. It feels less like a mausoleum."

Tatiana followed him into the kitchen, still considering what he'd said. Why did he choose to live in a house that was so sterile, anyway? She wanted to believe it was an outward display of the cold man he was inside, one so incapable of being truly intimate with someone that he'd nearly sprinted from her bed. Only that dark view of him didn't fit with his actions since that morning. Instead of running away when she'd told him she was pregnant, he'd proposed and given her space in his home after she refused. Not any place, either, but the only part of it where he felt comfortable. Was there a chance that she might be wrong about him?

"Are you hungry?" Without waiting for an answer, he pulled out a block of parmesan cheese and some sort of meat out of the refrigerator.

"Famished." Tatiana had been too nauseated most of the day to eat, so her appetite was making up for it now. She didn't mention that she was also so exhausted that her limbs felt numb.

"Why don't you go downstairs and wash up while I make something? There are towels in the linen closet."

"You don't need to cook for me. I'm pregnant, not bedridden. Anyway, you're already giving me a place to stay, and—"

He waved the hand holding the cheese as if to brush away her comment.

"I have to eat, too." Setting the refrigerated items on the counter, he stepped to his pantry and pulled out a box of jumbo rigatoni. "I'm used to cooking for one, and I can easily double that. Since you're now eating for *two*, we need to make sure you're getting regular meals.

"Go on then. If you'd like something to change into, I can probably find some comfortable clothes that you—"

She shook her head before he could finish. "Really. I'll be fine until we pick up my things. Anyway, you and I have different definitions of 'comfortable.'"

He glanced down at his clothes again and then frowned at her. "Beggars can't be choosers."

"Good thing I wasn't begging."

She slipped out of the kitchen before he could offer again. She'd retreated from situations more today than she ever had, but the last thing she'd needed then was to breathe in his lingering scent on some old sweatshirt, if he even owned something that casual. She didn't need more reminders of their night together. Didn't need to recall the rough brush of his fingers over her skin, their calluses a surprise from a man who completed most of his work on a laptop. She was already remembering too much just being in his home. *His* home? It would be theirs, at least for a while.

Her weariness multiplied with each footfall on the stairs to the lower level and down the hall to the guest suite. Tatiana stepped into the bathroom, but then headed across the hall into the bedroom. Covered with a cozy-looking gray comforter and a mess of navy and white pillows, the bed was the most inviting thing she'd seen all day.

She needed to lie down. Just for a few minutes. Then she would be ready to explain to Travis why she couldn't stay in his condo. But as she sank back into the amazing mattress and onto the softest pillow ever made, images of the man a floor above her sneaked into her thoughts. Memories of that smile, those warm eyes and those gifted hands drew her into sleep.

Chapter Five

"Wake up, Sleeping Beauty."

Tatiana awoke to the words and blinked in the darkened room, the only illumination coming from some unfamiliar hallway. Who was speaking? Where the heck was she? A click of a switch and the burst of a lamp's light answered her questions. Travis stood in the doorway, his face partially hidden in shadow.

"Oh. It's you." The rest of the details filled in quickly. She searched the table for a clock. "What time is it? I just wanted to lie down for a few minutes."

"That was—" he paused to glance at his watch "—about an hour ago."

"What?" She pushed up on her elbows and shot a glance at the open slats of the blinds. Either he was telling the truth or dusk was coming extra early for this time of year.

"I called you when dinner was ready. Several times, in fact. Then I came down here to make sure you were okay. You were sleeping peacefully, and you'd looked so tired earlier, so I let you rest for a while."

Tatiana sat up quickly, immediately regretting it when Travis's face shifted in and out of focus. After waiting a few seconds for her head to clear again, she tossed back the comforter that she'd pulled over her and shifted her feet to the floor. "Jet lag."

"And a baby," he added. "Here. You're going to need this."

From under his arm, he pulled out a zippered gray Detroit Lions sweatshirt and tossed it on the bed. He'd had one after all, though she would bet her first paycheck that he'd dug it out of the back of his closet and that it had never been worn.

But as she slid her arms into the sleeves, the scents of sandalwood and musk from his cologne enveloped her. That triggered memories too pleasant for him to be standing in the bedroom doorway while she still lounged on the bed. Clearly, she would have lost that bet.

"I know you said you didn't need it, but it gets cold in this house, especially downstairs."

He pointed to the shawl-collared cardigan he'd pulled on over his "casual" dress shirt. Now that she would have expected.

"Thanks. I appreciate it." As she slid on the sweatshirt, she glanced past him out the doorway. "Did you say 'dinner'?"

"I did. It's cold now, too."

She pointed to the door. "Lead the way."

Within minutes she was seated in one of the straightback chairs across from Travis at the kitchen table and forcing herself not to shovel in her dinner with her hands. She swallowed another bite of amazingness before pausing to take a drink from her glass of milk.

"Dinner is great. What did you say was in it again?"

"Prosciutto, peas, pinot grigio, mushrooms and the pasta." He washed down his bite with a swig of milk and then wiped his mouth with a napkin. "I've cooked off the alcohol. Don't worry. All those things are mixed with the healthy stuff. You know, butter and heavy cream."

"Are you trying to feed me or fatten me up like a Thanksgiving turkey?"

Tatiana took another bite, closing her eyes to savor it. When she opened them again, she caught Travis watching her. He quickly looked away.

"How'd you get to be such a great cook?"

He shrugged. "I like to eat. Since I was a bachelor and determined to stay that way, I figured I needed to learn. At least until I could afford a cook."

"You could afford one now, couldn't you?" She didn't even touch on the other subject. When he'd told her six weeks before that he was a confirmed bachelor, she'd held back from asking why he'd made that decision. Now that he'd offered to trade in his bachelor card for her just that afternoon, she was more interested in what had changed.

"I could. But somewhere along the way, I started to love to cook." He grinned at that. "Anyway, watching you eat, I have to wonder if you've had a decent meal in months."

"I've been so hungry lately." She brushed her fork back and forth through the rigatoni and peas. "That is, when I haven't been too nauseated to eat."

"Sorry if I added to the problem by delivering the bad news, you know, about your dad. That could make anyone lose her appetite." He popped up from the table and returned with a pan. At her nod, he ladled a second serving.

"I should have known better than to believe it would just go away."

"Why's that?"

She cleared her throat. How much had she given away? Just because she recognized that the bizarre story would linger in Grave Gulch didn't mean she'd suspected why it should.

"I mean, big news stories like that don't fade away in small cities like Grave Gulch. Even after suspects are exonerated."

He stared at her, his fork pausing on the way to his mouth, so she dipped her chin and took another bite. This one was more difficult to swallow.

"You still don't believe your father is guilty?" He lowered the fork to his plate again, the noodles he'd stabbed still laced through its tines.

"Why do you care so much what I think?" Now she was the one watching *him.* Was she naive to think only of his generosity in proposing marriage and then offering her a place to stay, without considering his motives? She should remain on guard around Travis until she knew what was in it for him.

"I just figured you haven't had many people to talk with about it."

Her fork dropped to her plate, so she quickly reached for it. "You think I don't have friends?"

"I didn't say that. I just thought you could use some support. After today."

He was right that she hadn't spoken much about it with her few remaining friends in Grave Gulch. Mostly because no one bothered to ask. So, no matter how much of a risk it was to trust anyone, she couldn't resist answering.

"The truth is I don't know what to believe."

"I get that. You heard what Troy and Bryce said though. The police have DNA evidence to place your dad at the scene. Maybe they don't know *why* he did it, but they know he did."

"They were certain last time, too."

Travis pushed his plate aside, planted his elbows on the table and cupped his chin in his hands, appearing ready to listen.

"When my father was arrested, the idea that he could be a murderer seemed ludicrous to me. He couldn't have killed anyone. Dad told me there had been a mistake, and he wouldn't let me visit him in jail, so…"

She shrugged, considering whether to share the rest. "I needed to get away. I don't even know how I settled on Paris other than it was on the other side of the world. I took a vacation from work like I never did, hunted for a short-term apartment rental, and booked a flight. I knew I was running away, but I couldn't help it."

"No one could blame you for that."

"If you'd met my dad, you'd understand why none of this made sense to me. A great father. A devoted husband. I couldn't get him to leave Mom's bedside for more than a half hour at a time during the whole week before she passed."

"I'm sure there were—*are*—good things about your father."

She pointed at him from across the table with her fork. "Please don't tell me that some serial killers spoil their cats or take their kids to Sunday school."

"I wasn't going to say that." At her glare, Travis added, "Not in those *specific* words."

"At least you're being honest. I would probably tell you the same thing if our roles were reversed."

"And I would be declaring Frank Colton's innocence from the nearest rooftop, whether I suspected him or not and whether he would have done the same for me or not."

Part of his comment would have made her squirm about her own suspicions if the second part hadn't caught her attention. She would have asked what those words about his father had meant, but he shifted in his chair and looked away. There were no murder suspects in his family, but clearly, the Coltons had their problems, too.

"I hate to admit it, but I was *relieved* when the supposed evidence disappeared."

"You heard what my cousins said about Randall Bowe, the forensic scientist, right? He's accused of falsifying evidence in many cases. Like one where a woman was accused of bludgeoning her husband with a paperweight and another in which an innocent man was convicted of killing his boss. He's also facing charges that he removed evidence, causing not one but *two* murderers to go free."

His sad look served as a reminder that her father was one of the suspects in question.

"Now I don't know what to think," she admitted. "Could my dad's case have been a setup, too? Was evidence falsified? I don't even think my dad knew that Bowe guy. Could someone have had something against my dad? If he hadn't said—"

"Who said?"

Tatiana's shoulders tightened. What was she doing? She knew better than to let her guard down around Travis Colton. She'd done that once. Look where that had gotten her. To buy time, she took another bite of pasta, which was getting cold again.

"Who said?" he repeated.

"I meant *they.* Your cousins. They said, you know, that there's more evidence."

He pinched his brows together, as if he didn't believe her, but then his forehead smoothed again. Had he bought it? She needed to be more careful in what she said to Travis. It didn't matter that he was easy to talk to. Yes, he seemed to be concerned with her safety as the mother of his child, even if he didn't technically care about *her.*

"I wouldn't lead with that when you meet with the police again."

"With what?"

"That you were glad the evidence went missing. You might not want to tell them that if you expect them to believe the rest of your statement." He sank back into the chair, grinning, but then he sat up again. "I won't be there to help you next time."

"I doubt your cousins will be sad that you'll miss it. I'm definitely not looking forward to another meeting with your family."

"Then there's something you should know."

"What do you mean?"

As if to answer his question, the doorbell rang to the tune of the song "Reveille." She turned in the direction of the entry.

"You told the police to come *here*? Why'd you bother sending them away the first time? Did you just want to get them out of the office?" She clenched her jaw. "I knew I shouldn't have trusted you."

A flash of hurt appeared in his eyes before he turned away and started toward the door.

"It's not what you think. Really." He flipped the switches for the interior and exterior lights, tapped the code on the security system, and opened the front door.

A woman in a heavy coat stood on the porch, an equally bundled child in her arms.

"Hey, Desiree," Travis said. "Good to see you."

"I really appreciate this."

"No problem at all."

As Desiree stepped inside her hood fell back to reveal a mass of long, brown curly hair, falling loose around her stunning face and accenting her light-brown complexion. Something about the shape of her deep brown eyes struck Tatiana as familiar, but she didn't think they'd met before.

"Hey, little man." Travis stepped closer and brushed his fingertips over the boy's beanie.

The child's hazel eyes stared out at them both before he buried his face against the woman's coat.

"Someone's being shy tonight," he said.

"You remember Travis, don't you, Danny?"

But even as Desiree reassured the child, twin lines of worry appeared between her delicate brows. She shifted the boy's weight on her hip, the diaper bag slipping off her opposite shoulder and catching on her elbow.

Clearly, the woman wasn't an on-duty police officer, but who was she, and what was she to Travis? For that matter, what was his relationship to the child? Was Tatiana's baby the only one Travis had fathered? Danny didn't seem to know him too well, but that didn't mean the boy couldn't be his.

After Travis relieved her of the items she carried, Desiree pulled off Danny's hat and unzipped his coat.

"You know, I wouldn't have asked if, well, I wasn't—"

"Desperate?" he finished for Desiree. "Don't worry. My feelings won't be hurt if I wasn't the first person you called. Or the second or…"

He paused, as if waiting for her to fill in the blank.

"The sixth," Desiree admitted.

"Ouch."

"But I also didn't expect you to say yes. The others told me not to bother asking you. Usually, you wouldn't even be home at this time of night."

As the two of them spoke, Tatiana couldn't help watching the boy, with his crop of messy brown hair. Would her own child have a lot of hair at birth? Would he or she be shy like Danny or outgoing?

Desiree glanced at Tatiana, who leaned against the wall, as if only then noticing she was there.

"You didn't tell me I was interrupting something."

"You're not," he said.

Tatiana gestured toward Desiree. "You haven't told me what's going on here, either."

Travis gestured toward his guest. "I'd like you to meet Desiree Colton and her son, Danny. He's a big boy. Twenty months."

"Sister or cousin?" Tatiana asked, her cheeks heating. Had she really been jealous of one of his relatives? They weren't in a relationship, anyway. She had no claim over him at all.

"Cousin," Desiree said.

No wonder she'd looked familiar. "Troy's sister?"

"You know my little brother? I take no responsibility for any boneheaded thing he said."

Tatiana turned back to Travis. She should have known better. What had she told him about her dad? Was there anything that he could relay to the police to help them find him?

"Does she work at the police department, too?"

Desiree answered for herself. "Just part-time, so I can be home with this little guy. I'm a sketch artist."

Tatiana pinned Travis with her stare. "It wasn't enough that you let those two guys ambush me at work today. Now you're distracting me with delicious food so you can have another law enforcement agent show up to do a sketch of my dad? They have his *mug shot* on file."

Desiree stared wide-eyed at her. Her son's bottom lip trembled.

"No." Travis shook his head several times. "You've got it all wrong."

"What is she talking about?" his cousin wanted to know.

"Desiree, this is Tatiana Davison, my co-CEO at Colton Plastics. And current houseguest."

"*Davison? Houseguest*?" She spoke both words as though they were equally shocking. "Maybe I should just call the station and say I can't come in, after all."

"Now why would you do that?" Travis held out his arms to Danny, but the boy only stared at his hands without moving. "He'll be fine with me. With both of us."

"You didn't tell me someone else would be here when I called," Desiree insisted.

"Don't worry. He'll be safe. We won't let anything happen to him again."

Again? Tatiana was trying to make sense of his words when he finally turned back to her.

"Desiree was called in last-minute to the department for a case. She phoned while you were napping. She was looking for an emergency sitter for Danny. I volunteered us."

"Oh." Tatiana couldn't decide which surprised her more—that a single man with no children had volunteered to provide childcare for his cousin or that he'd intended to do it with her. Was this a statement about his future role as a father or the way they'd co-parent their own baby?

To keep from asking those questions in front of his cousin, Tatiana spoke to Desiree instead. "I'm sorry for overreacting to your showing up here. It's been a really long day."

"That's okay. I've had a few of those myself," Desiree said.

Tatiana cleared her throat. "Did Travis say that something happened to Danny?"

His cousin nodded. "In January, he was abducted."

Tatiana gasped. "That's awful. I'm so sorry."

"Thanks. He was recovered quickly, with no injuries, but I've never been so scared in my life. So, you'll understand if I'm just not comfortable—"

"I totally get it. I would be so nervous to even leave if it were," she paused to clear her throat, "my son."

She couldn't imagine the fear and agony she would have experienced if someone had taken her child. Though she hadn't even met her baby yet, the thought of a loss like that nearly dragged her to her knees.

"You do what makes you most comfortable," Tatiana

told her. "But I am happy to help Travis with Danny if you decide you can leave him."

Desiree nodded but stood staring at her feet.

Travis stepped forward. "Remember, Tatiana isn't accused of any crime. And we can't help who our fathers are."

His rough attempt at humor must have helped her escape from her dark thoughts as she glanced up and chuckled. "You've got that right. Why do you think I'm a single mother by choice?"

"So?" Travis pressed. "Do you feel comfortable enough to leave him? Remember, the whole family will descend on me like a wildfire if I so much as tear his fingernail."

"That's true." Finally, Desiree nodded. "Danny, you get to play here for a while."

Tatiana approached slowly then, the child regarding her with caution. When she was close to them, Danny reached out and came willingly into her arms. She wasn't prepared for the warmth that spread inside of her. Perhaps it was the hormones from the pregnancy or simply the anticipation of holding her own child that autumn, but the sensation was startling and new.

As Travis closed the door, after receiving Desiree's promise that she wouldn't report at the station that Tatiana was staying with him, he turned back to her. They exchanged a look as tender as the range of emotions filling her.

"Guess, for tonight at least, we're in this together."

Didn't he see that because of the existence of their own baby, his words spanned beyond a single evening? They were connected now, whether they liked it or not. She wouldn't read more into their relationship than was there though. She'd made that mistake with him once before.

But that didn't contain her curiosity. She wasn't sure what to make of many things about him today, from his protectiveness of her and amazing cooking to his kindness involving Desiree's child. Tatiana was certain of one thing though: she really liked this softer side of Travis Colton.

Chapter Six

An hour later, Travis sank with a sigh back into the cushion of the sectional next to Danny, who sat with his legs spread wide as only toddlers could do comfortably. A pile of solid-wood blocks buried his tiny legs. Every minute or so, the child would try to toss a block over the back of the sofa, or, worse, into Travis's lap, narrowly missing parts that were important to him.

"Guess the blocks weren't a great idea," he said, as he tweaked the little boy on the nose. He hadn't thought the whole babysitting plan through, either, but it hadn't turned out too badly with Tatiana there. How was he supposed to use this time with his cousin's son to show off his childcare knowledge when he had almost zero of it? Was this supposed to convince Tatiana that he would be a good father to their unborn child?

His lack of experience with kids was just one of the reasons Desiree had been nervous about leaving Danny with them. Who could blame her for being cautious after her son had been kidnapped? If he'd informed her that Len Davison's daughter was staying with him, cousins or not, Desiree would have turned him down flat. That was why he hadn't mentioned it.

"Probably not the O's cereal, either," she said, as she pulled her head away from the cushion.

Tatiana pointed to his end of the sectional. "You'll be finding those little treats in your sofa for weeks."

"Now you tell me."

"I tried. You weren't listening."

She pulled the blanket she'd tucked around her lap higher so that it covered part of her blouse. Though she'd napped earlier, she still looked as though she could have fallen asleep right there, even with the boy's constant chatter.

"More," Danny announced as he slid down and smeared his grimy hands over the coffee table.

Travis reached for the damp paper towel and tried to wipe the toddler's hands again, but it quickly transformed into a chase game with a trail of giggles in its wake. Yeah, he could get used to this, he thought with a grin. Well, if he could learn to put up with a little more dirt. And if he could do better job with those little tab things on diapers than he had that night.

"I think you've had enough, buddy," Travis told Danny, still laughing.

"Want more." The toddler's bottom lip quivered.

Travis froze. He didn't know a lot about kids, but he recognized that waterworks were coming.

"Help," he said out the side of his mouth.

Tatiana grinned. "CP co-CEO brought down by an opponent less than three feet tall."

She climbed down on the rug centered beneath the coffee table and tucked her knees under her skirt, her pink-painted toes peeking out on one side.

"Want to build a house, Danny?" Already, she was

gathering some cylindrical and triangular-shaped blocks off the floor and piling them on the table.

"House?" Danny called out.

Cereal forgotten, the toddler grabbed blocks from the floor and dumped them on the tabletop.

"Thank you, sir," she told him, not batting an eye over the noise or the mess.

Tatiana collected more from the floor and set them side by side for a base. The next layer she rested lengthwise to construct a perimeter, and then she stood a few more on their ends. The boy squeezed in front of her and knocked the whole structure off the table. She just laughed. Caring for Danny was easy for her. Effortless. Would it ever be that way for him, even with their own child? Would he be able to let go and really enjoy being a parent? Would he love his child for the person he was instead of trying to make him or her into someone else?

"Hey, are we building houses or crashing them?" Tatiana asked, and then caught the boy around the waist and tickled his belly. More giggles erupted.

"That was a cool trick."

"What do you mean?" She started putting the blocks back on the table, with Danny knocking off each one as she did it. "Are you talking about distraction? That's an essential babysitting skill."

"You must have babysat a lot."

"Just a few times for neighbors. But, if I were to guess, I'd say this is the first time you've ever watched anyone's kids."

"Guilty." He chuckled and shook his head. "Was it so obvious?"

"There were a few hints. Like when you offered Danny some water. *In a glass.*"

"Good save, finding that sippy cup in his bag." He frowned, imagining the disaster that could have been.

"The O's, too. I was surprised you let him eat or drink anything in here." She waved her arm to indicate the great room.

"I'll admit, it was tough, but in the end, it's just a house."

She gave him an odd look. "I was so glad that Desiree decided she could trust us with Danny. I'm not sure I would have been brave enough if the roles were reversed."

Having heard his name, the toddler looked up from his demolition project, but the attraction of crashing blocks drew him back to it again.

"It was an awful time for our whole family," Travis admitted.

"I didn't remember the names of the people involved, but I had read about the abduction when I was here for my interview."

They exchanged a look as they did every time either of them mentioned her earlier visit. Then she brushed her finger over Danny's cheek, causing the child to squirm.

"I'm so glad everything turned out okay. Desiree must have been so worried. Didn't the kidnapper turn out to be a grandma or someone, desperate to get police to look at her relative's murder case again?"

"You have a good memory. It was a grandmother. Hannah McPherson was trying to help her granddaughter, Everleigh Emerson, who was accused of murdering her estranged husband. She was later exonerated, though."

"You mentioned that case before. Do you know these people personally?"

"I do now. Everleigh's my future sister-in-law. Engaged to my brother Clarke, the private investigator. He started out protecting her from her husband's real murderer, and then, well…" He let his words fall away and then grinned.

"He was really attentive to his assignment."

She tilted her head to the side in that endearing way he remembered from that night he was supposed to forget.

"Exactly," he managed. "It was when Clarke and the GGPD started looking closer at Everleigh's case that they started seeing inconsistencies in some of Randall Bowe's other cases."

"Guess we know how that turned out."

"Sorry," he said.

"I'm glad it worked out well for your brother and his fiancée."

"That's kind of you. I know it wasn't great for your dad."

The sadness filling her eyes squeezed something inside him that he couldn't quite define. Did she feel alone like he did? At least she had an excuse. She was an only child who'd lost her mother, and her father must have become a stranger to her. How could his situation even compare to that when he was surrounded by more Coltons than should ever live in one city?

Tatiana lowered her gaze and started building again. With a squeal, Danny scrambled over once more to begin his demolition work. Travis couldn't resist getting in on the action, sliding to the floor on the opposite side of the table and starting his own construction project. Delighted with that idea, the toddler moved between them to destroy both castles by turns.

"You're going to be a great mom." Travis licked his lips, surprised by his own words. But he wouldn't take them back, either. He could easily picture her with their child nestled at her breast.

She lifted a brow when she looked back at him. "How do you know that? Just because I can distract a busy almost-two-year-old?"

"You're a natural with him."

"You're the one who claimed to be a confirmed bachelor and just happened to have a whole set of blocks around the house for a kid to play with."

"They weren't so bad after all?" He waited for her headshake before he continued. "I only kept a few things when Mom insisted that my brothers, sister and I go through our stuff and clear it out of her house. I didn't need any Little League trophies, but I wanted the blocks."

He considered for a few seconds whether to admit more and then did it anyway. "I have the metal and the plastic brick building sets, too, but I thought the pieces might be too small for the little dude here."

"Good thinking about the choking hazards. Your cousin will never leave him with anyone again if he ends up at the ER tonight."

"She's definitely had more than her share of parental scares."

Tatiana pointed to the blocks that Travis had started lining up in a train track of sorts, which the boy was busy scattering with his foot. "Didn't your siblings want any of that stuff?"

"I told you I had nothing in common with them. While they were playing cops and robbers, I was off in the corner building a skyscraper or an amusement park."

"It's no wonder that you ended up founding and building Colton Plastics. It was in you from the beginning." Travis swallowed and kept working on his failing train track. He couldn't risk looking at her. Was it because of her own engineering background that she just seemed to *get* him?

"My focus at Colton Plastics has always been on building a solid *company,* more than a specific product. Plastic businesses design and manufacture parts to meet other companies' needs, like car interiors and exterior cases for printers, and I wanted CP to stand for quality in that arena." He stopped as Danny dismantled the last piece of his railroad and shook his head, grinning at the mess.

"My business degree made me the right person to build CP, but it never would have worked without the engineering expertise that Constantine Niarchos provided." He gestured to her destroyed block building on the table and smiled. "Now you'll fulfill that critical role with a more appropriate title as co-CEO."

She shook her head. "I didn't mean to suggest you needed an engineering degree. I'm just saying that all the building you did as a kid showed you had a vision of making something."

"Not everyone thought it was inevitable that I would start a company. Or thought it would succeed when I did."

She lifted her chin. "Well, you proved them wrong, didn't you?"

"I guess so."

"They have to be proud of you."

"You would think."

Frank Colton's face appeared in his son's thoughts

then, always supplying just enough apprehension to make Travis doubt himself.

Tatiana squinted as if his comment confused her.

"What parent wouldn't be bragging about what you've accomplished? CP is not just surviving. It's *thriving*. I did my research. I would never have agreed to join the company if it hadn't been in a good position."

Her thoughts must have drifted in the same direction as his then, as she swallowed visibly and turned to stare out the wall of windows into the darkness beyond.

"I hope it stays that way," she said after several seconds.

"CP will weather all this fine," he said. "We all will."

He wished she would look at him, so that he could give her an emphatic nod, sure enough to convince them both.

"Do you think they'll ever leave me alone to be able to raise my baby?"

She pointed into the darkness and then this time met his gaze. He couldn't allow himself to feel hurt that she hadn't included him in the question. She just didn't know yet how determined he was to be involved in his child's life, and he could be stubborn when he wanted something.

"Do you mean the police or the media?" he asked, stalling for time until he could come up with a better answer.

"Both."

"Honestly, I don't know. Until they locate your dad, I don't think so."

She pointed to the window.

"Do you think the police are out there watching us now?"

"After all the trouble we went through to get you here? I don't think—"

He stopped himself since they had no way of knowing. Even if Desiree had said she wouldn't inform the others that Tatiana was staying there. Would she keep her word?

"One way to find out." He marched into the foyer, switched into his boots, and pulled on the parka he only wore when he used the snow blower on the driveway. "Would you mind staying with Danny a few minutes?"

"That's fine." She picked up the boy and held him close to her until he squirmed to get down. "Be careful out there."

"It'll be fine. We're probably just getting spooked." He knew *he* was.

He flipped off the outside lights and then darkened the foyer as well. This was silly. He was a Colton, even if he was a square peg trying to squeeze in the round holes on their family tree. The GGPD wouldn't waste time tracking his whereabouts or even those of his houseguest. They had to have better leads on Len Davison than that.

Still, rethinking his first idea, he jogged down the stairs to the lower level. Without turning on any lights, he enabled the security system and exited through the sliding door. He moved as quietly as possible across the small backyard, trying to recall the obstacles he needed to avoid, all hidden beneath the eight inches of snow that had collected within the perimeter of the privacy fence. At the back of his property, he carefully unlatched the gate, hoping the squeak he'd battled with in the fall hadn't returned. Thankfully, it hadn't.

He kept one hand on the wood as he crossed behind

his property and the next. As he neared the edge of his neighbor's fence, he held his breath and then peeked around the corner.

He spied a patrol car parked on the side street. Its headlights and taillights were turned off, but its engine was running. Also, he would have recognized the dull light of the laptop mounted in the dash anywhere. He backed away from the corner, whirled around and retraced his steps to his property. After rounding the corner, he carefully slid along the fence toward the street, hoping none of his neighbors picked this moment to get nosy.

Just like on the other side, another patrol car was parked in front of the next building. He had to force himself not to move too quickly, but he needed to get back to Tatiana. Was it because he wanted to shield her again? He wasn't sure.

Once inside, he paused to disable the alarm but sensed he wasn't alone. As his eyes adjusted to the near absence of light, he recognized the outline of Tatiana, who sat on the steps.

"Hi," she whispered.

He flipped on a floor lamp, and the rest of the picture filled in. She cradled a sleeping Danny in her arms. He'd imagined a similar scene earlier, though that baby had been theirs. If he hadn't already felt protective over her and their unborn child, this image would have awakened that instinct, but now it magnified that need into something visceral. He had to protect her, and something told him it was from far more than only police working a murder investigation.

"How'd you get him to sleep?"

She held her finger to her lips and then spoke in low

tones. "One minute he was sitting by me, knocking down more towers, and the next, he was curled up on the floor by the couch. Guess he ran out of gas."

He nodded, relieved that his baby cousin, and the woman holding him, were safe.

"I checked outside," he began. He dreaded having to share what felt like a betrayal. Not of his family. Of *her*.

Her lips lifted, but her smile was a sad one.

"You don't have to tell me. I know they're out there. You were right. They're never going to leave me alone."

He yanked his cell phone from his back pocket, scrolled through the contacts, and clicked on one to dial. The recipient of his call answered on the second ring.

"What's up, Travis?"

"Hey, Melissa. You know exactly what's up. I thought it was time for you to come over for a little brother-sister chat."

Chapter Seven

After his doorbell rang for the second time in thirty minutes, Travis sneaked a peek at Tatiana, who'd been pacing since they'd returned upstairs. More so since Desiree had picked up her son. Maybe he should have run the idea of Melissa's visit past his houseguest before he called in the chief of police.

"You okay?"

Tatiana nodded, though it was clear she wasn't. He resisted the temptation to rush over to comfort her. There was already one woman on her way over, who'd be furious when she arrived.

He crossed to the entry and pulled open the door.

"Hello, *brother*. Thanks for the nice invitation."

Melissa stood on the porch with her puffer jacket unzipped over a Michigan State sweatshirt, her hair shoved up in a messy ponytail. The cuffs of her jeans were half in and half out of her boots. She pressed by him without waiting to be invited in. A big sister's prerogative, he supposed, though he would have preferred that she at least take off her footwear.

"I saw Desiree leaving here with Danny."

"You weren't in one of those stakeout cars, were you?"

She rolled her blue eyes, the one trait that she had in

common with all three of her brothers. "It's not really a stakeout if the cars are marked. But, no, I wasn't in one of the surveillance vehicles."

"I still can't believe Desiree left me here taking care of her son while she went into the station to report on my houseguest. And what are you doing about the leak at the GGPD? The press knew Troy and Bryce would be questioning Tatiana today, and you haven't even made a public announcement about the serial killer theory."

"Desiree didn't tell us," she said, addressing his earlier comment first. "We already knew Tatiana was here, little brother. It was an easy guess after you were protecting her like a Doberman at the office."

"I wasn't—"

Melissa lifted a hand to interrupt him. "And I'll handle the leak *if* there's one in my department.

"Anyway, I can't believe you summoned *me* over here when I was in my comfy pj's." She tapped her collarbone over her coat. "I'm the *chief* of police."

"Sorry I didn't follow your chain of command, but you're the only sister I have at the police department."

"I don't know what you were thinking when you allowed—"

"You mean *invited*?"

She dismissed Travis as only an older sister could. Then she stepped over to Tatiana. "Miss Davison, I'm Chief Melissa Colton. I wish we'd met under better circumstances."

Tatiana stared at her outstretched hand for several seconds before gripping it. "Thanks for that. It's Tatiana."

Travis stepped between them. "Now that we're all friends, you can tell us why you're tracking her like she's a suspect."

"Well, she—" Melissa paused and focused on Tatiana "—*you* weren't a cooperative witness this morning, so…"

"You tracked us here, hoping your suspect would show up in town and take his daughter out to dinner?"

"Something like that," his sister admitted. "Now we all know that Ms. Davison is a guest in your home. What we don't know is *why* she's staying?"

"I'll tell you why," Travis began and then cleared his throat. "She needed protection from both the police and the media, and she wasn't going to get that in an extended-stay hotel."

"And you're going to take responsibility for protecting her from these perceived threats?"

Melissa's expression showed just what she thought of the idea and his assumptions about the police.

"I have a security system, and I'll make sure she isn't alone. Those are at least two things I can do for her. She is my co-CEO, after all."

The last part he added too late. This time his sister stared at him, not buying anything he'd said.

Tatiana rolled her lips and couldn't have appeared more uncomfortable if she'd made it her life's work.

"I do appreciate having a safe place to stay, at least until I find something more permanent."

Melissa shook her head. "Well, I wanted to let you know there have been some developments in the case since this afternoon."

Tatiana's posture straightened, her eyes widening. "Was it like before? Has the evidence against my dad been proven inconclusive? Or was it somehow lost?"

"Those items had help getting 'lost' the first time, but, no, this is different."

"In all the accusations made against my father, no one has even suggested that he had a motive. He had no reason to commit these crimes."

"Remember that not all details in the case have been released publicly." Melissa glanced at her watch. "It's ten o'clock. You can at least learn more if you turn on the news."

"Why don't you just tell—" Travis began, but he stopped himself. Even before she'd climbed the ranks of the Grave Gulch Police Department, his sister had been one of the most stubborn people he'd ever met. Once she made up her mind about something, no one could change it.

Travis walked across the great room and grabbed the remote. The spray-tanned blonde news anchor who appeared on the screen was a familiar one. Delilah West, if he remembered correctly. The image that appeared in a cameo at the lower right corner of the screen, though, was the one he'd dreaded.

"Questions abound in the investigation of two Grave Gulch Park murders, but tonight new developments may have changed the narrative completely," Delilah said. "We'll have Val Cornish on the scene right after this."

Tatiana rushed over to stand behind the sofa, her hands curling into the overstuffed back cushion as the broadcast went to commercial after the teaser. His sister hung back, watching. At least one of them knew what was about to be said.

The field reporter, who'd probably been one of those milling outside Colton Plastics all afternoon, stood in that same parking lot now. The new headquarters Travis had been so proud to open a few years back was behind her, outlined in nighttime safety lights.

"Thanks, Delilah," the reporter said. "Grave Gulch Police questioned Tatiana Davison, new Colton Plastics CEO and daughter of at-large murder suspect Len Davison, earlier today at Colton Plastics company headquarters. But tonight, new developments have investigators reeling. Len Davison is wanted in connection with the murder of Jonathan Manelli last month at Grave Gulch Park."

The reporter went off on a history lesson about Davison's arrest for the earlier murder of Vincent Gully, so something told Travis that she was holding back on the most important part of her story. That Tatiana continued to stare at the screen, her fingers probably digging holes in the sofa cushion, told him she recognized it, too.

"Are they ever going to tell what happened?" Travis said.

"Wait for it." Melissa pointed to the screen, still carefully observing Tatiana instead.

Then the image switched to some grainy security-video footage.

"Len Davison was spotted today in New York City and was pursued by police, though the trail quickly went cold," the reporter said, finally getting to the meat of the story. "In this video, obtained exclusively by WOGG News, Davison is seen dashing into the Grand Central subway station."

The video showed an older man who looked eerily like the suspect's photo that had been published in the local newspaper and flashed on the screen of several TV new stations.

"Is it him?" Travis asked, though he had no doubt it was.

"He's in New York?" Tatiana asked at the same time.

"You really didn't know?" Melissa added a third question to the mix.

Tatiana blinked several times and then focused on the police chief. "No, I didn't know where my father was. I kept telling the police officer and the FBI agent that, but no one would believe me."

She slid around the couch and slumped into its cushions, planting her elbows on her thighs, and propping up her head.

"You'll want to see the rest," Melissa said in a low voice.

"You're hearing it here first," Val's voice called out from the TV again. "WOGG has confirmed that there has been a *third* murder in Grave Gulch Park. Police were called to the scene tonight after joggers discovered a body near the main walking trail. The victim has not yet been identified."

"Another murder?" Travis called out. The reporter had buried the lead, all right.

But Tatiana only continued to stare at the screen.

A taped segment showed Melissa in her dark blue uniform as she talked to reporters outside police headquarters. The almost purple sky in the background suggested that the impromptu press conference had been recent. Travis didn't know why she'd bothered to take questions at all. She'd confirmed only two details: someone had found a body in the park, and the death was being investigated as a homicide.

"I cannot comment on that as the GGPD is involved in an active investigation," she repeated for the fourth time.

The reporter must have given up on getting any more details as she spoke directly to the camera.

"Is there a serial killer in Grave Gulch? Or just a copycat whose fascination has been transformed into murder? We'll be following this story, and we'll bring you the answers when they're available. This is WOGG. We're on your side."

Travis gestured toward the television. "You taped that interview tonight?"

"About an hour ago," Melissa said. "I'd just gotten home and changed when you called."

Tatiana leaped up from the couch and stepped between them.

"You saw the proof. My dad was in New York today. Nowhere near Grave Gulch or the park. That has to mean he's no longer a suspect."

Travis exchanged a look with his sister. Had Tatiana missed the reporter's conjecture about a copycat criminal?

"He can't be, right?" Tatiana pressed.

The hope in her eyes squeezed Travis's heart. Did she still want to believe her dad was innocent?

Finally, Melissa answered for them both.

"My department is unable to release any details on the incident at the park today, other than the information given at the press conference. But even if date and time of death would rule your father out as a person of interest in that case, he would still remain the prime suspect in two other murder investigations, one with DNA evidence placing him at the crime scene."

Tatiana nodded, her shoulders curling forward.

"Everything's going to be all right," Travis blurted.

Melissa frowned at him, though he already knew he shouldn't have been promising Tatiana that. Nothing could fix the broken pieces of her family.

"I'm sorry," Melissa said stiffly. "I know how difficult all this must be."

Tatiana had been staring at the floor, but now she looked up at her.

"You have no idea," she spat. "Just wait until *your* father is the one accused of murder, and there's not a thing you can do to help him."

Travis expected his sister to get in Tatiana's face over that, but de-escalation training all cops had to undergo must have been effective. Melissa only nodded.

"You're right about part of that. I shouldn't have said that because I *don't* know. I can't even imagine what it's like to have something like this shake your whole foundation. But you're wrong about the second part. There is something you can do for your father."

"You mean, turn him in?" Tatiana shook her head.

"Not exactly. You could get him to turn *himself* in. If he's guilty of these acts of violence, and we believe he is, your father needs help."

"And you think he'll get that help in prison?"

Melissa licked her lips and didn't answer the question. They all knew that the correctional system and the rehabilitation it promised often were mutually exclusive. "At least if you convince him to come in, you can keep him alive."

Tatiana stared at her hands, as if she hadn't considered the possibility of her dad dying while on the run.

Travis stepped forward again, the need to protect her and their child pushing past his good sense.

"Come on, Melissa. I mean, Chief Colton. Do you really expect her to do your work for you?"

His sister gave him the kind of look that would have sent him running when they were kids. Then she turned her attention back to Tatiana. Why had he asked Melissa to come in the first place? Had he really thought that would help? His sister and Tatiana's father were on opposite sides of the law, and Travis's meddling had done nothing to change that.

"Or I could help him prove his innocence," Tatiana announced defiantly.

"That's a possibility, too, once he's in police custody." Melissa's expression was a mask of professional distancing. "He'll get his day in court with proper representation."

"Then he'll be acquitted. As I said, you don't even have a motive for him." For several seconds, Tatiana stared out the window, appearing lost in her thoughts.

"Look, Miss Davison. *Tatiana.* Your father is wanted for violent crimes. To your question, proof of motive is not required for a criminal prosecution. Anyway, that will be handled in the courts. As police, our job here is only to enforce the law and investigate crimes."

"And I'm sure you do a bang-up job," Tatiana said with a sigh. "But, as I told the officers many times, I don't know— Well, I *didn't* know where my father was. Nor do I know why he was in New York, or where he'll go next."

"All you have to do is tell us about some places that held meaning for your family. Places your father might return now since they would make him feel safe."

"But he's my *dad.*" Tatiana spoke in a small voice, but it was as if she'd shouted. All her fear and heartbreak seemed to have been squeezed into those four tiny words. The emotion gathering in Travis's throat surprised him as much as the heaviness that settled into his limbs. Her loss seemed to become his own.

Melissa opened her mouth as if to reason with her, only to close her lips again without speaking.

"You might be able to track down my father and send him to jail, but you'll have to do it without my help," Tatiana said.

Then she hurried from the room. Soon her footfalls could be heard on the stairs to the lower level. Travis grimaced as he stared in the direction she'd disappeared. They hadn't made it back to her hotel yet, so she didn't have any clothes or toiletries.

"You've really stepped in the middle of it this time."

Melissa stood facing him with her arms crossed.

Travis copied her stance. "If you're going to tell me that Colton Plastics should withdraw its offer, save your breath. She's a great addition to the company, and we couldn't withdraw at this point without risking a lawsuit, anyway."

"I'm not talking about the job." She made a sweeping gesture of the room around her. "But did you have to let her stay here? I get it that you don't want to be associated with the members of our family involved in law enforcement, but did you have to give us a slap in the face by inviting her to stay with you?"

"This might come as a surprise, but not everything is about you. Or even about the GGPD." He held his hands wide. "Besides, Tatiana isn't even the suspect in a case. Clarke couldn't say that about Everleigh."

"At least Tatiana isn't a suspect *yet*. But if she's harboring a fugitive—" She stopped and stared at him, wide-eyed. "Wait. Are you *dating* her? Or trying to? After avoiding relationships for years, this is the one you choose? Not only do you work with her, but also, well, you know…"

"I'm not dating her," he spat, hoping to hide his discomfort, even if he hadn't lied.

"Then why is she here?"

"She just returned to the US. She's all alone. And everyone's coming after her. Your department. The press. Maybe even eventually her dad."

Melissa tilted her head to the side. "This protective side of you is new, and any other time I might appreciate it, but you have to realize that Tatiana Davison isn't your responsibility."

"Sure she is," he said before he could stop himself.

"How's that?"

She watched him the way she probably did suspects during questioning. Like they must have, he couldn't help squirming, so he moved to the window before finally turning back to her.

"She's the … Well, like a told you earlier, she's the co-CEO at Colton Plastics."

Her expression told him that, like earlier, she didn't believe him. If she only knew. But, for once, Melissa didn't call him on his bull.

"I guess you know what you're doing."

"I do. Now you need to get home. I bet you haven't seen Antonio all day."

Bringing up his sister's fiancé, Antonio Ruiz, was unfair, but he needed to convince her to leave so he could get back to Tatiana.

"Guess I'll call him to say good night." At the door, she turned around once more. "If your co-CEO tries to hide her father, I will arrest her, even if I have to do it in your home."

"Noted."

"And if you help her do it, I'll—"

"I get it."

She lifted both hands in frustration, but finally she exited and closed the door behind her.

Travis barely waited for the patrol car to pull from his drive before he rushed downstairs. He wasn't sure what he would say when he reached Tatiana. Somehow, though, he had to convince her that despite his mistake in bringing in another Colton to harass her, his place was still where she needed to stay. What he couldn't decide was whether it was for her and their child's security—or his.

Chapter Eight

The dog walker rounded the corner just as the last patrol car pulled away from the entrance to Grave Gulch Park. His yellow Labrador retriever trudged beside him, her fur nearly blending in with the snow. He'd done such a good job of disappearing into the night himself, with his dark hat, coat, and boots, that he'd risked their lives every time they'd stepped off a curb around all the unobservant drivers.

Why weren't the police worried about *those* menaces to society, endangering the lives of innocent pedestrians and pets? But no. They were focused on following poor Tatiana, as if they expected her to flip on her own dad. The cops were sniffing along the wrong trail this time. He smiled into the darkness. Tatiana Davison was no more a snitch than anyone could call him *innocent*. Not after tonight.

"She's a good daughter, Polly. Just like you're a good girl."

The dog sat on the sidewalk, which was a narrow trench between two snowdrifts, and stared up at him, whining.

"Now don't complain. How many times do you get a good long walk like this one? Anyway, you've got a fur coat, plus that sweater and boots. I'm the one who's freezing."

He zipped his parka higher and tugged on the leash. After a little reluctance, the dog plodded forward again. She wasn't as enthusiastic as she'd been two hours earlier when he'd driven her from his house on the unfortunate east side of Grave Gulch Boulevard to a spot near the park on the west side. But he never had to question Polly's loyalty. Unlike so many others he knew.

At the next corner, he stopped and glanced back at the park. It looked empty and forlorn now that the flashing lights from patrol cars and the ambulance, plus the crowd of nosy neighbors, were gone. He would still find crime-scene tape if he followed the bike trails into the park. It just wouldn't be the same.

The rush after firing his nine-millimeter semiautomatic and watching a dark hole bloom on his target's chest had been so amazing that a weaker man would have squeezed the trigger a second time. Even with that silencer, that hadn't been nearly as quiet as he'd hoped. Still, he was too disciplined to lose control like that. Though he'd found staging the body less, well, *satisfying* than taking the original shot, and quite messy, he'd carefully stuck to the plan. He'd arranged the guy's arms over his abdomen and had taken only cash, though that wallet had contained a half dozen credit cards, one of them platinum.

But an homage had to be perfect. A single gunshot wound to the chest. Hands folded just right. Only cash missing.

Len Davison deserved to be honored, if for no other reason than he'd made headlines in the *Grave Gulch Gazette* with a name other than Colton. A serial killer right in his town? Davison would put Grave Gulch, Michigan, on the map. The shooter had been shocked by his good fortune, and that was *before* he'd learned that Davison's beautiful daughter was returning to town and would be working at Colton Plastics.

If that wasn't kismet, he didn't know what was.

For weeks, he'd been planning tonight's events to co-incide with Tatiana's arrival. No detail was too inconsequential if he hoped to impress Len Davison's only child with this tribute to her dad. And it had played out perfectly. Even the victim had arrived in the park alone, saving him from the moral dilemma of having to separate a pet from its owner. That was the one thing about Davison's work that hadn't quite fit for him, leaving an animal stranded.

What kind of deviant walked on a winter night without a dog, anyway? Well, he had earlier, out of necessity, but he couldn't have created the scene accurately with Polly there. Also, he needed to protect his dog from seeing sights that might upset her.

Tatiana would be so impressed with his efforts. She was a daddy's girl, after all.

"It's as if you brought Tatiana to me as a gift," he said to Len and to the darkness.

When his dog whined again, he startled and glanced around to ensure he hadn't been overheard. He would need to be more careful now that the police would be hunting for Davison in the area.

"Okay, girl, let's go home. We both deserve treats tonight."

Polly picked up on one of her familiar words as she danced around, pulling on the leash. He tugged it a little tighter and looked back at the park once more, farther away now and swallowed by winter and night.

Even if his trigger finger didn't tingle the way it had earlier, and his heart was no longer beating out a hard-rock drum solo, he was content as he returned to his SUV and opened the passenger door for Polly. If the pattern held, Len Davison would one day be immortalized in true-crime books alongside some of his other favorite serial killers. He couldn't wait to add those volumes to his collection. Whenever he read them, he could relive that exhilarating moment when he'd watched that guy hit the snow, already spattered with his blood. Even better, Davison's daughter would be cuddled up next to him while he read.

TATIANA STEPPED INTO the elevator at Colton Plastics two mornings later, grateful to have survived her first solo walk-through in the lab on the first floor. She hadn't felt alone, however, when she could see and feel the gazes of so many employees on her, some blatantly gawking while others were more covert.

She couldn't blame them for their curiosity. Travis might have sneaked her into the building again that morning, using the same company van and procedures they'd employed since Monday night, but the rest of the staff had been forced to pass reporters shouting questions for two days. Didn't the media think it was premature to ask them all what it was like to work with a serial killer's daughter when she'd been there less than a week?

As the elevator doors closed, Tatiana sighed. At least she would have a two-minute break from having to feel like a bug in an insect collection. How would she ever be an effective manager and earn the respect of the employees when she was already the focus of break-room gossip?

The doors stopped and reversed course, as if someone had pushed the up arrow too soon.

"Sorry about that," Jan Kennedy said as she boarded the elevator. "But this thing takes forever to return if it reaches the third floor. By tomorrow, you'll see why almost everyone takes the stairs most of the time."

"I'll make sure to wear comfortable shoes."

"You'll be glad you did." Jan pointed to the low-heeled, sensible walkers she'd worn with her navy slacks and sweater.

Tatiana glanced down at her own high-heeled boots below her long skirt. The footwear and probably most of the clothes that she and Travis had retrieved from her hotel made more sense in fashion-forward Paris than a small city in Michigan. She clearly had some shopping to do.

"Have you made it through the pile of résumés on your desk?" Jan asked as she checked off items on her list. "Call me and I'll schedule the interviews."

"I'll finish those today. Travis is lucky to have you as an assistant."

The older woman smiled at that, deep dimples denting her cheeks. "I let him know that every chance I get."

"Well, good," Tatiana said as the doors slid open. Jan looked up from the emails on her phone and started out the door. "Oh, Jan." She waited for the other woman to turn back. "Sorry about Monday morning. It was an intense first day. At least yesterday was a little better."

"Don't give it another thought. I imagine it was quite a surprise when the police arrived."

"And about the other thing later, sorry for that, too. Jet lag really got to me, so I wasn't feeling great, and then the police showing up was so upsetting…" Tatiana paused, running out of excuses.

Jan brushed her hand through the air as if to push Tatiana's worries aside. "None of my business, but I hope you're feeling better."

Though Tatiana suspected that Travis's assistant knew more than she was letting on, she couldn't help her momentary relief. Keeping her secret would be tough if she spent every morning in her office restroom getting an up-close view of the commode.

"I do feel better."

"Good to hear."

After half a dozen crackers, anyway, Tatiana was confident that the breakfast Travis had insisted that she eat would stay down. Her lips lifted at the memory of the hot bowl of oatmeal, plate of fruit, and glass of milk that had been waiting for her when she made it upstairs that morning.

How was she supposed to keep up her guard around him when he kept doing nice things like that? She wasn't even holding a grudge over his misguided decision to set up a chat with his sister the other night. The least she could do was to be a little suspicious of his protectiveness over her, but the temptation to, just this once, let someone take care of her was too strong. Anyway, his attention was kind of sweet.

Jan took off down the corridor at a good clip with Tatiana trailing behind her. They shifted to the side as they came upon three employees, too caught up in their own conversation to pay attention to hall traffic.

"I've been on the phone with them all morning,"

the pale woman with a short cap of red hair was telling them.

The older man, a ring of salt-and-pepper hair topping his olive-hued face, stepped into Jan and Tatiana's path without looking up from the tablet in his hand. "If we can't get the plastic-injection-molding shop to put a rush on that repair—"

The third employee, with an umber complexion and a clean-shaven head, reached out his arm like a tollbooth bar. "Watch out."

The three managed to stop without a collision, but Tatiana still pressed her back to the wall. They trampled each other's apologies.

"Good morning, everyone," Jan said. "Have you met our new co-CEO, Tatiana Davison?"

All three shook their heads. The odds were still fair that anyone they passed would require an introduction, even after two days. Jan gestured to the woman, then the older man and finally the younger one.

"Meet Christa Zimmerman, Enzio DeLuca and Blake Foster. Three of our finest engineers."

"The backbone of the company, of course," Tatiana said with a grin as she shook their hands. "But as an engineer myself, my opinion might be slanted in your favor."

She pretended not to notice when they sneaked glances at her while continuing the trip past the elevator toward the east stairway.

"It'll get easier," Jan assured her as they stopped at Tatiana's office.

"I appreciate that."

"Oh." The assistant held up her index finger. "I'm supposed to let you know that sometime tomorrow, the guys from the IT department, either Lucas McAllister or Dylan Evans, will be doing some work with your computer."

"Is there a problem with it?"

"No. They're just updating your security. And don't be surprised if you get another call from human resources. They'll want to register you for some diversity and anti-harassment compliance training."

"Good to know. Hopefully, I can hire my AA this week, so you won't have to split your time between Travis and me."

"I don't mind. Makes him appreciate me more," Jan said with a grin.

Tatiana hurried into her office and sat behind her desk. Getting up to speed on her work was taking longer than she'd hoped, so she promised herself she would finish evaluating résumés before lunch. That while in her office she could avoid curious stares from the employees and glimpses of reporters were bonuses, as far as she was concerned.

Unfortunately, the silence also gave her mind too much freedom to wander. Instead of the words on the pages citing candidates' qualifications, she could only see that news broadcast from the other night. For just one moment, she'd believed that it had all been a bad dream. If her father couldn't have committed one murder, then maybe he was innocent of the other two. Chief Colton had dashed that hope with talk of more DNA evidence. But then, Len Davison had done a fine job of crushing her belief in him when he'd phoned after his release from jail.

I'm sorry, dumpling.

The words replayed in her mind like a song on repeat.

Those three words, the only ones he'd spoken before hanging up, hadn't been part of an outright confession but enough to make a daughter question her own father and then despise herself for her disloyalty.

I'm sorry, dumpling.

Now the words covered her like a weighted blanket over her head, pressing her chin to her chest and suffocating her breath by breath. The body count had grown to three, murders connected through either participation or mimicry. Though she'd desperately wanted to hold on to her belief in her father's innocence, her fingers were being pried away from that conviction, knuckle by knuckle.

Tatiana shook her head and took several deep breaths, waiting for her stomach to settle. When it did, she set the résumés aside and opened her folio instead. She tapped her finger down each bullet point in her list from "meet each member of the engineering department" to "familiarize self with primary suppliers." At the bottom, she'd added "buy sensible shoes" and the more cryptic "schedule checkup" to indicate the next day's appointment with the obstetrician to confirm her pregnancy.

More focused now but not yet ready to tackle evaluating potential employees again, she launched the email software on her laptop. How could she already have thirty unread messages, all marked "high priority?" She would work her way through those and then return to the résumés.

She clicked on each of the first few messages. The ones Travis had promised to send, with internal documents on CP's short-and long-term goals, would be helpful to her in flattening her learning curve. She was pleased to know that in addition to the ability to make a mean rigatoni dish and his skills in some more private areas, Travis Colton was good at his job. More than that, he seemed to respect her role there, treating her as a true equal, though she hadn't had the chance to contribute yet.

As she scanned the list, a message in the middle of her screen caught her attention. In the subject box, it said, "Welcome Tatiana Davison!" Since it was probably a new employee packet from HR, she nearly passed it for more critical messages, but the company title in the email address made her look twice.

"'Friends of Tatiana Davison?' What's that all about?"

She hesitated a second before clicking the message to open it. Her jaw dropped as she read.

You belong with me. And since you're Daddy's Girl, I'll make sure nothing changes.

Her pulse thudding in her temples, Tatiana leaned forward in her office chair and stared at the mysterious words. Was this a joke? A prank on the new employee, who was such an easy target because of her father? But the chill scaling her spine in icy fingers told her there was neither a punch line nor rascals hiding in her office closet ready to shout "serial killer's daughter" through the company hallways.

"I 'belong?'" she asked aloud. The choice of words was particularly cruel since she didn't feel comfortable anywhere lately.

Her hand hovered over the external mouse, her fingers trembling. Should she report the message to company security? The police? Was it even that serious? She twirled the arrow on the screen until it pointed to the trash can at the top of the page. She considered putting it there. No one would have to know about the note. And, if it had been a joke, she would get the last laugh.

But as she shifted the mouse to the X to close the email, the message scrolled higher, showing another line farther down the page. One she'd missed.

PS You look beautiful in that shade of blue.

Slowly, Tatiana lowered her gaze to her blouse. Silk. Office-appropriate. *Royal blue.* Someone was watching her? She gasped. Her gaze darted to each corner of the office. She hadn't noticed cameras before, but had she been looking closely enough? When she still didn't see any, she rushed to one of the windows that looked down on the courtyard. Only two second-floor offices, hers and Travis's, had that garden view. Still, the window-lined hallways would have made it possible for someone on the opposite side of the building to see her from several vantage points.

She scanned the deserted hallway once more and then hurried back to her desk and grabbed her office phone. As she started to dial, her gaze lifted to the top of her laptop where the tiny circle of a built-in camera looked back at her. She slammed the lid shut and dialed an internal number without hesitation this time.

Travis answered on the first ring. "Hey, Tatiana. Everything okay? Did you run out of crackers?"

She cleared her throat, her gaze flicking back to the laptop once more. "Could you come to my office right away? We've—I mean, *I've*—got a problem."

Chapter Nine

Travis slammed down the phone and hurried from his office to hers. He would have sprinted if he hadn't passed Gordon Littleton, the day shift foreman. Littleton was good at his job but always seemed to be lingering near the executive offices when he should have been on the production floor actually doing it.

"Good morning, boss. What's the rush?"

"It wouldn't be a day at CP if there weren't a dozen or so mini crises for me to handle at the same time," Travis said without bothering to stop. Rounding the corner, he rushed past the empty desk outside Tatiana's office and through her door. He didn't stop to knock.

"What is it? Are you okay?" He approached the desk where she was hunched over, then bent and spoke in a low voice. "You're not having, uh, cramping, are you?"

She squinted her eyes as she looked up at him. "What?"

Her gaze flicked to her belly and then lifted again. "Oh. No. It's not that."

Travis puffed up his cheeks and blew out a sigh. Didn't she realize that his thoughts would automatically go there? What she couldn't know was how much he dreaded the possibility that she could have been experiencing a miscarriage.

How could that be? A few days ago, the idea of having kids was nowhere on his radar, and now he was almost looking forward to lullabies and sleepless nights. What had changed, he wasn't sure, but he had the strange suspicion that he wouldn't have been looking forward to fatherhood at all if the mother had been anyone other than Tatiana Davison. Now that he couldn't explain at all.

"It's probably nothing. Could be just a prank. I'm sure I overreacted."

Tatiana wrung her hands and didn't look up at him. She'd been pale that morning from her nausea, but she looked downright ashen now.

"Just tell me. What did you overreact about? Did a reporter manage to get inside? Did the police call again? What is it?"

"This." She opened her laptop, hit a few keys, probably entering her credentials, and turned the machine to face him on her desk.

"What is that? From 'Friends of Tatiana Davison?'"

Then he stopped and read those chilling words. *You belong with me*? *Daddy's Girl*? He braced his hands on her desk as spots danced before his eyes. The temptation to lift her in his arms and race from the building was so overwhelming that he had to force himself to sit in the guest chair to keep from rounding her desk.

"Where did you get this?" he barked. Then he tried again in a lower voice. "I mean, *when*?"

She closed the message and showed him its time stamp.

"We could have been hacked, I guess, but it also

could have just been an outside email making its way inside. You don't think it's a prank, do you?"

"No. I don't." If it were just a joke, would his heart have been beating as if it were trying to break out of his chest?

She nodded, her front teeth sinking into her lower lip.

"It says you're wearing blue." He couldn't help looking around the office as he said it, a shiver scaling his spine.

"I know. But that doesn't have to mean that whoever sent this is inside the building. There's a camera in my laptop. We could have been hacked. It happens all the time. You know that."

She seemed to be trying to convince herself as well. It was probably easier to consider corporate espionage than to accept that whoever had sent that cruel note might be right inside the building with them.

"Someone is watching you inside our office. The creep has hacked in or installed cameras to do the same thing."

"You make it sound worse when you say it like that. Do you think it's the media?"

She'd asked the question, but they both shook their heads to answer it.

"That wouldn't make sense," she said. "They want to get the story that's already there, not create a new one."

He wouldn't give the local outlets that much credit, but he didn't tell her that.

"And after the murder last night, they have a bigger story to work on than anything about me." She pulled the computer back to her. "I have two choices. I can report it, or I just take extra precautions. Obviously, someone's having fun at my expense."

"How about *we* do both?"

She must have noticed his emphasis on the word *we* because her gaze narrowed. "Are you saying you think I should call the police?"

"Why don't you let me do that?"

"I can handle this myself. I've been taking care of myself for a long time." She lifted her chin and crossed her arms.

"I'm sure you can, and I'm sure you have."

Travis didn't point out that she'd called him for backup not ten minutes before. The last thing he wanted right now was for her to spurn his help.

"But there's one thing I have that you don't," he said. "A family full of law enforcement officers."

She opened her mouth and then closed it. "Fine."

Instead of reaching for her office phone, he pulled his cell from his pocket and tapped through his contact list.

"Who are you calling? A sibling or a cousin?"

"Neither." His gaze flicked to hers. "But she's the best."

Travis paced to the outer office and spoke in quiet tones. He'd already messed up once, and here he was approaching a member of the GGPD a second time. Tatiana was still sitting there, gripping her hands when he returned.

"Okay, pack your laptop in your bag, and we'll head out again through the service entrance."

"If we're going to the police department, right in the center of town, why are you bothering to use the van again? Someone will see us, and our photo will be on page one tomorrow. So why don't we just skip it and give my stomach a break?"

"First, you might not be front-page news tomorrow

because of the new murder." He shrugged. "Maybe only page two. And, second, we're not meeting her at the police department."

"Meeting whom?"

"Ellie Bloomberg."

"Who?" She squinted and then shook her head. "Wait. I remember her from school. She was a year behind me. Is she a police officer now?"

He shook his head. "The department's tech guru."

"Where are we meeting her? This city's too small. Not everyone will recognize my face, but they'll know yours. If we show up at Mae's Diner or Paola's Pizza or, heck, even the Grave Gulch Public Library, they'll put two and two together."

"That's why we're not meeting nearby," he told her.

"You convinced Ellie to meet outside town, you'll be sending me in that awful van again, *and* you talked Miles into carting me all over Oceana County in the middle of the afternoon?"

"Yes, yes and no."

"How's that?"

"Yes, Ellie is meeting us, and you'll be a passenger in the van. But Miles won't be involved this time. You know your driver, though. Me."

TWENTY MINUTES LATER, Tatiana sat in the passenger seat of a Colton Plastics delivery van, eating French fries right out of the bag, as they traveled on US 31 toward Muskegon. Every few minutes, she would sneak a peek at the driver, but her timing must have been off, as Travis kept catching her doing it. At least she hadn't been forced this time to stay in the back where the molds and manufactured products were usually transported, so she hadn't required a bucket and a mop. As soon as they'd reached the outskirts of Grave Gulch, he'd pulled off the road so she could move to the front and buckle in.

"Have you killed everything in there now? I wanted to warn you that the bag isn't edible."

"Funny." She frowned, though he had a point. She'd eaten her hamburger, the last few bites of his and both of their fries already. She took a swig from her bottled water, the only concession she'd made for a pregnancy diet during their drive-through stop on the way out of town. At least while she was eating, she didn't have to worry about why they'd taken off on this midday road trip in the first place.

"Hope you enjoyed your lunch. There won't be anything left to eat when we get to the rest stop. Your OB is going to frown on you eating fast food, anyway."

"Good thing I don't have my appointment until tomorrow. Technically, no one has confirmed that I'm even pregnant yet."

He shook his head. "I was impressed by how much you were putting away."

"I'm *probably* eating for two, you know."

"And you've *probably* just given both of you indigestion."

He returned her frown with a grin.

"You never told me how you convinced Ellie to come all the way out here to meet us," she said.

"It wasn't that difficult. The GGPD will do almost anything to get information from you. Didn't you figure that out after talking to Melissa the other night?"

"You're sure that's all it is?" She waggled her index finger at him. "Did you and Ellie date or something?"

"No, we didn't date."

Though Tatiana had been kidding him about it, her discomfort over the idea that Travis could have had a history with Ellie unsettled her.

For a few minutes, they drove in silence, and then Travis pointed to the computer bag between the bucket seats.

"You doing okay?"

Tatiana swallowed, surprised she'd been thinking of anything other than that email. As she stared down at the bag, the message replayed. *You belong with me.* Who would write something so possessive? Who would want to play with her mind, using the tragedy of her father's fugitive status to get to her? She turned toward the side window so that Travis wouldn't see her face.

"I guess so."

"You don't sound convincing."

She didn't bother responding since they both knew he was right.

"You've been hit with a lot in the past few days. It already had to be overwhelming. And now that." He gestured toward the bag again.

"Definitely not the way I'd planned to start my new job."

"We're going to find out who sent it. I won't stop looking until we do."

"I know." The words were out of her mouth before she could stop them. Why did she continue to feel safe with Travis in the swirl of everything that had happened this week? Why was he the first person she'd called after receiving the creepy email? Letting her guard down around him was too much of a risk.

She shifted in her seat, causing the shoulder strap to

tighten over her chest. "Can we talk about something else for a while?"

"What did you have in mind?"

She pointed to his hands on the steering wheel. "You're doing a far better job of driving the van than I would have expected. Do you even have a commercial driver's license?"

"Thanks, I think."

"You don't have to be a great driver, though. Your sister could fix a ticket if you ever got one."

At that, Travis chuckled. "Melissa would never do that for me. In fact, she told my brothers and me on the day she made chief that if we had traffic citations or got our butts thrown in jail, we needed to forget her phone number. Not as if I would have taken her help, anyway."

Now that claim Tatiana had no trouble buying. Travis didn't seem to be the kind of man who easily accepted assistance from anyone, so it made no sense that he'd sought it on her behalf twice this week.

"Besides," he continued, "I do have my CDL. In the early years of the company, I had to fill a lot of roles. Marketing. Mold contracting. You name it. I even emptied trash cans and scrubbed toilets when it needed to be done."

"Given the stock numbers, and that fancy ladies' room in my office, you've come a long way in growing the company."

"Too fast, some would say."

"Who says that?"

He lifted his shoulder and dropped it but kept his gaze on the road. "My dad, I guess. Let's just say that Frank Colton wasn't entirely on board when I decided to do something crazy like start a plastics company.

He didn't want me to use Colton in the name, either, in case the business didn't make it."

"Nothing like having your family in your corner."

"Even now he pops in with a warning whenever I take any growth risks. Or any risks at all. It didn't help that he was right about Aubrey."

"Who's that?"

"My ex-fiancée."

"You were *engaged*?"

He nodded. "Seven years ago. For about a month."

She considered that for a few seconds, surprised again by how uneasy it made her feel. What was she doing? Travis had already rejected her once. She only risked more pain if she allowed herself to believe there could be more between them than the child she carried.

"Then what was all that about the confirmed bachelor?" she asked after a long pause.

"Aubrey helped with that confirmation."

"How was your dad right about her?"

His jaw tightened briefly, then relaxed. "He said to watch out. I thought I'd finally found someone who got me, and he was convinced she was just out to get my money since CP was starting to take off. Guess which one of us was right?"

She swallowed. It didn't matter that Travis had humiliated her on their one night together. She still couldn't believe that Aubrey had hurt *him* that way. "I'm sorry. That stinks."

"Thanks. Everything she'd told me was lies, too. Her past. Her job. And then there was a friend who wasn't just a friend." He shrugged. "You get the rest."

She also understood more about Travis Colton now. Why he avoided relationships. Why he'd told her he didn't lie. Even why he had such a complicated relationship with his father. But what it didn't explain was why he'd proposed to her when one fiancée had already burned him. Did he feel safer in knowing that the marriage would be only a business transaction to give a Colton heir his name?

"Then your dad's probably blowing up your phone with messages this week. My presence at Colton Plastics is definitely a risk. And then if your sister told him you'd invited me to stay at your place, you're lucky he didn't show up on your doorstep before breakfast the next morning."

"I can handle him."

What he hadn't said spoke as loudly as his words. He'd faced off with his cousins and his sister on her behalf. Now he was promising to do the same with his own father. Or he already had. Why was Travis going to all that trouble? Sure, it might have involved the baby, but he'd tried to insulate her from his cousins in law enforcement before he knew she was pregnant. She could continue to tell herself that he was trying to help them capture her father, but that theory was full of holes and starting to drip like a cheap umbrella.

Tatiana knew she should let the subject go, but she couldn't help wanting to know more about the enigmatic Travis Colton.

"You said you were a maverick—well, before." This wouldn't go well if she brought up things that he'd said on the night they weren't supposed to discuss. "Was that because your dad wanted you to go into law enforcement or personal protection like your siblings and your cousins?"

"You have to understand that some in my family

consider police work a higher calling. It has to do with my Uncle Geoff's first wife, Amanda. She was killed during a home invasion when Desiree and Troy were just toddlers. That crime was never solved."

"That's terrible. I'm sorry for your loss."

"Thanks."

She might have been pushing too far, but she needed to know the rest. "Was your dad disappointed that you didn't have that higher calling, too?"

The side of Travis's mouth lifted. "He didn't exactly say that, but since I didn't have the same career aspirations as my siblings did, and I was the first son, he expected that I would be the one to follow him into the shipping business. Antiquated, I know. Also, though he'd worked his way up to become an executive, he wanted to make things easy for me, helping me to make the right contacts."

"He didn't want to give you the chance to earn your own success and deserve it?"

"Guess he didn't see it that way."

But the side glance he gave her showed his surprise that she did. Why would it shock him so much that she understood him? Travis, who'd been so determined to protect *her*, had his own tender spot. He was a full-grown man, still chasing and not quite receiving his father's approval. She'd appreciated him sharing his strength with her, and certainly his kindness, but that he'd let her see his vulnerability touched her in a way she couldn't explain.

He didn't say more as he took the exit for the rest stop and parked. Though there were plenty of semis filling the longer spaces in the back, only a few cars dotted the spots closest to the picnic areas.

"It doesn't look like she's here yet." He opened the door and climbed out, anyway.

Tatiana had just finished buttoning her coat to the top and pulling on her hat and gloves when he rounded the van and opened the door for her. "You're sure this was a good idea?"

"Got a better one?"

She shrugged and reached for her laptop bag. "Glad I ate in the van. No way I could hold on to a French fry with my gloves."

They'd just reached the first picnic table two hundred feet from the rest stop facility and had sat on the facing benches when a dark-colored SUV pulled into the spot next to the van. The woman Tatiana immediately recognized as Ellie hopped out of her vehicle, yanked her hood over her blowing dark hair and stomped over to them.

"This had better be good, Travis." She glanced from him to Tatiana and then to the table that had a thin film of snow on it.

"It is." He gestured toward the bench.

"It's been a while," Ellie said to Tatiana while pulling the tighteners on her hood to close it around her face. "I'm sorry the circumstances aren't great."

"I appreciate that. But thanks for coming all the way out here."

Ellie watched her for several seconds, her blue eyes narrowing. "I get the idea that you and I think I'm here for different reasons."

Then she pinned Travis with a look. "Am I right?"

"Someone is threatening my new co-CEO," he said. "Through email. And we need your help."

Instead of answering, Ellie started away from the

table and gestured for them to follow. "Well, if you think I'm working out here in the cold, then you don't know me at all."

Chapter Ten

"So, this is what stakeouts are like?" Travis patted the crate he sat on in the van's cargo area. Then he gestured to Ellie and Tatiana in the captain's seats. Though he tried to joke about it, he hated sitting back there, watching, when he should have been doing something.

Ellie glanced up from Tatiana's laptop and frowned. "As a matter of fact, they aren't. We put way more thought into them than this. If nothing else, you could have given me a heads-up about what I would be walking into here."

"I wasn't sure you would still come," he said.

She shrugged, neither confirming nor denying his claim. "You're lucky this van has Wi-Fi, or we would be forced to operate from the hot spot on my phone."

As Ellie scrolled through the list in his co-CEO's email box for what had to be the fifth time, Tatiana shivered visibly in the driver's seat. Her coat, plus the van's heater, which she'd turned on at regular intervals, weren't keeping her warm. No matter what she'd tried to tell him earlier, she wasn't okay. That he couldn't do a damn thing about it frustrated him even more.

Ellie paused her message search and reached into her coat pocket to withdraw a pad of miniature sticky notes. She stuck one over the laptop's camera and went back to work. "That should be covered up whenever it's not in use. Webcams are easy to hack."

"Do you think that's what happened?" Travis asked.

"Anything's possible."

Ellie clicked on the message from "Friends of Tatiana Davison" again, and Tatiana startled when it opened, as though it came as a surprise.

Travis gripped his hands together to keep from reaching out to her. "What's your best guess about where it came from?" he asked Ellie instead.

"I don't guess," she said without looking up. "I follow trails of electronic clues that lead me to more complete answers."

Tatiana turned in the seat to face them both. "Is that what Travis told you to convince you to meet us? That you would be getting *answers*?"

Ellie pushed out her bottom lip and blew a breath that ruffled her bangs. "He said that Tatiana Davison was with him, and she was ready to talk, though she would only speak to me."

Tatiana's gaze flicked to him then, and she nodded, as if acknowledging that on part of that statement, he'd told *her* the truth. What would it take to get her to trust him? He waited for her to look away before turning back to the other woman.

"And, like I said, she *is* here with me. I was surprised you bought the rest. I mean, you might have known each other in high school, but you weren't best friends or anything, so why would she insist that she talk to *you*?"

"I let my curiosity get the best of me. I'm also not so magnanimous that I wouldn't accept the credit for taking down a—" Ellie stopped and jerked her head to look at Tatiana. "I mean, closing an open case."

Travis leaned forward into the wide area between the seats. "Sorry I brought you here under false pretenses. But we needed your help, and we couldn't march into the GGPD with everyone watching. Besides, I don't think we should file a police report."

Instead of answering him, Ellie focused on Tatiana. "You're sure you don't have more you want to share about your father?"

Tatiana shook her head. "As I told all the officers, I don't know anything. I was as surprised as anybody to learn that he was in New York."

"I had to try." Ellie shrugged and then glanced over her shoulder at Travis. "Why wouldn't you want to file a report? You need a record of this. Anyway, I'm not a free technology service. I work for the city."

Then her gaze narrowed. "Wait. Are you just trying to keep your company out of the newspapers? It's a little late for that."

"Yeah. Everyone keeps reminding me," he said, frowning. "But it's not that I'm trying to avoid publicity. Well, at least not for the reason you probably think. And the guy—at least I'm guessing it's a guy—hasn't technically committed a crime yet. I just need to know who he is, so I can stop him."

"Planning a little vigilante justice?"

Ellie looked back and forth between Travis and Tatiana. He braced himself to be asked why he would break the law for her. How was he supposed to answer that? Was he sure himself?

"Well, don't," Ellie said instead. "Also, you're wrong about no crime being committed. Stalking *is* a crime.

If this vaguely threatening message is the beginning of that pattern, there needs to be a report on it. I'm not even a police officer, and I know that.

"And another thing—we already have a possible copycat murderer. What if it's someone else wanting to get in on the act? Even in Grave Gulch, we have our share of kooks who might like fifteen minutes of fame."

He shook his head though what she'd said unnerved him. "Those things aren't connected. Anyway, we've had reporters camped out on our parking lot for days. Maybe not as many now, since that third body was discovered. But we can't give reporters *another* story to follow involving Colton Plastics. That might make it easier for *him* to blend in if he's hanging outside the building."

"You think it could be a reporter?" Ellie asked.

"I'm not ruling out anybody."

"I hate to tell you this, but the guy might already be blending in if he's inside your building." She pointed to the screen. "Look here. He knew you were wearing blue."

Travis's whole body tightened, so he leaned forward and rested his elbows on his knees. Tatiana's reaction was more obvious as she pulled her coat closer around her neck as if to hide her blue blouse.

"We know." If only he could have kept the exasperation out of his voice. "That's why we need you to figure out who sent that message and only share that information with us. At least for now. We have to know if one of our employees sent it."

Tatiana hadn't said anything for so long that it startled him when she spoke up again.

"I haven't gotten weird vibes from any of the male employees I've met so far, but there really hasn't been time."

"No one's asked you out?" Ellie wanted to know.

"Hardly." Tatiana cleared her throat.

"It's only my third day. I haven't even been alone with any of them. Other than Travis's admin."

He wished he could tell her to slow down, but that would have made her nervousness more noticeable. She was walking a fine line between truth and lies and stepping off a few times into gray areas that threatened to blacken. No one had asked her out, but someone had *proposed*. And she hadn't spent any time alone with male CP employees, but she'd spent intimate hours with one executive, who was also now her roommate.

"What about when you first interviewed?"

Travis shifted his head to the side so Ellie couldn't see his grin. Tatiana must have gotten wise and answered that one with a head shake. But he couldn't linger on the memories of their night together, that sweet blur of moments they'd agreed to forget.

"I just worry we might be overreacting to what could have been a prank on the new CP exec," she said.

"Did you find it funny?" he asked before he could stop himself.

"No, but—"

"Neither did I." He straightened and crossed his arms. "If we find out that it was one of our employees, I think you'll agree that it's time for him to move on."

"I do."

Finally, he turned back to Ellie, finding her watching them so closely that he shifted on the crate. "So, what steps do we take next?"

"What *I* should do is tell you to either file a report or I won't help you," Ellie said. "You're the chief of police's brother, for God's sake. You want me to go behind my boss's back."

"We're not asking you to commit a felony. Just to track the source of an email so that we know whether we just have a prankster with a lousy sense of humor or a creep who might be coming after my co-CEO."

"We have to find out for sure," Tatiana added.

"And remember," he paused, waiting until Ellie met his gaze, "though she might be *related to* a fugitive, Tatiana is just a local resident now, one who hasn't even been accused of a crime."

"I know." Ellie brushed her hand through the air.

"And, of course, we'll pay you for your freelance work."

"Oh, no. I'm not taking your money. It's enough of a conflict now, and I won't make it worse by—"

"Does that mean you're going to help us?" Tatiana said, interrupting her.

Ellie tucked her chin, defeated. "Fine. But I'll need to take Tatiana's work laptop."

"No problem." Travis sneaked a few quick breaths, trying to slow his racing pulse. He was more relieved than he should have been that Ellie had agreed to help and too invested in Tatiana, who still could have been lying to them all. "I'll have her use my backup, so we won't make a big deal about hers being missing."

Ellie tucked the laptop under her arm. "Sounds good. Then I'll figure out whether the email is internal or external and, possibly, if the sender breached the firewall protecting your company's VPN."

She shot a glance at Tatiana. "That's the virtual private network."

"I'm an engineer," Tatiana said. "I know what that is."

Ellie shook her head. "I knew that."

Travis pointed to the computer. "You'll also be looking at IP addresses, that is, if the guy wasn't using a random IP generator, right?"

Ellie frowned. "If you two know all this stuff, you don't need me, so—"

"No. No. You're the expert," Travis said. "We need you to find out everything you can about whoever sent this message."

"I will. But since this isn't official police business, I won't be working on it during my regular shifts. I'm working days. Don't call me at work. Ever. And if we figure out who sent the message, you are *not* to take this matter into your own hands. You will turn it over to police."

Travis nodded more times than was necessary, but he couldn't seem to stop. "Thanks. And thank Mick for us, too," he said, referring to her longtime boyfriend, Mick Hanes. "We appreciate him sharing you during your off-work hours."

"We're really grateful," Tatiana chimed.

"With as busy as his work has been lately, he'll barely notice," Ellie said with a shrug. "Good thing for you he's as big a workaholic as I am."

With the computer still under her arm, Ellie opened the van door, stepped out and closed it behind her. After Tatiana slid from the driver's seat to the passenger one, Travis opened the side door and climbed out. Ellie had just bent to tuck the laptop on the floor in her SUV's passenger seat, but she turned back to him.

"One more thing."

"What's that?" He eyed her cautiously, certain that whatever was coming wouldn't be good.

"If I get in trouble with the chief for this, I'm taking you down with me."

BY LATE AFTERNOON, Tatiana had made it to the bottom of the résumé pile, which was a feat, considering her pace had been tortoise slow. How could it not have been when she'd felt compelled to track down every random noise in her office and had catapulted out of her seat each time a ding on the borrowed laptop announced a new email?

Her office windows had become an enemy as well. How was she supposed to work when she couldn't shake the sense that someone was watching her?

After one more look around the office, she read the final cover letter and résumé. That decision came easily for her, and she quickly placed them facedown on her *no* pile.

The candidate's qualifications looked fine, but something about the tone of the cover letter seemed odd to her. As if the woman had a chip on her shoulder. That wasn't a vibe she needed in her office. Tatiana would already have to work harder than she'd ever expected to prove her worth at Colton Plastics without adding employees who brought negativity with them.

"Sorry, Miss Oliver. I have enough problems of my own."

At a knock outside her office, Tatiana jumped again,

this time whacking her knee on the underside of her desk. She yelped, and the door swung wide.

"Are you okay?" Travis asked.

She leaned forward in her chair and rubbed her sore knee. "I'm fine. Just a little jumpy this afternoon."

He wasn't listening, though, as he stepped to the window, his hands fisted at his sides.

"Guess I'm not alone in that."

He whirled to face her. "What?"

"I'm not the only one who's jumpy."

"Right." He shook out his arms and then stretched his neck. "Sorry about bursting in here like that. I heard voices and—"

"Mine. I talk to myself when I'm working sometimes. I'll have to be more careful to whisper in the future."

Travis shifted his feet. "No. It's your office. It's just— I don't know."

"It was nice to know that the cavalry would come if I ever call out for help."

Frowning, he glanced out the window again toward his own office on the opposite side of the courtyard. "I don't know what we were thinking when we designed this building where you can see inside the offices."

"Transparency, maybe?"

"We might have considered that there's no place to work in privacy. No place to even think."

"Did it bother you before?" she couldn't help asking.

He shook his head but didn't look back. "Things change."

Neither had to mention that her arrival at Colton Plastics was the biggest recent development, one that appeared to have thrown the company on its ear.

"I've asked Jan to schedule for the decorator to order blinds for our two offices." He shrugged. "The designers wanted to do that from the beginning, but I thought it ruined the aesthetic."

"Good idea" was all she could say. She hated that he was making so many changes to the company for her benefit, but she couldn't deny his actions reassured her.

Finally, he stepped away from the window. "Were you able to get any work done this afternoon?"

He scanned her desk, his gaze falling on the laptop that she'd closed and pushed to the corner.

"Some." She pointed to the two stacks of paper. "I'm ready for Jan to schedule interviews."

"At least one of us finished something." He indicated one of her visitors' chairs with a flick of his hand. "You mind?"

She shook her head. He sat and pointed to the piles of résumés.

"Maybe you were more productive because of that nap you had on the way back to the office."

She dipped her chin. "I still can't believe that I fell asleep. One minute I was mulling over the things Ellie said, and the next you were waking me up at the CP loading dock."

"With a bit of drool on the corner of your mouth," he said with a smile.

"You weren't supposed to notice that."

He probably hadn't intended for her to see the tenderness in his eyes when she'd awakened, either, but she had. Her heart still fluttered at the memory of it, though she still wasn't certain what it meant.

"I hope you didn't sit in the parking lot, waiting for me to wake up. I can sleep pretty hard when I'm tired."

"To be fair, it was only for a few minutes," he admitted.

It was the second time in two days he'd watched her sleep, and yet she didn't feel creeped out by it. In fact, she found it almost comforting. As if she would be okay knowing that Travis Colton was the one watching over her. She was a strong, independent woman. Since when did she like the idea of having a protector?

"You might have been fighting against your exhaustion, but our growing baby won."

And there it was, the reason for his attentiveness. The baby. She should have been grateful, she supposed. Some guys denied paternity, and Travis had been on board from the moment she'd told him, even without a DNA test. She needed to remember that everything he was doing—the proposal, the offer of shelter, all of it—was for their child. Those were all good things, but she couldn't allow herself to think that he might care about her, too. Travis Colton might have offered her marriage but never love.

"How's the belly feeling?"

Automatically, her hands moved to her abdomen, which had become an unfortunate habit in the past two days. She had to stop that if she planned to keep the pregnancy a secret.

"You know, after the fast foodfest."

She nodded. "You should be a medium. You did a great job at predicting the future."

"I'll remember that if Colton Plastics goes under."

"Don't even joke about things like that," she said. "Do you want to tempt fate?"

She knocked on her wooden desktop in a superstitious tradition, and he leaned forward and did the same.

"Hope it wasn't too bad."

"The fate tempting?"

He shook his head. "The indigestion."

She pulled out the trash can from beneath her desk and tilted it so he could see inside.

Wrappers from both sleeves of saltines that she'd brought from the condo that morning were crumpled at the bottom.

"At least it wasn't what I thought you might be showing me."

She frowned over his lame joke.

"Sorry you've been feeling crummy. I'll make us something healthy when we get, uh, back to the house."

He'd almost said *home*, and the word rang hollow in her ears, anyway. She no longer had a place she'd come from or where she could return when she needed to recharge. Though she'd been back in Grave Gulch for days, she hadn't been able to drive by the old place that her father had sold right after her mother's death. At least she had a place to stay until they tracked down whoever had sent the email, but his home wasn't and would never be her home.

Travis cleared his throat, possibly realizing that he'd touched on a sensitive subject.

"You know what I've been doing all afternoon?" He waited for her to shake her head before continuing. "Digging through employee records down in HR."

Relieved for the change in subject, she glanced up at him again. "You don't mean *physical* records, do you? Don't we have all that stuff on the company network in the encrypted files?"

"They are. But if someone has hacked into the network, we don't want them to see where we've been looking. We keep a physical copy of employment records in the locked file room."

"Good idea avoiding the network."

At that, he smiled. "I'd thought so, too, until the head of HR started hanging around asking me if she could help me find what I was looking for."

"Find out anything?"

"Other than employees paranoid they're going to lose their jobs? No." He scooted the chair closer to her desk and planted both elbows on it. "I looked at all the men, and nothing seemed to be off in anyone's backgrounds. It still could be one of them."

"What about the women?"

"I haven't looked yet, but I will." He closed his eyes and shook his head before opening them again. "I still get the idea that it's a guy."

"Or someone who wants us to think so."

"We'll also have to take extra precautions at work to ensure you're not alone with any of the employees, except for Jan or me—and your own assistant, once you have him or her in place."

Travis shook his head. "I hate to think someone got past one of our screeners. We check references, work histories, and social media profiles. We always try to root out any potential problems before we bring candidates in for interviews."

"It doesn't always work, though." She shrugged. "The board hired me."

He leaned forward and met her gaze. "You had my recommendation. And I wasn't wrong."

"Your father would probably disagree," she said with a chuckle.

"I wasn't wrong," he repeated.

She searched his eyes, but he didn't crack a smile as he stared steadily at her. Finally, she had to look away from the intensity of his gaze. Whether his determination came from his opposition to his father or his support of her, she wasn't sure, but how could he not see that bringing her into Colton Plastics was probably the biggest mistake of his professional life? Just like taking him into bed had been her worst mistake, personally and professionally, no matter how deeply they'd seemed to connect at the time.

Travis sank back into the chair, folded his arms and crossed one leg over the other.

"Sorry. I shouldn't have brought your dad into this discussion. I wasn't playing fair, and he had nothing to do with it."

He shrugged and then uncrossed his arms. "You're probably right about what he would think, anyway."

Travis laced his fingers and glanced over at the line of windows again, likely seeing images in his memories instead of whatever was outside. An idea that had been playing at the periphery of her thoughts came into clear focus then.

"If you were in HR, you should have been able to see the parking lot from those windows," she said. "Were there still a lot of reporters out there?"

"Yeah. Some. Fewer even than this morning, though. They might not be here because they're at my condo, waiting for us to return from the office."

She hoped that wasn't the case, but it was a possibility. "Or maybe they're hanging around the police station, waiting for your sister to give an update on the murder from yesterday."

After standing up slowly to avoid the head rush, she

collected both piles of résumés. "Wait here. I'm going to drop these off with Jan and have her shred the extras."

He started to stand as well, but she gestured for him to stay seated. "Just stick around. I'll be right back."

She did as she said, hurrying to the opposite side of the building and returning only minutes later.

"Okay, what did you want to talk about?" Travis asked as she moved to her seat.

Instead of answering immediately, Tatiana grabbed the laptop and lifted its lid.

"Better pull the chair closer," she said.

Though she'd signed into her email on the new laptop, she avoided checking her messages again. This was more important for her to take care of right now. Travis had done so much for her, from preparing healthy meals to checking in on her at work to that drive out of town to meet Ellie. It was time she did something for him.

"Why? Are you making another list?"

"No, I have to write a statement, and I'll need your help."

"I don't think this is how it's done, though," he said.

"What do you mean?"

"I try to know as little about this subject as possible, but to make a statement to police you have to be in the presence of an actual police officer."

She opened the document and started typing. "Good thing it's not that type of statement."

He tilted his head, squinting. "Then what is it?"

"It's time for me to speak formally to the press."

Chapter Eleven

Just before five o'clock, Travis reluctantly stood at the revolving door in Colton Plastics' huge, slate-tiled lobby. Outside, several reporters were perched on curbs, probably freezing as they ate their dinners from takeout containers and talked. In minutes, they would pop up as his employees rushed out the front door and tried to escape without being cornered and questioned.

"You're sure you still want to do this?" he said over his shoulder to Tatiana, who was behind him.

She didn't look up from the document they'd prepared together. "Yes, I'm sure. Relax. It'll be fine."

She wasn't even peeking around him at the wolves about to devour her. Instead, she waved at the two day-shift security guards, who were getting more entertainment than they'd had all day.

"Listen," he said.

"What?"

"You're used to controlled trials in an engineering lab. You won't have any command over what happens once you step out in front of them. They could ask you anything. *Anything.* And if you don't answer it, you'll be on camera not commenting on it."

She held her gloved hands wide. "I can do this. Trust me."

"I do trust you. I don't *them*."

"You sound like my dad before I went out on my first date."

He glanced back in time to see her eyes widen over what she'd said.

"We can still bail," he suggested.

"I want to do this. I'm sick of riding in the back of a cargo van."

He would have asked her what the van had to do with her stepping out in public this way, but a few of the reporters and camera operators started shifting outside as if someone had seen them.

"Don't say I didn't warn you."

They stepped through the revolving door. Once outside, they continued together down the walk to the area where the press had been kept at a distance with lighted barricades. Reporters, some familiar, some not, rushed up with either their notebooks or huge microphones.

"Good evening. I'm Travis Colton, founder and co-CEO of Colton Plastics. Our new co-CEO will be reading a prepared statement, and then she will take a few questions." Or none, if he had anything to say about it. "So, I'll turn this over to Tatiana."

She stepped in front of the collection of microphones. "Hello."

Immediately, she bent her head to look at the statement in her hands, appearing nervous and stiff.

"My name is Tatiana Davison—"

"Hey, Tatiana," someone called from the back. "What's it like to have a dad who's a serial killer?"

She froze, her eyes wide, her jaw slack. But move-

ment continued all around her as other reporters, freed
from the decorum of a press conference, began to shout
questions at her from all directions.

Travis held up both hands to stop the noise. "Please
allow Tatiana to speak, or we will end this press conference immediately."

Finally, the crowd quieted.

"Read," he said in a low voice.

She blinked several times, then lifted the folder and
started reading again. But he knew her well-crafted
statement had already lost its impact. No matter what
she said then, the TV footage would show the deer-in-
the-headlights look that had flashed across her face
when that awful question was lobbed at her.

"Please allow me to address the situation involving
my father, Len Davison. Grave Gulch Police have informed me that my father is wanted for questioning regarding a murder that took place in Grave Gulch Park."

As she continued to read, her voice became stronger, and her shoulders straightened. This was the image
she'd wanted to portray to reporters and the public.
The one they'd planned. He couldn't have been prouder
of her for that recovery. Still, his hands twitched as
he searched the crowd for the reporter who asked that
awful question. Good thing he couldn't identify the
guy, or no one would have been able to guarantee that
hack's safety.

"Also, be aware that all Americans, including my
father, are entitled to a fair trial," she continued. "He
has not been convicted of any crime.

"I ask that you please respect my privacy during this
challenging time for my family. Also, please refrain

from questioning Colton Plastics employees regarding this private matter. Thank you."

Travis leaned into the microphone. "Now we have time for a few *appropriate* questions."

A familiar woman with an olive complexion and a long black ponytail stepped in front of the others and extended a tiny microphone.

"Ms. Davison, I'm Dominique de la Vega, investigative reporter for the *Grave Gulch Gazette*. Can you tell me if you've spoken with Len Davison since his release in December, following the disappearance of compelling DNA evidence connecting him to the murder of Vincent Gully? And are you familiar with a GGPD forensic scientist named Randall Bowe?"

"Uh. I don't think—" Tatiana shook her head. "Sorry. Could you repeat the question?"

Dominique dutifully asked again.

"Um, no, I haven't. And, yes, I have been informed about the case against Mr. Bowe."

Travis held his breath as she answered the second question about Bowe. The strange thing was that though he didn't know all of her story, he sensed that Tatiana had lied when answering the first question. The one about speaking to her dad. If that was true, she'd also lied to him.

After a few more questions that Tatiana handled better than the first two, Travis ended the press conference and ushered her back inside the building.

"That went okay, right?"

She squinted as she asked it, hinting that even she recognized it hadn't been a perfect appearance. He was tempted to take her in his arms and comfort her—and also to shake her for talking him into conducting a press conference when she wasn't close to ready. He had re-solved to hire a public relations director for CP. If he'd had one already—and that director had allowed the two co-CEOs to make that appearance—Travis would have fired the guy on the spot.

"It wasn't *bad*, right?"

Tatiana lowered her head as she trudged past the el-evator to the stairs. "Then it must have been even worse that I thought it was…and I thought it was awful."

"It wasn't your fault," he said from behind her as he climbed. "Someone lobbed a verbal grenade at you for your first question, then they didn't even step up and take credit for it."

She reached the second-floor landing and turned back to him. "I should have expected it, though. Maybe wrapped up in pretty, distant words, but I should have known that question was coming and had a response ready."

"That would have been a good idea."

Travis followed her as she returned to her office and they both dropped down in the seats they'd occupied earlier. "I shouldn't have rushed it," she admitted, plant-ing her elbows on her desk. "Obviously, I had to speak to them at some point, but I should have waited until I was ready. *Really* ready."

Because she would get no argument from him on that point, he didn't say anything at all. Like he'd told her, he'd made no mistake in recommending her for the position of co-CEO, but he couldn't say the same for so many of the decisions he'd made involving her since then.

"Do you think they're going to trash me on the nightly news?" she asked after a long pause.

He shook his head. "It will probably be all right. They know that the question the guy asked was a low blow."

"You don't have to sugar coat it for me, you know."

He shifted in his seat. "What do you mean?"

"You know they'll make me look like an idiot, which I made awfully easy for them. So, don't lie."

"Funny that you should say that…"

"What do you mean?"

Travis stood up from the chair and crossed to her office door. He hated lies, but she'd told falsehoods to him and gotten him to cover for her to his cousins about the messages she ignored in Paris. Whether or not she'd asked him to lie, he was a fool to set aside his moral code to protect her when she refused to tell *him* the truth.

He considered not answering her question at all, but as he opened the door, he couldn't stop himself.

"If you don't think we should lie to each other, then tell me this. When did you really speak with your dad last? And why did you lie to *me* about it?"

Then he stepped outside and closed the door behind him.

TATIANA HAD DONE her daddy proud at that press conference, in his opinion. Well, except for the part where she'd looked shocked after that amazing first question came from the gaggle of reporters. *Go big or go home. Am I right?*

But the question seemed to surprise his lady love, which in turn had shocked the hell out of him. How could she not have been prepared for someone to ask that? Reporters and everyone else who would watch or read the articles later would be dying to know what it was like to be Len Davison's daughter. *Dying.* He chuckled over his word choice. A little insider humor, and he'd earned his spot in the club.

If he hadn't known better, he might have thought she wasn't as proud of her father's accomplishments as she should have been. He was in on the gag, though. Tatiana was a brilliant woman, too smart not to realize that Len Davison was a celebrity, a hero and a mystery. No one would even have heard of Grave Gulch if not for his work. The fear and shock in Tatiana's beautiful hazel eyes had to have been part of her performance, making for better television. Who could blame her? She would be interviewed in documentaries for years to come, and she needed to start building her innocent persona now.

It was unfortunate that the media presence at Colton Plastics was smaller tonight. But those reporters who missed the press conference had no one to blame but themselves for relaxing their vigils outside the headquarters.

He guessed he couldn't blame them for choosing, instead, to wait outside the Grave Gulch Police Department for updates on the newest murder. So many bodies, so little time. They were going by the old journalism adage "if it bleeds, it leads," and the freshest one was still painting the snow red.

He tried to ignore the extra little thrill that came with knowing that Chief Melissa Colton would be updating the press on *his* work this time. But that day he couldn't help standing a little taller among the reporters finishing their feeds or hanging around for quick interviews. Too bad he would have to watch the event at the police department on TV. He also needed to remember that a protégé must not try to overtake the notoriety of his mentor. At least not right away.

There was plenty of time for that later, after he and Tatiana consummated their match made in, if not heaven, somewhere awfully close. He couldn't wait to introduce her to Polly, too. His dog was going to love her, though his furry friend might balk at giving up her side of the bed. He couldn't wait to share his books with Tatiana and teach her about some of the most fascinating serial killers of their time, some more infamous than her father. He might even allow her to flip through the books herself one day, but only if she promised to wear cotton gloves and never to fold the pages.

He smiled as he replayed the press conference in his mind, Tatiana's hair tied back in a way he would never permit her to wear it. It had been so like a Colton to horn in on an event that should have been Tatiana's moment to shine. Something about the way Travis Colton had hovered left him grinding his molars. The Colton Plastics founder had taken over the show, introducing her and then stepping in again the moment she'd faced her first question. The familiar way he'd tucked his hand under her elbow to guide her to the microphones had grated on him as well.

Like a father. Or a *lover*.

Immediately, he shot a glance to the revolving door through which Tatiana had vanished with her protector. Now it made sense who'd helped her disappear each day after work. Had Colton taken his sweet, innocent Tatiana to some undisclosed location? Or even his own home? Had he been trying to seduce her, or had he already tasted her charms? He fisted his hands so hard that his nails bit into his palms through his gloves, and he chomped down on the inside of his cheek so hard that he tasted blood.

Colton needed to know that not everything could be his with a snap of fingers. Some things were intended only for those who'd earned the right. The guy would pay a price for trying to take what was rightfully his. But for now, he needed to be patient. To observe. To plan.

Good thing he'd thought ahead to record the evening news on WOGG and competing stations. No way had he planned to miss broadcasts of this press conference. He'd expected that the recording would be a lovely keepsake of the early days of his and Tatiana's romance, but now he'd made it that much better.

Each time they watched it together, they would hear that amazing first question, happy to know that the voice coming from the back was his. What a wonderful surprise for her. He couldn't wait to tell her someday soon. It was almost a marriage proposal on live TV... Only the bride didn't know the groom yet.

Chapter Twelve

The cold, silent ride back to Travis's condo, this time riding in his fancy new SUV, led Tatiana to a baked chicken dinner, where the only sounds were the occasional scrapes of knives and forks and the clinking of ice cubes. She wanted to shout that Travis was too old to use the silent treatment and tell herself she was too far away from childhood to let it get to her. But by the time that Travis walked across the kitchen and returned with a bowl of fresh fruit for dessert, she'd had enough.

She stood up, took the bowl and spoon from his hands, and pointed for him to sit again. He frowned but, after a few seconds, obeyed.

"Okay, I lied," she said as she set the fruit on the table. "Does that make you happy?"

"Why would that make me happy? I hate lies." With jerking movements, he scooped fruit salad, made of oranges, pears and grapes, onto their plates.

"I meant are you glad I admitted—" She shook her head and then shrugged. "It doesn't matter. I'm sorry for doing it."

Travis sat up straight, as though he wasn't ready to accept her apology.

"Then you *do* know where your dad is hiding?"

She'd been scooting around the fruit with her fork, but at his question, she stabbed an orange slice and looked up. "Of course, I don't."

"How do I know you're telling the truth *now*?"

It stung more than it should have that he'd believed her capable of keeping quiet if she knew where her dad was hiding. When had what Travis Colton thought of her become so important?

"But you *did* speak to him."

His stare dared her to deny it.

"Yeah. Once. Right after he was released. Police had told him not to leave town, but I'm guessing he already had."

"He didn't tell you anything?"

"It was a really brief call." She shifted her shoulders and finally set her fork aside. She couldn't eat more, anyway. "So, it felt like a little white lie when I said it during the Colton Plastics interview. A short conversation. With no real details. And it only happened that once."

She was talking too fast, but she couldn't make herself slow down. Not with her father's damning words swirling through her thoughts again. Should she tell Travis what her dad had said? Could she trust another person with the suspicions that had weighed on her heart for so long? If she did tell anyone, why would she choose Travis, the man who had a tougher time in naming relatives who *weren't* cops than those who were?

"I know of other things that happened *only once* that weren't so trivial," he said.

They exchanged a meaningful look before his gaze lowered to her tummy. Clearly, he was trying to lighten the mood by introducing a different subject. Only that one was just as heavy.

"Guess not," she conceded.

"And, technically, it was one night, but it wasn't once."

She shook her head, but one side of her mouth lifted. Leave it to a guy to break it down to something so basic. She pushed aside memories she shouldn't have been recalling and lifted her fork again. Maybe she could get a few more bites down.

Travis made a strange sound in his throat, as if remembering that they'd declared *that* subject off-limits.

"Why'd you feel you had to lie about talking to your father?"

She reluctantly looked up from her plate. For her, both topics—her dad and their night together—were equally dangerous.

"You have to understand that his arrest was humiliating for me. How could my own father be accused of murder? I believed the cops must have made a mistake, that he was innocent. After his release, I wanted to pretend it never happened. That's why I ignored the phone messages from police, too."

"So, when the matter came up during your interview with the board, you just wanted to separate yourself as much as you could from your father."

"I guess so." She shrugged. "I wanted to be like any other job candidate, judged only on my own merits rather than my father's infamy."

"I get it. I hate being judged because of my relatives, too."

Her gaze flicked to his then, and he lifted a brow. On that night six weeks before, he'd only described himself as a maverick *after* she'd lumped him in with his police relatives.

"I'm sure you do. Sorry."

Travis planted his forearms on the table and folded his hands. "Since we're sharing a home right now, I have to ask. Was that the only lie you told me, or are there more that I should know about? I will tell you now that I have zero to report."

She couldn't help smiling at that. "None come to mind, either, but I'll let you know if I remember any others."

"Seriously. I have to be able to trust you. It's only a matter of time until the press figures out that you're staying here. And neither of us knows what's going on with your stalker, whether he's just trying to frighten you or is a real threat. I need to be sure we're on the same side."

Tatiana dampened her lips as she realized he wasn't joking anymore. He probably had no idea how refreshing his words were for her to hear. After her father's arrest had painted all her childhood memories with a fuzzy brush, Travis offered her and requested from her a friendship based on both honesty and clarity. It was the best gift anyone had ever given her.

She met his gaze directly. "You can trust me."

"I hope so."

"Do you want me to tell you what he said?" She spoke the words before she could talk herself out of it.

He blinked a few times and then watched her for several seconds.

"That depends on whether you're just trying to prove something by telling me, or whether you *want* to do it."

"Can it be both?" As much as she needed him to

know that he could count on her as they searched for answers about the stalker, she also wanted him to understand the dilemma she'd carried since her last conversation with her father.

"I guess it can."

She sat higher in the chair and took a deep breath before plunging forward. "He just said three words—'I'm sorry, dumpling.'"

"That's it?"

She nodded, though her hand automatically lifted to her mouth, a sense of betrayal landing on her like a crushing weight. Travis's gaze moved from her hand to her eyes and then down to his own plate.

For what felt like an eternity, neither spoke. Tatiana squirmed in her seat, wondering again if she should have kept that information to herself. Just when she was ready to call out, "Say something," he finally did.

"It was only three words. Were you even certain it was him?"

"I know his voice. And dumpling was a term of endearment he often used when I was a little girl." Just recalling it hurt now, the memory bitter instead of bittersweet.

"So, it was him. Then do you have any idea what he was sorry for?"

"What do you think?"

He shook his head. "It's more important what *you* think."

Tatiana stared at her folded hands. "I feel like a lousy daughter for believing it, but how can I not? He had to be saying he was guilty of that murder in Grave Gulch Park, even if there was no longer any evidence to prove it."

"Maybe you're reading too much into a cryptic message. He could have as easily been trying to protect you from knowing the truth about him."

"Who's reading too much now?" She smiled, wishing she could accept Travis's sweet take on the story but understanding she couldn't. "If you believe that anything he told me was for my benefit, then we don't need a new PR exec at Colton Plastics. You're already a spin doctor."

"Okay, maybe he didn't do it for *you*," Travis said, "but that call wouldn't count as the briefest confession in GGPD history, either." He stood and stacked their dishes into a neat pile. "There are many reasons he could have apologized. For disappearing when he should have stuck around for you. Or because he regretted that his arrest caused you embarrassment. Or even that he's sorry you lost your mom, but he misses her too much to stay where everything reminds him of her."

Instead of answering, she grabbed the glasses and stepped past him to the sink. That was easier than facing him while he gave the same excuses that she had been telling herself for three months. They sounded even less believable coming from Travis.

"You don't believe any of those things, do you?" she asked. She moved out of the way so that he could reach the sink. He rinsed, and she loaded the dishwasher.

"We don't know anything for certain yet."

Tatiana slid a glance his way, but he didn't look back at her. He'd admitted that he hated lies and said he would tell her the truth, yet he was spinning this story to shield her from heartbreak. She no longer wanted to make excuses for her father, but Travis was sweet to try. A girl could fall in love with a guy like Travis if she wasn't careful.

"I'll be sure to tell him to hire you as his personal publicist if he's ever caught," she said to bring them back to reality. Then she closed the dishwasher with a click.

"Do you think he ever will be? Caught, that is?"

His questions triggered another set of emotions. How could she even joke about his capture? This was her *father*, the guy who always held her hair when she was sick since her mom had a weak stomach, who'd taught her to drive and bought her first car, then made sure she knew how to check her oil and change a tire before he let her operate it. If he were taken into custody, he would face murder charges. Nothing could make that funny.

Travis must have recognized her internal battle, as he didn't press for an answer. Instead he grabbed the teakettle off the stove, filled it at the sink and returned it to the burner. Then he grabbed two mugs from the cabinet and a wooden box from a drawer and carried all of it to the table.

"I guess I never asked if you like tea," he said as he arranged the mugs and spoons.

"I do."

"There're all kinds in here." He lifted the lid off the box. "I'm guessing you'll want herbal?"

"I was planning on skipping the caffeine, but thanks for the reminder." She crossed to him, pulled out a bag of vanilla chamomile and plunked it on the table. "You might have no interest in being a real law enforcement officer, but you have the diet police thing down," she joked. "Are you going to get worse after my ob-gyn appointment tomorrow?"

"Probably." He laughed.

"At least you warned me," she said dryly. "Then you should be aware that I might balk. Probably a lot."

"I wouldn't expect any less."

Only when they were seated again with steaming mugs in front of them did Tatiana tackle the question he'd asked before.

"I don't know if he'll be caught," she admitted. "Dad's a smart guy with a real technical mind and street smarts. He also always loved those survival shows and liked reading about people who lived off the grid. Guess we know why now."

Travis dunked his bag of Earl Grey in his own mug several times and then used his spoon to squeeze it out before setting it aside.

"Those are the kind of details that the police were asking for when they interviewed you."

She nodded, trying to decide if she regretted not sharing at least that much information with police.

"Did your mom have strong technical skills, too, or did that come from your dad?"

"None," she said with a smile. "She couldn't even put a contact in her smartphone, no matter how many times I showed her how to do it. But all the important things, like patience and empathy, I either learned or inherited from her."

"I bet there were other good things from your dad, too."

She planted her elbows on the table and lowered her face into her hands. "If only I didn't question everything that he taught me now."

"I get that. The same guy who probably guided you in your values has put you in conflict with them—because what kind of daughter wants to see her dad go to jail?"

For several seconds, she could only stare at him. How had he figured out and then put so succinctly the battle waging inside her?

"This isn't some ploy to get me to give up all my secrets so you can report in with Chief Colton, is it?" She chuckled, lifted her tea, and took a sip.

"I thought you said you didn't know anything that would help police."

At Travis's words, she set her mug on the table with a thud, the liquid sloshing over the top. As he sopped up the mess with a napkin, he grinned at her. Clearly, she hadn't been the only one trying—and failing—to get a laugh from the other.

"You make it too easy." He took a drink and set it aside.

"Glad I could help." She rolled her eyes. "You think I should tell the police about the call, don't you?"

"I never said that."

"But you said—"

He shook his head until she stopped. "I told you they were looking for that type of information. There's a difference. It was, and is, your choice how much you share."

"So, the call?" Her chest felt tight as uncertainty filled her.

"It makes him *sound* guilty, but it doesn't prove anything," he said. "Anyway, they have DNA evidence on the second murder charge. I'm sure the police would like to hear about it in connection with the first charge, but it's up to you whether you tell them. If you did, then maybe they would check your phone records to determine his location at the time of the call."

"Location would be all it showed," she said. "It was probably a burner phone. I remember because I didn't recognize the number and almost didn't answer. I told you. He's a smart guy. He wouldn't have left clues like that."

"What about the first two murder scenes? Police found DNA evidence *both* times."

"That I've never been able to make sense of. Maybe he left clues on purpose. He could have wanted to get caught." She lifted her hands, palms up. "But then I never really knew Len Davison, either."

"Don't say that." He shook his head. "Maybe you knew him when he was his best self. You don't know what losing a life partner can do to someone. Something could have snapped in him when your mom died last year. What if he just couldn't cope?"

It would be so easy to believe Travis. He offered her a convenient escape from a maze with too many turns and dead ends, but the path he'd cleared had left her without the real answers she craved.

"We still don't know if there were other victims." Her heart ached at just giving voice to the suspicion. "Dad's job might have been just one of the reasons we moved around a lot."

He nodded, as if he'd considered the same possibility, but his eyes were filled with such compassion that she straightened her back. "I don't need your pity."

"Good. Because I'm not offering any. But you need to know that no matter what Melissa, Troy and Bryce said, you aren't obligated to help them build a case against your own father."

He held his hands out in an imaginary scale. "If you knew something important like the location of a murder weapon, that would be different. And you could be forced to testify if the case ever went to trial, since you're a daughter, not a spouse."

"But Troy said I should help them stop him, or I'll feel responsible—"

"They're trying to catch someone they believe is a serial killer. But whether you help them any further or not is up to you. You've answered questions the best you could at the time. Twice. That can be enough. Our best has to be good enough."

That he lowered his gaze and started stuffing napkins and used tea bags into their empty mugs made her wonder if he was speaking of more than just her situation with her father.

"Parents make mistakes. A lot of them," she told *him* this time. He needed to hear it. How could he have so much understanding for her father and be so uncharitable to his own? "We'll make them, too."

He looked up from the mugs to where her left hand rested on her belly.

"And all parents worry," she continued, "that someone will hurt their children. That they won't be able to protect them. Could that be what your dad has tried to do with all his caution about the business? Could he have been trying to shield you from failure?"

Travis shook his head, closing his eyes, as if he didn't want anyone to defend his father. But then he opened them again and pointed to her abdomen.

"No one's going to hurt *this* child. Not if I can help it."

His pronouncement made her smile, but then sadness

filled her instead. "I just worry that the odds will be stacked against this little one. How could they not be? You heard what that reporter asked? What was it like to be a serial killer's daughter? Our child will never be able to escape that lethal legacy. He or she will always carry the DNA of a criminal. Just like I do."

"That's where you're wrong."

"How could I be—"

He shook his head to interrupt her. "*This child* will know only love and unconditional acceptance. From both parents. *This child* will wake every morning and go to sleep every night confident that his mom and dad have his back."

Tatiana's eyes fluttered, and her heart raced like she'd been running up a staircase. How could he be so committed to her baby—*theirs*—when they'd known about his or her existence such a short time? How could he make a commitment to this little person when she and Travis hadn't figured out the boundaries of their professional relationship or the possibility of a personal one? Was it instinct that caused her to splay her fingers over her belly in protectiveness?

"You don't know what will happen in the future." She shook her head for emphasis. "Whether my dad will be captured. Or what will happen with the company. We haven't even told anyone about the baby— Len Davison's grandchild. And then there's someone coming after *me*, making a normal life impossible for us in Grave Gulch."

"I don't have to know what will happen in the future. And I don't care *whose* blood flows through his veins, as you said it the other day. This is our child—

yours and mine—and we'll do whatever is necessary to protect him."

He reached out a hand so that it was only inches away from the one she'd rested against her body.

"May I?"

Something fluttered inside her though it was too soon to have been the baby's movement, but finally she nodded. He rested his right hand on top of her left one, his so large that only her fingertips peeked out. Time could have frozen, or maybe it was just her, as they stared down at their hands. Travis shifted his, though, and so easily their fingers laced, a matched pair, their only mission sheltering their child. She'd once welcomed him inside her body, but no contact until that moment had ever felt more intimate.

After what felt like seconds but must have been minutes, Tatiana lifted her gaze to find Travis staring back at her, his eyes wide, his pupils so large that there was barely a ring of blue around them. He cleared his throat and slid his hand away from hers.

"Sorry. I shouldn't have—"

But Tatiana couldn't allow him to apologize away that perfect moment. Not when it seemed like two sides of an angle, coming together at a perfect point. Not when nothing else had felt so right in the six weeks since she'd left Grave Gulch. Since she'd left *him*. So, she did the only thing she could think of to stop the flow of words, even if it meant ignoring her own gut shouting that she would regret it.

She leaned in and kissed him.

Chapter Thirteen

Tatiana's swoop toward him came in slow motion, and yet he still started when she touched her lips to his. But even if it took a moment for his mind to catch up, the rest of him was immediately on board. His arms closed around her and pulled her to him, and his fingers sank into the silk of her hair, still tied at the back of her neck. Her scent, her taste, the satiny feel of her skin all enveloped him in a heady concoction he couldn't have resisted, even if he'd wanted to.

And right now, he didn't want to.

From that first touch, Travis couldn't imagine how he'd resisted doing this since the moment she'd returned to Grave Gulch, and they'd been forced to walk the same hallways and breathe the same air. Now he couldn't get close enough to her, couldn't stop rolling his mouth over her sexy, pouty bottom lip. And when he dabbed his tongue to the seam of her mouth, and she opened for him, he couldn't sink deeply enough into her sweetness.

What was wrong with him? He'd been with women before. He'd been with *her* before. Sure, it had been a while since he'd last had sex. Yet something was different now. It was as if his most ardent desires had become entangled in that mass of hair and in those haunting eyes.

He traced a tiny circle on her neck with his tongue, her pulse thudding beneath it, and reached behind her to free her hair. It cascaded down her back. Then with a gentle tug on her shoulders, he pulled her into his lap, blessing his decorator this time for choosing the armless chairs that made it so easy for her to straddle him.

When Tatiana scooted closer and fitted herself to him while kissing her way up his neck, he decided to send flowers to his interior designer the next day. Or his new co-CEO. Or both.

Before now, he'd longed to forget that night, a painting he'd only been able to recall in broad strokes. Now he resented those large swaths of color, craving the precision that too much wine had dulled. Much of it was coming back to him, though, as he skimmed his hands down her sides and then traced his thumbs over the hardened tips of her amazing breasts. But as he settled them into his palms, heavier and fuller than he remembered, Travis stilled his hands.

Something was different, all right.

Was he craving her more now because she carried his child? His reaction to her had been primal before, but the intensity of it now shocked him. His eyes opened in time to see Tatiana squeeze hers closed in what looked like pain rather than pleasure.

"Ouch," she said, her lids lifting.

Hands shifting to her elbows, he eased her back from him. Immediately, she crossed her arms over her chest. Then she curled her shoulders forward so that even her own arms wouldn't touch them. "I'm really sore there."

"Sorry. I'd forgotten that was a thing."

He helped her off his lap and back into her own chair, not missing when her gaze slipped to his lap, where the evidence of what she did to him was *hard* to hide. He leaned forward, wishing he'd worn darker slacks. Or stopped her before she'd kissed him. Or at least avoided trying to repeat their activities of six weeks before. Tonight, he didn't even have an excuse.

"I, uh, don't know what *that* was," he said.

She stared down at her crossed arms. "I think that's fairly obvious."

"I'm sor—"

"Don't worry." She rushed over his words. "It won't happen again."

That wasn't what he was worried about. How could he tell her that he would think of nothing else until she was in his arms *and* in his bed again?

"It's not your fault. I was the one who let the conversation get so—I don't know—*intense*. The one who went all caveman about the baby."

"Good analogy, but you don't have to make excuses for me." Tatiana grabbed the mugs he'd started to put away before and carried them to the sink. "I'm a big girl. I get it."

She didn't. That was just it. But he couldn't afford to explain it to her right then. The truth was that he couldn't protect her if he became so distracted by her. Nor could he safeguard their baby, or the interests of Colton Plastics, when it would be so easy for him to become lost in her. When he might be tempted to toss away his road map to their relationship and stay happily adrift for good.

Hadn't he learned his lesson with Aubrey? He wasn't a great judge of character. Tatiana had already admitted she'd lied to him, too. He couldn't be certain that there weren't more to go with that one, hers dangerous because of her connection to a fugitive from justice. She'd told him he could trust her, but could he?

"Let's just forget about this. We should get to bed, anyway." He cleared his throat and shifted his feet. "I mean, you should get to bed *downstairs*, and I'll go to my room up here."

"Glad you clarified that."

He could have sworn she was grinning when she looked away from him, which made his jaw tighten, but he continued anyway. "We have to be at our best if we're going to fool your stalker into believing we don't have him figured out."

"Since we're not even close to determining who sent that message, we won't have trouble pretending."

"Guess not."

When Tatiana started from the room without looking back, Travis followed her into the hall. She kept her head high, though she had to believe that he'd rejected her not once but twice now. Even with all those reasons he'd given himself for keeping space between them, he had to force himself not to chase after her, pull her into his arms, and show her just how wrong she was.

She glanced back at him when she reached the top of the stairs. "See you tomorrow."

He should have let her go, but he couldn't resist a parting comment.

"Tatiana?"

She stopped and looked over at him.

"If this were another time, another place, then…" He stared at his feet before looking up again. "Anyway, I'm—"

She tilted up her chin so quickly that he stopped, those eyes that had been filled with passion only moments before now appearing more raw than angry.

"Please don't apologize again." She cleared her throat. "Look, if anyone should apologize tonight, it should be me. I kissed you. So, sorry. I shouldn't have—" She blinked several times as her voice faltered, and then she stared down at her hands. Again, he was tempted to go after her, and this time, he took one step. As her eyes widened, he stopped.

"Good night."

She fled down the stairs. Though she didn't stop or look back when she reached the lower level, Travis stood staring down at the empty steps, watching after her for a long time. When the sound of a door closing to her suite filtered up to him, he shook his head.

What was he doing? He'd made every mistake possible since inviting her into his company and into his life. He seemed to only be gearing up for more and hurting her in the process. However, this wasn't only about protecting her. He'd told himself he would never be vulnerable to a woman again, and he'd already opened to Tatiana in a way he never had with anyone before. Did he have no sense of self-preservation? Could he take a risk on the serial killer's daughter, who still seemed to have something to hide?After the sounds of her movement died down, he began the ritual of turning off all the lights, checking the doors and arming the security system. Grave Gulch used to be a place where people didn't worry about dangers from outside. Not anymore.

When he'd finished the evening tasks, he returned to his master suite, which felt emptier than ever. Though he didn't need one anymore to cool his body, he climbed in for a punishing cold shower. Then, shivering afterward, he snuggled in the blankets and prepared himself for the sleepless night ahead.

AFTER HER LUNCHTIME appointment that next afternoon, Tatiana parked Travis's SUV in his assigned spot and headed back inside the Colton Plastics headquarters. She hurried past the few straggling reporters still hanging around the parking lot, one of a few reasons that Travis had been unable to go with her to the appointment. A secret pregnancy wouldn't remain concealed for long in a small city if Travis Colton had been seen entering an ob-gyn office.

After passing through security, Tatiana skipped the elevator and took the stairs. She planned to get extra steps since her doctor had said walking was one of the best exercises for *women like her*.

The words of the older ob-gyn she'd chosen made her smile. At least the lady hadn't said "in a family way" like her grandmother would have. And the doctor hadn't blinked when she'd asked if it would be possible to get a noninvasive prenatal DNA test. It was kind of Travis not to ask for one, but he deserved to know for certain that the child was his.

Tatiana patted her tote bag, which carried precious cargo now but no laptop. She was going to be a mom, and she had an ultrasound photo in there to prove it. Despite her embarrassment over his rejection *again* last night, and though they'd been dancing carefully around each other all morning, she still couldn't wait to share the news.

She couldn't think about how mortified she'd been while escaping downstairs to hide in her room, feeling alone without his arms around her and still aching for his touch. None of that could matter today when she could confirm that Travis was going to be a father.

As employees who passed her greeted her, Tatiana returned the favor, but didn't stop to chat. The two IT guys—Lucas and Dylan, if she remembered correctly—waved from the break room. One of the female engineers she'd met the day before greeted her at the bottom of the stairs.

"Hi, Tatiana. Hope you had a nice lunch," the woman said. "Try anyplace new?"

"No. Just running errands on my lunch hour." Tatiana tried to recall her name. "It's Christa, right?"

"Good memory." She waved and continued toward the lab.

She was on the fourth step when someone spoke from behind her.

"Hey there, Tatiana."

The deep male voice set her nerves on edge, but she'd been jumpy most of the morning, anyway. At least, when she hadn't been in her private restroom pacing and trying to decide if her breakfast would be making a return visit.

Stopping, she gripped the handle and looked back at him.

"Oh, hi…" She milked her memory again, but this time, it came up dry.

"Enzio DeLuca," he said. "Engineering."

"Right. Enzio."

"Don't worry. You'll get the names down soon enough."

"I appreciate the support." She took a few more steps up, holding the rail tightly in case she became dizzy.

"I never have understood how women can manage to walk across the room in heels, let alone to navigate the stairs, but you're doing a fine job. You look lovely in that skirt, by the way."

And she'd never understood why some men felt the need to comment on a woman's appearance while they were positioned to get a great look at her ass or her legs beneath her skirt. And she was his boss!

"We do our best."

Tatiana didn't answer his other comment, given that he shouldn't have made it, and he was giving her the creeps. She made a mental note to talk to Travis about the company's sexual harassment policies and either have HR add additional training for everyone or insist that the older engineer have a refresher course. She would also make a trip to the shoe store a higher priority on her to-do list.

As she exited the stairs, she gave Enzio a side glance. He waved and, without looking back at her, continued to the third floor.

She barely had time to hang up her coat and stow her laptop bag before her gaze caught a vase of yellow roses on the bookshelf next to the window.

"Subtle," she groused.

Still, she brushed her fingertips over her lips that suddenly tingled again. He would stop apologizing to her over his kiss if he knew that the memory of those tender moments would keep her warm through many lonely nights ahead.

"Knock. Knock."

She whirled to find the man she was thinking of standing at her open doorway but waiting to be invited in. That she appreciated. She waved him inside.

"How'd it go?" Travis asked.

"What?" She shook her head. "Oh. You mean my physical? It was *positively* delightful."

He glanced behind him to the open door and then stepped over to close it. When he faced her again, he was grinning. "Then why don't you look happier? I know it was kind of a surprise, but you're okay with it now, aren't you?"

"I am. Really."

Tatiana tried to smile, but the incident on the stairs was still bothering her. She'd told Ellie that she hadn't felt strange vibes from any of the male employees. That was no longer the case. Could Enzio be the man who'd sent her the email?

"Then what is it?"

"We'll deal with that later. First, let me show you this." She pulled a notebook out of her computer bag and opened it. Inside lay a small square ultrasound photo, showing a mostly white blur, with a black oval in the center and a tiny shape attached on one side.

Travis stepped in front of her desk and reached for it but then looked up in a silent request for permission to touch it. At her nod, he lifted it and turned his back to hide the picture from anyone peering inside the office windows. Then he pointed to the tiny spot in the pond of dark.

"That little bean in the middle is our kid, right?" he asked, grinning.

His happiness was contagious as her excitement from earlier washed over her again, and tears welled in her eyes. The circumstances of the conception didn't matter anymore. They were having a baby together, and no matter what, they would be great co-parents for this child.

"I take it you've seen an ultrasound photo before."

He nodded, still beaming. "You might have noticed, but I have a lot of relatives around here. More if you head to Grand Rapids."

"Well, according to my doctor's calculation, another Colton baby will be born somewhere around October the ninth."

Travis sat forward in the chair. "And there was a heartbeat?"

"I got to hear the little whoosh-whoosh-whoosh, and everything appears to be fine."

Her own heart beat a little faster as she recalled the sound from the Doppler stethoscope. The photo had made their baby real for Travis, but for her, it was hearing that wonderful confirmation of what she'd already known. Their child was growing inside her body, its heart beating out a healthy rhythm, and she was already in love with that tiny person she'd never met.

She reached for the photo that he'd gently rested on the notebook page. "I do have to agree that our child looks like a bean, which has led me to a possible name. If it's a girl, Bean, and if it's a boy, well, Bean."

"At least you're consistent."

"And since he or she bears a resemblance to a shrimp, too, it's going to be a while before I want shrimp cocktail again." She paused, grimacing, as a wave of nausea sprang out of nowhere. "Maybe never."

He rolled his eyes. "Did the doctor give you other details?"

She shared as many as she could with him, surprised that he was interested in hearing them all. For a guy who'd just found out he'd made a woman pregnant by accident, he seemed to be enjoying every minute of it. So much so that she hated to end his good mood by reporting on other events at Colton Plastics.

"Are you ever going to tell me?" he asked.

"I think that's about it."

"I mean, when will you let me know about what was bothering you when I came in? Has there been another email?"

She pointed to her borrowed laptop on the corner of her desk. "I took my bag with all my paperwork but not the laptop to the doctor's office."

"Then what is it?"

As Tatiana told him about the conversation with Enzio on the stairs, Travis's hands fisted against his pant legs, and his jaw flexed, as if he were gritting his teeth.

"I'll fire him."

She raised a hand in a signal for him to stop. "Now we don't know that it was him. He might just be an old-school guy who doesn't realize he lives in a post–Me Too world. Would I say we might want to have the staff go through another round of sexual harassment training modules? Probably. But that doesn't mean that Enzio is the person who sent that email."

Travis frowned, clearly not ready to give the engineer a pass. She tried not to grin over his protectiveness. It wasn't exactly office-appropriate, either, but it was endearing.

"Did he make you uncomfortable?"

"Well, sure—"

"Then we need to call him in and—"

She shook her head. "Do you plan to haul every

guy in the building into our offices? Because I'm nervous around all of them. I can't help feeling I'm being watched."

Travis flexed and unflexed his hands. "But I have to do something."

"Then watch and wait. Remember that Ellie made us promise not to take anything into our own hands. I'm going to hold you to it."

"Fine." As he slumped back into the chair, Travis turned toward the window and pointed to the roses. "Those are nice. Who sent you flowers?"

Tatiana froze, a chill starting somewhere deep inside her and worming its way out. "I thought," she began, then cleared her throat. "I thought they were from *you*."

Travis leaped up from the chair and crossed in three long strides to the vase on the bookshelf. He picked it up just as someone knocked at the door.

"Come in," Tatiana called out.

Jan turned the handle and leaned in.

"I didn't realize you were both in here." She pointed to the roses. "I just wanted to make sure you got the beautiful flowers."

"Do you know how they got in here?" Travis asked.

She stepped inside the room, her brows lifted. "I brought them up after they were delivered to the security desk." Jan smiled at Tatiana. "I hope you don't mind that I unwrapped them for you. We don't get a lot of roses around here between Valentine's and Mother's Day."

"That's fine," she assured the assistant.

Across the room, Travis didn't appear to be listening any longer as he pulled the tiny white envelope from the long plastic prong in the arrangement.

"I didn't open the card. None of my business." Jan turned to go but stopped at the doorway. "All the interviews are set for tomorrow."

"Thanks, Jan. I really appreciate your help."

The woman left quickly, as if she, too, felt the chill in the room. Only then did Travis set aside the flowers and carry the card to Tatiana's desk.

"You weren't *expecting* flowers, were you?"

"Expecting?" She tried to make sense of what he'd said. Then she understood. He'd accepted with no more than her word that the child she carried was his and suddenly had a reason to question whether there might be other men in her life.

She shook her head. "There's no one."

"Then who…?"

Both stared down at the tiny, sealed envelope. Finally, Tatiana reached for it and slid her thumb under the seal. She took a deep breath, and, with trembling fingers, she flipped open the card.

Her breath caught, and blood seemed to freeze in her veins as she read the typed message on the florist's card.

Cheering you on in your new position, Miss Co-CEO. Don't forget to make snow angels. You'll always be my little girl.

Love, Daddy

TATIANA LAY IN bed that night, the white card clasped in her hand appearing more eerie under the soft yellow lamplight. She should have left it at the office to show to the police later like Travis had suggested, but she'd wanted to look at it again. Needed to think. So, she'd slipped it in her purse when they'd left the office. For unlike Travis, who still had the luxury of believing that the flowers could have come from the same person who'd sent her the email—someone who was fixated on her father, her or both—Tatiana knew better.

They were from Len Davison himself.

She should have told Travis right away that her father and not the copycat obsessed with him had sent the flowers. But she'd panicked. Why had it been so easy not to correct Travis when he'd assumed that they were dealing with only one suspect? What was wrong with her? She'd promised not to lie to him, even if it was a lie of omission.

Lies were far from her only problem, she decided, as she stared down at the card in her hands. The one that proved her father was nearby. *You'll always be my little girl.* As they had then, those words on the page made her shiver, and bile backed up in her throat. Whether it was revulsion from her father's actions or fear on his behalf, she wasn't sure. Would he hurt *her*? She shook her head against the pillow, refusing to believe that. But she'd been wrong before. Now she was more convinced than ever that he'd murdered those two men in the park.

My little girl. She didn't know why she kept focusing on that part of the message when the yellow roses and the snow angels had been the most telling parts of the note. Those things would have appeared innocuous to someone who didn't know better. Yellow roses were supposed to mean friendship and joy, and snow angels were almost a given for any Michigan childhood. Both also were symbolic in her family.

Those blooms had been her mother's favorite. On those Friday nights when Len brought Marcia flowers, he'd always included at least one of them in the bouquet, even in the winter when the rest didn't match. What would Travis have thought if he'd known that she'd experienced a moment of profound loss when he'd tossed her roses into the dumpster, and an explosion of lemony petals flew up from the bottom?

The reference to snow angels on her father's card was equally significant. It brought back both happy memories and a location she could still see clearly. She couldn't be sure where her father was, but he'd practically shouted that he was headed to the ice-fishing cabins they'd rented as a family.

Cheering you on... She hated that her father's approval still mattered. That the lingering, hopeful side of her wanted to believe he'd sent those flowers just to celebrate her new position. The developing cynical side knew better. He hadn't called her since December or reached out with a card or a text. Nothing. So why now after he'd been spotted in New York and was more vulnerable to capture? He'd made national news, for God's sake.

Love, Daddy. And suddenly, she knew exactly what the gift had been: a test of her loyalty. Would she tell Travis that the flowers were from her father and report her suspicion about dear old Dad to the police? Her face felt hot, and her stomach churned in a way that had nothing to do with the baby. It was worse than that she'd kept the truth from Travis, and that was bad enough. She'd convinced him to hold off before reporting the gift or even giving Ellie a call. The delay might have prevented her father's capture.

How could she do that to Travis? He'd been so kind to her and so accepting of the pregnancy, and she'd repaid him by involving him in covering up for a murderer. Travis had been right to reject her a second time.

She didn't deserve him, and she didn't deserve to be the mother of their child.

After tucking the card under her pillow and flipping off the lamp, Tatiana lay in the darkness for several minutes. She hugged her knees beneath the covers. Her dad might have intended this as an examination of her devotion to him, but it really was two tests in one. She could honor her dad, or she could earn the trust of her baby's father. Her heart squeezed with the truth that she'd passed Len Davison's test and failed Travis's at the same time.

Chapter Fourteen

A familiar sense of dread settled on Travis's shoulders that Saturday night as he pulled off the quiet lane of massive lakefront properties onto the curved driveway. That wasn't the feeling that he should have when returning to his childhood home, but there you had it. Less ostentatious than most in the west side neighborhood, the yellow wood-frame house had a cross-hipped roof, superior craftsmanship and a feel of old money that disguised the new. It also had a view of Lake Michigan from the bluff out back that could take your breath away.

Travis pushed open the door as quietly as possible, hoping for a moment of calm before the onslaught of family. After leaving his boots in the slate entry with all the others and stowing his coat in the closet, he stepped in his socks on the hardwood that led through the molded-panel, arched hallway to the great room. The scents of his mother's amazing roast beef and the dried lavender she always had in containers throughout the house brought him back to less complicated times.

He paused as he emerged from the tunnel to look out the wall of windows, formed by a set of French doors and three sets of sliding doors with grid-covered windows at the top, connecting them all. Outside, the gun-metal sky stretched down to meet the water at some point, but since March sunsets still collided with the dinner hour, he couldn't see where.

Around the corner and past the staircase, the chaos of a Colton family dinner was already underway in the kitchen. Clarke, the oldest sibling and the one with hair and coloring closest to Travis's, was stuck at the stove stirring something he probably hadn't cooked and scrolling his phone with his free hand. He'd either shed his sweater down to his fitted black T-shirt, or he'd skipped it entirely, since their mother always kept the house warm enough to boil potatoes without lighting the stove.

Youngest brother Stanton set the eight-foot, dark-wood dining table in the great room, his tousled brown hair falling over his piercing blue eyes girls always loved. Funny how Stanton was able to effectively run Colton Protection, an elite agency that provided security services for movie stars and politicians, but he couldn't get the dishes right that he placed around the table. At least their mother, Italia, must not have thought so. She followed behind him, redoing his work.

Even the new Colton recruits had been called into action for the dinner. Clarke's bride-to-be, Everleigh, chopped vegetables at the counter, occasionally using a forearm to push her short blond hair out of her face. Melissa's always well-dressed fiancé, Antonio, was probably sorry he'd worn a suit jacket to a family dinner, since he was stuck helping Frank lift the huge lidded roasting pan from the oven and set it on top of the stove. The local hotelier had a good chance of impressing his future father-in-law with his effort.

At the wet bar, Melissa appeared almost relaxed in her cashmere sweater and dress pants as she opened two bottles of cabernet, but Travis didn't buy her act. Until the suspects in the Grave Gulch murders and the evidence-tampering cases were taken into custody, Chief Colton wouldn't be getting any sleep.

She poured the wine into a glass to sample, but when she caught sight of Travis, she hurried over instead.

"About time you got here," she said as she sidled up next to him.

"It's great to see you, too, sis." He dipped his head to drop a kiss on her cheek. "Looking a little fancier than you did the other night."

She glanced down at his black V-neck sweater and gray wool-blend trousers.

"And you look as fancy as usual. You're lucky I didn't show up in my pajamas the other night. Where is your *houseguest*, by the way?"

The emphasis she placed on the word grated on him, but he refused to let her get to him. "She's at home, but I'll let her know you asked after her."

"Were you too afraid to invite her here?"

This time, he couldn't keep his jaw from flexing. Travis was afraid, all right, but it had nothing to do with bringing Tatiana to a Colton family dinner and everything to do with the creep who'd sent that email and now those flowers. Could they have been the same person, or had Len Davison himself come out of hiding to congratulate his daughter on her new job?

Both of those possibilities made him want to rush out the door right then to get back to her. He wouldn't have come at all if he hadn't been able to hire at the last minute a security guard to stay with her at the condo. His connection to Stanton had paid off there.

"Whoa, it's that bad?"

Travis lifted his gaze to find her observing him in a way that was far more suspicious police officer than concerned sister. He couldn't afford to drift off in his thoughts around her tonight. Melissa was trained in the art of questioning, and he needed to remember that she was curious about *him* this time.

"As a matter of fact, I *did* invite Tatiana, but she wasn't feeling well."

Her exact words had been "not in a million years," so he'd figured his odds of talking her into coming were low. He couldn't blame her for wanting to nap on the sofa under a fuzzy lap blanket until it was time to go to bed for real. It had been a hell of a week for her— for them both—and she had the added stress of a tiny human growing inside her body.

"Besides, you know I can't bring a female friend to a family dinner without giving Mom ideas about grandkids again."

He coughed and turned away to cover it. Though his brothers and sister had joked about who would make Italia Vespucci Colton a grandmother first, he'd never dreamed he would be the one to do it. Now he couldn't wait to tell her.

"I'm worried about you, little brother," she said.

"Don't be," he assured her. Even with the challenges he faced, he'd never doubted that the Coltons always had each other's backs.

"Did I hear you say you are bringing a woman to dinner?" Italia nearly floated across the room to Travis, her short and perfectly arranged brown hair barely moving, though the pearls she always wore swayed. She greeted him with air kisses on both cheeks, a custom she'd brought with her from her native Italy. "How are you, my son?"

She held his face between her hands and stared into his eyes in another tradition, this one purely hers. His artist mom stared at him as if recording his features for one of her paintings or even memorizing the shape of his face for a sculpture.

"Nobody's coming with me, Mom. I'm doing well, though," he said when she stepped back. "Apparently, you are, too. Your hearing is practically bionic when it comes to matchmaking."

She only smiled at that. "It is not good for you to be alone."

His mother couldn't have been more right about that, though there was no way he would tell her now. Sometimes it scared him how right it felt seeing Tatiana every day at work and then at dinner each night. He could get used to that life.

Melissa took that opportunity to step forward. "Don't worry, Mom. Travis isn't alone. He has his new roommate. He invited her tonight, but she couldn't come."

"*Her?*" Italia asked.

Travis glared at his sister, taking back every kind thought he'd had about her being on his side.

"He didn't tell you?" Melissa continued. "The woman who just started as his co-CEO at Colton Plastics. He's invited her to stay with him for a while."

"Tatiana Davison?" Frank appeared with them as if he'd already been part of the conversation. He turned to his wife. "She's the daughter of a suspected serial killer. *Len* Davison."

Italia's eyes widened. "Is that right, Travis?"

It was clear which of them watched or read the news, but his dad didn't seem surprised that Tatiana was staying with him, either. Had Melissa told him about that?

Instead of waiting for his son to answer his wife's question, Frank posed one of his own. "Are you sure that's a good idea, son?"

Frank shoved his hand back through the tiny island of salt-and-pepper hair that remained on top of his head. It was a gesture of frustration that Travis recognized from having been the source of it so many times.

Why had he gone to the dinner at all? This was just like the night last month when he'd made the announcement about his new co-CEO at that gathering at police headquarters. Their parents hadn't been in attendance, so it shouldn't have surprised him that they might have a repeat of that mess tonight.

"Hi, Dad. Good to see you, too."

"Yeah. Good to see you."

Frank managed a smile of sorts as he extended his hand. Travis shook it and then pulled back. The moment was no more or less awkward than any of their greetings in years.

"Oh, Frank, my love, is it not wonderful having Travis home? It has been so long." Italia slid up next to her husband and leaned her head on his shoulder, working her magic on him like only she could.

Frank smiled, despite his obvious attempt not to. "Yes, it is, sweetheart." Stanton must have seen this as his chance to break for the kitchen, where Antonio,

Everleigh and Clarke stood in the wide opening, close enough to hear but wisely out of the line of still possible fire. Stanton leaned close to his sister as he passed.

"That was cold, Melissa," he said in a loud stage whisper.

And they wondered why he didn't visit more often.

Their father spoke up again. "I heard from my brother, Geoff, that Miss Davison was with you when you babysat little Danny the other night, too."

That explained his father's lack of surprise. He'd had extended-family help in collecting the details.

"Glad to hear the Colton gossip line is in great working order." Travis raised both hands as if he'd been arrested. "Guilty of helping out a cousin in need. I'll make sure not to pick up my phone next time anyone calls."

He resisted the urge to rub his temples, though his head was already aching. Why was he being asked to explain himself? He was thirty-four years old. Didn't anyone see that? Because he couldn't stand the silence any longer, he started anyway.

"I would have told you all myself… Anyway, after the recent events involving Tatiana's father, she and I decided it wouldn't be safe for her to stay alone right now. She lost her mother, and her dad is—" he paused again and shrugged "—missing."

Italia stepped forward, wringing her hands. "It is kind of you to offer your help, but it is not your responsibility, no?"

"Sure, it's my responsibility." He wasn't sure how he'd managed not to say *she*. If he'd done that, he would have had even more to explain.

"Tatiana is my co-CEO. Let's forget for a minute that she's only recently returned to Grave Gulch and has no support system. Or that, as members of this family, we were taught to help others when we could." He shot glances at his siblings, whose actual jobs involved that calling. "Even pushing those things aside, the truth is, whatever happens to Tatiana Davison ultimately affects Colton Plastics."

Frank crossed his arms. "Which is why I'm surprised that you agreed to bring her into the company during this volatile time. Her association with her father might be problematic for the company."

Surprised. Travis had heard that word before. It was code for *disappointed*, and he'd had enough of that to last a lifetime.

"We'll be okay, Dad. My associates know who my father is, and they're still willing to do business with me."

Frank blinked several times and pressed his lips together at the slight, but he didn't respond. In all the time that his dad had been discounting his ideas and armchair quarterbacking his dreams, it was the first time Travis had stood up for himself. What had changed?

Clarke clapped his hands loudly as he stepped out from the kitchen. "Well, this has been fun. I don't know about the rest of you, but I want to eat before Mom's roast beef gets cold and tastes like shoe leather."

"As if that would ever happen," Stanton chimed in.

The dinner scramble resumed, though maybe there were fewer smiles than there had been earlier. Italia hurried into the kitchen, donned a pair of heavy oven mitts, and pulled the steel lid off the roaster.

"Perfect," she called out. "The beef tenderloin has had just enough time to rest."

Longer than it needed but Travis appreciated her fib this time. He shot a look of gratitude to Clarke as well for stopping him from saying something worse to their father in the heated moment. The special bond the two of them had always shared required no words. In his former role as "the Colton on the wrong path," Clarke understood what it was like to be an outsider.

Within minutes, they were sitting around the massive table, their parents on the ends per tradition. Some of the dishes they passed were slightly cold or overdone, including the gravy Clarke had been stirring. Yet no one dared to complain as they inhaled all the side dishes, most of the roasted potatoes and the massive hunk of still perfectly cooked meat.

As Travis took his last bite, Italia leaned closer to him and spoke in a low voice. "You must do what your heart tells you is right."

Travis shifted to look at her. His mother's usually smiling eyes were shinier than usual. Great. Now he'd made her cry, too.

"Thanks, Mom. I appreciate your support."

He glanced at the other end of the table and found Frank looking back. Dad and son looked away again, two fighters retreating to their corners between rounds.

"You father supports you as well."

Travis didn't bother looking up this time. "Does he? I don't see it."

"He does, of course. He worries also." She cleared her throat. "As do I."

His mother's words echoed Tatiana's from a few days before, and yet he still didn't believe it. Even if his father *was* only concerned about him, that didn't give him the right to question only his decisions and not those of his siblings. When he couldn't come up with anything to say that wouldn't hurt her, he patted his mother's hand instead.

"I'll be careful. I promise."

"I know you will do this."

As usual, his mother's easily offered faith in him softened the edges of his father's skepticism. He wished he could tell her about the bean in the black-and-white photo. More than that, regardless of what he'd said earlier, he longed to introduce her to the baby's mother. Clearly, the time wasn't right yet, but maybe sometime soon it would be.

Regular conversations had resumed along the table, and in this crowd, that meant talking about two subjects: police work and wedding planning. Travis even had the chance to tune out as Melissa and Everleigh discussed the pros and cons of having outdoor ceremonies.

Antonio caught Travis's attention and rolled his eyes. "As long as the reception is at my hotel, I told Melissa I'm up for whatever she likes."

"Are you sure you want that, Antonio?" Travis said. "Our family doesn't have such a good record for wedding receptions at the Grave Gulch Hotel. There tend to be kidnappings and mayhem instead of just a big cake."

Antonio shook his head. "Don't remind me."

Everleigh raised both hands in a sign to stop. "Bad joke. Bad joke."

"Yeah, who let him get past the censors?" Clarke agreed with his fiancée.

An awkward pause followed, and then someone—it could have been Stanton—started laughing, and then they all did.

"Not funny yet?" Stanton asked.

"No, not yet," Clarke and Everleigh said in unison.

Frank leaned his forearms on the table to take charge of the conversation. "Well, I believe that a lot of good came out of that night, too. Our daughter found her future husband. And information came out to clear the good name of our son's beautiful fiancée." He gestured first at Antonio with Melissa on one side of the table and then at Everleigh with Clarke on the other.

"He's right," Stanton said. "Danny's doing fine, too. Just ask Travis, the kid's new babysitter."

Everyone got a good laugh out of that one.

"Yeah, it wasn't all bad." Clarke paused to lift his bride-to-be's hand to his cheek and then lowered it but kept their fingers linked. "Even Everleigh's grandma doesn't seem to mind home detention at all with her new flat-screen TV and several streaming services."

"So, what's the scoop on Randall Bowe?" Stanton asked Melissa, who sat next to him. "Anyone track him down yet?"

At least someone had asked the questions, Travis figured, because they all had to be curious.

Melissa only shook her head.

"Crafty little scientist. Maybe that's why he got away with tampering with evidence for so long," Stanton added.

"It's a mess, all right," she admitted.

She received several murmurs of agreement on that one, though none of the Coltons wanted to admit that the GGPD might have been asleep at the wheel when it came to Bowe's collection of questionable results. It was enough of a headache for Melissa, who was ultimately responsible for her department.

"Trail's going cold on that one." Then she sat straighter

in her seat. "But Bryce is getting some good leads in New York City, looking for—"

She cut off her words and shot a glance at Travis across the table before exchanging a look with Clarke.

Travis planted his hands on the table and pushed his shoulders back. "Are you kidding? You can't talk about the manhunt for Len Davison because *I'm* here?"

"No, that's not it, bro," Clarke said.

Melissa wouldn't meet his gaze. "I shouldn't have brought it up at all. I can't really discuss an active investigation."

Travis crossed his arms and sank back into the upholstered chair. "But you were going to until you realized that the enemy was here."

"The enemy?" she scoffed. "Well, it is awkward, since you're *living* with the suspect's daughter."

"What do you think I'm going to do? Race out of here and tell her everything you said? And what's she supposed to do, pass it on to her dad by carrier pigeon?

"She told you she doesn't know *anything*." He jumped to his feet then, no longer able to stay seated. "Until that newscast, she didn't even know where he was."

Melissa carefully folded her hands. "Let's just take a breath. Then we'll talk."

"Do not use your de-escalation tactics on me."

"I'm not," she said. "But if you think Tatiana doesn't know more than she's sharing, then you might want to ask yourself how you can be so certain about a woman you barely know. Do you have blinders around her?"

Travis managed to stop himself from saying something he could never take back. "I can't do this."

He glanced from one end of the table to the other.

"Thanks for dinner, Mom and Dad. I'm sorry I won't be around to clean up."

Then he strode away from his family and through the tunnel. He grabbed his things and was out the door before any of them could come after him. They didn't trust him. They never had.

He hurried to his SUV and backed out of the drive. Only when he could no longer see the big yellow house in his rearview mirror could he finally breathe again.

Chapter Fifteen

Tatiana had never appreciated the sound of a garage door opening more. That meant Travis was home. Relief flooded through her as she sat up on the sofa where she'd been pretending to sleep for the past hour. It wasn't that Micah Lowe was a bad guy. She hadn't even been uncomfortable having him inside the condo with her, as he seemed competent in his job, regularly checking the security system, and he was beefy enough to take an intruder with one hand. But if he gave one more Detroit team sports statistic, she would run outside and beg her stalker to abduct her.

"Sounds like your guy's back early," Micah said.

"He's not my guy," she said automatically, though the idea of it wasn't as distasteful as it had been a week before. Sometimes, it seemed downright appealing.

"Whatever you say. I was just hired to do a job."

"Thanks for doing it, especially on such short notice."

Micah grinned, flashing a chipped front tooth that he'd probably earned on the job.

"People in my business can be accommodating for the right price."

She was sure Travis had paid it, too. If Micah hadn't

been available, there was no way Travis would have left her alone.

"Tatiana. Micah," Travis called out as he entered the house. "Everything okay?"

"In here," Micah said.

Travis made it to the great room too quickly to have been walking. He still had one arm in his coat sleeve. His movements were sharp, agitated. Something must have happened at his parents' house.

"I didn't expect you to get back so early," she said once he'd stowed his coat.

"Me neither." He crossed into the room and sank on the other end of the sofa, resting his head on the back pillows and closing his eyes. "Didn't make it to dessert. And it was Mom's legendary raspberry cobbler."

"Then it must have been bad. It would take a lot for me to skip even average cobbler." She'd hoped her joke would lighten the mood, but Travis didn't respond for several seconds.

"It was a lot," he said finally.

She was tempted to crawl over and curl up next to him. Would he find her presence comforting? Would he push her away a third time?

Micah cleared his throat, reminding her that he was still there. He hadn't been that quiet all night. She clasped the lap blanket to her, feeling strangely exposed.

The bodyguard stepped around to the front of the couch and grinned. "I hate to interrupt this family moment, but there is the matter of my payment."

"Right. Sorry." Travis stood and fished in his back pocket for his wallet. Then he pulled out some bills. A lot of them.

"Any reports from tonight?"

Micah shook his head. "Not a one. House is locked up tighter than a drum, and no suspicious movement near the perimeter. No repeat dog walkers, either."

"Good." Travis pressed the money into Micah's hand. "I came home earlier than we discussed, but it's all there."

"Thanks, man. Awfully decent of you."

"I don't do anything just to be decent," Travis said. "I just want to make sure that if I call you up, last-minute, again, you'll fit me into your schedule."

"Unless I have Red Wings playoff tickets, I'm all yours."

Travis gave the other man a strange look, but Tatiana shook her head to warn him not to ask. He showed Micah to the door.

"What was that all about?" he asked when he returned.

"That man loves sports," she admitted. "I thought security guards were supposed to stay silent, or is that just in the movies?"

He plopped down again, propped his feet. "Sounds like you had as much fun tonight as I did."

"I'm guessing you had more. What happened?"

"Which do you want to hear about first? The faceoff with my dad *before* dinner or the one with my sister right over the table?"

"You sound like the life of the party," she said dryly.

"I guess you could say that. Somewhere between those fun moments, I managed to eat my mother's roast beef. You missed out on that, but I'm glad you didn't come tonight."

She turned on the couch so that she sat crisscross facing him. "Why's that? Because you wouldn't want me to see the arguments, or you wouldn't want to share the roast beef? Or were both fights about me?"

"In part, I guess."

"I shouldn't be staying here. It's hurting you both at work and with your family." And maybe she cared about that—and him—more than she wanted to admit. He shifted on the sofa to face her and sighed. "We've talked about this. You can't stay alone. We still don't know who sent the email or the flowers or if they're even connected."

"Still, you didn't bargain for all this when you recruited me."

"Neither of us did. I don't think you came back to Grave Gulch hoping to have your dad be at the center of another murder investigation and, as a bonus, have a stalker pursuing you."

Tatiana rolled her shoulders, not wanting to continue this conversation. If she did, she might be tempted to tell him the truth about the flowers. How could she tell him now when she'd already lied to him? It was too late. Would she see the betrayal in his eyes if she admitted she was a liar? He would never forgive her, and she only now realized that life without Travis Colton would be no life for her at all. Because she wasn't ready to face those consequences, she took the coward's way out and asked about his father instead.

"As usual, he didn't think a few of my decisions were good ideas."

"Working with me at Colton Plastics and letting me stay here?"

"Those exact two."

"He's right that neither is in your best interest."

"He's not right. About that or any other of his *suggestions*."

"Like I said before, parents worry."

He lifted a brow. "Are you sure you weren't there tonight? My mom said almost the same thing."

She watched him for so long that he shifted on the couch and crossed his arms. "What?"

"You don't have any idea how lucky you are, do you?"

"How's that?"

"You have two parents and three siblings who at least want to be involved in your life. I'm sure they drive you crazy. They probably stick their noses in your business and offer unsolicited advice, but what I wouldn't give…"

"I'm a big jerk, aren't I?"

She couldn't help grinning. "No, just a small one."

"Well, thanks for not disagreeing. I keep complaining about not fitting in with my family, and you're—"

Tatiana appreciated that he stopped himself before saying "alone," but it didn't prevent emotion from settling in the back of her throat. She had to clear it before she could speak again.

"Someday Bean here will want to get to know his or her grandmas and grandpas." She rested both hands on her belly, lacing her fingers. "I won't be able to give my child that. Mom's gone, and Dad will either be in prison or on the run.

"If our child is ever going to have a relationship with grandparents, they will be *your* parents. So, do what is required to heal that relationship so you can share them with your child."

"I will."

Though he continued to look forward toward the television, he watched her out of his side vision.

"You haven't spoken a lot about your mother. Does it hurt too much to talk about her?"

"I haven't?" Guilt filled her that she hadn't shared more about Marcia.

"Were you two close?"

Immediately, those last days filtered through her thoughts again. So much regret tied up in an already tragic situation.

"We were." She stopped because it hurt too much to say the rest.

"But you were closer to your dad, weren't you?"

"How did you know that?"

"The media portrayed you as a 'daddy's girl,' which must have been where the stalker got it. But I sensed it was true."

She tightened her arms to her sides, not sure whether to appreciate that he'd understood her or resent her own transparency. "Dad and I just always seemed to understand each other. I don't know what that says about me."

"It doesn't say anything."

She shrugged. "I felt bad about always being closer to him, particularly after Mom died. I wondered how often she must have felt left out of our inside jokes."

"That's why you got the tattoo."

Automatically, her hand moved to her rib cage, where the pink ribbon painted her skin. Of course, Travis had seen it. He'd viewed, touched and tasted so many areas that night. But this patch had been more private than the rest, and at that moment, she was glad she'd shared it with him.

"It's more that I wanted to keep part of her with me,

and I guess permanently on my skin was as close to forever as I could make it. I felt terrible that I hadn't tried harder to get to know her. Hadn't tried to have our own inside jokes."

Travis surprised her by scooting closer on the sofa. She held her breath, not sure if this would turn into a repeat of the other night, but when he was close enough to touch her, he gave her shoulder a gentle squeeze, and then he moved his hand away. Strange how a platonic touch had never felt so personal before. She felt its absence deeply, too.

"I'm sure she was proud that you were her daughter and probably didn't feel as left out as you thought she did. But since you were closer to your dad, that must have made his arrest even harder on you."

She couldn't look at him as she answered. "Nothing like learning that your whole life was a lie."

"Yeah. I can't imagine. Do you think your mother ever knew?"

"Gosh, I hope not." She considered it for a few seconds and then shook her head. "No, I don't think so. Mom thought that the sun rose and set with him."

Good thing she'd never had to see all the darkness behind all that light. Len had saved that opportunity for Tatiana.

Neither spoke for a few minutes, and then Tatiana looked up. "You see, your family situation could be a whole lot worse."

"I was thinking the same thing." He pulled his phone from his pocket and started typing.

"What's that?"

"A group text apology to my family," he said as he continued drafting his message.

"For getting into arguments?"

He tapped the arrow to send and then looked up again. "Kind of. They didn't want to talk about the search for your dad because we're roommates. Can you believe it? They didn't trust me not to tell you what they said."

"Would you have?"

"Probably."

"Then I guess you do owe them an apology."

He lifted an index finger to ask her to wait, and then he typed a second message. He gestured to the phone when he was finished. "I told them I probably wouldn't have trusted me, either."

She chuckled, but the sound felt forced. He wasn't the only one who needed to apologize, but how was she supposed to tell him the truth about the card now?

He must not have noticed as he leaped up from the couch. "Could you eat anything?"

"Depends on what it is." She followed him into the kitchen, anyway. "What did you have in mind?"

"First, we'll scare up something healthy for you. Then I'll make up some chocolate chip cookies. My mom's recipe. I didn't get any dessert and—"

"And you're my hero," she finished for him.

"But I'm warning you, I won't let you lick the bowl no matter how many times you try to tell me that raw eggs are fine for pregnant women."

"What kind of animal are you?" she joked.

"Wow, that was quick. From hero to animal in record time."

That was how it would be for her when she admitted she'd lied to him. Again. He'd done so much for her. He'd taken on his whole family for her. And all he'd asked for in return was the truth. She couldn't even give him that.

It didn't matter that she just might be falling for him. He'd been through something like this with his ex-fiancée, and he wouldn't repeat it for her. When he found out the truth, he would walk away from her as fast as his feet would carry him. And she would be exactly what she'd been before and what she deserved to be again: alone.

TRAVIS ENTERED THE outer office in Tatiana's executive suite early Monday morning, pulling up short when a young woman with dark skin, a tall bun and a wide smile stood up from the desk and stepped into his path. Of course, the new administrative assistant was supposed to begin work that day.

"Excuse me," she said.

She lifted her shoulders, trying to appear taller, a feat since she barely broke five feet.

"Were you wishing to see Tatiana? Do you have an appointment?"

"I guess I don't. You must be Haley Rollins." He extended a hand. "I'm Travis Colton. It's nice to meet you."

"Oh, Mr. Colton. I'm so sorry."

He waved away her apology. "It's Travis. And don't be sorry for doing your job. My administrative assistant wouldn't let anyone get past her, either."

At least someone was trying to protect her when he had to be in his office on the opposite side of the building. It wasn't as if he could be with Tatiana every minute when they both had work to do.

"Is that Travis out there?"

Tatiana opened the door and stepped behind her new assistant. She looked like she'd seen a ghost, her face ashen, her arms pressed close to her sides.

" I was just getting to know your new assistant."

"Oh. I'd planned to introduce you after your meeting with suppliers."

"Saved you a step. We're already old friends, aren't we?"

Tatiana cleared her throat and looked around again. "Well, it's good that you're here. I need you to look over that financial report."

"Then I have good timing."

She turned back to her assistant. "No calls, please, Haley."

"Yes, ma'am."

Haley quickly turned away and returned to her desk. Tatiana waved him inside her office.

He followed Tatiana inside and closed the door. She didn't stop until she'd rounded her desk and dropped into her chair.

"What is it? What happened? Another delivery?"

Instead of answering, she stared at her computer screen. She'd been acting strangely ever since she'd received the flower delivery that could have come from the stalker. They needed to take the card from those flowers to police. He shouldn't have let her talk him into delaying. With every unfamiliar vehicle in the parking lot, he became more concerned about her and the baby's safety. He sensed that someone was recording his and Tatiana's every move as well. Even now he'd shown up in her office since he couldn't bear to have her out of his sight.

Finally, she turned her laptop toward him. "There's another one."

Her in-box was open on her screen, with one message visible. The heading said, Tatiana Davison—Colton Plastics New Co-CEO, but the words in the body of the email were terrifying.

Did you see my work at the park? I knew you'd love it. Just like your daddy's. I'll make you both proud.
PS Call me Daddy. I like that.

Travis's breath froze in his throat. He had to swallow several times before he could speak again. "The guy just confessed to murder."

Tatiana stared at the back side of the laptop, curling her shoulders forward as if she was trying to hide.

"He says he killed that guy, Patrick Kowalski, for—" She stopped and shot a look at the office window. "For *me*?"

"When did you get this?"

"Just now. I was leaving a message for Ellie because the guys from IT keep insisting that they have to load some software on my computer that I don't have, and—"

"You called Ellie? At work?"

She crossed her arms. "*That's* what you're worried about right now?"

Travis shook his head and lowered into the seat across from her. He didn't care that she hadn't invited him to sit. "No, that's not what I'm worried about."

"We thought the first message was a prank. I think we were wrong."

"I think so, too." He was ashamed now that he'd ever allowed himself to believe it. How could he have put the mother of his child at risk just to avoid drawing more attention to Colton Plastics? The panic that flashed in her eyes tempted him to pull her into his arms, even with Haley right outside the door and the windows allowing anyone on the second floor to see them.

She pushed back from her desk and stood up to march across the room to the window before he had the chance.

"Why didn't we put those things together right away? Even Ellie suggested the possibility that the stalker might be trying to make news like the copycat murderer. Why didn't we consider that it could have been the same guy?"

"Neither of us wanted to believe something like that," he admitted. He still didn't. How was he supposed to protect her from this person, who could be anywhere? The guy had killed before. What would stop him from murdering Tatiana if she didn't return his creepy affections or didn't show proper appreciation for his flowers?

"We have no choice now." She spun to face him. "It's time."

"For what?"

"For us to go to the police." She stared down at the floor a few seconds and then looked up again and nodded. "And for me to tell them what I can about Dad, too."

"Are you sure?"

"I am."

His phone vibrated then, so he pulled it from his pocket to read the text. "It's from Ellie. She said you shouldn't have called her while she was working."

"Tell her I'm sorry," Tatiana said.

He clicked reply and started typing a response, but

the phone rumbled in his hand before he was finished. He read the second message and looked up at her again. "You're sure you're ready to talk to the cops?"

She nodded, though he would have sworn she'd seemed less confident than before.

"Well, good, because Ellie just said that first email you received was internal." He waited for the enormity of those words to sink in. Her eyes widened with what could only have been a fraction of the fear threatening to close off his throat. "Someone at Colton Plastics might be a murderer."

Chapter Sixteen

Less than an hour later, Travis and Tatiana sat in Chief Colton's office, at the far-left corner of the GGPD building, receiving the dressing-down that Tatiana knew they both deserved.

"You should have come to *me* right away." Melissa crossed her arms over her uniform, causing the bottom tines of her shiny silver badge to point at them across the desk. "Not my department's tech expert."

Travis shifted in his seat like a student in the principal's office.

"After all that fun the other night at Mom and Dad's, did you really expect me to come to you?"

"Don't give me that crap, Travis Colton. You asked Ellie to help well before that dinner with the family. Anyway, it doesn't matter if you're mad at your sister. Right now, I'm talking to you as the chief of police, and you took unnecessary risks by waiting so long to file a report about the stalker." She pointed at Tatiana. "You took risks with Miss Davison's safety."

She must have known that her words would hit a mark with her brother. When he glared at her, her lips lifted slightly.

"Fine." Travis spoke the word in a huff. "We didn't

think it was a big deal, and we wanted to keep it quiet if we could."

"Oh, just your run-of-the-mill stalker instead of one who might be a murder suspect as well," Melissa said.

He dampened his lips. "When you put it that way—"

"How am I supposed to put it, Travis? You *knew* the GGPD had open investigations for multiple, possibly related, murders, and then you held back information on someone targeting a prime suspect's daughter. And you knew it was a big deal. Otherwise you wouldn't have gone to Ellie Bloomberg for help. She's in hot water, too."

"Don't blame Ellie," Tatiana piped up. "We begged her to help us. She tried to get us to go to the police."

"I'll deal with her later. For now, I need you to tell me everything you know about your stalker, no matter how unimportant you think it is."

Melissa paused and looked at Tatiana with the same intensity she had her brother moments before. "And when you're finished with that, I hope you're ready to tell me everything you can about your father. Whoever is targeting you is fascinated with him. You won't be safe until he's taken into custody. Neither of you."

Tatiana swallowed and slid a glance to Travis. What kind of awful person had she been to let him put himself in danger to protect her?

"There're just those two emails." She pointed to the printouts resting on the police chief's desk. "Ellie only knew of the first one, which she told us came from someone *inside* Colton Plastics."

Travis cleared his throat. "Aren't you forgetting about the flowers?"

Tatiana shook her head, her shoulders lifting toward

her ears before she forced them back down. "Right. And the roses."

Since the gift hadn't really come from the stalker, they'd been too easy to forget. How much should she tell? Should she share the whole truth now? Could she?

"There were flowers delivered to the office the other day." Travis filled in the information for her when she didn't speak up right away. "They came from a local florist, and they had a card with them, too, but it was preprinted. It's back at the office."

"Oh. I have it with me." As Tatiana produced the card from her purse's outside zippered compartment, she purposely focused on Melissa, but she could feel Travis's gaze on her. Had he figured out that the flowers had really come from her dad? Had he realized that she'd lied? She was in a trap of her own making, and there didn't seem to be any way out.

Eventually, she would tell him the whole truth, but for now she would share the vital details that would allow the police to pursue her father. She hoped that would be enough. Melissa read the card and flipped it over to examine the blank back. Then she set it on top of the two printed emails. "The note is pretty general. Could it really have come from your father?"

"I don't know." The words tasted sour in her mouth, but in her hierarchy of lies lately, this was a mild one. Even after Travis had told her how much he hated lies, so much of what she'd told him lately had been peppered with them.

"Do you have any guesses about who the stalker could be?" Melissa asked. "Anyone who made you uncomfortable in the office?"

Tatiana shrugged. "Ellie asked that question, too.

And, after she asked it, everyone seemed suspicious to me."

"Anyone specifically?" Melissa tapped her pen on her notepad, waiting.

"Well, there was Enzio DeLuca, an older engineer, who at least might need a sexual harassment refresher. And Miles Kettering, the van driver. Too many jokes about things that happen in vans."

"They said those things?" Travis stared at her with wide eyes.

Melissa cleared her throat. "You can fire them all later, Travis. Right now, we need to find a stalker."

He shook his head, his eyes closed, and then they popped open again. "Then you'll need to look at Gordon Littleton, the day-shift foreman. He always seems to be lurking around on the second floor instead of down on the production floor where he belongs."

"Any others?" Melissa wrote the names on the list. "I agree that anyone with an interest in your father could have written it. It talks about your new job and then has references to a little girl, which would correlate with a daddy obsession. The unidentified suspects in both the copycat murder case and the stalking one we'll file today could be fixated on your father, if not you *and* him."

Tatiana couldn't keep herself from shivering, a reaction that neither Travis nor his sister appeared to miss.

"Why us?" she asked before she could stop herself.

"I'm not a psychologist, so I can't explain it, but people harboring obsessions over murderers are more common than you think." She pointed to the card. "I'll have my detectives follow up with the florist to see if it produces any leads."

It wouldn't. Tatiana could have told her that much. Her dad was too smart, probably using a fake name and purchasing with a prepaid credit card. At least nothing they found would show that she'd lied.

When Melissa shifted the printouts to the top corner of her immaculate desk, Tatiana recognized that they'd moved on to the second, riskier topic.

"We used to rent a cottage every summer on White Lake near Muskegon," Tatiana blurted and then cleared her throat. "I mean, that's the kind of information you're looking for, right?"

Melissa flipped the page of her notebook and started writing again. "Do you know specifically where it was? If we used a satellite map of the lake area, would you be able to identify the cottage?"

She tilted her head back and forth. "Maybe. It's been a long time."

"Is that the only place you can think of?"

"I think so." Could she tell them about the place she really believed her father might be? Could she live with herself if she didn't? She stared at her gripped hands and then finally lifted her head.

"No. There's one more place. Not far from White Lake, there's a smaller body of water, Walleye Lake or Steelhead Lake or something like that. The guy who owned much of the area had a bunch of ice-fishing cabins that he moved right out on the water each year when the lake froze solid. We rented those several times, too."

She blinked away the memories of snow angels and the wiggling fish that they'd reeled in through the openings built into the cabin floor. Again, she couldn't look at Travis. If she did, he would know she hadn't told him the truth and was still protecting her father. She couldn't bear knowing she'd hurt him with her lie.

Travis leaned forward in his seat. "Okay, sis, she gave you what you wanted. Now what are you going to do to protect *her*? If this guy is telling the truth, we already know he isn't afraid to murder someone just to impress her. He'll have no problem killing again to get what he wants."

"My detectives will move as quickly as they can," Melissa told him. "And we'll increase patrols in your neighborhood, but you know we're not a security service. You two will have to do your parts as well. At work, you should behave as if you know nothing, while making sure that Tatiana isn't left alone. And at the house, you'll have to be diligent, locking doors and checking locks."

Travis folded his hands together. "So, you're willing to admit that it was a good idea, after all, that Tatiana is staying at my place."

Melissa shook her head, but one side of her mouth lifted. "I won't go that far. But it could have been worse if she'd been alone."

"That's a start."

The police chief studied Travis and Tatiana, probably still wondering about the depth of their relationship. Tatiana was less certain of that herself now. They were more than coworkers, friends and prospective coparents but still less than lovers, if that one unwise night could be discounted. Even in all the mess surrounding them, it was becoming harder by the day for her to deny that she wanted more from him.

Melissa stood, signaling the meeting was over. "I'm going to have you two sit down with Officer Grace

Colton to complete your official report. We will keep the report quiet for as long as we can."

"Another Colton? Sibling or cousin?"

"Cousin," Travis and Melissa chorused.

Tatiana couldn't help but to laugh at that. "Looks like I'll meet the whole family before too long."

"It'll still take a while," Travis told her.

As Melissa guided them to the door, Tatiana recalled why she'd sought information from the police department that day in the first place.

"Is there any chance I'll get my laptop back? The guys keep hounding me about updates."

The chief shook her head. "'Fraid not. That computer is official evidence now."

"But what am I supposed to do when—"

"You're going to have to be evasive," Melissa told her. "You've proven you're skilled at that."

Travis crossed his arms. "Why do you keep saying that? She told you what you wanted to know."

That Melissa glanced down at her notes rather than answer the question suggested Tatiana hadn't given her all the information she needed.

"Just don't try to save the day, little brother." She touched his arm as they exited her office. "You chose not to be in law enforcement, so I want you to leave the heroics to those who get paid to do it legally."

"I'll try," he told her.

"Try hard, or you'll be spending the night in a jail cell, too."

TROY RAPPED ON the door to Melissa's office a half hour later and waited. The door swung open instead.

"Travis, I don't want to talk about—"

"Sorry. Wrong relative," the detective said with a grin. "I thought that was my cousin rushing out of here with Tatiana Davison a few minutes ago."

Melissa frowned, then pulled him into the room and closed the door. She looked exhausted, and it was barely noon. The spike in violent crime in Grave Gulch was taking a toll on the whole community, but, as chief, his cousin was under the most pressure.

"The two of them were here to fill out a report. Someone's been stalking Tatiana with emails and flowers, and now there appears to be a connection between that suspect and the copycat murder."

"Travis really stepped in it this time, didn't he? What was he thinking, bringing her into his company and his home?"

"I don't know, but we have to deal with the situation as it is now. We're going to try to keep it out of the news, but we haven't had much luck with that lately. We have a leak somewhere in this department."

"You still haven't figured it out?"

Her jaw flexed, and she shook her head. "No. But when I do…"

Troy shook his upper body. "Man, I wouldn't want to be the one with a big mouth."

Melissa updated him on the recent murder case and gave him an overview of the stalking situation. When she was finished, she handed him the copies of the emails and the card from the flowers.

He focused on the most recent message first. "He said 'my work at the park,' which hints at a murder confession, and then he wants her to know that he did it for her dad *and* her."

Melissa leaned forward, more alert as she had the

chance to discuss case details and relive her former role as detective.

"If he's really guilty, instead of just taking credit for someone else's crime, then we already know that he made some mistakes in the murder," she said. "The first two victims each had a single gunshot wound on the left side of the chest cavity, but the third victim's injury was on the right side."

"His other mistake was in the staging of the body," Troy said. "He had Patrick Kowalski's hands folded over his chest, not over his abdomen like the two other victims."

"Good thing for us Davison made a few mistakes of his own." She glanced down at her notebook. "But I have to wonder if he wanted to get caught. I can't believe he left DNA at both crime scenes. It seems he would have improved his skills the second time. If it was only the second."

Troy had wondered that himself. "We'll need to look at other communities where the Davison family lived. Apparently, they relocated frequently. But back to differences, the copycat killing didn't follow the pattern there, either. Not a spot of *human* DNA evidence at the crime scene. Just some blond dog fur, which is hardly conclusive, since everyone walks their dogs in the park. At least they did before all this."

"We have to stop them both." She pressed her lips into a line. "We have to take our town back."

Troy pointed to the second email. "Then if we are to believe that the stalker is also the copycat murderer, we know he's smart and methodical in some ways and impulsive in others. He couldn't wait to tell her that he'd killed for her."

"Tatiana is part of his obsession." She stared at the pages on her desk and then looked up again. "So, what do you think he'll do if he discovers there's something going on between the Colton Plastics co-CEOs?"

"You think they're a thing, too?"

"I don't know if there's something between them yet, but from the way my brother was looking at her just now, I know he *wants* there to be."

"Bryce and I wondered the same thing when we interviewed her with Travis in the room. He was so protective over her that we could barely ask our questions, and then he wigged out at us after she got upset and ran out of the room."

"Travis sure knows how to pick them."

"You're not going to bring up Aubrey now, are you? Their engagement was like seven years ago. Still a mother hen, protecting your brothers?"

Melissa harrumphed, but eventually she smiled. "Never cross a guy's sister."

"I'll try to remember that," he said with a grin. "But we're talking about Tatiana Davison here, not Aubrey. If there is or might be something between her and my cousin, Tatiana's worst crimes appear to be having a dad who's an accused serial killer and, possibly, being too loyal to him."

"The second part is what I'm worried about. Tatiana finally told me some places where her father might have gone in Michigan. I've been in contact with the Muskegon Police Department and the Muskegon County Sheriff's Department, and they're sending out patrol cars to check out those areas. But I still get the feeling she knows more."

"You'll know the answer to that soon enough."

Melissa crossed her arms as if suddenly cold. "On the other case, I told Travis we will increase patrols around his condo. But we don't know what this guy will do if she doesn't return his affections or isn't impressed with the crime that he committed for her. Or if the woman he believes should be his wants someone else."

That was the crux of the situation. She was too close to these cases, particularly the one involving the stalker. She couldn't protect her brother.

"He's a smart guy, Melissa. He'll be okay."

She waved away his comment. "Of course, he will. I just hope he doesn't get so focused on shielding Davison's daughter that he ends up becoming a target himself."

Chapter Seventeen

Travis stood at the top of his stairs, looking down to the level below, where Tatiana had disappeared the moment that they'd arrived home two hours before. As angry as she'd been during the ride back home, he didn't want to go down there and talk to her, but he couldn't wait any longer. She had to understand that he'd determined that they would both work remotely for her safety, even if he'd had to overrule her to do it.

"There's food up here if you're hungry," he called down and waited for a response.

Just when he was convinced none would be coming, she rounded the corner and stood at the bottom of the steps. "Did you think you could draw me out with food?"

"I figured it was worth a try." He didn't dare mention that it had worked.

She started up the stairs. "I might as well have dinner. Looks like I'm going to be stuck here, anyway."

"You need to eat something for the baby."

He didn't miss her glare. "This might not be the best time for you to tell me what to do with my body. Or the baby. You already pulled rank at the office when we were supposed to be equals, and so you'd better not try it at home."

"Okay. I'll keep quiet about that." At least he'd convinced her to come upstairs. He hadn't been sure that would ever happen tonight.

"Dinner had better be something good."

"Wow. Demanding."

She'd started toward the kitchen, but at his comment, she glanced back. "You're calling *me* the pushy one?"

The words *demanding* and *pushy* didn't mean the same things, but this wasn't the time to point that out.

She entered the kitchen and took her seat at the table he'd already set. Then she lifted her chin, closed her eyes, and sniffed. "Wait. What is that wonderful smell?"

"Hamburgers grilled on my stove and French fries." He carried a tray of burgers and grilled buns and a basket of fries to the table, where he'd placed a vegetable salad.

"You must really be trying to make this up to me."

"Well, I did make the fries in the air fryer, but I wouldn't mind if dinner earned me a few steps out of the doghouse."

"It's going to take more than food to dig you out of that shack."

But even as she said it, she reached for a bun and a burger. She took her time stacking on a tomato, some lettuce and a squirt of ketchup before taking a big bite. He had to hide his grin. It wouldn't help his case. He fixed his own sandwich and waited a few minutes before bringing up the subject he dreaded.

"You have to know that I made the right decision."

The fury in her eyes told him he could have found a better way to broach the topic.

Instead of answering right away, Tatiana used the tongs to put salad on her plate and dragged several fries through her puddle of ketchup before downing them in quick succession.

"That's just it," she said. "*You* made the decision. What happened to co-CEOs? Was that only for the company letterhead?"

"What was I supposed to do? When we got back to the office, I don't know about you, but there was no way I could have gotten any work done."

Just the thought of it brought back that moment of panic when he'd realized he couldn't protect her or their child from an enemy he couldn't identify. If only he hadn't at the same time made that discovery and had the sudden conviction that his feelings for Tatiana had long since bypassed platonic. Had he overreacted? Possibly. But he wouldn't admit that to her.

"I don't know. You never *asked* me if I was okay to work. Your sister told us to act like everything was fine while they were conducting the investigation."

He blinked and then shook his head. "I'm sorry. You just looked so freaked out that I—"

"Did I really look that bad?"

"No. Not bad." He considered her words for a few seconds and then sighed. "Fine. It was me. I was the one who was freaking out. Each time one of the guys passed me, all I could see was him dragging you from the building and holding a gun to your head. The gun he used to blow a gaping hole in the chest of a stranger, just to impress you."

She paused with a fry midway to her mouth and then lowered it to the plate instead. "That was…graphic."

"For about a minute, I considered temporarily shutting down the whole company, but—"

"It would have been a little obvious?" she finished for him.

"Well, that, too, but mostly, I couldn't do that to the employees without any warning. They count on their paychecks."

Tatiana pushed her plate aside, though she hadn't touched the salad. "You're sure it didn't have *anything* to do with attracting more press attention and causing speculation that Colton Plastics might collapse? There's no such thing as bad publicity, you know."

He rolled his eyes. "We both know there is."

Her lips half lifted but then straightened again, as if she remembered she was mad at him.

"Having both co-CEOs take leave at the same time will cause speculation, too. We've been lucky not to have the press in your front yard so far, but they'll be here now."

He shook his head, though he knew she was right. "It'll be fine. We're not taking leave, anyway. We're working remotely. It's the in thing now."

"But you didn't even take the time to discuss it with me. You had me find out by *email*, no less."

"There just wasn't time," he insisted, his argument dripping through its many holes now. "We had to get you out of there, and Stanton said my condo would be the easiest place for him to guard."

"I don't care what you were cooking up with your brother. I should have had a vote."

"You would have voted no."

His anguished tone surprised him, and her dazed

expression told him she hadn't missed it, either. For a long time, neither spoke, and Tatiana dragged a fry in her ketchup without looking up from her plate.

"I had to keep you safe," he admitted in a voice that probably lacked the strength to show that he could.

Finally, she nodded. At least she didn't look up at him right away. He needed time to regroup. When she did speak again, he braced himself for more questions he couldn't answer.

"Are you going to eat that?" She pointed to the tray where one lone burger sat next to a bun.

"Well, I was pretty hungry." He grinned, relieved that she'd let him off the hook, at least for now.

"Hungrier than a pregnant woman?"

"Hmm. That's one thing I never will be able to judge, but you're welcome to it." He passed the tray over, and she loaded up the burger.

She glanced up from the bun. "You don't happen to have any horseradish sauce or spicy pepper rings, do you?"

"You really are pregnant."

He stepped over to the refrigerator and pulled out a jar of horseradish, checking the date before carrying it back to the table. She put a large dollop of it on her burger and dug in.

As Tatiana finished eating, Travis stepped out onto the deck into the day's last light with darkness creeping in from the edges to enclose them. A shiver scaled his neck, and gooseflesh peppered his forearms beneath his rolled sleeves. Anyone could have been right outside. Watching them. Waiting.

"We'd better get dinner cleaned up," Tatiana said as

she stood up from the table and carried her dishes to the dishwasher.

"What's the rush?" Since he hadn't told her that Stanton would be popping by at any time to introduce himself, he could only guess that she was off to brood in her room again.

"We have some online Colton Plastics shopping to do."

He stacked dishes and followed her to the counter. "What for?"

"If we're going to be working from home, we'll need a second desk."

Travis finished loading the last of the dishes. "I'm sure you'll find something nice that can be delivered tomorrow. I already have mine in the office."

"That's where you're wrong." She waited for him to glance back at her and grinned. "That desk is in my part of the house. We'll need to order another one for you."

TATIANA STARTLED WHEN the doorbell rang an hour later, but she'd been jumping at every sound all day. She hadn't been able to complete a single task at work earlier. How could she when she was certain that someone was watching her and listening to her every breath? Maybe Travis had been right to have them take a break from the office, though there was no way she would admit that to him.

"Are you expecting someone?" she asked him as he leaped up from the sofa and headed to the door.

He paused with his hand on the latch. "I guess I didn't tell you. Stanton."

The only other Colton she could recall from her high

school class stepped inside. Stanton turned back to lock and bolt the door and then approached her without taking off his coat. He shoved his dark hair out of his eyes and jutted out his hand to her over the back of the sofa.

"Hi, Tatiana. Good to see you again."

She looked at his hand and then finally accepted it. "Thanks for coming."

Travis stepped around the end of the sectional. "I take it I don't need to introduce you two."

"Nope," Stanton told him before turning back to Tatiana. "I'm not sure I've seen you since graduation. Well, except on TV the other night."

"I hope they showed my good side." She'd wanted to break some of the tension with her joke, but when she recalled that interview, she sat forward on the couch and then stood. It hadn't been a shining moment for her.

Stanton traded a look with his brother and then smiled. "I'm sure it's been a long couple of weeks."

"More like a year."

Tatiana crossed her arms, preparing for the interrogation. "I've been questioned by a lot of people lately, so do your best."

Stanton brushed away her comment with a wave of his hand and then stepped to the front of the couch and plopped down not far from where she stood. "I'm not here to question you. I'm a bodyguard and the owner of Colton Protection. I'm here to *protect* you and my brother, if he'll let me."

She relaxed her shoulders and returned to her seat. "Good to know."

"But I'll need to ask a few questions in order to do my best work."

When Tatiana jerked her head to look at him, Stanton was grinning.

She shot a look at Travis. "Your little brother's a comedian."

"But not a good one. That's why he's a bodyguard instead."

Stanton leaned forward, his expression serious. "Travis wants me to stand guard until your stalker is caught. You and my brother need to stay in this house until then."

"I already got that memo."

Stanton must have missed the look that she exchanged with Travis as he continued. "I'll have two of my guards on the team with me, watching this location. We'll be trying to draw out the stalker."

"You're wanting to bring him here?" she couldn't help asking.

"I hate to tell you this, but he probably already knows where you are."

At that, she shivered. She couldn't help it. *Call me daddy, too.* If only the guy's words would stop sneaking behind her defenses, like cloying hands determined to touch.

When Travis's phone rang, he excused himself and went into the kitchen, leaving Tatiana behind with his brother. Once he was out of earshot, Stanton caught her attention.

"Travis is a good guy."

She squinted at him. "I know that. What are you trying to say?"

"He's been hurt before by a woman who wasn't who she appeared to be."

"He told me about Aubrey. But I'm not, I mean, *we're* not…"

Stanton's eyes widened when she mentioned his brother's ex's name, but then he schooled his features. "Like I said, I will protect you from the stalker. I've guarded celebrities and politicians I didn't necessarily trust, either."

"Either?"

He shrugged. "I'm just saying that none of the Coltons will look kindly on anyone who hurts Travis again."

"Point taken, but, as I told you—"

"That was Melissa," Travis said as he reentered the room.

Both jumped to their feet, caught in a conversation they shouldn't have been having.

"What'd she say?" Stanton asked.

"Police in Muskegon reported back that there have been no signs of Len Davison at White Lake. Not the other location, either. The one with the ice-fishing cabins is called Pike Lake, by the way."

Tatiana folded her hands at her waist, hoping her grip didn't look as tight as the squeeze between her fingers felt.

"I'm sorry. Those are the only places I know to look," she told them.

Travis watched her for so long that she had to force herself to stay in place.

"She wanted me to ask you one more thing."

She licked her lips. "What's that?"

"She wants to know what else you're holding back."

Chapter Eighteen

Travis tiptoed to the lower level the next afternoon and moved down the hall, past the bedroom, on his way to the office. *His* office that she'd commandeered. He'd almost reached the door when a desk drawer slammed.

"May I help you with something?" she called out.

He peeked his head inside. "No, but maybe I should help you. Looking for something in particular?"

She glanced down at the desk. "Yeah. Do you have a stapler *anywhere*?"

"Sure, I do."

He stepped into the office, but instead of stopping at the desk, he moved to the supply closet and opened the folding door. The stapler was on the shelf at about eye level. He grabbed it and handed it to her.

"Why don't you keep it in your desk?"

"What can I say? It's *my* office."

"Not for a while," she said with a grin.

He returned it, but it felt forced. Her excuse for digging through his desk seemed reasonable enough, so he hated that he was checking up on her. How could he not, though? His sister's question about Tatiana hiding something had compounded his own concerns after meeting with Melissa the day before. The more that

Tatiana insisted she wasn't hiding anything, the more certain he became that she was.

Why had she been carrying that card in her purse, anyway? She'd forgotten all about the flowers and wouldn't have mentioned them to the chief of police at all if he hadn't reminded her. Was there some other reason she had it with her?

"You haven't said why you're in here," Tatiana said without looking at him as she typed on her borrowed laptop.

"I wanted to remind you that it's quitting time."

She glanced at the bottom corner of her screen. "It's six thirty already? I can't believe it. This is the first quality time I've had to do my work since starting at Colton Plastics."

If only he could say he'd had a successful workday, too. But then the shallow basement windows didn't offer the same view of the street that the new desk in his bedroom did. Even with the guards parked outside and regularly checking the perimeter, he couldn't help watching each car that passed and wondering if the driver might be the one who would hurt Tatiana and their baby.

"Don't tell the board about your lack of productivity earlier," he said.

"Mum's the word."

He cleared his throat. "I made some stew in the slow cooker, so we can eat if you're ready."

"That's the wonderful smell that's been filtering through the vents. I could definitely get used to this."

So could he. That was the worst part. Even wondering if she was hiding something—and his gut told him she was—he still was enjoying their captivity far more than he should have been. It felt like playing house, and the game was becoming irresistible to him. Stanton and his crew were only monitoring danger on the outside of the condo. Travis was convinced he was far more at risk indoors.

He was more certain of it after dinner as they sat in the great room, and he couldn't help splitting his time evenly between watching television and watching *her*. In an unconscious habit, she traced her fingers back and forth over her slightly rounded belly, covered by leggings and a tunic. He couldn't look away, couldn't stop imagining the soft fingertips on his skin instead of the cloth.

"What are you looking at?" she asked when she glanced over and caught him.

"I've been thinking that you should reconsider my proposal." It was true that it had been on his mind, just not technically right then.

"That's a super-romantic offer, but I think I'll pass."

"Would you say yes if I piled on the romance?"

"Well, when you put it that way," she said with a chuckle.

Neither mentioned that she'd said she wouldn't marry without a forever kind of love. Was he ready to give her what she needed? He knew he wanted to protect her and the baby. The thought of someone close to them with malicious intent brought out a rage in him like he'd never experienced before. But was that love? Would he know it if he felt it? He'd been wrong before.

"What brought this up, anyway?" she asked. "With the rest of the mess we have going on, why are you even thinking about that now? In case you've forgotten, there's a manhunt underway for my dad and a stalker who's murdering for my personal entertainment."

"Because of *that*." He pointed to her stomach.

As Tatiana looked down, her fingers stilled. "I can't seem to stop doing that. It doesn't make any medical sense, but sometimes it soothes the nausea."

She straightened her top over her leggings. "These clothes were more comfortable for work, too. I can't believe the waistlines on some of my skirts are already starting to pinch."

"That's just a reminder that no matter what else is going on in our lives, in seven months, we are also going to have a baby who needs two parents. I have to know how we're going to make it work if you still won't marry me."

She sat up on the seat and planted her feet on the floor. "I've told you before that we're living in the twenty-first century. Unmarried couples have babies all the time. Some even raise them together as coparents."

"Is that what you want us to be? Coparents?" he asked.

"I don't know what I want anymore."

"Well, I know I don't want to abandon my child." Could that have been what she was holding back? That the baby wasn't really his? He dismissed it immediately. What reason would she have had to claim the child was his, when her involvement with a Colton had only complicated her life? He was almost relieved that Melissa remained suspicious of Tatiana. She knew nothing about the baby, and yet she still had questions.

Tatiana turned to face him, her knee drawing up on the sofa cushion. "You would never do that. There's not much I'm positive of lately, but of that I am."

"I'm glad." Her faith in him drew him in, made him long for more of a connection with her than she'd offered. "I will be here for the child, no matter what his choice of profession. Or no matter whom she chooses to love."

"We're a pair, aren't we?"

He turned to find her watching him, her lips lifted. "Why do you say that?"

"My dad appeared to offer me unconditional love, and all of it might have been hogwash," she said. "And yours probably loves you the way he should and has no idea how to show it."

He narrowed his gaze. "Hey, you've never even met my father. How do you know what he's incapable of showing?"

She shrugged. "It's just a guess, but I'm hopeful for the both of you."

"If our dads were so messed up, then how'd we both turn out so perfect?"

"Our moms," they said at the same time and then laughed.

When they stopped, they glanced down to see that they'd scooted closer on the sofa, so close that their knees, lifted on the cushion so they could face each other, nearly touched.

Before he could talk himself out of it, Travis reached for her hand where it rested on her leg. Their fingers laced so easily, as though his hand had been formed with the sole purpose of linking with her far smaller one.

The room went still, the walls and tables and decor that she'd rightly guessed hadn't been his choice all seeming to hold a collective breath. Without seduction, with barely a touch, the moment had become more intimate than any he'd experienced.

Yet the longing that had drawn him to her in the first place pulled him deeper, closer to her, until only a breath separated him from lips he'd tasted before, recalled in exquisite detail and couldn't wait to touch again.

The doorbell rang then, causing them both to jump back. Her heavy-lidded eyes popped open again.

"You've got to be kidding," he growled.

But as he stepped away from the couch on his path to the door, Tatiana rested a hand on his arm to delay him.

"I'm going to need a rain check for that."

TATIANA'S CHEEKS BURNED as Stanton stepped inside the condo, just as he had the night before. Only last time he hadn't arrived just in time to catch them on the verge of a make-out session that, if she had her way, would end in something even more thrilling.

"What took you so long?" Stanton asked Travis as he looked back and forth between them.

Travis crossed his arms. "I wasn't waiting right inside the door for you to ring the bell."

"I told you I would update you on any developments."

Tatiana stepped to the doorway between the great room and the entry. "Did the police catch the stalker?"

"Not yet" came a feminine voice that she recognized as Melissa's.

Stanton pulled his cell from his pocket and pointed to the screen that showed his sister on a video call.

"What's going on?" Travis asked Stanton.

"I told him I would update you at the same time," Melissa answered for him from the screen.

"Apparently, Davison was sighted coming out of one of the ice-fishing cabins, parked on the frozen Pike

Lake," Stanton told them before holding up the phone to allow his sister to tell the rest.

"Special Agent Colton told me—"

"Come on, Melissa," Travis said. "It's just us."

"Fine. *Bryce* told me that Davison appeared stunned to see the police officers and FBI agents storming the cottages, but he still managed to escape, taking off in a snowmobile, right across the ice."

Travis leaned forward so his sister could see him on camera. "They weren't prepared for the possibility that he would try to get away?"

"Do you want to hear this or not?" she asked.

Tatiana was positive she didn't. Her legs were so shaky that she was surprised they still held her at all. She'd betrayed her father, and he *knew* it. No one else would have heard about their trips to Pike Lake, and he'd let her know he would be there. It was her fault he'd almost been caught. Could she have lived with herself if he had?

"So, I wanted to thank you, Tatiana, for providing the tip on the location. But, unfortunately, I need to ask if you have any other information that might help us bring in your father safely. Any little detail that might help."

"I don't know *anything* else." Her voice was sharper than she intended, more filled with the anguish of a daughter who'd failed her father.

Tatiana didn't miss the look that passed between the two brothers, but there was nothing she could do about it. She'd already shared too much.

"Leave her alone, Melissa," Travis said. "She told you all she knows."

Then he looked up from the phone to Stanton. "You haven't said anything more about the stalker."

"Yes. Anything you haven't updated me on, Stanton?" Melissa asked from the screen.

The bodyguard shook his head. "We have kept our clients safe and the perimeter secured, but none of my guys have noted any unusual suspects making repeat visits to the area or coming too close to the property. No other new developments.

"What about you two? You're still on Colton Plastics' VPN, right? Have you been monitoring your email?"

"I have," Travis answered and shifted his gaze to Tatiana.

"I checked a few times today."

"No wonder you were able to get work done," he said.

"Want to check one more time tonight?" Stanton said.

Tatiana nodded.

"I'll grab her laptop for her." Travis took off down the hall to the stairs before anyone had the chance to argue.

Stanton stared in the direction his brother had disappeared. "He's efficient."

"And protective of people he barely knows," Melissa added from the phone.

"Your brother's a good man," Tatiana said before she could stop herself.

The bodyguard blinked several times, but no one spoke after that. Neither of Travis's siblings could argue with what she'd said.

Travis returned so quickly that he had to have run once he reached the basement. He carried the laptop into the kitchen and set it on the table. Tatiana and Stanton followed him with Melissa still on the video call.

At the table, though, he stepped back and gestured

for Tatiana to take the seat. The two men crouched behind her, with Stanton turning the phone so that Melissa could see the screen as well. They wouldn't find anything, Tatiana told herself, but her hands trembled, anyway, as she opened the computer, signed in and clicked on her email.

Her stomach squeezed as the last message downloaded. Its title read Missing Tatiana Davison.

I'm disappointed in you, my darling. There are guards all over Colton Plastics. And you're living with Travis Colton himself? I'm sure you regret your mistake, but you'll still need to be punished, I'm afraid. You belong with me. Looking forward to sharing my favorite stories with you. Just know you'll love Polly and my macabre heroes as much as I do.
Love,
Daddy

The words swam on the screen in front of her. "He knows where I am," she whispered.

Travis squeezed her shoulder. "I should have gotten you out of Grave Gulch."

Stanton, who was supposed to protect them, shivered visibly. "He calls himself 'Daddy?' Yuck."

"Get it together, will you, everyone?" Melissa called out from the phone.

Stanton stuck the cell in front of the laptop screen and flipped the image so they could all see the police chief's frown.

"Tatiana, keep your head low." Melissa cleared her throat before continuing. "I'm sorry this is happening to you."

She stopped again, clearly uncomfortable with seeing Tatiana as a victim rather than an evasive witness. Then she turned her head on the screen.

"Now, Travis, you watch out for her, though you would probably do that no matter what I said. And Stanton, you guard them both. Then let the GGPD do our jobs. We'll get an arrest."

"She's right," Travis announced.

In front of his brother and the screen version of his sister, he spoke to Tatiana alone.

"We're going to figure this out. With the GGPD and Stanton working with us, we're going to stop this guy." He paused, shook his head and then added, "He'll never get close enough to share his creepy stories with you. He'll have to get past me first."

His suddenly startled expression suggested that he'd realized he'd said too much. Rather than to call him on it, his sister made a sudden excuse to get off the phone, and his brother told them he needed to relieve one of his staff members at his post.

Travis was probably embarrassed over his declaration, but Tatiana had never felt safer. She'd been unable to trust anything she'd accepted as truth over the past several months, but at that moment she believed one thing with all her heart: Travis Colton would lay down his life to protect her and their child.

Chapter Nineteen

"That was intense," Tatiana said as she returned to the sofa where she and Travis had almost kissed less than an hour before. It seemed like months. Decades.

He didn't even look up from his spot on the opposite end, his shoulders curled forward, his elbows on his thighs and his chin leaning on his cupped hands. "That's an understatement."

Something had changed from earlier, when he'd all but promised to put himself between her and the man threatening her. Had he realized that it was a mistake to endanger himself and so many of his relatives just to keep her safe? That they'd all be better off if he put her back on a plane to Paris?

"We sure are lucky to have Melissa, Stanton and the rest of your family members working on this case." She paused, watching for his reaction. "I'd hate to be the stalker with a team like that tracking me."

"I guess so."

She studied him for a few seconds longer. "I don't get it. A few minutes ago, you were confident we had this thing under control, and now you're—I don't know— deflated, maybe."

"Your dad's going to know that you were the one who let police know where you thought he might be."

Tatiana didn't need him to remind her of that. Melissa had said her father had appeared stunned when police had arrived, but he had to have been mostly shocked that his own child had turned on him. She cleared her throat. "That's true."

"And the creep who's after you knows you're here with me. If he's aware of that, does he also know about the baby?"

"How could he?" Still, she shivered just as she had when she'd read the eerie message. The guy was aware of too many things. A voyeur who'd been inside her office and, perhaps, behind the camera in her laptop. He might know more than they realized. "We haven't told anyone."

"Who the hell is Polly, anyway? And what are 'macabre heroes'?"

"Your guess is as good as mine. We're trying to figure out someone who clearly doesn't have a good grasp on reality."

Travis let his hand fall to his side on the sofa cushions. "What if we don't?"

"Don't what? Try to figure him out?"

"Have it under control. What if it's not enough?" He puffed up his cheeks and blew out a long breath. "What if I can't *protect* you?"

He wouldn't look at her as he said the last, but his anguish squeezed her heart. That was what had changed. Maybe it had been naive of them to ever think they could take on the forces of human evil and illness just by holing up in a condo, but his announcement in front of his siblings had meant more to her than he would ever know. No one in her life, other than her parents, had ever committed to put her first, and at least one of them had lied. And now she was doing the same to him.

"I told you before that I was positive you would never abandon your child. Besides that, there hasn't been anything I've felt confident about since the moment the police arrested my father for murder."

"You deserved none of it. And then I made it worse by bringing you into the company, convincing you to expose your father and putting you at risk from him and the stalker."

When he finally looked up, she smiled. "You didn't let me finish."

"Go ahead."

"I was saying there hadn't been anything else I'd felt sure of since then." As she met his gaze, she added, "Until now. I know you'll keep us safe. What does it say that the only two things I can believe in have one thing in common? *You.*"

For several heartbeats, Travis stared at her, his brows furrowed as though he didn't believe her. Or couldn't. Then he scooted toward her and lowered his lips to hers in what felt like a single, inevitable move.

Her brain barely had time to register the gentle touch before he pulled back, his eyes wide, his lips still hovering near hers. Travis seemed to be asking for permission. The sweetness of it made her smile. She lifted her chin and pressed her mouth to his and then waited until his arms closed around her, warm and welcome. This had been what she'd been telling herself she *didn't* want? Her eyes closed, and she reveled in the feel of his mouth moving over hers, sampling, testing, remembering. Her fingers slid behind his neck to settle in the feathery softness of his hair.

Her own memories of those stolen moments at her hotel before flooded her thoughts again, but the tastes and sensations were clearer and more potent now without the blurred edges from wine. She couldn't get enough, returning Travis's kisses with a desperation she couldn't explain. She drank him in, drew on his tongue to bring him closer and clung too tightly.

Tomorrow, she would think about her father knowing she'd betrayed him and wonder if he would make her pay for it. Tomorrow, she would worry about the stalker, who knew too much and seemed to be closing in. But for tonight, she wanted this. *Him*. She wanted to bring them together inside a cocoon of safety, give herself to Travis and take whatever he offered in return. It might not be the kind of forever she'd always dreamed about, but it had to be enough. At least she would have the chance to show her truth, even if she wasn't ready to say it out loud: she was falling for him.

A moan of protest escaped her when he drew his mouth away from hers, though he only moved to her neck, where he traced a line of kisses from the base to the sensitive spot just behind her ear. As Travis returned his lips to hers, he gently lowered her to the sofa cushions. Then he balanced over her and settled himself at the juncture of her thighs in an imitation of the intimate act that they would share. Hopefully soon.

The thin material of her leggings leaving no question about the intensity of his need for her, she moved against him. Needing more. Needing all. She smiled against his cheek when he drew in a sudden breath between his top and bottom teeth.

"There's no rush, Ana," he breathed against her neck.

Her eyes fluttered open at the name she'd once banned him from calling her. It had become a sweet intimacy again.

When they were both breathless, Travis slid his lips away from hers and rested his forehead against hers. "I could kiss you all night."

"You're not going to, are you?" Her whining tone embarrassed her, but that didn't stop her from sliding her hands down his back to grip his behind and press him tighter against her.

His chuckle rumbled through his chest and into hers. "Always so demanding."

But he must have taken pity on her then, as he shifted them to their sides so he could trace his fingertips over the new lushness of her breasts. He reached for the bottom of her tunic and slowly skimmed it up her body, teasing burning skin along the slow journey from hip to shoulder, then over her head.

"I could never get over how beautiful you were."

Her eyes, falling closed as he traced mesmerizing circles over sensitized skin, popped open again. "What do you mean? You couldn't say you were sorry enough or run out of that hotel room fast enough."

"What can I say? You scared the hell out of me." He grinned. "I knew I was getting into a workplace nightmare. I couldn't blame it on the wine. But that wasn't what terrified me. It was wanting you again when I'd just had you. And it was hoping for—" he paused, shifting his shoulder "—I'm not sure what."

"Yeah, that would have scared the hell out of me, too." She chuckled, trying to make light of a moment that was anything but.

Travis traced his fingertips from her sternum to her navel and then splayed his hand over her belly.

"Does it bother you to know that I think it's incredibly sexy that I've already put my child in here?"

"It's not super feminist."

"I don't know. It's definitely pro-woman." He bent to kiss her stomach. "This woman."

As he traced his fingers farther down her body and followed that trail that he'd blazed with his lips, Tatiana found she agreed with him.

"Would you like to go to the bedroom?" she asked.

"Why? Are you uncomfortable?" he asked as he lifted his head.

"As a matter of fact, I'm delightfully comfortable."

"Then I thought we'd stay here. This room is a little stuffy and could use some shaking up."

"Then here it is." She started with the buttons of his dress shirt, and once he'd shed that, she pulled his undershirt over the top of his head.

Travis peeled away her leggings until she shivered, lying naked on his couch.

He handed her the throw she'd napped with several days before and popped up from the seat, standing in his khakis that left little to the imagination.

"Just a minute. I need to—" He stopped himself and grinned. "Hmm, I guess I don't need to."

"There are some advantages to me already being pregnant." She reached for the waistband of his pants and pulled him closer.

"I can get into these advantages," he said as she undid the button and the zipper, freeing him.

"Still want to kiss all night?" she asked as she closed her hand over him.

His eyes fluttered, and a hiss of air escaped him. "That, too."

Travis stepped back, out of her reach, grinning, and then moved down to her feet. Starting with one arch, then the other, he kissed his way back up her body, paying close attention to all the sensitive areas he encountered on his journey. When he finally settled over her again, she writhed against him, no longer able to wait.

"Please, Travis," she whispered against the side of his mouth.

"Can't disappoint a lady."

He brought them together easily, as if they'd been made to fit each other. As if their bodies recalled their moments together as clearly as their minds. The groan that escaped her was part desperation and part appreciation.

"Why didn't we do this sooner?" he said with a sigh.

At that, she laughed. "I think we did."

Travis captured her mouth then, making good on his promise to kiss her all night, as they began moving together.

As Tatiana lifted herself to him, she opened her eyes and found him staring down at her. He didn't look away, didn't try to hide the raw emotion.

"This is perfect," she whispered. Only it was another lie. It wouldn't be perfect or even close to it until she told him the whole truth.

Tomorrow. She would make it right with him then. But for now, she moved with him. Breathed with him. She swallowed his sighs, never trying to hold back hers. Because if he refused to forgive her in the morning, this night and his child would be all that remained of him when he left her.

THE DOG WALKER made one last pass by the condo—two was his maximum, since the guards were still there watching—and noted the darkness inside the house.

"Come on, Polly. Let's go home."

The dog picked up her step, excited to get back to the car, but he'd parked at the back of the condo complex. Maybe he could only *walk* by twice, but he'd driven by a couple of times as well, that night and the night before. By now those bodyguards probably believed he owned a unit in the complex. It was so easy to drive with Polly, park in the back, take her on a walk and then drive back out. None of the guards were the wiser.

He glanced back at the darkened condo and ground his molars, imagining Travis Colton involved in all sorts of debauchery with *his* woman. How dare he touch her. Colton was so entitled. He must have believed that everything inside Colton Plastics belonged to him just because he'd started the company.

Well, he was wrong this time. Tatiana Davison was *his*.

He should have just ended the guy right in his fancy CEO's office months before. He could have done it, too. But until Len Davison had made a true name for himself, he'd had no argument with the man. Tatiana's arrival had changed all that. He couldn't even blame Travis for sniffing after such a beautiful woman. She was at fault for not following the rules.

"Maybe one more pass by, Polly?" He shook his head. "No, you're right. Too risky."

He was far too disciplined for that. This was a necessity in his new role. He could be a patient man, too. Someone would let his guard down, and he would be there to rescue her from all those Coltons. Davison would expect nothing less in a new son-in-law, and he would never let his hero down.

If Travis Colton got in the way, he would have to be dealt with as well. All wars had unfortunate collateral damage. Only this war was a battle for greatness.

Chapter Twenty

Travis pulled his SUV into the garage and slipped inside the condo just after sunrise, making as little noise as he could. He was surprised he'd finally been able to convince the other members of Stanton's team to let him out of his cage. Tatiana was safe, and he wasn't the target, but if they'd known what he'd planned to do on his errand, they would have argued that it wasn't an essential outing.

He found Tatiana just where he'd left her, rolled up in the blankets in the center of his bed, with only her face and her tangled mass of hair popping out the top. At some point during the night, they'd relocated from the couch to his king-size bed, where the expanded space gave him a better opportunity to explore and cherish her.

Under the first light streaming in the panes of his room's circle-top windows, she dozed peacefully now, her brows smooth and relaxed instead of furrowed as they'd been so often lately. At least sleep had held her worries at bay for a little while.

His smile spread as her lips, slightly parted and still swollen from his kisses, inspired memories of sweet tastes and shared delights that even now made his skin tingle. Impossibly, his body tightened again with need for her, his conclusion that he would never be sated disquieting.

The other new discovery of the morning unsettled him more. Despite his promise to himself never to be that vulnerable again and his practical offer of a marriage without the complication of feelings, he was falling in love with her. If he were honest with himself, he'd lost that battle for his heart on that first night they were together.

Did the fact that she'd made love with him again mean she was ready to accept his proposal? Would she believe him when he said he could now offer her the kind of relationship she'd said she wanted? He shook his head. He wasn't ready to tell her yet. Besides, he didn't know if she felt the same way, and he'd discovered that he wanted that, too.

"Are you watching me sleep again?" she murmured, startling him. "That's becoming a bad habit, you know."

"Busted. Sorry." At least they weren't going to have another awkward morning after, though technically he hadn't stayed until daybreak the last time. Waking up with Tatiana in his arms was the reason he was beginning his day in such a good mood, despite the trouble swirling around them. Well, one of the reasons.

"What time is it?" She yawned and stretched her arms out of her blanket nest.

"Practically afternoon."

"Are you serious?" She tossed back the blankets, and then noticing her nakedness, clutched them to her chest again.

He tried not to let her impulse bother him. Was she the one with regrets this time?

"No, it's still morning. But I've already been out to pick up a few things."

"The guards let you leave?"

He met her gaze until she shrugged and looked away as reality set in. No one was coming after him. Just her.

Tatiana sat up straighter in bed, carefully arranging the blankets under her arms. Did she even know how sexy she looked, with her hair mussed like that and her bare back still visible? He was tempted to climb back into bed with her and not emerge until after noon.

"What did you have to buy?"

"Just a couple of necessities. Before I get them, I was thinking about a good use for that front bedroom that gets all the morning light."

She yawned and stretched. "What's that?"

"Well, I was thinking…a nursery. Filled with a crib, a rocker, plenty of storybooks and too many toys."

At first, she stared at him, her eyes wide. But as he continued describing it, she couldn't help grinning. He would require a nursery in his home even if they planned to only coparent their child, but he needed her to know he wanted more.

"I can picture you in that rocker, our baby at your breast."

This time, she smiled. "You really have thought this through, haven't you?"

"I think of everything. Speaking of which. Be right back."

He hurried to the kitchen, where he'd left his packages, and returned with the vase in one hand and the box with paper plates and napkins on top in the other.

"Those were your emergency supplies?"

"Never said it was an emergency."

She grinned at the green tissue–covered flowers and the box that said "doughnuts."

"Oh my gosh. This is like Christmas. Bring those over here."

"Sure your morning sickness isn't too bad?" he asked with a grin.

"I feel okay so far. I'll risk it."

She immediately opened the box and grabbed a jelly-filled doughnut, taking a big bite and then closing her eyes to savor it.

"What can I say?" she said after she swallowed and opened her eyes. "I'm pregnant."

"I guess so."

He handed her the vase. "I hadn't done anything yet to celebrate the baby."

She ripped away the tissue paper to reveal an arrangement of six pink roses with a light blue ribbon tied around the neck of the vase.

"Sorry I couldn't do more. My options were limited at seven o'clock in the morning."

"I love them. They're beautiful."

"I didn't know your favorite color, but I was making a statement with those." He wasn't sure why he was rambling, worried she wouldn't like his gift.

"Mom always loved *yellow* roses. Each week Dad would—"

She froze, her eyes wide, as she must have recognized what she'd revealed. Ice filtered through his veins, his pulse thudding in his temple.

"You knew all along that the flowers in the office and that card were really from your father, didn't you?"

Her mouth opened, as if she wanted to argue his point, but then she pressed her lips together and nodded.

"He was sending you some kind of message. Snow angels?"

"We used to make them right on the ice at Pike Lake."

She adjusted the blanket around her again as though the warm down covering could hide what she'd done.

"You have to understand," she said in a small voice.

"Oh, I *understand*, all right. That you lied. To the police. And to me. *Repeatedly.*"

"I didn't know what to do."

"Not when your father, the fugitive, told you exactly where he was going?"

"I wasn't positive that was what he was saying." She stared at her lap as she spoke. "I mean, I thought I knew, but—"

"Stop lying!" He planted his hands on his hips. "Do you even know how to tell the truth?"

"I *did* tell Melissa the truth."

He refused to see the hurt in her eyes when she looked up again. He wouldn't acknowledge her plea for understanding. She didn't deserve it.

"And I betrayed my own father by telling your sister where police might find him." She shook her head, closing her eyes. "He'll never forgive me for it."

Though her words chipped at the seams in his armor, he couldn't let her slip past this time. "You waited *days* to tell. Precious hours when police could have been staking out the lake with the ice-fishing cabins. And then you still made them figure out which lake you were talking about when you know that in Michigan, you are never more than six miles from a body of water."

He paused, considering whether to add more, and then spewed the rest. "If not for all that, he might not have gotten away."

"Are you blaming me for a police swarm that failed?"

"You did everything you could to ensure he wasn't caught."

She shook her head, tears welling in her eyes. "That's not true."

"Really? You let me believe that those flowers were from the stalker instead and convinced me not to go to police when I knew we should." He paused, his skin hot, his jaw clenched so tightly he couldn't speak.

"Even when you finally decided to share *some* of what you knew, you wouldn't have told Melissa about the flowers if I hadn't mentioned it."

"I told her enough. Too much."

"You played me for a fool. You let me defend you to my whole family, and to become a part of your lies, without ever trusting me with the whole truth."

"I did trust you, Travis. You know I did. But even you said I wasn't obligated to help police build their case, and since I wasn't sure—"

He crossed his arms and glared at her. The words he'd spoken before seemed silly and naive now. "If that's what helps you to sleep through the night, then go ahead and believe it. I never will."

The memory of her pulling that white card from her purse taunted him then, something that had bothered him at the time, though not enough. He didn't want to hear the answer to his question, but he had to ask it, anyway.

"If you never intended to tell police that the flowers really were from your father, then why were you carrying around that card in the first place?"

She curled her shoulders forward as though she longed to fold into herself and disappear.

"It was from *my dad*," she said finally.

Another day he might have accepted her words, might have pitied her for the impossible situation she'd been in, but he couldn't do it now. Just like Aubrey, Tatiana had betrayed him. He'd swore he would never allow himself to be vulnerable to another woman, never give her the power to destroy him, and yet he'd done it again. Only the first had had been a pinprick when compared to this sledgehammer strike.

"I don't know who you are. Maybe I never did."

She shifted as if to climb from the bed and then pulled the blankets tighter, as she must have realized her clothes were still in the great room.

"You do know me. Better than anyone does. And I know you."

"I thought both of those things were true for a minute."

He hurried from the room, returned with her clothes and turned his back so that she could dress. No way he would torture himself with seeing her again and risk longing for someone who was so toxic to him.

Finally, he turned back, finding her fully dressed, sitting on the edge of the bed and watching him.

"I'm so sorry," she began. "I never meant to—"

"It doesn't matter now. What's done is done."

She folded her hands together in what looked like a plea. "It does matter. I would never want to hurt you. I *love* you."

He hated that his disloyal heart immediately raced over her confession. Apparently, he would never learn. "You'll have to forgive me, but I find it hard to believe anything you say now."

"But it's true. I do."

To that he didn't know what to say. Of course, he couldn't believe her, but he wanted to, which was worse. He trudged to his closet and returned with a duffel that he automatically started filling with shirts, socks and underwear.

"Where are you going?" she wanted to know.

"I can't stay here."

"Please don't leave. I need you."

They were words he'd wanted to hear, and now they sounded *empty*. Even the tears escaping the corners of her eyes had to be a ploy she would use against him. He wouldn't fall for it this time.

"Don't worry. The guard detail will still be here to protect you." From his closet, he collected shoes and a few pairs of khakis, and returned to tuck them in his bag. "I won't let anything happen to my baby. Or the child's mother."

He might have gone one step further to question the child's paternity since Tatiana had a lousy honesty track record, but as stricken as she already appeared, he decided to wait. That could always be completed following the birth.

"But this is *your* house," she insisted, wringing her hands. "I can't throw you out of your place."

"That's what I get for inviting people I don't know to stay with me, isn't it?"

"I can just go somewhere else where the stalker

doesn't know where I am." She hurried for the door of his room.

"What's going to keep him from finding you this time?" he asked her before she made it into the hall.

He refused to acknowledge her shiver, trying to convince himself it was forced.

"Where will you go?" she asked.

"Does it matter?"

Travis hefted his bag on his shoulder and rushed past her, careful not to even brush her arm. In the entry, he collected his coat and boots. He couldn't have answered her question, anyway. He had no idea where he would go next. The only thing he was certain of was that he couldn't stay there with her. He couldn't see her every day and be reminded that he couldn't trust his instincts. Maybe she'd done him a favor by letting him know once and for all that his search for a connection was fruitless. Love was only meant for the lucky ones, and he was like a craps player holding two dice, each with six blank faces. The reality was becoming clear that he was meant to be alone.

TATIANA LIFTED HER head off Travis's pillow, damp from the tears she had no right to cry, and she rushed to the master bathroom to be sick again. The jelly doughnut that had seemed like such a wonderful gift earlier haunted her with its return visit.

After washing her face in the sink, she took a good look at her ruddy reflection in the mirror. The face of a liar. She was more like her father than she'd realized. He would have been proud of how adept she'd become at subterfuge, capable of saying anything necessary to get what she wanted. She winced and splashed her face again, her skin refusing to cool.

When she was relatively sure she was finished being sick, she dried her face on a hand towel and stared at her reflection once more. The woman looking back at her was a stranger. When had she lost her ability to differentiate between right and wrong? When had she disappeared in this battle of allegiances?

She could say she'd had no choice but to cover for her father, but was it true? She'd always had a choice, and she'd picked a side. Travis had recognized it hadn't been his. Now she would have to live with that decision.

As Tatiana continued to watch the stranger, her gaze lowered to her abdomen, which she sheltered with her hands. She knew how difficult it was to betray a parent, but now that she knew she was going to be one, she should have been a better example.

"Your mom's really messed things up this time, Bean." She should have treated Travis better as well.

I love you. The words sounded strange and empty in her head, her heart aching with loss over something she'd never had. It wasn't the way she would have chosen to tell him, either, but no matter what she'd said, he wouldn't have believed her. Could she blame him? She'd lied about everything else. How was he supposed to know the difference?

Nervous energy had her moving around in the condo, making up Travis's bed, folding the throw blanket on the sofa and then heading back to his room to carry the gifts he'd given her into the kitchen.

The home gave her the creeps now that Travis wasn't there, an empty, yawning place, devoid of joy. In the silence, she couldn't shake the sensation that she was being watched there. How was she supposed to bang around its vacant rooms without losing her mind?

"I'm going to make this right with your dad. I promise."

How she would do that, though, she hadn't a clue. What had made her hold back information about her father, anyway? Why had she felt compelled to protect him when she knew he was guilty? She'd thought of it as a loyalty test, but could it have been something more? What if it hadn't been at all about who her dad was but who *she* was? Not about her family of origin but the family she would create with Travis once the baby was born, whether or not they ever married.

Tatiana pushed aside the internal, philosophical debate as she started downstairs to shower. Until the copycat killer was caught, she couldn't worry about redeeming herself anyway. So, the image that flashed in her mind then in full color surprised her. Why was she recalling her mother's grave site with such clarity when until now she'd always viewed it through a curtain of tears?

That was it, she realized, stopping in the middle of the staircase and clinging to the rail to keep from plummeting to the bottom. Of course, that was where her father might have gone. Why hadn't she thought about it before?

She reached the lower-level bathroom and withdrew her phone from the pocket in her leggings. Before she even undressed, she dialed the number, but waited to hit Send. Just because she probably had no chance to heal her broken relationship with the man she loved didn't mean she couldn't help *him* mend some scratches in his own family bonds. She still had the chance to do the right thing, even if she was late coming out of the gate.

She straightened her shoulders as she stood staring into another mirror and clicked the button to make the call. Now was the time for her to show not what Len Davison's daughter, but what *Tatiana Davison* would do. It was long past time for her to be the person and the mother her child deserved.

Chapter Twenty-One

Tatiana directed Melissa to the kitchen table at Travis's condo an hour later, the police chief eyeing her suspiciously as she passed.

"You know, I think you have the wrong idea about my job description," Melissa told her as she sat in the seat next to the box of doughnuts.

"I know it's highly irregular for you to make house calls, but I can't exactly pop by the police station when I'm basically under house arrest here." Tatiana poured herself a glass of milk and gestured to the jug to offer Travis's sister one.

Melissa shook her head. "I wouldn't mind a cup of coffee, though."

Both women turned to the restaurant-worthy espresso maker on the kitchen counter, but Melissa missed Tatiana's grimace over the smell that nauseated her every morning.

"I gave up coffee recently." Tatiana asked, "You have any idea how to use that thing?"

"Your guess is as good as mine. Forget the coffee." Melissa glanced past her through the doorway to the great room. "Where's Travis, by the way? I figured he would be here."

"It's just me this time." She cleared her throat. "Travis went out."

There was more to the story, but at least what she'd told her this time was true. She carried the milk and two plates to the table and gestured toward the doughnut box. Melissa shook her head, and neither took any.

"If you've called me out of the office, this had better be good. Are you ready to tell me all of it now?"

Tatiana chewed her bottom lip but forced herself to meet the police chief's gaze.

"Yes. I'm ready."

"Well, go ahead."

"I've thought of another place where my father might be."

Melissa pulled her notebook out of her purse, opened it, and waited. "You were right before, so maybe we'll get lucky again."

Tatiana wasn't sure she would call it lucky, but she nodded anyway. "There's a place near the tiny cemetery where my mother is buried."

Melissa looked up from the paper, frowning. "We've already thought of that. We've instructed the cemetery groundskeepers to keep an eye out for him."

"No, not there. A couple of miles from it. There's an old campsite. I noticed a sign for it last week when Travis drove me to the cemetery."

"That's your best guess?" Melissa lifted a brow.

"I think it's a good guess. I can see Dad being drawn there. There are probably all kinds of places he could hide at that type of campsite."

Melissa closed her notebook and set her pen next to it. "Well, I'll have an officer check it out."

"You seem like you were expecting something bigger than that."

Travis's sister shrugged. "Kind of. I knew you were holding something back. Thought it might have more fireworks than that."

Tatiana opened the doughnut box to have something to do with her hands, but when the syrupy-sweet scent hit her nostrils, roiling her stomach, she closed it again without taking one. The police officer narrowed her gaze but didn't say anything.

"Then this is probably the part you're looking for. I think my dad sent me those yellow roses."

Calm, cool Melissa Colton blinked several times. "But I thought you said…"

"I never said anything. It would have been easy for me to jump to the conclusion that it was the stalker, too, if there weren't enough hints to convince me otherwise."

Melissa opened her notebook again. "Such as?"

"My mother loved yellow roses." Tatiana filled her in about the single rose in every bouquet her dad had brought her mom.

"That's why Travis, not you, mentioned it when you brought in the emails from the stalker." At her nod, Melissa continued. "Anything else?"

She told her about the snow angels on Pike Lake.

"So, you weren't trying to be quite as helpful as we thought you were."

"Split loyalties. Think about if it were your father."

The compassion in the police chief's eyes surprised her.

"Makes sense. But we were almost able to capture him, based on information that you provided, so that's something." Melissa tapped her pen to her front teeth a few times, thinking. "Then that makes the fact that the copycat wanted you to call him 'Daddy' just dumb luck."

"Appears to have been."

"Do you have anything more to tell me?"

Tatiana considered for a few seconds, and then she told her about the phone call from her father. Once the words were spoken, she was relieved, too. Even if it still felt like a betrayal of her father, she believed it was the right thing to do.

"What about those?" Melissa pointed to the vase of pink flowers on the counter. "Is there anything I should know about them?"

"No." That she'd almost said *not yet* made her cheeks burn. Soon enough, they would all know about the newest Colton baby. "Doesn't have anything to do with my dad."

"Pretty."

Melissa studied her for several seconds. "Well, thanks for helping us out. We need to take Mr. Davison into custody as soon as possible."

"I hope you find them."

Melissa tilted her head and watched her. "Why did you decide to tell me about the flowers from your father now? My detectives followed up on that florist, and the trail went dead almost immediately."

Tatiana glanced out the window, where it had begun to snow again. "Travis has done an awful lot for me, and I haven't done much to show that I appreciated his faith in me, whether it was earned or not. He's also had to take a lot of questioning from family members. I just want to make sure that everyone knows what an amazing brother and cousin you all have. And he didn't make a mistake to help me get on my feet."

By the time that Tatiana was finished, the corners of Melissa's mouth were turned up. "Where's my brother?"

"I don't know. He left."

Melissa closed her notebook and stood. "Well, when he gets back, you might want to be sure to tell him something important."

Instead of telling her that she wasn't sure when he would be coming back, she asked, "What's that?"

Melissa didn't look up from the engagement ring on her left hand. "That you're in love with him."

TRAVIS STEPPED INSIDE his parents' house two hours after he'd left Tatiana at his condo. The lengthy drive had been necessary for him to work up the courage to go home again, especially with *this* request.

"Clarke, are you out there?" Frank called from the back of the house. When he didn't receive an answer immediately, he called out again. "Stanton, is that you?"

"It's me, Dad. It's Travis."

"Oh. Hey, son." Frank appeared from the arched hallway. "Don't usually expect to see you in the middle of the day. Who's watching the store at Colton Plastics?"

"I didn't expect to see you at home, either, Dad." *Hoped* was a better word for it, but he didn't want to start a fight this soon.

"Wait. You didn't come to tell me that CP went belly-up, did you?" Frank pointed to Travis's duffel that he'd set next to the front door and chuckled.

"As a matter of fact, I didn't. Wait. You aren't announcing that you're taking forced retirement, are you?"

His father's features shifted when Travis's joke struck him: a low blow.

"Ouch. What was that all about?" Frank asked him.

"Just joking around, like you." Leaving the bag by the door, Travis hung his coat in the closet.

"Didn't feel like a joke. I've been doing some work from home."

"Yeah, me, too." He crossed through the tunnel hallway to the back of the house and spoke over his shoulder. "Where's Mom?"

"Hair appointment."

Great. No one to run interference. On the long dining room table, Frank had spread a couple binders open next to his laptop. Travis leaned against the clear end of the table.

"What's the bag for?" Frank asked when he reached him.

"I was wondering if I could stay here a few days."

"What's the matter with your house? Heard that Stanton has been guarding your pretty guest there."

He pushed away from the table and started for the front door again. "Just forget it."

"Travis, stop. Talk to me."

He halted but didn't turn around.

"Have a seat. There's coffee in the pot."

Travis considered for a moment and then turned back and lowered into one of the chairs. His father stepped into the kitchen and returned with two steaming cups. For a few minutes, they both sipped in silence.

"What's going on?" his father asked finally.

"I can't do this anymore."

"Can't do what? You mean having Miss Davison in your condo?"

"I mean with *you*."

"What are you talking about?"

Frank drew his brows together as if he didn't know what his son meant. Travis might have bought it if he didn't know better.

"Is this about what your mom was telling me the other day? That you think I don't support you?"

"Mom told you?"

Frank's lips lifted. "We've been married a lot of years. We don't keep secrets."

"Then, yes, it's about that." Travis had picked up his cup, needing the caffeine after a night of little sleep, but he lowered it without taking a sip. "I'm sorry I didn't pick a heroic gig like my brothers and sister or follow you into the shipping business. I'm sorry I'm such a disappointment. That I routinely make huge mistakes in my business and life that you feel compelled to tell me about."

Frank shook his head, appearing perplexed.

"I don't know what you're talking about."

But this had been coming for a long time, and Travis was on a downhill roll. He didn't even *want* to stop it.

"You might not know this, but my company is a fricking success. It's publicly traded, for God's sake. It's large enough now to warrant having co-CEOs."

Travis would have said more, but his father started shaking his head, his usual smile flattening into a straight line.

"I'm so sorry, son. I've allowed *my worries* to make you feel as if I'm not proud of you. That's just the opposite of the truth. I couldn't be prouder. Instead of just having pipe dreams like the rest of us, you've turned your idea into an amazing company."

Travis could only stare at his father, words he'd never expected to come from the man's mouth spilling freely. Worries? Tatiana and his mother had been right that Frank's suggestions had been more about parental concern than second-guessing, even if he hadn't presented them well.

"But I thought…"

"I'm just sorry I ever made you think I wasn't solidly in your corner. That's where I am. Always."

Travis could find no words, so he lifted his cup and took three long sips in succession before lowering it again.

Frank blew out a long, slow breath. "You'll find out what it's like someday if you're ever a parent, but it's hard to get past that instinct to shield your kids from things that will hurt them. Including failure. But we forget sometimes that through failure our kids learn how to succeed."

"Dad, you know I'm thirty-four, right?"

Frank shrugged, his smile back in place. "You'll always be my kid."

His father drank down his coffee, which had to be cold now, and then set the cup aside. "So, are you ready to tell me what's really bothering you this morning? It has to do with Miss Davison, right?"

"Her name's Tatiana."

Frank grinned. "What is the issue with *Tatiana*, then?"

Travis considered for a few seconds and then decided just to put it out there. "She lied to me about information she had regarding her fugitive father's whereabouts. Now I can't trust her. I can't be with a liar. Unfortunately, I'm still in love with her."

He waited for the fatherly warning to pour out, but Frank only nodded. "Tough spot."

"It's just like Aubrey." Travis shook his head, the memory of those mistakes still shaming him. "You warned me. You knew she was a liar and a cheater. That she was only after the money I hadn't even made yet. I just didn't see it."

"Are those situations that much alike?"

Travis took another sip of his coffee, so cold now that he had to gag it down. "They both lied."

"But you said this young woman was trying to protect her father. We can't help who our parents are, and you should know as well as anyone that we can't help but to love them despite their shortcomings." He put his hand to his chest as a reminder that they'd just discussed his. "Can you blame her for loving her dad?"

Travis lowered his chin to his chest and shoved both hands back through his hair. "I don't know."

"Well, you're going to have to figure this one out all on your own."

"No fatherly suggestions?"

Frank shook his head. "Not this time. You're the one who has to decide if she's worth the trouble and what sacrifices you're willing to make. Only you know those things."

Travis nodded, realizing he already knew the answers to those questions. Whether he was brave enough to follow through with his convictions was still a question, though.

"One more thing, Dad."

"There's more?"

"I *am* going to be a father. Later this year."

"Well, congratulations. And I look forward to meeting the baby's mother."

Neither bothered mentioning the obvious thing: that the woman he'd been so upset about and the mom-to-be were one and the same. Frank rounded the table and hugged his son, something he rarely did. He might have said more, but the beep of the security system announced the front door had opened, and voices could be heard from the entry. Frank returned to his seat.

"Can you keep that to yourself for just a few days? I have some things to figure out before I go public with it."

His father nodded as his mother and Clarke reached them.

"What's going on here? And what's that bag by the door?" Clarke asked.

Frank stood and stepped over to drop a kiss on Italia's cheek and compliment her on her hair.

"Travis is going to visit for a few days," he announced. "That'll be great, right?"

"That's wonderful," Italia agreed as she stepped over to greet him with air kisses.

Clarke and Travis exchanged a handshake.

"You're staying *here*? I thought Stanton's team was guarding both you and Tatiana at your place," Clarke said.

"Long story."

The oldest Colton brother grinned. "Those are always the best kind."

Travis was relieved when Clarke's phone pinged before he had the chance to ask questions.

Clarke pulled it from his pocket and hurried from

the room to make a call. When he returned, Travis sent him a curious look.

"What's going on?"

"Randall Bowe, the GGPD's forensic scientist who's been on the run, is playing a game of cat-and-mouse with police right now. He sent a group text to several officers from a burner phone." He pulled out his smartphone again and swiped through a few screens. "Melissa forwarded it to me."

He held it out so his brother and parents could see it.

You'll never catch me. Sinners never prosper.

Travis shivered involuntarily. Bowe was playing God and the courts all at once. Len Davison and who knew how many other suspects were free though they were guilty, or incarcerated despite their innocence, because of choices Bowe had made.

"At least that will give the investigators something new to look at in the case," Clarke said. "Oh, and Melissa told me Troy's going to be revving up his search for Bowe's brother, Baldwin."

The search for Randall Bowe was fascinating, but Travis was far more interested in two other investigations right now. Both involved the same woman. So, he retreated to his childhood room to think and regroup. He might not have been with her just then, but he was every bit as committed to help stop those who might hurt her.

Chapter Twenty-Two

Travis parked in front of the tiny Grave Gulch Book Shop late that afternoon and hurried to the glass storefront. Why it had taken him so long to figure out this connection, he wasn't sure. He'd been lying back on top of the twin bed in his childhood room, rereading copies of the emails from "Daddy," when some of the information inspired him to do a little research of his own. Now, though he still hadn't figured out who Polly was, he had a good idea where he could learn more about "macabre heroes."

"Welcome to Grave Gulch Book Shop," called out an enthusiastic clerk with Henry on his name tag. "May I help you find something?"

"Hello, Henry. I'm Travis. I've just recently gotten into reading true-crime books. Do you have a section of those?"

"Do we ever." The clerk guided him to a tiny, clearly marked section, just over from the storage room door. "Do you have an area you're particularly interested in?"

"Definitely serial killers."

The clerk moved through the section and pulled out a few titles, stacking them in Travis's arms.

"Oh, while you're here, Henry, I've been thinking

about starting a true-crime book club. Do you know of any clubs in Grave Gulch? I wouldn't want to reinvent the wheel if there's already a group I could join."

Henry tapped his index finger to his lips, closing his eyes. Then he opened them again.

"You're in luck. I'm pretty sure yours will be the first in the area. At least if there is a true-crime group locally, the members aren't ordering their books here."

Travis rubbed his hands together. "Great. Now you don't happen to know anyone who might be interested in joining a group like this, do you? I'll post notices at the library and Grave Gulch Coffee and Treats, but I figured since you would be an expert on your readers' genre choices, you might be able to suggest potential members."

"I think I might have someone. My boss doesn't like us giving out names or information about our customers, but I don't think he'll mind this time." He crossed to the cash register and flipped through a traditional business card file. "This is it. Dylan Evans."

Travis's arms jerked, and he had to juggle to keep from dropping the books. "Dylan Evans?" Somehow, he kept his voice from squeaking, but his limbs felt frozen in place. The little weasel was supposed to be working on upgrading the computer systems through the IT department, not using all that access to stalk the woman Travis loved.

"Yeah, as many true-crime books as he purchases, he's probably got a great library of them at home," Henry said.

"Oh, I can't wait to see it. You don't happen to have an address for Dylan, do you?"

"Sorry. I know my boss would frown on that. But I

can tell you that Dylan works at Colton Plastics. I saw his work badge, which I'm sure isn't a secret."

"Oh. Thanks so much. I'll be sure to get in contact with him."

Travis started re-shelving the books one by one.

"Are you, uh, going to buy any of those?" Henry asked.

Travis grinned. "Of course."

He handed Henry the two remaining titles and went to check out at the only cash register. He used cash. No use having Dylan know that he was on to him if he came in to buy books.

Once Travis was outside the shop, he had to force himself to wait until he reached his car before making his first call. Melissa answered on the second ring.

"This had better be a social call, little brother. Remember, this is my personal cell. I already had your girlfriend ask me to come over to the condo today to give me details—"

His mind caught on the word *girlfriend*, but he couldn't think about that now. He couldn't worry about anything else until he ensured that Tatiana and their child were safe.

"I know who he is," he blurted.

"The suspect?"

Travis put the call on the car's audio system, pulled out of the parking space and drove down Grave Gulch Boulevard, forcing himself not to speed. "His name is Dylan Evans. He works in my IT department. I'm getting ready to call Stanton to have his team lock down Colton Plastics. Could you send some patrol cars?"

As soon as he ended the call, he gave the verbal command to phone Stanton.

"Got updates?" his brother barked into the phone when he answered.

"I have a name. Dylan Evans. I need you to lock down the whole building until he can be located. I don't care if it's five o'clock. He's in the IT department. I also need his address off the file in HR."

"I've got some news for you, then."

Dread crept up his back like a steadily spreading ice-water spill. "What is it?"

"I'm at the security station. Evans signed out of the office for the day before noon. The form here says 'illness.'"

"Damn! I'm headed to the condo."

"Why weren't you already there?" Stanton asked.

"I'll explain later."

"Luke's on duty."

"I'll call him."

He hung up without saying goodbye and then tried Tatiana's cell. That one went to voice mail. His heart beating furiously, he dialed Luke from his contacts. Voice mail again.

"If you hurt her, you son of a bitch…" he breathed through gritted teeth.

His last call was to his sister again.

"She's not answering, and Dylan left the office around lunchtime." Even he could hear the panic in his voice.

"Now calm down," Melissa said. "She might just be away from her phone."

"Stanton's team member isn't picking up, either."

"Oh." She was quiet for a few seconds. "I'm headed to your place. Don't go inside until I get there."

Since Melissa went in without the siren or lights and

had to maintain regular speed, Travis reached the condo first. He immediately noticed that although Luke's car was still parked on the street out front, no one was inside it. Deciding against entering through the garage, Travis parked in the driveway and rushed up the front walk.

Behind the hedge, Travis found Luke propped against the side of the house, a blood-soaked scarf pressed into a head wound.

"Sorry, man," Luke said. "He got her. Couldn't stop him. Surprised me."

Travis swallowed. "Don't worry, buddy. We'll find her."

He said it as much to assure himself as the wounded bodyguard.

"What did he get you with?" Travis asked as he took a cursory look at Luke's injury, making sure not to pull the cloth away and start the bleeding again.

Luke leaned forward and then swayed, so he rested against the wall again. "Snow shovel."

"Ouch."

"Did you already call an ambulance?"

Luke shook his head. "Asshole took my phone."

Travis pulled out his phone and placed the call himself.

"Police will be here in a few minutes, too," he told the other man before he opened the front door and rushed inside.

The front part of the house was trashed with broken glass pieces; there were clear signs of a struggle. But, like Luke said, she was gone.

He rushed back out the front door just as Melissa ran in. "I thought I told you not to go inside."

"Couldn't wait." He gestured toward Luke. "I called for an ambulance, but you might want to ping Luke's phone. Dylan took it so he couldn't call for help."

As Travis rushed down the driveway, a woman in a long parka marched up it.

"Are you looking for the tall, skinny guy in the white SUV?" she asked. "He forced the lady inside. She was yelling."

"Did you call 9-1-1?"

She shook her head. "Didn't want to get involved."

"Story of my life," Melissa said as she approached. "I'm Chief Melissa Colton. One of my officers is going to need a statement from you."

"I'll look for them." Travis yanked open the door.

"Wait. We don't even know where he's taking her. Why don't you leave it to law enforcement? We'll find her."

"I left her here. Don't you get that?" He looked away, trying to block all the horrible scenarios invading his thoughts. If anything happened to Tatiana or to the baby, he would never forgive himself. "I have to try."

TATIANA WIGGLED AGAINST the nylon zip ties holding her wrists behind her and her ankles together, as she sat in the front seat of the guy's car. She would have yelled again, but the gag between her top and bottom teeth put an end to that. The sound she made was supposed to say, "What do you want with me?" but it ended up sounding more like a series of grunts.

"I'm sorry, Tatiana. I tried to take the gag off, but you just wouldn't be quiet. You have no one to blame but yourself."

His tsk-tsk-tsk sound made her want to yank out all

his bushy blond hair. As if she didn't want to already. His voice sounded familiar, though muffled behind the mask he wore over his nose and mouth. She vaguely remembered him as someone from inside the Colton Plastics office, but so far, she hadn't been able to recall his name.

Where was Travis? Would he even try to find her after the argument they'd had that morning? He was a good man. He would certainly search, at least for the baby's sake. Just the thought of the innocent human inside her made her chest squeeze with loss. What would her abductor do to her when he realized she was pregnant with Travis's child?

She made another sound behind her gag that was supposed to be "where are we going?" It must have had some similarities to the real words, as he answered her.

"I decided against Grave Gulch Park. Too predictable. And too much of a police presence there lately. So, the cemetery it is. I found your mom's grave recently and have been visiting every chance I get."

"You stay away," she attempted to say, but again, he must have understood her muffled words.

"Sweetheart, you're going to have to get used to it. You and I and Polly will have a wonderful life together, and your daddy will be so proud.

"I was thrilled when I learned you would be coming to Colton Plastics. It was fate. As if he brought you to me. You almost messed it up, though, by getting involved with Colton. He doesn't deserve you. He'll never understand how much you value your role as a serial's daughter. I know. That's why you're mine."

Right then, he pulled off his mask and even in profile she recognized him as one of the IT guys she'd been putting off from working on her computer.

"Remember me? Dylan. You'd know me better if you finally had let me install the software on your computer, but I get the feeling you didn't have that laptop anymore."

As he pulled the SUV into the tiny cemetery where her mother was buried, the sorrow she always felt when she visited was magnified as the man's fixation on her father's murders seemed to desecrate Marcia's memory.

"Come on. We get to enjoy this for the first time together." He reached in the center console and pulled out a handgun and tucked it in his pocket. "In case you get any ideas."

He came around and opened the passenger door and then hauled her out.

"Let her go, Dylan," Travis called out from somewhere in the darkness.

Tatiana couldn't breathe. She'd wanted him to come for her, and now she wanted him to be far from there and out of harm's way.

"Hello, Colton." Dylan yanked her closer to him and held the muzzle to the small of her back. "You're out of your league here. Do you really think Tatiana Davison would choose *you* when she has someone who understands the superior mind and venomous instincts she inherited?"

"Why don't you let her choose, then?"

Tatiana stiffened as Travis's voice seemed to come from a different place this time. Closer. "Get back, Travis. He has a gun."

"That was a mistake, my love." Dylan whipped out

the gun and used it to whack her across her cheekbone before she had the chance to move.

Tatiana screamed, a white-hot flash of pain searing her face. The sharp pain was replaced by a constant pulse of it, signaling the swelling had started.

Then it was Dylan's turn to yelp as Travis attacked from out of nowhere, a loud thud of a fist connecting to bone, fracturing the silence again. Her abductor lost hold of her, and she fell forward into the snow. She tucked her limbs in so that she rolled before she reached the ground, trying not to land on the baby.

"Run," he called out, unaware that her feet were zip-tied.

As the two men wrestled for control of the gun, she crawled behind a larger tombstone and closed her eyes, waiting for the worst to happen. Travis disarmed Dylan instead, tossing the handgun and then landing several sickening-sounding punches.

Suddenly Travis was at her side, sliding his arms under her and lifting her. "You're going to be okay, Ana."

"Where did he go? And where's the gun?"

"I can't tell. He ran."

As if in answer to that question, the headlights of the white SUV came on, and Dylan aimed the much larger weapon at them, mowing over gravestones as he went. With Tatiana in his arms, Travis ran and dived behind a tree. The SUV hit it dead-on.

The tree won.

Both airbags deployed, trapping the driver inside. The cemetery was awash then with lights as several police patrol cars, an ambulance and even a fire engine lined the drive.

Travis and Tatiana lay in the snow, their lungs heaving. He pressed his forehead to hers.

"I should never have left you alone."

"You had every right to be angry. I shouldn't have lied. I should have trusted you."

"Oh, Ana. He could have—"

"But he didn't. Because of you."

"I love you so much," he told her.

"And I love you."

She nestled close to him, and he pressed his lips to hers. Their kiss tasted of tears. Maybe hers. Possibly his. Theirs.

"If you two could stop making out, we need to have the paramedics check you out."

They looked up to find Melissa grinning down at them. As soon as Travis stopped kissing her, the pain returned. It was becoming more difficult for her to see out of the sliver of her swollen eye.

Travis pulled back. "He hit her with the gun."

"That's right. You said you threw it, so we'll be out here combing through the snow for an hour to find it." She frowned. "Thanks for that. It's probably our murder weapon."

Melissa whistled, glancing in the direction of the SUV where Dylan, already handcuffed, was being treated for his injuries.

"Hey, over here," she called out to emergency workers.

She shook her index finger at her brother. "You're lucky you didn't get yourselves killed. I told you not to play the hero."

He shrugged and then brushed back Tatiana's hair

from her face. "Sometimes you just do what you have to do."

"Well, for our non–law enforcement brother, you didn't do a half-bad job," Melissa told him.

"How'd you get to us so fast, anyway?" Travis wanted to know.

"Luke's phone. Just like you suggested."

"Oh, make sure that someone goes back to Dylan's house to get the dog," Tatiana said. "It's not her fault her owner is a schmuck."

"We're on it," Melissa said.

Travis and Melissa stepped back to let the paramedic examine Tatiana, using a penlight and his moving index finger. But as he continued with his exam, the chief of police moved closer again.

"Be extra careful with her, because she's important to my little brother." She caught Tatiana's gaze. "And be gentle. She's pregnant."

"How'd you know?" Tatiana asked as soon as the paramedic stepped away after she promised she would go to the ER for a full exam.

Travis studied her as well. "How did you?"

"Have I ever told you I'm really good at my job? Maybe I have an instinct for protecting family." She pointed to Tatiana's belly. "And that baby is Frank and Italia Colton's first grandchild."

Travis grinned at her but then stepped forward and took Tatiana in his arms again. "Yes, this baby will have that weighty title but will have a more important role as well. He or she will be Travis and Tatiana's *first* child."

Chapter Twenty-Three

On the last Sunday in March, for the second time in a month, all four of Frank and Italia's children, plus a pledge class of new recruits, were gathered around the mammoth table in Frank and Italia's lakeside home for dinner.

Travis was particularly happy about the newest attendee, who wasn't quite official but would be by the end of the meal, if he could help it. Already they'd devoured most of the glazed ham with roasted potatoes and cheesy garlic asparagus, so if he didn't act soon, he would miss the dessert course as well.

Gathering all his courage, Travis pushed back his chair and stood. "I have an announcement to make. Tatiana Davison and I will welcome a child—the first Colton grandchild—on or about October ninth of this year."

He bent to kiss her cheek, which still held a green-yellow reminder of the stalker, who could have taken this amazing life from them both.

Everyone set aside their forks for a round of applause.

Stanton stood on the opposite side of the table. "And if there's anyone at this table who hasn't heard this news, please stand."

Immediately, he sat as laughter broke out around the room.

Travis frowned. No one was going to make this easy on him. "Remind me never to tell any of you secrets that need to be kept."

At the head of the table, Frank tapped the butt of his knife on the wood. "Duly noted."

"But seriously," Travis said, grinning, "we are so excited to welcome Bean into our lives and into this family."

Italia lifted a hand. "I nominate one Italia Vespucci Colton as official babysitter."

Travis rolled his eyes. "Thanks, Mom."

"Go, Grandma," Stanton said. At her frown, he said, "I mean, *Nonna*."

"Excuse me," Travis said. "Can I try this again?"

"You mean you weren't finished?" Clarke chimed.

After his comment earned him a glare from Travis and a poke from Everleigh, Clarke held out his hands, palms up, and returned the floor to his brother.

"Thank you. Well, a few of you have asked me how you should refer to Tatiana." He grinned at her, and her face immediately pinkened. "Should I call her my friend? Sure, she's that, but so much more.

"And what about 'girlfriend'?" He shook his head. "So, if you don't object, Tatiana, I would like to call you something infinitely more precious. First *fiancée*, then *wife*."

He stepped around his chair, reached into his jacket pocket for the box and lowered to one knee. Then he popped it open to reveal a sparkling round solitaire diamond engagement ring. Her eyes automatically filled with tears.

"Tatiana Davison, ours has been a whirlwind romance. Please be my wife, and our whole life will be that slow courtship we missed. Every day can be our first date, and every kiss can be our first. I bring to you a large, messy family that you will some days see as a reward, others as a consolation prize. So, will you accept this ring?"

She had been doing okay until he'd mentioned family, but at that moment, tears spilled from the corners of her eyes. He reached over to wipe each side with his thumbs.

"Well, will you take us?" Stanton asked.

"Yes. Absolutely."

After slipping the ring on her finger, Travis pulled her into his arms for a kiss that was indecently long. It earned applause all around.

Clarke wiped the back of his hand across his forehead. "Sure glad that's over. I never thought we'd make it to dessert."

More laughter, jokes and hunks of chocolate-walnut torte followed.

When the last of the crumbs had been consumed off the dessert plates, they returned to the fifteen-conversations-at-once plan that was a Colton staple. Somehow Melissa still managed to take the floor.

"Have any of you seen the recent social media posts from Dominique de la Vega, the investigative reporter from the *Grave Gulch Gazette*?" she asked. "She's been posting about asking sources for info about corruption about the GGPD."

Clarke nodded. "I've seen them. The way she's talking about the story, you would think she was looking at the keys to the Watergate Hotel. Who's going to be her Deep Throat, do you think?"

Melissa frowned. "Thanks for that historical comparison, dear brother. You make me feel so much better."

"I'm sure it's going to be fine," her fiancé, Antonio, offered out of obligation.

She leaned forward and continued. "Anyway, she's asking for anyone with information about the GGPD, and especially its former forensic scientist, to contact her. This could be awful for all of us."

Clarke leaned in and glanced down the table at his only remaining uncommitted sibling.

"Didn't you two used to be a serious couple?"

Stanton shifted in his seat and frowned. "Why'd you have to remind me of that?"

"You could be the one to explain to her how dangerous this investigation is," Clarke said. "And then you could convince her to leave the investigation to us."

Stanton scoffed at that. "No problem. I'll just do that on my lunch hour tomorrow."

Frank, who'd kept quiet most of the meal, spoke up. "What's that supposed to mean?"

"I'm telling you, any time I've run into Dominique in the past two years, she's glared at me and walked in the other direction." Stanton shook his head. "So, I'm definitely not the man for that job."

"Hey, I thought that was *all* women when they saw you coming," Travis said, earning the laugh he was going for.

Stanton chuckled, too, but he wasn't his usual jovial self. He was clearly unnerved after hearing Dominique's name.

The party broke up soon after, which was just as well

since Travis needed to get his new fiancée back to their condo and hopefully wrapped in something much more comfortable. Like him. With their life already so perfect, he'd worried that adding marriage as well might be asking too much. But he would never forget the look on her face tonight when she'd said yes.

A short while later, as they lay sated in the soft sheets, Travis smiled down at her.

"How are you feeling, future Mrs. Colton?"

"Can't complain," she said, dreamily, as she lay draped across his chest.

"So, you made it through another night with the Colton clan showing no visible scars."

She shook her head. "Your family's amazing, and you know it. You're so lucky."

"You're part of that family now, too."

She became quiet then, as she often did when they spoke of family.

"Thinking about your dad?"

Her lips lifted. "Is it so obvious? I'm glad your sister didn't bring him up at dinner."

"Melissa understands. Still no sightings of him since the lake?"

She shook her head against his skin. "Since I led the police to him. I'm not sorry. I still worry he'll follow the pattern and kill again in two months though."

Travis brushed his fingers through her hair. He couldn't remove her pain or her worries, but he could be there to support her as she faced them.

"Do you think the copycat threw him off his pattern?" he asked.

"I hope so."

"Either way, you can be at peace knowing you did the right thing."

"I am," she said without hesitation.

He brushed her hair until she drifted to sleep, her arm still covering him.

Travis continued to stare down at the amazing, beautiful woman, who'd just tonight agreed to be his wife. A man who hadn't fit in anywhere and a woman whose whole world had collapsed had found a home in each other. He couldn't wait for the moment they would become a family of three.

* * * * *

MILLS & BOON

THE HEART OF ROMANCE

A ROMANCE FOR EVERY KIND OF READER

MODERN

Prepare to be swept off your feet by sophisticated, sexy and seductive heroes, in some of the world's most glamourous and romantic locations, where power and passion collide.
8 stories per month.

HISTORICAL

Escape with historical heroes from time gone by. Whether your passion is for wicked Regency Rakes, muscled Vikings or rugged Highlanders, awaken the romance of the past.
6 stories per month.

MEDICAL

Set your pulse racing with dedicated, delectable doctors in the high-pressure world of medicine, where emotions run high and passion, comfort and love are the best medicine.
6 stories per month.

True Love

Celebrate true love with tender stories of heartfelt romance, from the rush of falling in love to the joy a new baby can bring, and a focus on the emotional heart of a relationship.
8 stories per month.

Desire

Indulge in secrets and scandal, intense drama and plenty of sizzling hot action with powerful and passionate heroes who have it all: wealth, status, good looks…everything but the right woman.
6 stories per month.

HEROES

Experience all the excitement of a gripping thriller, with an intense romance at its heart. Resourceful, true-to-life women and strong, fearless men face danger and desire - a killer combination!
8 stories per month.

DARE

Sensual love stories featuring smart, sassy heroines you'd want as a best friend, and compelling intense heroes who are worthy of them.
4 stories per month.

To see which titles are coming soon, please visit

millsandboon.co.uk/nextmonth

JOIN US ON SOCIAL MEDIA!

Stay up to date with our latest releases, author
news and gossip, special offers and discounts, and
all the behind-the-scenes action
from Mills & Boon...

 millsandboon

 millsandboonuk

 millsandboon

It might just be true love...

GET YOUR ROMANCE FIX!

MILLS & BOON
— *blog* —

Get the latest romance news, exclusive author interviews, story extracts and much more!

blog.millsandboon.co.uk

MILLS & BOON
True Love
Romance from the Heart

Celebrate true love with tender stories of
heartfelt romance, from the rush of falling
in love to the joy a new baby can bring,
and a focus on the emotional
heart of a relationship.

MILLS & BOON
MEDICAL
Pulse-Racing Passion

Set your pulse racing with dedicated, delectable doctors in the high-pressure world of medicine, where emotions run high and passion, comfort and love are the best medicine.

MILLS & BOON
Desire

Indulge in secrets and scandal, intense drama and plenty of sizzling hot action with powerful and passionate heroes who have it all: wealth, status, good looks… everything but the right woman.